Lyn Andrews was born and raised in Liverpool. The daughter of a policeman, she also married a policeman and, after becoming the mother of triplets, took some years off from her writing whilst she brought up her family. In 1983 Lyn was shortlisted for the Romantic Novelists' Association Award and has now written thirteen hugely popular Liverpool novels. Lyn Andrews still lives in Merseyside.

16| Sept 2007..

Love

Kathy

x

When Tomorrow Dawns

Lyn Andrews

headline

For Maeve Binchy, who has been an inspiration,
confidante and mentor, and also ᴅo ᴄᴏo
ᴀɴᴀᴄᴏᴄhᴀʀᴀ. Where would I be without you,
Maeve?

First published in 1998
by HEADLINE BOOK PUBLISHING

First published in paperback in 1998
by HEADLINE BOOK PUBISHING

15 17 19 20 18 16

ISBN 0 7472 5806 6

Typeset by Palimpsest Book Production Limited,
Polmont, Stirlingshire
Printed and bound in Great Britain by
Mackays of Chatham plc, Chatham, Kent
HEADLINE BOOK PUBLISHING
A division of Hodder Headline PLC
338 Euston Road
London NW1 3BH

Chapter One

'Well there it is, luv, what's flaming well left of it.'

The stocky woman standing next to Mary, her cheap, well-worn brown coat buttoned up tightly and a scarf tied firmly under her chin, seemed oblivious of the fine August morning as she pointed towards the Liverpool waterfront.

Mary looked puzzled. The three magnificent buildings looked to be intact. They stood out sharply in the early morning sunlight, black with soot after half a century of standing in air that was heavily laden with grime. Above them the sky was a clear bright blue with a few wisps of cloud, like white satin ribbons, twisting and trailing across it. The reflection of the sky turned the water of the Mersey to a pale shimmering blue. They had come up the river past the lighthouse on Perch Rock and then the fort at New Brighton. They'd passed the *Franconia* which seemed enormous in comparison to the ferry. She was on her way to New York and as she went by the three deep blasts of her whistle made Mary jump.

The river was calm and what ships there were moving left a silvery wash trailing behind them. The foamy white bow

1

wave of the *Leinster*, the British and Irish Steamship Company's regular overnight ferry from Dublin, drew closer. At the landing stage ready to leave were the Isle of Man ferry *Lady of Man* and the gleaming white-hulled *Empress of France*.

They were nearly there, Mary thought. This was the city where she would make a new and different future. Whilst saving for her fare she'd dreamed about Liverpool. She had big plans but no money to implement them, yet. Oh, she knew things were hard in the city and she missed Colin so much, but life had to go on and Liverpool would become her new home.

Her grip on her little son's hand tightened as the boat drew closer to the landing stage as the *Lady of Man* drew away. Now she could see the devastation for herself and it horrified her. She was too young to remember the similar destruction of the buildings on O'Connell Street and the Dublin quays by the gunboat in the Liffey after the Easter Rising. The Troubles, as her mam and everyone else called those awful days. Days that had led to the creation of the Irish Free State. But their new status as a separate country had had little impact on the inhabitants of the Liberties. The overcrowding and poverty there hadn't changed.

She raised her hand to shield her eyes and squinted ahead in the sunlight. St Nicholas's church was just a pile of rubble. Only the blackened spire remained standing. She could see the heaps of rubble and the shells of burnt-out buildings in what had been Derby Square. The statue of Queen Victoria alone seemed untouched.

She was appalled, and softly voiced a thought aloud without even realising she was doing it.

'Sure to God, is this what I left Dublin for?'

The woman beside her drew herself up and bristled with indignation.

'Well, we got no help from youse lot. "The Emergency" youse lot called it! The flaming Emergency! Six years with one half of the world killing the other half, and it's not finished yet with those little yeller heathens. Holy God, the number of ships and men that sailed from here on them convoys and hardly any came back. Them U-boats was just waiting for them. That's why I've not seen me sister for years. It wasn't bloody safe. Oh, *they* said it was and people did go, but *I* remember the *Lusitania*. It was fortunate that the *Munster* wasn't full of passengers when it was sunk in the dock. Some Emergency! You weren't here when night after night them Jerry planes came and half flattened the city. I was. I've 'ad murder with me sister in Ardee Street about it. I tell you, girl, it'll be a long time before I go to see that one again, even if she has given me some bits of food. Her son sitting in safety stuffing himself with food we 'aven't seen the like of for years while his cousin, his first cousin mind, is buried in a war cemetery in France.' She sniffed indignantly.

Mary's younger sister Breda Nolan cast her eyes upwards to the blue sky. Everyone was always moaning about wars, emergencies and troubles. Why keep harping on and on about it?

She wasn't in the least upset about going amongst strangers, as her mam described it. No, she was looking forward to it. Whatever state the city was in, it had to be better than the Liberties. There'd be a rake of things to do, but best of all she would be away from the Mammy and the neighbours who spied on you all the time and then went carrying tales.

Though Breda at seventeen was not as tall as her sister, they were very alike. Both had the black hair, deep blue eyes and pale skin that proclaimed their ancestry. But that was as far as the similarity went. Breda knew she was pretty, and she used her looks to further her own ends in ways which included flirting shamelessly. Where was the harm in that? she often asked indignantly. Wasn't it just a bit of fun?

A bold strap of a girl, the Mammy called her, and if the Father caught you even just laughing with a lad after Mass there was holy bloody murder and you were marched back home and then the Mammy would belt you to bits. No, there wasn't much in the way of fun in Dublin.

Mary thought back over the past six years. She'd argued and pleaded with Col when he'd come back from seeing a recruitment film. *Step Together* it had been called. There had been recruiting posters in bookshops and in places like Boland's Bakery, Blackrock Hosiery and Bradmola for a long time, and the rally in College Green, when Mr de Valera and Mr Cosgrove stood together to explain Ireland's precarious position, had been the final push Col had needed. After that the membership of the Local Defence Force had risen to 130,000 and the British Army had over 20,000 new recruits.

'I'm going to help protect *us*, Mary, and to earn more money. Aren't we a new country? The Treaty was only signed just over twenty years ago. Sure, how can we stand up to the Germans on our own when even Britain with all its empire is having to fight for existence? Hitler could invade us and we could do nothing, *nothing*, Mary. Wouldn't it be worse to have our freedom snatched away again after so short a time and crushed under a jackboot?'

She'd had no answer and had clung to him, weeping.

4

Gripping Kevin tightly she turned on the small woman, an expression of anger on her face. There was sadness in her eyes, but her back was straight and her head held high.

'Let me tell you, missus, that I'm a widow. Yes, a widow at twenty-four and with himself here to bring up, so I won't be having strangers making a mock and a jeer out of us. Aren't you a fright to say things like that. I begged and pleaded with my husband not to go but no, he went to help protect Ireland from invasion. And we *did* have rationing, *and* a blackout, and Dublin was bombed a few times too. My poor Col was dead set on going and dead is what he is. He's buried somewhere in a desert in Africa. I don't even have a grave to tend. If I only *knew* I could go and see it . . . him . . . It would be a comfort to me.' The tears sparkled in her eyes as she turned away.

The woman patted her arm contritely. 'I'm sorry, girl, I didn't know. There were a lot of Irish lads who joined up looking for a bit of excitement, more money, and, like your feller, to feel they were protecting their country. A lot of them never came back and it wasn't even their war.'

She crossed herself. 'It wasn't as bad in some ways as the Great War. Jesus, Mary and Joseph, the slaughter, the sheer slaughter of those lads! And they were only lads – some were only sixteen and seventeen. There was 'ardly an 'ouse or a family in our street that 'ad no one killed or wounded. People got embarrassed if their lads came back unhurt.' She decided to change the subject.

'Have you anywhere to go, like, when we get ashore? The housing's shocking. We was overcrowded before the flaming war, and now there's people who 'ave been bombed out two and three times, God 'elp them. And all these fellers

5

coming over for work will have to find lodgings as well.'
She jerked her head towards the crowd now assembling near
where the gangway would be let down.

'Yes, an aunt, if she's still got a roof over her head.' Mary
hadn't really noticed that the ferry was mainly full of men,
young and old, who were hoping to get jobs clearing the
rubble and starting to help rebuild a port and city that lay
in ruins.

Breda had noticed, though. She'd spent the first minutes
of the trip trying to look seductive and fluttering her eyelashes at one or two she thought seemed handsome and
well set up.

'Breda, will you behave and not be making cow's eyes
at that lot, showing us all up? Try to get some sleep,' Mary
had said sharply.

'Sleep, is it? With the noise out of them all and these
wooden seats?'

Mary's patience had snapped.

'Oh, shut up, Breda, for God's sake! Haven't I enough to
be worrying about? We at least *got* a seat; some people are
having to sleep on the floor. I wish I could have afforded a
cabin for us.'

'Aren't the cabins reserved for the gentry?' Breda asked.

'Not if you've got the money, but we haven't,' Mary had
stated flatly.

She had been awake and worrying all night with her
six-year-old son tucked in against one side and her sister
leaning against her on the other. The noise level had abated
as people tried to sleep on the hard deck, but the saloon
stank of beer and tobacco. She thanked God it was a calm
night. The anxious thoughts went round and round in her
head. What if things went badly? She didn't have much

money after paying for the one-way tickets. There wasn't much left of her little hoard at all.

She'd sold or pawned everything, including her silver cross and chain and her precious wedding ring. She'd cried all the way home the day she left it with Mr Brennen, knowing she'd never have the money to redeem it. It had been a special link with Col. When she was feeling really miserable and lonely she'd used to twist it round and round on her finger to conjure up his expression on the day they were married at St Catherine's, or the look on his face as she'd stood and waved him off to join the British Army. That was before the *Munster* had been sunk. She certainly didn't blame the woman next to her for not crossing the water.

It had been a hard decision for her to make, to leave Ireland, and not only had she her son to look after, but Breda as well. Her mother hadn't wanted the girl to go.

'Won't you have enough finding work and taking care of him?' Kathleen Nolan had argued.

'Mam, it won't be that bad. I'll make some kind of fist of it. There's more jobs over there. There always has been. Sure, don't half the country take the emigrant ship?'

'You'll need your wits about you, Mary, in a huge place like that,' Kathleen had said earnestly.

'Mammy, for God's sake, isn't most of the population of Dublin living and working in Liverpool?'

'Well, that's as may be, but you'll have to mind that bold strap. She has the heart across me.'

Breda had begged and pleaded and Mary had championed her sister's cause.

'Mammy, you know what she's like. Left here without me she'll just run riot and have you destroyed altogether with the worry of it. You should have some peace and quiet. You've worked hard all your life for us.' Mary had glanced around the sparsely furnished room that had been her home for years. Both she and Breda would send money home, like every other boy and girl who emigrated.

So Kathleen had capitulated. It was a tearful Mary and Kevin and an impatient and highly excited Breda Kathleen Nolan had watched go up the gangway of the ship that would take them all to a new life, like so many before them.

Now the thump of the ship's side against the huge rubber tyres that acted as bumpers, and the shouts of the shorehands as they secured the hawsers, drove all thoughts from Mary's mind.

'Kevin, hold on tightly now to Mammy's skirt while I carry the case and the parcel.'

'God, we'll be crushed to bits!' Breda complained, clutching a large bundle to her chest with both hands.

'Then go and flutter your eyelashes at one of those grand-looking navvies, maybe they'll help.' There was a note of sarcasm in Mary's voice. It was a terrible crush and she was terrified that Kevin would fall and be trampled on. He was so pale and thin for the want of good food. Rationing had made no difference. All they could afford was bread and tea, a bit of brisket, ox heart or bacon with cabbage, or just scraps that Mammy used in a stew.

In the crush she lost sight of the woman in the brown coat. It was everyone for themselves, although a couple of the lads made room for them, with coarse innuendoes that she ignored but Breda did not.

'Breda, for God's sake stop encouraging them,' she snapped. She was beginning to regret that she'd saddled herself with such a responsibility. In a city like Liverpool there was plenty of trouble that bold strap could get into, but she'd done it for her mam.

One of the deckhands caught her eye and she shouted across to him.

He elbowed his way through to her. 'What's up, queen?'

'When we get off how will I get to Hornby Street, please?'

'Catch the number 20 or 30 tram. It's not far. Ask the conductor to put you off where Scottie Road joins Hornby Street. I think most of the houses are still standing, though maybe they've been pulled down as being unsafe. I don't know, luv, the whole of that area took a hammering. But we got our own back all right. Sometimes I feel a bit sorry for them now, with their whole country in ruins.'

'Well, they should 'ave thought about that before startin' a flaming war.' The woman in the brown coat was there again, hanging on to the deckhand's thick navy sweater with the letters 'B & I' on the front, having elbowed her way through the crush.

'It's all behind us now, missus. Come on then, let's get yer all off.'

Mary felt happier in one way and very apprehensive in another. Happy that he had taken the case and parcel from her, leaving her free to look after her son properly. But what if the O'Sheas' house had been blasted to bits? What would she do then? Although they were first cousins, she'd only met them once and she couldn't recall what they looked like. Apparently they'd come over for her mam's wedding and then to wake her poor da, but that was all. No communication whatsoever since then.

Eventually they disembarked, but there was no time to stand and look around. People were pushing past them, so she guided Kevin and Breda towards the row of green and cream painted trams that were lined up at the pier head. She found a number 30 tram and pushed her little brood aboard.

'Sir, could you put us off on the corner of Hornby Street, please?' she asked the conductor.

He grinned at her. 'I can tell yer not from round 'ere. I've never been called sir in me life before. I'm just a working feller, luv. I've a girl your age. 'Ave yer just come off the boat? 'Ere, I'll see to meladdo, you just find a seat. Yer look wore out.'

Mary smiled at his kindness as she ushered her son and her sister to a double seat. She put the case on the floor and gave the bundle to Breda. Kevin would have to sit on her lap; the tram was filling up.

When the conductor came for the fares, he shook his head at the proffered money in her hand.

'It's company policy to charge for meladdo as well, luv. It's supposed to be half price but what the 'ell. The bloody Corporation can afford to lose a few coppers now and then. Grasping owld windbags the lot of them.'

As the tram trundled down Chapel Street and Tithebarn Street, the trolley giving out sparks as it crossed the junctions, Mary couldn't believe her eyes as she twisted from side to side. Oh, they'd heard on the wireless and in the newspapers of the bombardment by the Luftwaffe on the cities over here. But seeing it with her own eyes she was horrified. Whole streets of houses, churches, shops and pubs were in ruins. It must have been terrifying, yet the Liverpudlians had gone on, day after day, week after week, month after month for six long years, trying to carry on as normal whilst encircled by chaos, loss, ruin and worry.

What kind of job would she get here? How could she make her dream come true? She held her little boy tightly. Oh, Col, why did you have to go? she said silently as the tears pricked her eyes. He'd not had a bad job as a coal heaver with Murphy's and they'd got a two pair front in a house in Balfour Square. Once the gentry had lived in the beautiful Georgian houses, with a rake of servants to see to their every need. That was many long years ago and the houses were now dilapidated, crumbling and overcrowded.

She'd furnished their rooms with second-hand stuff, painting or varnishing tables and chairs. She'd scrubbed floors and woodwork. When Kevin had been a baby she'd got a deep drawer from an old chest Mr Brannigan had in his yard and lined it with canvas, then calico and finally muslin. To cover the wood she'd made a deep frill with cheap gingham, and Mrs Dunne, who lived upstairs, had said it was like one of those fancy cribs you'd pay an arm and a leg for in Grafton Street.

She'd made curtains, cushions, quilts and all her own and Kevin's clothes. Oh, they'd not been doing too badly at all, and now she didn't know if these relations she'd scarcely met had a roof over their heads or would welcome her one little bit even if they had.

When she'd alighted, with some assistance from the conductor who wished her good luck, she looked down Hornby Street and her heart sank. There were houses, but there were huge gaps and mounds of rubble too.

The sun was warm on her back now and people had started to go about their business. A horse and cart passed slowly, the iron-shod hooves of the heavy shire horse seeming very loud as they struck the cobbles and echoed along the street. The cart was decorated with crudely painted daisies and was full of milk churns. It was followed by another proclaiming it contained the wares of 'Blackledge's. Bakers and Confectioners'. Mary ignored them, struck dumb by the sight of the dereliction that surrounded them.

'There's nothing left! It's a wild goose chase we've come on.' Breda was sure she'd not had a wink of sleep although Mary had said she'd slept all the way. She also had a headache. That was probably the half pint of horrible-tasting porter a young navvie had bought her when she'd managed to escape her sister's eagle eye for half an hour. She'd used the pretext that she couldn't stand the smell and needed some fresh air. Now it seemed as though they'd come to a place that was little better than the slum they'd left.

Mary glared at her but began to walk down the street, noting the condition of the houses that were still standing. They were 'landing houses', three storeys high, and had been built in 1900 to replace older slum houses. She could have shouted with joy and relief when she saw that the block that contained number 18 was miraculously still standing and was obviously occupied.

She put down her belongings while Breda leaned against the wall of the next house. Mary knocked loudly and after what seemed an age the door was opened by a large, rather blowsy-looking woman with greying hair and deep lines of worry on her face. She was Mam's age, Mary surmised.

'Mrs O'Shea?'

'Who wants ter know?' Maggie O'Shea's gaze swept over the little group on her doorstep. The obviously bored but beautiful young girl was trouble if ever she saw it. The whey-faced little lad was dressed in cutdowns that had been skilfully done and the haggard-looking young woman's wide blue eyes were full of anxiety.

12

'I'm Mary O'Malley. Didn't the Mammy write to you about us?' Mary paused. 'Mam . . . you remember her . . . your sister-in-law Kathleen Nolan?'

Maggie relaxed, her face transformed by a broad smile. 'I've gorra head like a sieve these days; it's all ter do with the war. Me nerves are strung like piano wires. Come on in, the lot of youse. Yer mam did write, I remember now.'

She led them down a dark narrow lobby that was devoid of carpet, rag rugs or lino.

'It's going ter be a terrible crush, like, with the six of us an' you three, but we'll manage. We're dead good at managing after six bloody years. As yer can see, we were dead lucky. We've still got a roof over our heads. Not much of a one, but there was a poor soul with a husband away in the Navy and a gang of kids living where next door used to be. She'd already been bombed out three times, and when that lot went she up and took them all off ter Kirkby. They took 'undreds of people out to the country places of a night ter sleep, things were that bad. The Yanks took them in lorries and brought them back in the morning.'

Mary wondered just how they would all manage with nine people crammed into this two up two down house. At home there was terrible overcrowding too but at least the rooms were bigger, and if you had a two pair back or a two pair front and decent clean neighbours it wasn't bad at all. Here they'd be all on top of each other. Still, she should thank God that the building was still standing.

She was taken into a small kitchen that served as a dining room as well. Over the range, the mantel was overloaded with bric-à-brac. The lino on the floor had definitely seen better days and there were stained newspapers covering the table in place of a cloth. That was all she could take in of her surroundings for Maggie was busy introducing the family to her, beginning with her husband Jim who was Mam's eldest brother and had come to Liverpool looking for work when he was just fifteen. He'd sent money home until he'd married, and that had helped. He was known as Big Jim and he was indeed a big man with a barrel chest and heavily muscled arms. Before he was demobbed he had sailed on the notorious Arctic convoys to Russia and counted himself lucky to be alive. He was jovial but very much in charge of his family.

'So, you've come ter see us at last, Mary O'Malley? You were just a twinkle in yer mam's eye the first time we were over. The second time was for yer da, God rest him.' He shot a look at his wife. 'And there'll be no bitter words in this house about Ireland being neutral. I'll not stand for it. Col O'Malley did his bit for us, and of his own free will too. He fought and died for our freedom and now it's our duty to look after these girls and the little lad too.'

'I wasn't going to make any such remark, Jim O'Shea,' came the spirited reply.

Mary learned that their eldest son Davie had been killed on D-Day. In one of the first companies to go ashore, he hadn't even made it to the beach. The weather had been atrocious for June and every man in the landing craft had been sick. Their uniforms were sodden, their packs so heavy and the swell so strong that he and many others had stumbled, fallen and drowned. Maggie had never forgiven the Army.

Bryan, who was twenty-two, had come through unscathed but tended to go on and on about his experiences in the King's (Liverpool) Regiment. When he'd been conscripted the turning point in the war had already been reached, and like his father he had already been demobbed.

Maurice O'Shea was a quiet gangly lad of sixteen. He hated his name because his mates called him Maury, and when he was introduced as such he complained, 'I 'ate being called that. It's like being called after the *Mauretania*. Me name's Maurice.'

Maggie glared at her son. 'Well, isn't that a nice way to speak to anyone?' Her words were heavy with sarcasm.

Two young girls in grubby nightdresses stared at the newcomers in silence. The smaller of the two had a mop of gold curly hair and had her thumb in her mouth. The other one was older and bolder and had untidy dark brown hair and eyes.

'I'm Patsy an' I'm eight,' she announced confidently.

'An' the other one's our youngest, she's six. Lily O'Shea, get that thumb out of yer mouth. I've told yer time an' again, yer mouth'll get out of shape an' when yer grown up yer won't speak proper,' her mother instructed.

'An' then yer'll never gerra feller,' Patsy jibed.

Maggie rounded on her. 'And since when 'ave you been thinking of fellers and the like, Patsy O'Shea? Did yer hear that, Jim? Eight years old and as bold as brass. Any more of that and yer da will take his belt to yer, yer 'ardfaced little madam, an' then I'll take you up to Father Hayes an' tell him about yer sinful goings-on.'

Breda's spirits began to droop. Maggie O'Shea sounded just like her mam, and at the look on Jim's face she inwardly cringed. Growing up without a da had meant she was subject to just her mam's giving out and chastisement. Now it looked as if she, like Patsy and Lily, would have to obey Jim's rules, like them or not.

Despite the sinking feeling in her stomach Mary managed a smile. It was like a circus in here, she thought. Were they like this all the time? But after six years of terror and grief and making do, who could blame them? She'd probably be the same herself.

Chapter Two

Breda looked with undisguised disgust at the small bedroom she was going to have to share with Mary, Patsy, Lily and Maggie. Jim and his two lads slept in the other bedroom and Kevin would have to join them.

'After work our Maury – or our Maurice as now he's taken the notion to be called – will go and get a couple of donkey's breakfasts,' Maggie raised her eyes to the ceiling, 'and our Lily and Patsy can sleep on them. We'll have the big bed. It's cramped but we'll have ter manage. We used ter have a saying "There's a war on" which covered everything people complained about, but it looks as if it's nearly over now, thank God.' Maggie patted the faded quilt covering the big iron bed that took up nearly all the space in the room.

Mary gulped and pulled herself together. Why some of them didn't sleep in the downstairs front room she didn't know. She voiced this thought and Maggie said that room was let to the lodger, Mr Fallowfield, a confirmed bachelor who kept himself to himself whenever possible. What his job was was anyone's guess, but he always paid the rent on time and saw to his own washing. In fact she'd wondered whether or not to up the rent because he sent his stuff out to the laundry, would you believe, but Jim had said to leave the feller alone. Mary kept her eyes fixed on the floor. After Col had died she'd gone back to her mam's, where she and Breda shared a double bed and Mam and Kevin had a single bed each. The rooms were bigger, too.

'That'll be great altogether. It's only sorry I am that we have to be putting you to so much trouble. I think we should all call you Aunty Maggie. It's more respectful.'

'Suit yourself. And it's no trouble at all, girl. There's whole families sharing rooms this size. We'll all muck in together.'

From what she'd seen so far 'muck' was a very apt description, Mary thought. Her own rooms in Balfour Square had been scrubbed twice a week and had been brushed every single day. She'd cleaned her windows with old newspaper. The carbon in the print put a real shine on them; a tip she'd got from Mrs Dunne upstairs. And Mammy wouldn't have you in the door with shoes or boots on, trailing the dust and dirt of the Dublin streets into the room. Mary's homes had always been spotlessly clean and that hadn't been easy to keep up in an area like the Liberties.

'What are donkey's breakfasts?' Breda enquired, trying to keep her emotions out of her voice.

'Ticking mattresses stuffed with straw. They're cheap and not bad to sleep on, an' it's still warm of a night.' Maggie crossed herself. 'Me own mam, God rest her, always used them. There were twelve of us. We was like a tin of those little fishes . . . sardines, but we was always warm in winter. Too flamin' hot in summer, though.'

Breda closed her eyes. God almighty, it got worse by the minute.

'Right then, I'll leave the pair of youse to get your bit of unpacking done. There's a couple of orange boxes with the kids' stuff in them. Chuck it all on the bed – we'll get more boxes ternight.'

When Maggie had gone Mary sank down on the bed and passed a hand over her eyes. There was already a faint throbbing in her head which she knew from experience would get worse as the day went on.

'Jaysus! Would you look at the place! *You* said we'd be grand here. *You* said it was a new life. *You* said—'

'Breda, in the name of God, *shut up!*' Mary was close to tears. She put a protective arm around her silent and mystified son.

Breda sat down and some of the anger left her eyes. 'I'm sorry, Mary. It's just that . . . well, I thought it would be . . . different. They're all mad. I've never seen such a carry-on.'

'Sure, it's different all right.' Mary turned up a corner of the quilt. There were no sheets, only the ticking covering the mattress which they'd have to lie on. There were no pillows either, just a long bolster, again covered in the stained, faded blue and white striped ticking. She bit her lip but straightened her shoulders.

'Well, once they've all gone to work or school or whatever they do all day, you and me are going to find the nearest second-hand shop and pawnbroker's. Even if we can only get sheets you can see daylight through I'll buy them and sew them ends to middle. I'm not sleeping on a bare mattress. Then we'll give the whole place a damn good clear-out.'

Breda stared at her mutinously. 'Why do we have to do it? It's *their* house and she doesn't seem to mind the mess. Old newspapers on the table, for God's sake! Mammy would have a fit, so she would.'

'Well, I *do* mind the mess, and you're right, Mam didn't

bring us up to live like this. Sure, we never had much but what we did have was clean.' She softened her tone. 'It's different for them, I suppose. Why struggle to keep a house looking like a new pin when the water mains and gas pipes are broken and it could be flattened by a bomb any time?'

'They don't have to worry about bombs now. The Emergency's over.'

'Not out in the East it's not.'

'Well, I can't see how any Japanese plane could get this far,' Breda said irritably.

Mary sighed, thinking about Kevin. He'd had friends at home and had seen how they lived, nearly all in dire poverty. One had died but that was often the fate of children. If you reared them over the age of ten you counted yourself lucky. But he'd never had to cope with such overcrowding, or having to share a bed. He'd have to go to school tomorrow too, but she'd take him there herself. She'd get all the details from Maggie later on.

'The quicker we get jobs the better,' Breda said petulantly.

'I don't see how that will change much. You heard her. The housing shortage is desperate.'

'Surely we can get one room? Three of us won't be too many for one room and we'll be out all day. It'll be easier to furnish, too.'

Mary sighed and got to her feet, weary already.

'For now we've no choice. I suppose we'd better go down and tell her we'd like to help with the cleaning.'

Breda pulled a face. 'She'll just sit there on her fat behind and watch while we do all the work. And she'll be giving out at us too. Wanting this done and that done.'

'Breda, that's enough. She's given us a home, we should

be grateful,' Mary stated firmly, but there was no note of
gratitude in her own voice.

When they went downstairs the kitchen was empty. The
room was a mess. Clothes and papers were piled on chairs.
Ash had fallen from the range, which was dull for the want of
cleaning. There were half-open cupboards and dirty dishes
everywhere. The rack that hung over the range, operated by
a pulley and rope system, was suspended to a height where
Maggie could just reach the items of clothing she needed.

Breda lifted the lid of the brown glazed teapot and
sniffed.

'It's stewed and half cold. Will I throw it out?'

'Yes, but go down the yard with it. I dread to think what
the sink in the scullery is like.' Mary shuddered.

She turned to her son who had remained silent, sitting
on the edge of the old sofa. 'Kevin, will you take up
your things in the parcel there for Mammy?' She squeezed
his hand.

The child looked warily up at her but seeing her smile he
did as he was bid. He was totally confused and miserable.
He didn't like this house at all. Suddenly his safe little
world, which had been bounded by his room and his bed
at Granny Nolan's, had gone. They'd left Granny Nolan in
Dublin. Mammy had tried to explain why they had to leave
but he didn't understand.

He'd left his friends too and there seemed to be no boys
of his age in this house. Tomorrow he'd have to go to a new
school amongst strange boys who might torment and bully
him. He clutched the bundle tightly to him. Last Christmas
Santi had left a knitted rabbit for him and it was his most
precious possession. He slept with his cheek resting on it

but now he wondered whether the others would take it off him.

'Will I keep my rabbit, Mammy?' he pleaded.

'Of course you will, why shouldn't you? Now go on up.'

She sent him into the lobby and stood watching him climb the stairs.

'Has Mrs O'Shea moved out, then?'

Mary turned, startled by the male voice.

'Who are you? Haven't you put the heart across me!'

'I'm sorry. I'm Chris. Chris Kennedy. My mam told me to come over. I've just got home. I've been demobbed. I live across the street.'

Mary regained her composure. She wasn't afraid of him. He didn't look like the desperate men she'd seen so far, although he was a good head and shoulders above her. He had dark hair like her own and a disarming smile.

'You'll be wanting Aunty Maggie, then? I don't know where she's got to but it won't be far, so you'd better come into the kitchen.'

'And who are you? Has she taken in more lodgers?'

'No . . . er . . . well, yes, I suppose we are lodgers. I'm Mary O'Malley. Mrs O'Malley,' she added.

'I see.' Chris nodded slowly as he followed her. His mam had said nothing about her but she was lovely and had a gentle calming attitude.

Mary turned and smiled at him. 'No, you don't see at all. I'm a widow. A war widow.'

'But you're Irish.'

'I am and so was Col. He was killed. He was one of Montgomery's Desert Rats. I have my little boy and my sister with me.'

'I'm sorry about your husband,' he said with sincerity. He'd seen so many men die that he shouldn't be surprised she was a young widow. The city was full of them, not only from the Army but the Navy as well.

'We only arrived this morning too, my sister Breda, my son Kevin and me. Aunty Maggie is being so kind giving us a home, and she after being overcrowded herself.'

Chris scrutinised her as she moved a pile of clothes off the armchair and indicated that he should sit down. She was young. Twenty-three or four at the most. She must have been a very young bride but he could certainly see what Col O'Malley had seen in her.

'How is it that Bryan is home already?' she asked, folding the clothes she'd just removed.

'Last in, first out, I suppose. I'm lucky to get out at all; there are plenty of lads who won't . . . oh, I'm sorry . . . I didn't mean . . . I . . .' He could have bitten his tongue. Col O'Malley hadn't been lucky.

'Don't worry at all.' She smiled sadly. This was something she was going to have to cope with: the men coming home alive and well and the rejoicing of their families.

'I'm truly sorry, Mrs O'Malley.'

'Don't I know that? And seeing as we're to be neighbours wouldn't it be better to call me Mary?'

'Only if you're sure?' He felt at ease with her again.

'I'm sure.'

'Well, I'm sure I've never seen such a mess in my life.'

Mary and Chris both laughed as Breda came back indoors.

'Your sister?' Chris queried.

'She is. Breda, this is Chris Kennedy, just home from the Army. He lives over the road.'

Breda nodded curtly in his direction.

'Isn't that a nice way of going on?' Mary chided her.

'I'm sorry. It's just that we're so tired and . . . and, well, things were . . . different at home.'

Chris didn't have time to reply before Maggie, who had nipped over the road to see Flossie O'Hanlon, walked into the kitchen, gave a cry of delight as he stood up, then almost smothered him as she hugged him.

'When did you get home? You look great, lad!'

'Thanks. Just half an hour ago. Mam sent me over and I'm glad I came.' He smiled at Mary and Breda and then at the pale, thin and scared little boy who had crept in behind Maggie.

'These are Jim's nieces from Dublin. They've come over to start a new life, although God knows why, the state this city's in. At least you'll not go short of work, being a brickie.'

'This is Kevin,' Mary said, her arm protectively around her son's shoulder.

'Hello, Kevin.' Chris smiled down at the child who remained silent.

'He's tired and shy,' Mary said.

'Well, I'd better go back. Mam was trying to find something for my breakfast.'

'Good luck to her. It's hard to find anything at all these days, but it's great to have you back, lad.'

Chris nodded to the newcomers before he left. They were a strange little trio, he thought.

'Here, Breda, luv, give me the teapot. I'll put fresh water on the leaves,' Maggie instructed.

'I threw them out. Haven't I just come up the yard from the ash pit?'

'You can tell you're not used to rationing. *We* have to use the leaves over and over again.'

'We did have rationing!' Breda said truculently, then fell silent as she caught the look on her sister's face.

'Will you have some tea and a bit of bread, Kevin? That's if you can spare it, please?' Mary finished appealingly.

'Ah, the poor kid. He's worn out, and so thin that if he turned sideways he'd fall down a grid. We're still on rationing, so you'll have to go and get ration books and clothing coupons.'

'We'll have to get jobs before we'll be able to buy clothes, with or without coupons. I can let you have five shillings a week for our keep, for three weeks. Where do you think we should go? For jobs, I mean?'

Maggie helped herself to a cup of tea.

'What can yer do? They're closing down the munitions factories now so the competition for jobs will be hard.'

'I can sew and cook,' Mary answered.

'But isn't your handwriting desperate? You'd think a spider had got drunk, fallen in the inkwell and then staggered all over the page, so you would,' Breda said disparagingly.

Maggie shot Breda a narrow glance. Pushy and hardfaced too was this one, but she'd soon put a stop to her gallop.

'Mary, I'd try Williams's. They make overalls. They've been turning out uniforms but they're back to normal now, or so I heard. And iffen I were you, Breda, I'd make meself presentable and go on up to the General Post Office in Victoria Street and see if they'll take you on as a clerk or something, seeing as yer so good with the writing an' all,' she finished sarcastically.

'We'll do that. Thanks, Aunty Maggie. But first we'd like to give you a hand with the cleaning, then we've a bit of shopping to do. Will that be all right?' Mary tried to sound casual.

Maggie was surprised but she didn't show it. She smiled at Mary. 'Oh, that'll be great, luv. The kids have the place looking like a rubbish dump. Yer can't do nothing with them, they're that flaming untidy. I've tried an' tried an' just given up.'

Mary pressed her lips together. Well, she certainly wasn't going to just give up, not even if she had to have a row every single day for a month. By the end of the week this place would be transformed.

Empty orange boxes seemed to be free and could be used for a dozen purposes. She'd yet to meet the neighbours but surely someone must have a sewing machine or know of somewhere she could borrow one. She'd run up some cheap cotton curtains in no time at all. Breda could teach Patsy to make rag rugs. That would keep the pair of them out of trouble for a while, for she sensed that despite their ages Patsy and Breda were alike. Even young Kevin and Lily could help, too. They could cut up the strips.

As she rolled up her sleeves she smiled grimly. When that lot came home from their jobs tonight working boots would be left in the scullery. She'd allow no dirty boots in at the door in future. Oh, there'd be opposition. She would be asked what right she, who had just arrived off the boat, had to order them about. All three of them worked on the docks, patched up and busy again now that there were American, Canadian, Australian and South African troops sailing for home, and at least now the merchant ships could bring in the much needed supplies.

By mid-afternoon they were sitting at a table that had been

scrubbed within an inch of its life, as had everything in the house. Mary and Breda's hands were red with it. They all had a bowl of soup and chunks of fresh bread that Maggie had bought from the corner shop run by Cissy Mathews. She'd taken Kevin to introduce him to Cissy and show him where the shop was, because he'd often have to run down for messages not only for herself but for neighbours too. Cissy was great, she'd let you put things on the slate but only if she knew you'd pay her at the weekend.

Maggie had also bought a ham shank with the money Mary had given her. It was simmering in a pan on the range and would be served up for supper with a mound of boiled potatoes and cabbage.

The girls were both exhausted, but knew they had to go into town to get the precious ration books. And of course they were citizens of a foreign country now, as Breda had remarked.

'Would we be here now, doing this, if Col had still been alive? Don't they owe us at least that much, Breda?'

'The pair of you had better get a move on before the flaming place decides to close. They're a bloody law unto themselves, that lot!'

Mary stood up to take her empty bowl into the scullery.

'We'll just get tidied up a bit first. Breda, bring the dishes out here. I'll wash them before we go.'

'Ah, leave them, queen. I usually do the lot after tea.'

Mary ignored Maggie and washed the bowls and mugs and left them upside down on the draining board to dry. She'd used the ragged tea towel as a floor cloth. It wasn't fit for any other purpose. When she was out she'd get a proper dish mop and she'd call in at Mathews for washing soda, a Dolly blue bag, bleach and Jeyes Fluid, plus a bar of carbolic soap for the men and one of Lifebuoy for the rest of them. They'd have to get some linen too. She sighed. All of this was eating into her savings. If they didn't get work soon they'd have nothing left at all.

Neither of them had ever experienced such sights as those that surrounded them as they travelled into Liverpool on the tram. There were more open spaces than buildings. Whole streets had been demolished. In the town centre a few of the big stores had survived. The Bon Marché, Hendersons, George Henry Lee, shops they would never have the money or status to frequent. Lewis's, Frisby Dykes and the smaller shops were just burnt-out shells.

They'd spent ages waiting in the queue only to face a barrage of questions from an over-officious, spotty clerk in a very shiny suit and grubby collar. Mary put the books in her handbag and tucked it tightly under her arm. She'd heard from the clerk that you could swop or even buy coupons. He'd warned her it was illegal, but legal or not it had also been an eye opener. They could sell some of their clothing coupons, and she would make all their things as she'd always done. Buying the material was much cheaper.

It was nearly half past five when they staggered back, laden with brown paper carrier bags and parcels.

'I'd given the pair of yer up for lost. Did yer get the ration books? They can be right snotty sometimes. Jumped-up little gets they are. A bit of power an' they think they're the Lord Mayor himself. They treated people who had been bombed out somethin' shockin'. Keeping them waiting and then sending them trailing across the city from office to office when the poor souls 'ad just lost their 'omes . . . and they had no money or anyone to leave the kids with. Flaming shocking it was.'

'We got them after we'd been through the grand inquisition,' Mary replied.

'What 'ave yer bought? Yer should save yer coupons, luv.'

'Oh, we have. Your man in that office told us it wasn't legal but people bought or swopped them. We can afford to sell some of the clothing ones. This is just some cleaning stuff, and I got some scorched sheets and pillowcases, bomb-damaged, that a man was selling cheap in that little road that runs off Church Street.'

'And didn't himself want four shillings for them, the creature. She beat him down,' Breda added.

Maggie looked at the two girls with astonishment. 'What do yer want sheets for? It only makes more washin'.'

Mary knew she was treading on dangerous ground already. 'We always had them at home. I ... I ... suppose it's like having a bit of home here. A bit of a comfort, a reminder.'

Maggie didn't seem to be put out. She nodded. 'Aye, our Kathleen had some queer notions when she got wed.'

Breda refrained from saying that if, as they hoped, they'd both be working, Maggie would have to do the sheets with the other washing on Mondays.

Mary hung up her cotton jacket. 'I'll wet the tea. I suppose we'll have the men all in on top of us soon?'

Maggie wrinkled her brow. 'No, Mary, luv, we won't see a sight of Jim nor our lads until gone half past six. They stop off at the Grapes for a pint or two.'

'Then won't the tea be ruined altogether?' Breda asked.

'No, queen, I just keep theirs hot. We'll have ours

first. I sent young Kev out to play in the street with those two little madams. I gave them all a conny onny butty.'

'A what?' Mary asked.

'Oh, the kids love them. It's just a bit of condensed milk on a piece of bread, keeps them going until their proper teatime.'

Mary smiled, but inwardly she thought conny onny butties sounded disgusting.

'I'll get these things put away and then I'll call them in to wash their hands.'

Maggie raised her eyes to the ceiling. Didn't these two have some very odd ways of going on? Still, they'd turn up their keep and help out with the chores, and if she played her cards right she wouldn't have to lift a finger hardly. Except for wash days, at the end of which she had the excuse of being worn to a frazzle to get out of having to cook or wash up.

The table was covered with a red and white check tablecloth they'd bought from another street trader and Breda had set out all the cutlery she could find.

'Take that milk bottle off the table, Breda.'

'There's no jug and the plates and mugs are all chipped and cracked,' Breda hissed back.

Patsy, Lily and Kevin had all been called in and given a good wash in the scullery sink. Kevin was used to this procedure.

'Kevin O'Malley, you little bowsie, I've never seen you so mucky. What have you been at?'

'Playing ollies in the gutter,' Patsy answered.

Mary cast her eyes to heaven. Patsy and Lily went to great

lengths to avoid soap and water at all and complained bitterly at having to come into contact with it now.

'You should be grateful it's the decent soap for you and not the carbolic, so stop all this nonsense,' Breda had snapped at Patsy who had been wriggling to get free of her cousin's grip.

Finally they were all seated at the table and Maggie and Mary served up the meal, Maggie slapping hands and telling her two daughters not to snatch and grab, to have some manners and not show her up. They were all halfway through their meal when they heard the back entry door groan protestingly on its rusty hinges.

'Trust them ter get 'ome early terday!' Maggie got to her feet.

'Sit down, Aunty Maggie. I'll see to them,' Mary instructed. She'd have to face them at the back door and she didn't know what kind of reception she'd get.

They were all grubby and their boots were thick with dust and dirt.

'You're all home early. Aunty Maggie said you'd be in later. Well, isn't it grand we can all eat together, like a family. You've just time to take off your boots and get a quick wash. Kevin will clean them for you later on.' She turned and went quickly back into the kitchen, leaving them staring after her in amazement.

'I'm not takin' me bloody boots off for that one!' Bryan blustered and Maurice muttered his agreement.

Jim had noted the tidiness of the scullery, the clean sink and scrubbed draining board, the new dish mop hanging on a rusty nail. The cleaning utensils were stored under the sink and his limited view into the kitchen showed that more changes were in store. They'd worked hard, both of them. Maggie wasn't getting any younger and she'd had a hard time of it bringing the kids up alone for six years and with the worry of him being away too. It was thoughtful of the two girls to ease the burden for his wife.

'You will and so will I. Those girls must have been scrubbing and cleaning non-stop since we left this morning.' He bent and unlaced his boots, placing them side by side against the wall.

'Well, I will, seeing as young Kev is going to clean them, though that's a bloody stupid waste of time as they'll only get dirty again tomorrow,' Bryan scoffed. He'd only had a brief conversation with his cousins, but they were both beautiful. Breda knew it, of course, but that didn't matter. He'd noticed the way she looked at him from under her thick dark lashes.

'I can see now where your mam and me have gone wrong bringing you lot up. No self-discipline, no pride in your appearance. Yer leave your things all over the place for yer poor mam to clear away. A right pair of lazy gets, that's what yer are. Well, I can see things will be changing and I won't hear any moans from you two either. Yer mam's had it hard these last years and she's not getting any younger and no one in the house lifts a finger ter help her, except the queer feller that lives in the parlour, if he's passing through, like.'

Big Jim O'Shea looked coldly at his sons and shook his head. The war had been hard on the women, they had double the responsibilities. Their men were away fighting or on the high seas. He'd been lucky and he gave thanks every day for it, for the convoys, whether Arctic, transatlantic or Mediterranean, had taken a terrible toll in ships and men. The women had faced that worry day after day as well as the shortages and the queues. Then the terror of the Blitz and the loss of their homes, no matter how poor they'd been. Many women cracked under the strain and all that was on offer was gin, strong tea and aspirins, a tonic from the dispensary and the sympathy of friends and relations. He was glad the two girls had come. Maggie's worries were over now.

The truculent expression vanished from Bryan's face as he went into the kitchen, noting how tidy it was and the proper tablecloth covering the table.

Breda and Mary were getting their meals from the oven, and as Breda put his meal down in front of him her fingers touched his own. It was deliberate, he knew that, as was the quick seductive glance she gave him before going back to her own place and resuming her meal, her eyes now fixed on the plate.

His heart lurched at the brief contact but it was a pleasant sensation. She was truly beautiful. All the girls of his acquaintance faded into insignificance. He hadn't been able to get her out of his mind all day and now, well, she'd made it clear that she found him attractive. Life was looking up.

Chapter Three

Kevin looked up apprehensively at the Christian Brother who was talking earnestly to his mammy. His mammy didn't seem worried but he was frightened of being left. He was six, a big boy now, he told himself, but it didn't help much.

Last night he'd clutched his rabbit tightly and lay on the edge of the bed as far away from his cousin Maurice as possible. Maurice had fallen asleep quickly and begun to snore. In fact they'd all snored. Uncle Jim, Bryan and Maurice. No one had snored at home or at Granny Nolan's. Oh, he'd wanted his mammy so much. He'd wanted to get up and go straight to her and say he wanted to go home now, this very minute. His salty tears had seeped into his only toy.

Mammy had got him ready this morning and walked with him to this new school. Patsy and Lily were nearly always late.

He'd been taught by the Christian Brothers in Dublin and some of them had been very hard men to please. In fact they were not very Christian at all. Some boys were beaten regularly and many were the raps on the knuckles with a ruler Kevin himself had been given. This one looked to be one of the hard type. Tall, thin, with a firm, forbidding expression on his face and a hooked nose like that of the big bird he'd once seen a picture of.

'Don't you worry about him, Mrs O'Malley, he'll get on fine with the other boys. Some of them are unruly but they don't get away with that, not in my class they don't. If he works hard and is punctual then I can't see there will be any problems.'

'He'll be no trouble. He's always been a grand little lad. He can write and read very well but he does take a bit of time to catch on to sums. Dividing and taking away and things like that.'

He placed a hand on Kevin's shoulder. 'Well, I'm sure we can remedy that.'

Mary twisted her hands nervously. She'd glanced down at her son and seen the stricken look in his eyes.

'Could you have a bit of patience with him, Brother Francis, please? He's very confused just now what with coming over here and being sort of thrown in at the deep end with my cousin and her family.'

'Mrs O'Malley, don't trouble yourself. He'll be as right as rain by the end of the week. We're sometimes prone to being "confused" ourselves. This school has been closed and reopened more times than I can count over the last six years.' He managed a grim smile.

He was a well-spoken, well-set-up man, Mary thought as she gently pushed a lock of hair off Kevin's forehead. Her son was so young and everything was so strange to him that tears were pricking her eyes. But she knew that the sooner she left the better it would be for him. Mary forced herself to step back while Kevin felt the tears burning his eyes. He *knew* his mammy loved and cared for him, but he wished he had a da like Patsy and Lily. He'd feel better if he had the protection a da could give. But Mary had to get back. Breda would be ready and waiting for her. They were both taking Maggie's advice. Breda was going up to the Post Office and she herself was going to Williams's. With any luck, by the end of the day they'd both have jobs.

Maggie had told her last night that in some ways the Blitz had been a blessing in disguise for some people. For the first time in years there had been full employment, for those who wanted it. Even Gerry O'Hanlon who lived across the road and was definitely workshy had worked full time and that had been a miracle. The dockers didn't have to wait on the stands to be picked these days. No, there was more than enough work for everyone. When all the men were demobbed from the forces it might be a different tale, though.

The morning had passed quickly, Kevin realised as the bell rang not only to signify the end of lessons but for the Angelus too. They all said the prayer to Our Lady, which they would repeat at six o'clock tonight, and then they were pushing, shoving, scrambling and laughing out into the playground.

Brother Francis had made him read out loud and that had scared him and caused him to stumble a bit, but his new teacher had said, 'Thank you, Kevin, you may sit down now.' Next they'd had a religious lesson which was easy and then they'd had to copy some words off the blackboard and been told they must learn them thoroughly by tomorrow as there would be a test.

Now he just stood and watched the other boys playing. Not one of them had spoken to him yet. He was so miserable that he almost wished Patsy and Lily were with him, but the girls had another part of the building where they were taught by nuns who always looked desperate. They'd walk him home, though. Mammy and Aunty Maggie had said they had to.

Suddenly he was confronted by two boys both bigger and

stronger than he was. He shrank back against the wall. One had a shock of ginger hair, freckles and crafty-looking eyes. The other one had black hair and a few pimples on his pasty face.

'We heard that you've come from Dublin,' the dark-haired lad said.

Kevin nodded, wishing his mammy or even Brother Francis was with him.

'Youse lot didn't go and fight. Cowards, that's what youse lot were,' the ginger-haired one said menacingly.

'Cowardy cowardy custard,' the other boy chanted, poking a finger in Kevin's face, then giving him a hard dig in the shoulder.

'We . . . we weren't frightened. Mammy told me why we didn't fight but I . . . I can't remember.'

The boy with the red hair yelled with mocking laughter. 'Listen to 'im. Mammy! Yer big baby!'

Tears of fear, misery and frustration trickled slowly down Kevin's cheeks, but he spoke up.

'My da went to fight. He went for you and us . . . and he didn't come back. He's buried in a far-away place.'

'Oh, yeah! Yer just sayin' that.'

'I'm not!'

'Just what is going on here, Thomas Rooney?'

At the appearance of Brother Francis both boys drew back.

'What have you been saying to this boy? I can't abide bullies and I'll have none of this. Go over there by the wall and kneel and say a decade of the rosary. In fact, make it three, and stay there until I call you in. Kevin, what did they say?' Brother Francis looked less forbidding now.

'They said I . . . we . . . were cowards, but my da wasn't. He joined the Army.'

The man nodded. This war had taken a terrible toll, not only on the citizens of this country but many others too. But they'd won. It was the triumph of good over the terrible evil that had spread across the world, contaminating everything and everyone it touched.

His tone softened a little. 'Go on in now and wash your face. Will there be anyone to meet you when we're finished for the day?'

'My cousins. Patsy and Lily O'Shea.'

Brother Francis's expression changed. Mother Superior had told him that if ever a girl was destined for damnation, and she'd seen many in her time, it was Patsy O'Shea. He nodded briefly and turned away.

The afternoon dragged on with sums and history and Kevin wished it was four o'clock. Tommy Rooney and Vinny Burns hadn't spoken to him again but they'd obviously been talking to the other kids in the class because he'd had a lot of sneering glances directed at him, so he'd bent his head over his exercise books and made sure he got out of the door quickly when Brother Francis dismissed them for the day.

'What's up with yer?' Patsy demanded irritably when he joined them at the gate to the boys' part of the school. She wasn't at all happy to have to wait.

'Nothin'.'

'There is. You've been cryin'. You've got dirty marks all down yer face.'

'I haven't! I haven't!' he cried defiantly.

Lily took hold of his hand. 'Don't you take no notice of them boys. I was so scared when I first came ter school I wet me knickers.'

Patsy glared at her. 'God, did yer have to say that, Lily? Now he'll be tormenting us with it for ever.'

'He won't, will yer, Kev?'

He shook his head, comforted by Lily's hand holding tightly to his.

'Tommy Rooney and Vinny Burns were tormenting me.'

'Why didn't yer belt them, then?'

'They're bigger than me and Mammy told Brother Francis I was a good boy and I didn't want to let her down on the first day.'

'For a start I'd stop calling yer mam Mammy. It sounds daft. No wonder they was skitting yer.'

The grip on his hand tightened as though Lily, with her straggling fair curls half hiding her face, was silently giving him more support.

'Well, aren't yer going to do anything about it, Patsy? He's family now and them two have always had big gobs on them.'

Patsy thought about this and decided her sister was right. The honour of the family had been called into question. 'Where are they?'

Lily pointed a grubby finger to a back entry and her sister was off like a shot.

'Will she take them apart, Lily?'

'You bet she will. Come on, Kev, our Patsy's dead good at belting people.'

Lily urged him into a trot and they arrived at the entry a little out of breath and just in time to see Patsy grab a handful of Tommy Rooney's hair and bang his head hard against the wall.

'That's for tormentin' me cousin!'

The boy yelled in pain. 'I never touched him.'

'Yer was skitting him.' This was accompanied by another bang to Tommy's head before Patsy turned to Vinny who looked a sickly grey colour. The pallor didn't last very long. There was a crack, followed by another, and the red marks of Patsy's fingers brought a stinging flush to his cheeks.

'If the pair of youse touch 'im or even call 'im names I'll batter yer both, and what's more so will our kid. Our Maurice will purra gob on yer and yer brothers an' all, so clear off 'ome.'

They ran.

Lily was looking at her sister with pride.

'I told you she was great, didn't I? They won't be at you again,' she said, still holding his hand tightly.

'Come on the pair of yer, let's get home. I'm starvin'!' Patsy said, preening herself at making short work of defeating the opposition.

'Thanks. Thanks, Patsy.' Kevin was really grateful.

She shrugged and ran on ahead.

Lily suddenly became shy and ducked her head so Kevin couldn't see her face properly. Her faded print dress was too short and she had no socks on, just a pair of grubby white pumps.

Kevin cast her a quick glance. It had been Lily who had pushed Patsy into getting their own back. 'I . . . I've got a rabbit, Lily.'

She looked up. 'A real one?'

'No, he's knitted. I got him at Christmas last year. I'll show you him, if you like.'

She nodded.

'I . . . I . . . might lend him to you for a couple of hours too.'

Again there was the squeeze of her hand and they smiled at each other, never dreaming that a friendship was being forged which would last for many long years.

When they got in Breda and Mary were in the kitchen looking highly delighted with themselves.

'Come here to me. How did today at the school above go? Were the lessons hard? Were the other boys nice or horrible?' Mary had been worried all day.

'Tommy Rooney and Vinny Burns from Lightbody Street were tormenting him so our Patsy belted the pair of them,' Lily said proudly.

Patsy just shrugged.

'Aye, it would be those two all right,' Maggie said with annoyance. 'I can't stand that Josie Rooney or Maura Burns. Sluts the pair of them. 'Usbands always fallin' down drunk. Reserved occupations they 'ad.' Maggie laughed cuttingly. 'Reserved for knocking back the ale in the pub!' Her tone was scathing.

Mary looked concerned.

'He'll be all right, Aunty Mary, honest. When our Patsy clouts someone she does it proper, like. She'll even go an' speak to a scuffer and that's a dead brave thing to do.' Lily tried to ease some of Kevin's mam's worry.

'What's a scuffer?' Kevin asked.

'A policeman. Don't you have them over there?' Lily asked.

Mary smiled at her. 'Of course we do, we just give them different names. The Guards, the Garda or the Garda Siochana, we call them.'

She liked Lily. She was a bright little thing, and washed and dressed properly, with a ribbon in her hair, she'd be very pretty. Kevin had seemed to have taken a shine to her, they were still holding hands.

'Well, are yer going to tell him the happy news then?' Maggie urged.

'I was just getting round to it. Mammy's got a job sewing overalls, and the faster I work the more money I'll be paid. Aunty Breda has got a job too in the big post office, sorting letters. Isn't that grand altogether?'

They'd both been lucky. The shrewdness of the manager in Williams's enabled him to judge that Mary would be diligent, punctual and fussy about her work, and the sorting office's head clerk had liked Breda. With her quick nimble fingers and command of the written word she would do well. Her looks had caused him a moment's concern but then he'd just mentally shrugged. She'd get on with the others, who'd stand no nonsense out of her.

Maggie beamed at them all. Two good extra wages coming in and Mary had plans. Tomorrow, in her dinner time, she was going to get some stuff to make curtains and God knows what else and then ask if she could stay late and run them up on the sewing machines at Williams's. Maggie could see life becoming easier for her by the minute. She'd have time now to have many a good jangle with Flossie O'Hanlon who lived opposite with Gerry and their three surviving kids. And with the Kennedys, her fortunate neighbours who still had their home in one piece. Yes, life was certainly looking up. That Breda had said Mary could work miracles with a pair of scissors and a needle and thread.

'Later on we'll go on up to see Father Hayes. It's time those two were getting ready for their First Communion. Was meladdo there having instruction back home, Mary, luv?'

'He was due to go in there at the end of the month.'

'Right then, they can go together. How in the name of God I'll get a dress and veil for her I don't know. An' it's no use Father Hayes saying it's not a fashion parade and he'd prefer to see them just neatly turned out. I'm not having 'er disappointed. Our Patsy wasn't.'

'Where's Patsy's dress?' Breda asked.

Maggie tutted. 'I got ten shillings for all of it from Flossie O'Hanlon for their Carmel and after she'd finished with it it was like a rag and the veil was in ribbons. Flossie's too soft with them kids.'

'Aunty Maggie, don't worry about that. I'll make her a dress and trim a veil and I'll make Kevin a pair of trousers and a shirt. They'll both look grand. I'll make Lily a nice headdress with wax flowers too.'

'Sure, she can make anything. She makes great hats altogether,' Breda informed them. 'And I'll get them both a nice pair of rosary beads and a holy picture just as a reminder of the day that's in it,' she added generously. She'd have her own money now so she'd spend a bit on them. She'd have to turn up her keep but there would still be a lot left over. She'd be paid twice what she'd get if by some miracle she was to land a similar job in the General Post Office in O'Connell Street at home.

Now there were tears in Maggie's eyes.

'God luv the pair of you. I just hope that these two of mine will grow up to be like you both.'

'That just might be the truth, Aunty Maggie,' Mary replied, her gaze flitting from her sister to Patsy, and then her son and Lily still holding hands. The sight caused a smile to cross her face. Kevin appeared to have found a true friend in little Lily O'Shea; maybe now he'd be happier.

Chapter Four

In the first election after the war Labour had swept the board, ending six years of coalition government.

'It's the people's party. Those fellers are all out for the working man and woman and about time too,' Jim stated, after reading aloud from the *Echo*.

'Do yer think they'll change much, Jim?' Maggie asked. She didn't understand much about votes and something called a 'manifesto'.

'They're bound to, luv. They'll have the country up and running soon and there'll be plenty of work for everyone as things get back to normal.'

'It'll take years and years to get back to normal. Half the city has gone. They're going to have to build thousands of houses. Flossie was telling me she'd heard they're putting people into "prefabs" now, whatever *they* are.'

'Prefabricated, luv. They come in flat pieces and then they put them together. All one level, mind.'

'Well, I wouldn't fancy that. What if they don't fix them together properly? The whole flaming house could come down on top of you. No, I'm staying put. That bloody Hitler couldn't shift me so no flaming Council is going to.'

'Just think, we'll be able to have bananas again,' Bryan said.

His mother cast him a disparaging glance.

'Oh, get him! Again! We never had them before. None of us 'as ever tasted one of the damned things. They were way above our means and don't you forget that, Bryan O'Shea.'

Bryan flushed with embarrassment, casting a quick glance at Breda and thankful that she seemed to be engrossed in her own thoughts.

'It says here that two big atom bombs, whatever they are, have been dropped on Hiroshima and Nagasaki.' Jim struggled with the names. 'There's not a building left standing and thousands were killed in a few minutes. A whole *city*.'

Maggie was incredulous. 'With just one bomb?'

'So it says here. Yer could see a big mushroom-shaped cloud for miles. It can't be long now before they chuck in the towel. Days, I'd say.'

'Will we 'ave a street party, Mam, like we did for VE day?' Patsy asked, her eyes lighting up with hope.

'Of course we will, luv, we've all been saving what we can.' Maggie looked across at her husband, engrossed again in the newspaper. He considered himself an ignorant man but he was educating himself by reading the newspaper from cover to cover. The likes of him didn't go and borrow books from what libraries there were left, he told himself. No, library books were for people who were educated.

Maggie turned to her son. 'What with all them troops going home there's been . . . well . . . things they didn't want or need, hasn't there, Bryan?'

He nodded sagely. 'Oh, aye, there were tins of stuff of all varieties that they'd cadged or paid for. The Yanks never seemed to go short of anything, and that included girls.'

'We'll get a day off school, Kev,' Lily said.

'Honest?'

'Cross me heart.' Lily made a sign on her chest with her finger.

'What's a street party, then?'

'Don't you know nothing?' Patsy demanded of him.

'Tharral do, you!' Maggie snapped. Patsy was going to be a real headache as she got older. She suspected the girl often got a belt from the nuns for her cheeky ways, but Patsy never told her because she knew she'd get another from her as well.

Lily pushed her hair out of her eyes. She had a thick fringe that needed cutting but she screamed and hid when Maggie produced the scissors.

'Well, everyone's tables are shoved into the street and the chairs and benches too. They put them in a line down the middle of the road and we has butties and pies, jelly and custard and tins of peaches and pears with Carnation milk. We have paper party hats and little flags and things and then we all sing and the grown-ups dance and get drunk—'

'And tharral do from you an' all, Lily O'Shea!'

'It sounds grand, Aunty Maggie. And why shouldn't people take a drop or two of the good stuff? They've got something to celebrate, after all. Do you still have the little flags and things from the last party? I'll be only too glad to make some more,' Mary offered.

'Thanks, queen, but we've kept them all.'

Patsy laughed. 'Yer should have seen it last time. It was great, really great. Big flags and little flags everywhere! Carmel O'Hanlon's da got so drunk he was talkin' to a lamppost thinking it was Mrs O'Hanlon, then he fell and went to sleep on their doorstep an' Mrs O'Hanlon left him there all night. Just shut the door on him. Carmel said there was a shockin' row next day!'

Maggie glared at her daughter. 'You've a gob on you like a parish oven. Any more of the lip out of you and it'll be the back of me hand you'll feel, melady.'

After that there didn't seem to be much news about Japan until on 14 August, very late at night, Mr Attlee, the Prime Minister, went on the wireless and told the country: 'The last of our enemies is laid low. Japan has surrendered unconditionally.'

It was Flossie O'Hanlon who came banging on the front door, getting everyone out of bed. The O'Hanlons had a wireless set, something Maggie viewed with disparagement. Flossie had all her priorities upside down.

'It's just been on the wireless, Maggie. Mr Attlee himself it was and our Gerry was still up. He let out such a roar I thought he'd fell and banged his head. It's over, it's really over. That emperor of theirs has had enough. It must have been them Yankee bombs!'

'Oh, glory be to God! Jim, did yer hear that?'

Big Jim lifted his wife, clad in a faded nightdress, off her feet and swung her around.

Maggie screamed.

'Put me down, yer fool, I've gone all dizzy like.' But she was laughing.

Everyone else, also in their nightclothes, was laughing and crying and hugging each other and Patsy, Lily and Kevin were jumping up and down. Lily as usual was holding Kevin's hand.

Mary and Breda felt strangely out of place although Mary thought she knew how it must feel. Mam had told her how people celebrated after the Treaty was signed in 1922. That was before they all fell out over it and started a civil war.

'Oh, Aunty Maggie, I'm so glad for you all!' She hugged the woman tightly, feeling her trembling with emotion.

Bryan O'Shea grabbed at the chance to sweep Breda, in her thin cotton nightdress that clearly showed the outline of her breasts, into his arms and kiss her on the mouth and get away with it. She didn't shove him away or try to stop him. In fact he thought she'd enjoyed it. There wasn't a second chance because young Maurice yanked her from him and hugged her. To Bryan's delight Breda shoved him away roughly when he tried to kiss her. So young Maurice has taken a shine to her too, he thought. Well, although Maurice was nearer to Breda's age than he was, he could see his younger brother didn't stand a chance.

'Jim, go an' get those bottles you got off them Yanks that you've hidden in the yard. There'll be no work tomorrow, or even the next day. I can't believe it! I just can't believe it!' Tears were streaming down Maggie's cheeks, and Flossie's, and Phil Kennedy's – Chris's mother who'd come running after Flossie's announcement. They were all on the brink of hysteria until Big Jim took them in hand.

'Stop that bloody noise! You'd think you were at a wake instead of a celebration. Get some of this down you and pull yerselves together! Grown women like you all whinging like babies.'

'He doesn't understand. Men don't,' Flossie said, drying her eyes on the hem of the apron she still wore.

'No, they flaming well don't. I think I've a right to cry, Jim O'Shea. We lost our Davie,' Maggie reminded him.

'You're right, Flossie, men don't have the same feelings. We've had to go through six years of pure hell. We've lost our sons, thousands of women have lost husbands and brothers *and* their homes, and the city is in ruins too. It's us who had to wait and worry. It's like a big weight being lifted offen you,' Phil added.

'Hadn't somebody better go and tell the queer feller in the parlour?' Flossie said.

'I think he'll already know, what with all this screeching going on,' Jim answered.

'I'll go and tell him formally,' Mary offered and promptly disappeared into the lobby. She was curious. She'd only ever seen him once, when he'd been passing through the kitchen to go to the privy in the yard. He'd just nodded to her. He was a tall, thin man with dark hooded eyes but he appeared pleasant enough. Maybe she'd be able to learn more tonight.

When the door finally opened he seemed taller yet there was nothing menacing about him.

'Mr Fallowfield, I'm sorry about all the noise in there, but I thought we should tell you the news. The war's over. The Japanese have surrendered unconditionally. It *really* is over now.'

He nodded. He had his own wireless set and already knew and had poured himself a small glass of rum.

'It's good of you to come to inform me.'

Mary smiled. There was no note of sarcasm in his voice. He was an educated man, you could tell by his speech, and she wondered why he stayed here in this madhouse where he had to share the basic facilities with the rest of them. Aunty Maggie took him a big jug of hot water each morning to pour into the old-fashioned bowl so he could wash and shave. He himself brought the jug back into the scullery.

'You are the niece from Ireland with the little boy, aren't you?' he asked in a quiet but interested tone.

'I am so. I've come here to work. Col – Colin, my husband – was killed at El Alamein and the poverty in Dublin is worse than here. Did you know we had rationing and a blackout too, because we got bombed as well? By mistake, I think. They thought we were Belfast where all the shipyards are.'

'Really?'

'It wasn't as bad as here, though. Will you come within and have a drink with us? Don't be worrying about coming in on top of us all, tonight's special.'

He seemed to hesitate, then nodded. 'I'll just put my dressing gown on.'

Mary had only been able to see his head round the door and now that had disappeared. She wondered what his room was like. The door hadn't been open enough for her to see inside the room where she might have glimpsed something that would throw some light on his strange, solitary life.

He came out wearing a thick grey flannel dressing gown that had red blanket stitch around the edges and was fastened by a red cord. In his hand was a half-bottle of Lamb's Navy Rum.

'Lead the way, girl.'

He actually looked as if he were going to smile.

'It's Mary O'Malley, Mr Fallowfield.'

'Very well, Mrs O'Malley.'

When he entered the kitchen everyone fell silent.

'Mr Fallowfield has come to have a drink with us all for the night that's in it,' Mary announced.

Jim pointed to a grubby upholstered chair. 'Sit down there, and I'll get you a glass. We don't see enough of you and you know you're welcome to mix with us in this house, isn't he, Maggie?'

Maggie nodded, still a bit taken aback.

'Isn't it great news altogether?' Mary tried to lift the conversation.

'It is.' He took the glass Jim held out and raised it.

'A toast. To the end of it all and let's hope that that's the last war for this century. Two in fifty years is two too many.'

Everyone raised their glasses and mugs and gradually the atmosphere thawed as Gerry O'Hanlon and Bob and Chris Kennedy arrived.

Phil looked at her husband and their eldest son who'd fought in France and tears filled her eyes. God had been good to her. She had her home and her family. She looked at Maggie and sighed and shook her head sadly, knowing that Maggie would be thinking of Davie.

Maggie leaned across to Mary.

'Slip into his room while we've got him in here. See if you can find out more about him,' she whispered.

Mary was horrified. 'I can't go doing that! It's a desperate thing to do.'

'Then I'll go.'

'You can't.'

'I can and I will. It's my house.'

'Oh, I'll go then. Now go and keep talking to your man,' Mary advised.

She felt awful. She was riddled with guilt as she looked round the room. It was sparsely furnished but that didn't matter as it was so small. It was also very clean and neat. A folded piece of notepaper lay on the top of the chest of drawers and she picked it up. Oh, God, this was desperate, she told herself, her hands shaking.

She scanned the lines and felt the blood drain from her face. A cold chilly feeling crept down her spine as though an icy hand had touched her. It was a letter telling Albert

Fallowfield to return to his duties as public executioner. Albert Fallowfield was the hangman at Walton Jail! She put the letter back. She was shocked but she could now understand why he kept himself to himself. No one would want to take such a man into their home. It was bad luck. She crossed herself before leaving the room.

She managed a smile as Maggie got up and came over to her, clutching another glass of cheap port.

'Well?' she hissed.

'There wasn't anything at all. Not a sight nor sign of anything that would give a person some idea,' Mary lied. There was no way she was going to tell Maggie. Besides, the man was a quiet person who had spoken civilly to her and was now chatting quietly with Jim about the future of the city, and after all *someone* had to do it.

'Did you open the drawers or cupboards or wardrobe and have a good root?'

'I did not! Sure to God isn't that taking it too far, and besides I didn't have time.'

Maggie turned away full of indignation, wishing she had a key for the room, but she didn't. She'd foolishly given him the only one. She wished now she'd had a spare one cut.

The next two days were declared public holidays as parties were held in streets in every city, town and village across the country. Bonfires were lit, too, and some got out of hand and did nearly as much damage as the incendiary bombs had done.

There was great activity in Hornby Street, as there was in every other street in the city. Tins of corned beef and Spam, pears and peaches, and even such exotic luxuries as pineapple chunks appeared as if by magic. The women had been hoarding them for months. Either they or their menfolk had bought them from the departing American troops, or found a broken crate that was being swung on to the dockside by the winch of a cargo ship. Damaged goods had always been one of a docker's 'perks' and both the foremen and the police on the dock gate usually turned a blind eye, unless of course you were greedy and tried to get too much out. They didn't bother for a bottle of something or a couple of tins.

The flags and bunting were got out again and the street was festooned with red, white and blue. There was excitement in the air and everyone was laughing and joking. Kevin was bursting with it, as were all the kids in the street, even those who had been too young to understand what the war was really about. They played street games and ran up and down and in and out of all the houses and got in their mothers' way and were yelled at and slapped and told to 'shift yerself from under me feet'.

'Go an' play in the next street, or preferably on the railway line!' Phil Kennedy added grimly. 'You shouldn't even be in this street at all, Micky Grady. Go back an' mither the daylights out of yer own mam!'

Despite the frenziedly hurried and makeshift arrangements the day went well. Dusk began to fall and people gathered in groups and danced and sang all the old favourites. 'Roll out the Barrel', 'We'll Meet Again', 'The White Cliffs of Dover' and 'It's a Long Way to Tipperary', the latter confusing Breda and Kevin until Mary told them it was a very old song the soldiers going to the Boer War had sung, while Ireland was still part of the British Empire.

Mary sat on the step and watched the festivities with mixed feelings. Happiness that the war was over but sadness that Col wasn't here to share that happiness with her.

Bryan sat down beside her. She was just as beautiful as Breda, but she was a widow, she'd know what it was like to sleep with a man. She'd be very experienced.

'Isn't it all great – or grand as you'd say?'

'It is so,' she replied a little tartly, thinking he was patronising her. He'd had quite a bit to drink too by the look and smell of him.

'Do you want another drink?' He indicated the empty glass she was holding between her hands.

'No. No thanks, Bryan. I've had enough. To be honest with you, it's ready for my bed I am. It's been a long day.'

He leaned closer and she drew back, away from the smell of beer on his breath.

'You wouldn't be worn out if it was my bed you'd be ready for.'

Her cheeks turned scarlet. 'How dare you speak to me like that!'

'It was a com- compliment,' he replied.

'Well, it's one I can do without.' She got to her feet, anger still making her cheeks burn, but he stood up too.

'Oh, come on, Mary. Don't I deserve even a quick kiss? It's a party.' He lunged towards her and instinctively she lashed out, her fingers leaving a mark on his cheek.

'Is he bothering you?'

Mary looked up to see Chris Kennedy at her side, his expression grim. She began to relax. She liked and trusted Chris. She'd seen him about a dozen times since they'd first met in Maggie's house and no one in the entire street had a bad word to say about him. She liked his easy way and his lack of embarrassment, and she was grateful now for his intervention.

'He is not. I've just clattered him.'

Chris caught Bryan's arm and gave him a hefty push. 'Clear off and look for someone else to annoy before I belt you. Your da would lay you out cold if he knew you'd been taking advantage of Mrs O'Malley. She's your cousin and a widow. Haven't you got a brain in your head?'

Mary hugged herself. For her the brightness had gone from the party.

'Thanks, Chris.'

'It was nothing.' He tried to shrug it off, but she looked so lovely, so young and somehow vulnerable, that his heart started to beat in an odd, jerky way.

'I'm fine, truly I am,' she reiterated, but anger was being replaced by the stirring of emotions she hadn't felt since Col's death.

'OK, then. I think I'd better get my da inside the house before Mam sees him. He's been at the hard stuff and he can't take it.' He managed a smile but he was longing to ask her to dance, just for the sake of having his arm round her waist. The feelings that had started when they first met had grown each time he'd seen her and now he was certain that he loved her.

Bryan had shrugged off both Chris's warnings and his stinging cheek as he walked away. He must have been mad to think she'd fall instantly into his arms – or, to be precise, his bed. She had a staid, 'touch-me-not' manner. Breda, on the other hand, was single, fancy-free and even more beautiful than her sister, with her flushed cheeks and shining eyes.

He didn't even bother to ask her if she wanted to dance. He just gripped her tightly round the waist, took her hand and moved to what he imagined to be a waltz.

'You're great, Breda. You're really gorgeous.'

'And you're drunk, Bryan,' she answered drily.

'I'm not. I've had a couple of bevvies but I'm not drunk.' He pointed to Gerry O'Hanlon, sitting on the kerb clutching a half-empty bottle and looking in danger of falling flat on his face. 'Now *that's* drunk.'

She laughed. She liked him, a fact she'd begun to realise over the past few days. He was a bit of a loudmouth but he'd fought in a bloody war, for God's sake.

'I've not long been demobbed. I had three years of it, though, and it was no bloody picnic.'

Breda looked at him with interest until Uncle Jim, who had heard his son's words, tapped him on the shoulder.

'You can give all that a miss. It's over and you're not the only one in this street who fought.'

Bryan changed the subject. 'Do yer like yer job, Breda?'

'I do so. What a strange thing to be saying!'

'I don't. I bloody hate mine, though it's better than it used to be.' He drew her closer and she didn't object or try to pull away.

'What would you be if you had the chance at all?' Her voice was soft and encouraging.

'Dunno, really. Go on the railways, that's a good job, with a pension at the end of it too. Or go to sea, now the bloody U-boats have all been sunk or scuttled.'

'And that's enough swearing out of you, Bryan O'Shea,' Maggie said acidly as she was swept by in the arms of her tipsy husband.

The incident with Mary was not completely forgotten. 'God, yer can't do nothing round here without someone sticking their oar in.'

'I'd noticed that myself,' Breda agreed.

'Should we go to the pictures one night, Breda? On the sly, like?'

She remained silent for a few seconds, then she nodded. 'Sure, where's the harm in it? I like you and you like me. When will we go?'

'Saturday night. We'll go to the Odeon. There's always good films on there.'

Breda smiled at him. Things were definitely looking up. She'd only ever been to the pictures once back home, with Mary and Bernadette Gallagher. Now she had a good job, money to spend on herself and a night out in the offing. She squeezed his hand to make her feelings known.

Their conduct hadn't gone unnoticed by either Mary or Maggie.

After Mary had watched Chris Kennedy walk away she'd turned and gone inside. Maggie had followed soon after.

'God, I'm spitting feathers. Put that kettle on, Mary, luv. Give me a good cuppa any day rather than that rotgut that passes for sherry and port wine.'

When the tea was made and poured out they took their mugs and went back to the front door.

'That's something we're going to have to watch.' Mary nodded her head in the direction of Breda and Bryan. She had no intention of telling Maggie of Bryan's conduct and thereby ruining the day for her cousin.

Maggie's expression changed. 'We will. They're first cousins and any romance will have to be put a stop to. Father Hayes would have a fit. They're too closely related.'

Mary nodded in agreement. 'Maybe now things are settling down we could persuade her to go out with the girls she works with. Then she'd meet someone else.'

'Oh, I know our Bryan. No girl over the age of sixteen is safe with meladdo over there. Thinks himself Jack the lad, he does.'

Mary sighed heavily. Maggie would belt him to bits if she knew he'd tried to kiss her, and Uncle Jim would take off his broad leather belt and flay the skin off him.

'If she doesn't go out with the girls and keeps this up there'll be murder. I know Breda. It's stubborn she is.' Her tone was firm.

Their conversation was interrupted by Chris Kennedy who had plucked up the courage and decided to ask Mary to dance.

Maggie smiled at him. At twenty-three he was the oldest of Phil's sons and was liked by everyone in the street. He was a bricklayer by trade and would never be out of a job for a long time to come, Maggie surmised.

'Mrs O'Malley, would you like to dance? You look a bit left out of things.'

'She doesn't need your pity,' Maggie replied but without any harshness in her voice.

He was indignant. 'It wasn't pity.'

Mary smiled at Maggie and then turned to Chris. 'I'd like that. It's a long time since I danced.'

'I'll try not to step on your feet.'

She laughed. 'It'll be the other way round so it will.

'They'll all talk, you know,' she said in a loud whisper as he drew her into the increasingly noisy crowd.

'Let them. It's a celebration, isn't it? They don't know anything about that young fool's pass at you, so why can't I ask a lovely young girl to dance? And you *are* still a girl.'

She ducked her head to hide the flush that was spreading over her cheeks. It was a long time since she'd felt like this. In fact she hadn't felt so young and carefree since Col had died.

'Because I'm a war widow. A *young* widow.'

'And a beautiful one too. Anyway, you're not on your own.

Half the young girls and women in the city are widows. There was one from Blenheim Street who was widowed twice and finally up and married an American bloke and went back with him. He was black and that caused quite a stir, I can tell you. Her mam's on her knees in the church morning noon and night and her da won't go into his local pub. He drinks further up Scottie Road now. Daft it is. I met him, he was a decent bloke.'

'And that's what would happen to me too. Aunty Maggie would probably send for the Mammy and she'd be over here like a shot and drag us all home.'

'Mary, you're a grown woman, not a kid. You're a mother yourself, for heaven's sake.'

She smiled again. 'Try convincing Aunty Maggie and the Mammy about that. Besides, I have plans for the future,' she said shyly.

'To do what?'

'I'm telling no one yet.'

He held her waist a little more tightly. 'Would there be a place for me in these plans?'

'I . . . I don't know. Anyway, haven't I enough on my hands just now with Breda?'

'That one will have half the fellers in the neighbourhood making fools of themselves over her.'

'Don't I know that already? But she seems to have taken to that eejit Bryan and she's on thin ice there. They're first cousins.'

Chris nodded, thankful she didn't seem upset. She was right. Bryan O'Shea was an idiot. 'Then you've got your work cut out.'

Mary sighed. 'I know. That's what I was talking to Aunty Maggie about.'

Before he could answer a girl with peroxided hair wearing heavy Panstick, rouge and lipstick pulled at Chris's arm. She was slightly tipsy

He sighed. 'Rosie, will you go and torment someone else? I'm dancing with Mary . . . Mrs O'Malley.'

The girl's expression changed and her eyes became hard. 'Then you're dancing with the wrong one. She's a widow with a kid. She should be wearing black and be up at the church praying for 'er husband. I'm single and fancy-free.' She tossed back her bleached hair and looked at him with narrowed eyes.

She'd been almost certain he was going to ask her out until that one had arrived from Ireland, and she had been mad about him for months. She was thankful that Breda seemed to be throwing herself at Bryan O'Shea. Single, and really beautiful without the aid of make-up, Breda would have been a rival she knew she couldn't compete with. In fact, she was beginning to hate both of them because of their stunning natural beauty.

And free with your fancy ideas too, Mary thought. The girl was the same age as Breda and she'd heard Maggie say that Rosie O'Hanlon had her mam's heart broke with the carry-on out of her. With all that make-up and dyed hair she should go up to Lime Street and make a proper job of it, Flossie had once yelled at her daughter. Gerry was no help at all either. He was too easy-going and nearly always in the pub with his cronies. Half the time he only had enough money for half a pint but his mates would stand him a bevvy, and it was their company he went for, that and to avoid the constant rows and arguments that went on in the house.

'I might go on dancing with Mrs O'Malley all night, but

then I might just save the last dance for you if you behave and don't have any more of that cheap sherry.'

He was treating her like a naughty child, Mary thought, and she was far from being a child. For some reason she'd taken a dislike to the girl, and it had nothing to do with the make-up and brassy hair. It was something she rarely did and she wondered if it had anything to do with the way Chris Kennedy was holding her.

Chapter Five

Work and rebuilding were in full swing as more and more men were demobbed and many women were laid off, especially the married ones. But Mary's savings grew. She was a fast and neat worker and earned the top rate.

She really didn't enjoy the job. Williams's was a nightmare world of heat, noise and frenetic activity. The room she worked in was like a big barn. There were rows and rows of sewing machines set in double banks facing each other, the motorised belt that drove them running on wheels slung from the roof.

Between the rows of machines was a shallow wooden trough where the finished garments were placed. Every worker relied on all the others to keep the line going. By the time she went home Mary always had a headache, having spent the day hunched over her machine, forcing the material under the drumming head of the needle. There were accidents, of course, most frequently when the needle pierced the top of the finger, often breaking and leaving half embedded in the nail itself. On one occasion a girl with long blonde hair had got it caught and but for the quick action of one of the pressers who cut her free would have been seriously injured. Since then every girl and woman (no matter how short their hair) was ordered to wear a turban.

John Harvey, the overseer, had taken a shine to Mary and often stayed behind while she made curtains, cushion covers, sheets and clothes for nearly everyone in the family. His presence made her use of the company machines less of a serious affair. Indeed, but for John Harvey's interest in her he would have refused point blank to allow her this practice.

'You know, Mary, you've got a bit of a talent there,' he said on the evening she was finishing off Lily's Communion dress.

She smiled up at him. 'So I've been told. All I know is that it saves us a lot of money. Material uses fewer coupons than the finished garment. This little dress would have been expensive in both money and coupons – if you could get one in the first place.'

He nodded understandingly. He was a kindly man and never spoke to her the way he spoke to some of the other women. Mind you, there were some who only understood his sarcasm and swearing.

He was married and she judged him to be about forty. His wife had been an invalid for years and they had no children. He knew her background, too. She'd told him over the weeks as he sat and watched her work, drawing on his pipe and nodding or shaking his head.

'Would you like to see what I've made for her headdress?'

She bent and pulled a brown paper bag on to her knee and gently and carefully drew out what could only be described as a small tiara of white and pink wax flowers with leaves made from the silver paper that lined cigarette packets.

'Mary, that's . . . that's just beautiful.' He fingered it gently, almost as if it were made of diamonds and pearls.

She smiled shyly. 'No one's seen it yet at home. Tonight we're going to have a sort of dress rehearsal, just Aunty Maggie, me and little Lily.'

'Well, she'll be made up with that. You know, Mary, you could make them in your spare time and sell them.'

She smiled again. 'That's what I intend to do. That's why I left Ireland, to open a millinery shop here. When I've got enough money.'

'I could lend you some, Mary. I'm a prudent man. I don't go in for a lavish lifestyle. It would start you off. Every woman and girl in the city wears some kind of a hat.'

Mary was in a dilemma. She didn't want to seem ungrateful by throwing his offer in his face, yet she didn't really want to be beholden to him.

'Aren't you kindness itself and I'd love to take up your offer, but I'm not settled yet. I've got a lot to learn about millinery. Ordering the materials and trimmings, even how to deal with the money side of it.'

He nodded. He could understand that. 'Well, if there's anything at all I can do, Mary, promise you'll ask my advice?'

'You won't tell anyone, though, will you? I'd feel such an eejit if nothing came of it.'

'Your secret's safe with me, luv, and I wish you the best of luck.'

'That's very kind of you, Mr Harvey.'

'Can't we drop the formalities out of working hours? It's John.'

'I . . . I . . . don't know whether I can.' She was blushing.

'Try.'

'Thank you . . . John.'

'Will you bring me a snap of the little one in all her finery?'

'I will so, and one of my Kevin, as well.' She was reminding him that she had a child too. She had responsibilities, but she'd bear his offer in mind.

After tea that night she, Maggie and Lily went upstairs.

'Why can't I come in too?' Patsy demanded indignantly when she was refused entry into the bedroom.

'Because this is special. She's the youngest and we won't have to go through all this again, that's why.'

'Well, can I see Kev in his rig-out then?' Patsy demanded, still feeling cheated although Breda had been excluded too. She really liked Breda, who told her fantastic tales about Dublin and what she got up to there.

'What do yer want to do that for?' Maggie demanded.

'Well, it's just not fair. I should be able to see one of them!' Patsy pulled a face and pouted but she'd already lost interest. It was only a Communion dress.

Maggie closed the door and Patsy went down the stairs with such thumping steps that a baby elephant would seem quiet by comparison.

Lily had had her hair cut. Maggie and Breda had held her down on the chair while Mary snipped at the thick, golden mane.

'Well, you'll not need to have rags put in, Lily, it curls up by itself.' Mary had smiled at the child. 'Once it's been washed, dried and brushed out your headdress and veil will look lovely.'

Lily had looked up at her with distrust. She and Kevin had decided confidentially that the only good part of the day would be the sandwiches, jellies and cakes afterwards.

'Don't you go saying anything like that, though, Kev, or they'll batter the pair of us!' she'd warned.

Kevin had already had the rehearsal, with his mam and Aunty Maggie ooing and ahing over him. He felt like an eejit in the outfit and why he had to wear a white satin sash he didn't know. The only thing that he took comfort from was the fact that Tommy Rooney and Vinny Burns would be dressed the same way.

Lily had already undergone a thorough scrubbing with the Lifebuoy soap, and now she was told by her mother to get out of that rag of a dress. She stood in her vest and knickers, wondering what she would look like with the white taffeta dress with the puffed sleeves and the pin-tucked bodice whose neckline was trimmed with a bit of lace. It had a wide sash and a sticky-out skirt that made a rustling sound when she moved. She liked that.

'Now stand still while I get these done up,' Mary instructed, fiddling with the small buttons down the back. She had decorated the hem of the dress with tiny hand-embroidered rosebuds.

Next she placed the short veil of net that she'd hemmed by hand over Lily's gleaming curly locks and secured it with clips. Finally she fixed the tiara over it. She'd bought the child a pair of short white ankle socks and Maggie had asked Jim to contribute to the pair of white buckskin shoes with the strap round the ankle.

The flowers that Lily would carry were going to be organised by Breda because she worked in town. She would make a careful selection from the flower sellers in Clayton Square. Maggie had told her to say they were for a First Communion so she might get them a bit cheaper.

'There!' Mary stood back and admired her handiwork. Lily was transformed entirely. Gone was the tousle-haired, scruffy little slummy.

Maggie dissolved into tears of gratitude to Mary and pride and love at the sight of her little daughter. 'Ah, God, Mary, queen, she's like an angel from heaven! I wouldn't 'ave been able to get her half of all that, and them flowers on her hair – she's . . . she's just like a princess, she is.'

'Mam, will I be best of all? Better than them with frocks bought from shops?' Lily asked eagerly.

'Of course yer'll be the best of them all, Lily, luv. Not one of them will have a crown like that. It must 'ave cost yer 'undreds, Mary.'

Mary smiled at Maggie's exaggeration. She'd soon found out it was a trait of all Liverpudlians.

'No, just some wax, wire, a bit of cochineal for colouring and silver paper from cigarette packets.'

'I want ter see myself,' Lily demanded. Judging by the expression on her mam's face and Aunty Mary's she looked lovely, but she wanted to see if they were telling the truth.

Maggie looked helplessly at Mary who was thinking quickly.

'Mr Fallowfield's got a long mirror on the outside of the wardrobe door. Will I go and ask him if just Lily, no one else, can go and see herself?'

Lily drew back. 'I'm not going in there. He's . . . he frightens me.'

Mary took her hand, thinking how terrified the child would be if she knew what he did for a living.

Maggie brightened considerably. 'We'll all go. After all, I'm her mam.'

Mary shook her head. 'No, Aunty Maggie. I'll just ask at his door and we'll wait outside.'

Maggie pursed her lips in indignation. It would have been the perfect time to see everything he had in there. Instead she waited in the lobby as Mary knocked, explained and then pushed the child inside.

When Lily emerged it was with a look of pure disbelief on her little face.

'Mam . . . Mam . . . was that *me* in that there mirror?'

'It was so, Lily. Didn't we say you'd look the best?' Mary replied.

The child held out something she'd been clutching tightly in her hand. ''E's nice. 'E said I looked like an angel from heaven an' he gave me this to wear.'

She held out a silver chain suspended from which was a silver crucifix.

Mary had to fight down the cry that rose in her throat. She suspected that he'd been given it by some unfortunate person in the last minutes he or she had spent on this earth.

Maggie was examining it closely.

'It's silver, real silver. An' he gave it to you? He didn't say you could borrow it?'

'No, he said it was for me to keep to remember,' Lily said firmly, holding out her hand for the cross and chain.

Maggie looked stunned. No one in the entire family had a piece of decent jewellery. All she had had was her wedding ring, and over the years that had been more in hock than on her finger.

'Well, isn't he a dark horse, then? A proper queer feller, like Jim calls him. Maybe I should put up the rent.'

'Aunty Maggie, isn't that a desperate thing to say altogether? It might be some heirloom, given him by . . .' she shrugged '. . . someone.'

Maggie took the point.

'Right then, up them dancers, Lily, and get that finery off before it gets all mucky.'

Lily looked petulant. 'Why can't Kev see me?'

'Because there'd be holy flaming murder with our Patsy and Breda. Upstairs now this minute,' Maggie explained.

She turned to Mary and hugged her. 'She does look like an angel, doesn't she, an' all because of you. God luv yer, Mary O'Malley.'

'They'll both knock the sight out of the eyes of the rest of them, you wait and see.' Tears pricked Mary's eyes as she thought of Col and Kathleen. How different things would have been if Col had lived. Then they'd both have had the joy of seeing their son take his place at the altar rail for the first time, and Mammy . . . well, Mammy would have been filled with the sheer joy of the day that was in it.

Bryan and Breda got away with their secret meetings until October when the leaves on the trees in the parks started to turn gold and red and brown.

'Oh, God, haven't I got this desperate feeling that we're going to be found out, Bryan,' Breda said as she clung to him, her back to a tree in Stanley Park.

They'd made excursions to all the city's parks and had found this one to have the most secluded walks and arbours of shrubs.

He wrapped his arms round her. 'Don't be so daft, Breda. It's just superstition, that's all.'

She shook her head. 'No. No, it's luck and I think we're running out of our share. They're not stupid. Just think of the lies we've told them, and . . . and what we've done.' She pressed her cheek to his.

'What have we done that's so wrong? I've kissed you, I've . . . well, I've touched you, but that's because I love you.' He thought back to the times when he'd gently fondled her

70

breasts and she had sighed with longing. Neither of them had dared to go any further than that. They both wanted to and they wanted to be seen out together, Bryan particularly. His mates would be green with envy, for she was so beautiful that heads literally turned when she passed.

'Have you told the Father in Confession?' she asked.

'Well, sort of. What about you?'

'No. Sure, I haven't the courage. What did you say?' She looked up at him with those deep blue eyes that he thought were just gorgeous.

'I said . . . I said . . .'

'You didn't say anything either. Oh, God, Bryan, what will we do?'

He didn't reply, just held her to him. For all his bluster and bragging he knew the day would come when someone saw them and her premonition had unsettled him. He did love her, in his own way, but they could never get married and that fact alone had made him carry on meeting her. She was a safe bet. Even if she let him make love to her and she got pregnant there could be no irate da to force them up the aisle.

Breda shivered, sensing his mood. 'We'll have to go now. It's already starting to get dusky.'

Bryan released her but put his arm round her shoulder as they walked over the grass verge and down the tree-lined path towards the gates which the keeper would soon lock. All the parks closed early at this time of year, except Newsham where there were houses in the park itself.

As they neared the gateway two paths converged with theirs and walking down one was Rosie O'Hanlon with a lad from Portland Street. Rosie was clinging to him and laughing loudly.

Instantly Bryan removed his arm.

Breda's heart plummeted. 'Oh, Jesus, Mary and Joseph! That's it now, Bryan. Doesn't your one over there hate me and Mary too?' The thought of what Rosie would say to Mary made Breda go slightly faint.

Bryan decided to brazen it out.

He was usually good at that.

'All right there, Rosie? Nice evening for a bit of a stroll. What's your feller's name, then? It's dead bad-mannered not to introduce people.'

'It's Joe, but don't think you're going to get away with that, Bryan O'Shea. I know you an' all yer talk. I used to think it was only talk but I've changed me mind now.'

'What do you mean?'

'Her.' Rosie pointed to the white-faced Breda, who was biting her lip. 'She's your cousin an' me mam told me yer da had given you a good talkin' to an' her sister had made her promise she wouldn't go out with you.'

Bryan's expression changed. Bluffing was useless with Rosie, he should have known better. She was as hard as nails.

'And I suppose you've been picking dandelions up there?' he said sarcastically, jerking his head in the direction they'd come from.

'Listen 'ere, lad, what we've been doing is none of yer bloody business,' Rosie's escort said belligerently.

'I'll make it my business and her mam's too.' He glared at Rosie who was smiling nastily at Breda.

'So you'll tell me mam I was out with a feller, so what? She knows I'm always out with fellers. I'm dead popular.'

'And we all know why too. The Hornby Street bike us lads call you. There's only two who haven't been with you, me and Chris Kennedy. We've got more sense.'

Even under the powder and rouge Rosie's face paled. A right bastard he was. She didn't care about her reputation or him but she did care a lot about Chris Kennedy. His jibe had hit home. The lad she was with lunged at Bryan but she caught his arm.

'Don't waste yer time with him, Joe. I know how to fix him good and proper, and her too.'

Again Breda felt faint. She knew Rosie meant it.

'I think I'd make yer name Walker, iffen yer know what I mean,' she said maliciously before linking her arm through Joe's and pulling him towards the gate where the keeper had already taken up his position, a big metal keyring in his hand.

Breda was in a panic. 'We can't go home, Bryan! We can't.'

'We'll have to. We can't walk the streets all night.' He was just as agitated as she was although he knew he shouldn't be, not after the sights he'd seen and the constant threat of death he'd suffered in the Army. But all that didn't seem real now. It belonged to another part of his life, one he had almost blanked out of his mind.

Breda was clinging to his arm. 'But she'll tell them all. She'll tell the entire street if she gets the chance and we'll be destroyed altogether. We'll be killed.'

'Who'll believe her? The cut of her and the carry-on out of her. I meant what I said about the bike. She's just a common little tart an' her mam knows it too. Doesn't Flossie drag her to Confession every single week, but she goes off and does the same thing next day with any feller she can get her hands on.'

'Oh, Aunty Maggie and Mary will believe her. They'll know she wouldn't make something like this up.' Tears of fright were filling Breda's eyes.

'Deny everything and I'll do the same.'

'Isn't it fine for you, Bryan O'Shea. You've got Michael Kennedy who'll swear you've been with him all afternoon. I haven't got an excuse like that.'

'What did you tell them?' His bravado was draining away as he thought of his mam and da. She was right. They'd be murdered unless she had a good alibi.

'I said I was going into town.'

'What for? Who with?'

'Nothing and no one. Just to wander round the shops.'

He was horrified. 'In the name of God, Breda, couldn't you do better than that? Couldn't you bribe our Patsy to say she'd gone with you?'

'No! No, I bloody well couldn't. I can't trust Patsy, even if I give her money. I'm watched, I know it. Mary's not an eejit and I've run out of all the good excuses.'

His heart sank and he felt cold. 'Then we're in for it all right. For God's sake don't tell them much. Say nothing about me . . . touching you.'

'Is it a complete eejit you take me for, Bryan? Jaysus, I'm terrified.' She broke down and sobbed.

He relented and took her hand. 'Come on, then, we'd better go and face the music.' He gave her hand a squeeze. 'She might not tell them. She might just be kidding us, out of spite.'

'She'll tell them.'

'Then keep your mouth shut, Breda,' he advised as the faint gleam of hope died.

As soon as he entered the kitchen he could tell that Rosie had called. There was no sign of the younger ones, not even Maurice. Both his mam and Mary sat at the table and glared at him, but it was the expression on his da's face that terrified him. Big Jim O'Shea was standing before the range, his legs planted firmly apart, his belt already in his hand and his face looking as if it had been carved from granite.

'Well, where is she?' he demanded.

'You mean Breda?' Bryan knew it was utterly futile to try to lie. It was far too late for that. 'In the yard. She's terrified to come in.'

Mary made to get to her feet. 'And isn't she right? I'll terrify her, the bold strap.'

Maggie pulled at Mary's arm and she sat down.

'Now, Mary, don't upset yourself, queen. Leave them both to me and Jim.'

With a face like thunder she turned her attention to her son. 'Go and bring her in here now!'

Bryan was out of the kitchen like a shot and returned half dragging, half supporting an increasingly hysterical Breda.

'Stop that screeching right now, Breda Bernadette Nolan!' Mary yelled.

'Right, the pair of you. How long has this been going on and what have you been doing?' Jim demanded, his voice quiet and steady and somehow more menacing than if he too had yelled at them.

'I've only kissed her, Da, and that's the God's honest truth.'

'Don't you speak of God and kissing that little madam in the same breath!' Maggie yelled at him.

'Maggie, leave this to me,' Jim instructed.

Mary covered her face with her hands. How could Breda disgrace them both like this? Maggie and Jim O'Shea had given them a home, had shared everything with them, in fact made them part of the family.

'Well, Breda? Stop that snivelling and say something.'

'We . . . it's true what Bryan said. We only . . . kissed. I know it was wrong.'

Jim finally raised his voice. 'Wrong! Wrong! You dammed well knew it was wrong. You know you're too closely related for anything to come of it. And the lies! What about all the lies the pair of you have been telling for months?'

Maggie crossed herself, a look of horror in her eyes. 'Oh, Holy Mother of God! The pair of them going to Confession every week asking for forgiveness with every intention of carrying on meeting and kissing. Who knows where it would have ended? Oh, I hope they won't be excommunicated! I couldn't stand it. We'd have to move, and after all we've been through with the Blitz an' all.' Tears of anger and hurt filled Maggie's eyes and Mary got to her feet.

'I'm sorry we've brought such shame on you and after you being so good to us. I knew what she was like, but she swore to me she'd behave. Well, it's a visit to Father Hayes we're after paying and right now this very minute and if she's to be excommunicated then she'll go home. We all will!' Mary grabbed Breda tightly and pushed her towards the door.

'Ah, God, Mary, don't make me go! I'll do anything . . .' Breda pleaded.

'You can promise to behave like an angel for the rest of your life but I won't believe you. Get out of that door, you bold little rossie. You knew you were doing wrong and you carried on. Aren't you a disgrace to Mammy and me, bringing down the shame on all our heads. Get out of that door!'

As she closed the scullery door Mary heard the first yell of pain from Bryan and she pressed her lips together grimly. He deserved a beating. He was twenty-two, a man, and one who had fought in a war and knew the ways of the world. Breda was only seventeen and had never set foot out of Dublin until they'd come here. Well, after tonight was over maybe they'd all get some peace. After the parish priest had got through with her sister, Breda wouldn't dare to even speak to her cousin again.

Chapter Six

Never again did Breda want to experience the wrath of Father Hayes. She'd been absolutely terrified as she'd stood, hanging her head abjectly, sobbing as words like 'eternal damnation', 'the fires of hell' and 'the whore of Babylon' had battered against her ears. Thankfully there was no mention of that terrible and much dreaded word 'excommunication'. That would have been the end of everything. She might as well be dead now and had it been mentioned she would have wished she *was* dead. When Mary had at last led her out and taken her home she'd sworn never to even look at Bryan again.

There had been no sign of him when they'd returned but Aunty Maggie had a bottle of camomile lotion on the table and pity was mingled with anger in her eyes.

She'd been sent straight upstairs and she could hear the groans that came from the other side of the thin wall. Breda had felt sorry for him as she lay there and her own sobs subsided. The worst was over for her but Bryan would go on suffering until the weals on his back healed. And really they hadn't done anything desperately wicked, except for all the lies. How that Rosie O'Hanlon got away with the things *she* did, she didn't know.

* * *

When they'd sat down with a mug of sweet tea each, Mary had passed a hand over her throbbing forehead. It had been a terrible day.

'We'll have to be going, Aunty Maggie. We'll be after finding somewhere else to live. I just thank God that Mam doesn't know anything about it. Since she was fifteen Breda's had the heart across Mam. Now she's thrown all your kindness and generosity back in your face and I can't stand the shame of it all.'

'He was as much to blame. More. He's older and should have known better. He was warned but he would go ahead and play with fire. Well, he's feeling the burn of it now,' Jim said grimly.

'There's no need for you to go, luv,' Maggie added. 'It won't happen again, we've all seen to that.'

'Don't I know it, but your one across the road will tell everyone and take a delight in it. She's a tongue that would cut the horns off a cow.'

'And who's going to believe a trollop like Rosie O'Hanlon? Oh, I know what the lads say about her. Me heart goes out to Flossie, it really does. Such a good-hearted woman, and she tries her best. It's a damned good hiding that their Rosie should have had years ago from her da, but he's always propping up the bar at the Grapes. God knows Flossie's tried but that little madam just doesn't care. If she was given a telling off from the Pope himself she wouldn't care. What kind of an example is she to their Jimmy and Carmel?'

'Maggie's right, Mary. As long as those two behave, act normal like, then no one will believe a single word from Rosie O'Hanlon.'

Mary had sighed and thanked them and gradually, as the

weather grew colder, darkness fell earlier and the winds rushing in down the estuary grew fiercer, things returned to normal.

Bryan and Breda spoke to each other only when absolutely necessary but, try as she might, Breda couldn't rid herself of the feelings she had for him, even after all she'd gone through, and she knew, from the occasional quick glance, that he felt the same.

He'd taken to going out in the evenings after work.

'God knows where. I certainly don't, and neither do I want to as long as he doesn't bring any trouble home here to us,' Maggie had remarked.

Their situation still disturbed Mary but she thanked God each day that Kathleen was ignorant of the whole affair.

'I hate November, it's dead miserable. You can't even play out in the street,' Lily complained to Kevin as they walked home from school. Both were muffled up in hats and scarves and gloves. The gloves were sewn to a long piece of tape which was threaded down the arms of their coats so they wouldn't lose them. Everything had been made by Mary. Their coats were second-hand and had been too big but because they were a good thick wool Mary had cut them down. Kevin had now settled in well after Patsy's threats to Vinny Burns and Tommy Rooney.

It was the first winter that Lily hadn't been shivering with cold on her way to and from school. She'd never had any of these comforts before and she was genuinely fond of Mary.

'Will we write to Santi, Lily?'

'Who?'

'Santa Claus. I think you call him Father Christmas.'

She looked at him enquiringly. 'What for?'

'To ask him for things. Haven't you ever done that?'

She shook her head. 'He just leaves us an apple, an orange and a shiny new penny, and sometimes a little toy, if he's got any to spare, like.'

'We'll write after tea and then you have to push the notes up the chimney so he gets them.'

Lily was a bit scornful; she'd never heard of anything like this before.

'How do you know he gets them?'

'Because he does, that's how, so Mammy says,' he answered emphatically.

So they both sat at the table after tea laboriously writing letters asking Santi for toys they suspected they'd never get.

'He wouldn't be able to get a bike down the chimney, Kev,' Lily said, seeing the practical side of it. She knew her soulmate was asking for far too much.

'But he might just leave it in the yard.' He was still hopeful.

Lily shook her head. 'He can't. I don't think it works like that.'

'What have you asked for, then?'

'Oh, any little thing and a doll, if he's got one to spare.' She was being just as optimistic. There was no harm in trying. Maybe this writing notes would make a difference.

'Carmel O'Hanlon says she hates Christmas 'cos her da's always drunk and her mam is so mad with him that she belts everyone in sight,' Patsy interrupted.

'Pity she doesn't belt their Rosie,' Maggie muttered as she tried to darn one of Jim's socks and as usual made a pig's ear of it. Mary had shown her but she still managed to cobble it.

Later that night Mary voiced her thoughts.

'Holy Mother, a bike! Does he know how much even a second-hand one costs?'

'No, but our Lily does. She was trying hard not to let him get too carried away. And where am I going to get a doll? There's our Maurice and Patsy to think of too.'

'I could make her one. I knitted his little rabbit the year he asked for a live one.'

Maggie turned to her husband. 'Is that doll's hospital still there up Mount Pleasant, or did it get bombed?'

'How would I know, for God's sake?' Jim retreated behind his newspaper.

'A doll's hospital?' Mary had never heard of such a thing.

'It's a shop and a sort of workshop. When kids break their dolls they take them there to be mended. Those that can afford to, anyway.'

'Then I'll go and see what they've got. Maybe I can buy one that's not too badly broken, mend it and dress it up.'

'Could you do that? Really?'

'I can and I will, but what am I going to do about a bike?'

Jim lowered his newspaper. 'Would he settle for a wooden fort and some lead soldiers? I don't mind helping out with the soldiers. There's a feller I know down the docks who knows another feller who can get things like that dirt cheap.'

Maggie raised her eyes to the ceiling. 'Isn't there always someone down the docks who can get everything.'

Mary had brightened up. 'Uncle Jim, aren't you an angel with your kindness.'

He grinned. 'Sometimes me halo does slip a bit.'

Maggie pealed with laughter. 'And sometimes he has to take his wings off to get into bed. But if you get the soldiers, Jim, what about the fort?'

'Go and see Chris Kennedy. He's not a chippy but he'll know someone who is.'

The two women had uttered the last phrase with him and they all laughed.

'Will I go now, tonight?' Mary suggested.

'Strike while the iron's hot, luv. Get your coat on and go over and ask him.'

Mary suddenly felt apprehensive. She'd spoken to Chris since the street party, of course, but they hadn't been long conversations. Even so, she always got an unexplainable warm, shaky feeling when she was with him and she suspected he did too.

Phil's house was clean and warm, now that she had Michael and Lizzie and Chris working. Theresa and Joey were sitting cutting strips of red and green crêpe paper to make decorations.

'At least it keeps them quiet,' Phil said as she ushered Mary into her kitchen.

'It's Chris I've come to see. I mean, I've come to see you too, but . . .'

Phil smiled. She was a big-boned woman but she was always tidy in her appearance, even on wash days, so Maggie said.

'I know what you mean, girl. Stop getting all flustered. He's in the yard with his da. The coal feller's been today and you should have seen the mess he made. I'll give him what for when I see him next. I'll give our Chris a shout.'

Mary wondered how on earth they could see the spilled coal in the darkness, then she remembered the street light on the corner of Vostock Street.

Chris was flushed with his exertions and the cold night air, but he smiled at Mary.

'Mam says you want to talk to me? Would it be by any chance to ask me out, Mrs O'Malley?'

She laughed with him, thinking it was only a joke.

'Ah, I'm afraid not. Uncle Jim suggested I get Kevin a wooden fort and some lead soldiers for Christmas. He really wants a bike.'

'So do half the lads in this city. He won't be on his own; they won't get them either.'

'We can manage the soldiers but do you know anyone who would make the fort, cheaply?'

Phil had returned and was poking at the fire in the burnished, blackleaded range.

'What about that Jimmy Marlow? Isn't he a carpenter?'

'I was just going to suggest I ask him, Mam. The only thing wrong with him is he's a bit slow.'

'Not when it comes to buying pints he's not,' Phil retorted.

'Mam, there's only him and his old mam living in that house. Do you blame him for having a bit of pleasure after a hard day's graft?'

'No. You know me, I never stop to think before I open my big mouth.'

'I'll ask him,' Chris volunteered.

'Will you ask him how much it will be, too?'

'Yes, but it won't be a fortune. He can use odd bits of wood from where he works. And I'll keep nagging him to make sure your Kev gets it on the big day.'

'Thanks. Lily wants a doll so I'm going to see what I can do about that. I'd hate to see them both disappointed.'

Phil grinned. 'They're a funny little pair, those two. When you see one you know the other is somewhere near by.'

'I know.' Mary laughed, stopping herself quickly from saying she hoped there was not going to be any trouble with them as there had been with Bryan and Breda.

'Well, I'd better get back.'

'Shall I walk you up the street?'

Mary felt herself beginning to blush. 'It's only a few steps.'

'Wash your hands and put your jacket and cap on. That wind will cut you like a knife through butter,' Phil urged.

'Really, there's no need,' Mary protested again.

Her eyes met those of the older woman. Phil was smiling encouragingly. She for one wouldn't object to her son's courting a girl like Mary O'Malley. Not only was she beautiful but she had a kind gentle nature, was a good worker and was thrifty. There'd be no objections from Phil.

They walked slowly, their heads bent before the icy blast.

'I'm grateful, but really there's no need for me to drag you out into the cold. Isn't it only a few steps.'

'I wanted to ask *you* a favour, Mary.'

She looked up at him. 'And what would that be?'

Chris took a deep breath. 'Would you come with me to the pictures on Saturday?'

She was taken aback and remained silent, still looking up into his eyes. She knew he liked her, as a neighbour and maybe a friend, but she had no idea how much. She'd never even thought about going out with another man since Col had died.

'You don't have to, Mary. I . . . I just thought . . .'

She saw the hurt in his eyes. 'No! No, I mean, yes! Oh, I'm a great fool. Yes, I'd like to do that, Chris. You just took me by surprise. I've never been out . . . since—'

'Then I'll call for you at seven?' he interrupted, not wanting to embarrass her or give her time to change her mind.

'That'll be grand, Chris,' she replied and went quickly through the yard door that he held open for her. She felt like a young girl again going out on her first outing with a boy. Oh, will you stop all this nonsense, Mary O'Malley, she said to herself. It was an outing, with a friend, that was all. She smiled to herself as she paused with her hand on the door latch. She could hear him whistling – or was it the wind? She preferred to think it was him.

She had told Maggie about his invitation and had seen the look of delight in Maggie's eyes.

'He's a good lad is Chris. Phil's brought them all up well, and you're still only a slip of a girl. There's a whole world out there waiting. Don't waste your life, living in the past. Col wouldn't want that, would he? Go and enjoy yourself, and who knows what will happen in the future.'

Mary smiled. 'Ah, come on out of that, Aunty Maggie. You're matchmaking.'

'Well, it's a match I wouldn't object to. Nor would Phil, despite Kevin.'

'What do you mean?'

'Well, there's plenty of women who wouldn't look kindly on a widow with a little lad as a wife for their son.'

Mary nodded. 'I just wish Breda would get herself a decent boyfriend. I've had a strange feeling lately that there's something she's hiding from me.'

'She goes out with that Maureen and Joyce from work now, and she's sure to meet someone sooner or later. She is only seventeen, Mary.'

Mary sighed. 'I know. But I'd feel happier if she found herself a steady lad.'

'There's plenty of time for that. Now stop worrying and go out and enjoy yourself.'

She'd washed her hair and decided to pin it up. Breda said it made her look more sophisticated.

'And what would that mean at all? That I'm looking older?'

'No, you eejit, more stylish and smarter. I read it in a magazine.'

'The things they put in magazines these days,' Maggie had tutted. Mary wore her best lemon-coloured blouse with its cutwork collar and her navy skirt. She'd borrowed the new coat Breda had bought and she'd made a navy hat. It was a small felt one without a brim and had a little piece of navy net covering the crown and the front of her hair. It was simple, but effective, she thought as she placed it over the new 'sophisticated' hairdo and gazed at the reflection in the tiny mirror on the bedroom wall. She felt that hundreds of butterflies were fluttering in her stomach and she noticed that her hands were shaking slightly.

When she at last came down the stairs she almost collided with Mr Fallowfield.

'Mrs O'Malley, you look very nice. Are you going somewhere special?' He heard everything that went on in the kitchen, he couldn't help it. He heard the rows particularly, and thought the one last month had been of a serious nature, involving a great deal of shouting and a beating. He deplored violence but sometimes it was necessary.

'Only to the pictures. I don't get out much.'

'I know. When you're not at work you're cleaning and scrubbing. The lobby looks a treat now.'

You couldn't help but like the man, Mary thought. He was quiet and educated and went to church on Sundays. He seemed to be completely at ease with his profession.

'Well, with so many of us living here Aunty Maggie doesn't get much time. Now we all share the chores.'

He stood back to let her pass. She was a very attractive young woman, he thought, but it was no use his thinking along those lines at his age. He doubted if there was a woman in the city who wouldn't drop him as soon as she found out what his job was.

Patsy had stationed herself by the window and as soon as she saw the yard door open she called to her cousin.

'He's here, Mary, but I don't know why you want to go out with him. You're both so old and you've got Kev.'

Patsy gave a yell as her mam slapped her legs hard.

'Old! She's far from old, you cheeky little get! And it's none of your business either. You're getting too hardfaced by half and I'm not having you end up like Rosie O'Hanlon. I'd kill you first.'

'I'll go out to him,' Mary said hastily, her cheeks flushed with embarrassment.

'I don't know why he didn't come to the front door. It's all above board, out in the open. Not like some others I could mention.' Maggie cast a quick glance at Breda who ducked her head. She was just putting the final touches to her own blouse before going dancing at the Locarno Ballroom with Maureen and Joyce.

Mary and Chris walked out of the entry and down the street, knowing they were seen. Mary wished they could run.

'You know we're being watched? Oh, they're all there lurking in their front rooms.'

'I know. Wasn't Aunty Maggie after saying you should have come to the front door.'

'I never gave that a thought, but I suppose I should. I'm sorry, Mary. I will next time.'

Next time, she thought. He intended to ask her out again. He must be serious about her.

When they reached the bus stop he took her arm and helped her on to the bus, but she was very quiet. Too quiet.

'Is there something wrong?'

'No . . . no. It's just been so long that I feel . . . I feel a bit embarrassed.'

'There's no need to feel like that, Mary, but I think I can understand.'

She smiled up at him. She really did like him.

The outing had been a success. She'd relaxed once the Pathé News was finished. They'd both laughed at the short cartoon that had followed and she'd wiped her eyes surreptitiously and tried not to sniff during *Rebecca*.

'Will you come out with me again, Mary?' he asked as he helped her off the bus, still holding her hand.

'I'd be delighted, Chris. It's been a grand evening, I've enjoyed it.'

'I'll call for you at the same time next Saturday.' He smiled. 'And I'll come to the front door.'

'You don't have to. I don't mind.'

'No, your Aunty Maggie's right. I should call properly.'

She could see from the look in his eyes that he was serious and he still held her hand. She made no attempt to pull away, for half-forgotten emotions were stirring again.

'Mary, would you mind if I kissed you goodnight?'

'I . . . I . . . don't think so, Chris,' she replied a little shakily.

He bent and kissed her gently on the mouth and then her arms were round his neck and she was kissing him back. When she finally drew away she felt dizzy and leaned against his chest. He still had his arms round her.

'Maybe it's too soon, and I don't want to upset you, Mary, but I think I love you. I've never felt like this about anyone else.'

She reached up and touched his face gently.

'It's not too early, Chris. I think I love you too.' An image of Kevin's face flashed across her mind. He had looked so stricken and lost in those first weeks at school. Chris would be a good father, she was sure of it, and she had to think of Kevin too, not just her own happiness.

They kissed and clung to each other until a couple of men on their way home from the pub passed them and one whistled.

'I'd better get you home.'

'I think you'd better, Chris. People will talk. I'll be called all kind of names, being a widow and carrying on like this in public.' She managed a smile but she didn't want to go home. She wanted to linger here and hold him and kiss him.

As they walked down Hornby Street, her arm through his, neither of them saw or heard Rosie O'Hanlon step out from the back entry where she'd been with Joe. Rosie's eyes narrowed and the hatred she felt for Mary increased. She wanted Chris Kennedy and now it looked as though the other Irish bitch had got her claws into him. Well, she'd taken care of that Breda and she'd do the same to Mary, if she could. She would wait for an opportunity and then she'd strike. Just as she had with Breda.

Chapter Seven

Despite the austerity Christmas passed with not a lot of material things or even food but plenty of cheer and goodwill. Lily and Kevin had been the most surprised and delighted.

'You were right about the notes, Kev. Look! Look, a doll, and all dressed too. She's even got knickers on!' Lily had shrieked.

Mary had found the body of one doll that was missing some fingers, and the head of another. It didn't matter if they didn't match, she'd told the girl in the shop named the Doll's Hospital.

Jim had put them together, joining them with tin tacks and then painting them over. She'd spent hours sewing the clothes because she had had to wait until Lily, Kevin and Patsy had gone to bed. You could never really trust Patsy to keep her mouth shut.

'He won't be interested in playing with you and that stupid doll!' Patsy had said spitefully. She'd got the usual apple, orange and new penny but only some plastic hair slides in addition. Mary had given her a set of scarf, mitts and tam-o'-shanter, all in bright red wool. Breda had got her a little bottle of scent, but her mam had said she was too young for things like that yet and promptly confiscated it. Took it to 'mind' was what she'd said. By way of compensation Breda had given her a silver florin.

'I'm sorry, Patsy. I should have known she'd take it off you, but I thought you'd like it.'

'Oh, I did, but thanks for the money, Breda. I can get something else now from Woolies in Church Street.'

'For God's sake don't get something else she'll say is too old for you. She'll take the pair of us apart and then all the money will be wasted and you'll have nothing at all,' Breda had warned.

Everyone at Mass on Christmas morning had been absolutely flabbergasted by the sight of Rosie O'Hanlon, face scrubbed clean of make-up, her bleached hair all tucked up under a beret, wearing a very plain brown coat. They were even more astonished when she went up for Communion.

'Do you think she's seen sense at last, Maggie?' Phil whispered. She was sitting next to Maggie and her family and all the O'Hanlons were in the row behind, Gerry looking decidedly pale and sheepish as a result of too much beer and a row with his wife earlier that morning. Flossie had yelled that she didn't care how much he'd had to drink or how bad he felt, it was Christmas and they were *all* going to Mass, even if she had to drag him there by the scruff of his scrawny, useless, idle neck.

'Well, something's changed her. Maybe Gerry gave her a good hiding at last, though from the look of him he couldn't punch a hole in a wet *Echo*. I definitely heard him singing as he came up the street last night. It was a shockin' row – the Ryans' dog sounds better. Of course it may not last very long.'

'You're right. It might just be a flash in the pan.'

But they were surprised when Rosie's new image did last, until New Year.

Christmas had been full of surprises for others too. Breda had dared to look Bryan full in the face, her eyes shining, when he'd given her the small box containing a cheap little brooch in the form of a shamrock. They did have fun together and he'd not given up hope of her letting him make love to her.

Obviously he still thought a lot of her, Breda surmised, he was handsome and anyway what right had Mary to tell her what or what not to do?

'I've nothing for you, except a card,' she'd said, their conversation masked by the noise level in the kitchen, the look on both their faces unseen as everyone's attention turned to present-opening, hugging and kissing.

'That's all right, Breda.'

'It is not. I should have got *some* little thing.'

'Just say you'll see me again; that'll be *my* best present.'

Her eyes had widened. 'Holy God! Are you mad? After what we went through last time? I'd be packed off into a convent and God knows what your da would do to you.' Despite her words she felt the emotions rising in her again.

'We'll just have to be more careful,' he whispered. 'They all think we've learned our lesson. If we keep up the not speaking bit it'll work. Rosie O'Hanlon seems to have changed.'

'Did you see the cut of her at Mass at all? She looked positively plain and dowdy.'

'I did . . . *and* she went for Communion. She's not done that for months, her mam wouldn't let her.'

'So . . .' She'd looked up at him.

'The park on Saturday at two?'

She had nodded and tried to hide the excitement she felt by telling everyone that she'd never had a Christmas as good as this one. Nor was it a lie. She hadn't.

For New Year Phil Kennedy, Maggie and Flossie O'Hanlon plus a few other neighbours decided they'd have a 'do'.

'This is the first New Year when all the fighting has stopped. Do you remember the Christmas of 1940, Phil?' Maggie asked.

'I do. A nice time that was. That lot decided to give us a good Christmas by bombing us. We nearly lost St George's Hall, the museum, the Empire Theatre, all our best buildings. Me sister-in-law was bombed out and ended up here with her tribe of kids. It was murder. I'll not forget that Christmas. But we've really got something to celebrate this time,' Phil said as they sat in her kitchen making plans.

'How much do you think we'll need? For the food and drink, I mean?' Maggie asked, looking at Carrie Quinne, whose eldest daughter Emily worked in Pegram's Grocers on Scotland Road.

'Our Em can get stuff a bit cheap but we'll still have to pool our coupons,' Carrie replied.

'I'll ask Gerry if that Ted Conway at the Grapes can let us have some ale. He owes us that at least. Our Gerry must be his best customer,' Flossie said sarcastically.

'The Ryans at number twenty-six have got a piano. It's a bit battered – it was flung across the room by the blast when the block next to them went up – but Dermot Ryan can play anything by ear.'

'I'll send our Rosie down the market to get some sheets of ribs and some pigs' trotters. They'll go down a treat and they aren't rationed now.'

Maggie seized the opportunity.

'She's changed, Flossie, hasn't she? Did someone finally talk sense into her?'

'No, it's all her idea. I was so staggered I couldn't open me mouth. "Mam," she says two days before Christmas, "I'm going to change. I've decided on it. I'm going to behave proper now, I mean it." And wasn't she off to Confession after chucking all her make-up and scent in the bin, along with some of those terrible common clothes she had. I tell you, Maggie, you could have knocked me over with a feather. It must have been all the prayers I said to St Jude.'

'And every other saint in the book,' Phil added.

'But will it last, Floss?' Maggie cautioned.

'God alone knows, but I pray it will. You all know how I've been out of me mind with her for years. Just couldn't do a thing with her.'

Everyone was excited about the forthcoming do, even Lily and Kevin, who had begged and pleaded to be allowed to stay up until midnight.

'It's really great at New Year, Mary,' Chris said as they sat together in a carriage of the overhead railway. Sections of it were still damaged from the Blitz, but it was still a good way to see all the ships in the eight miles of docks as well as the shipping out in the river itself.

'Everyone in the entire street comes out and we count the seconds down and then the church bells all over the city ring and the ships blast off their steam whistles and we all join hands and sing "Auld Lang Syne" and everyone kisses everyone else! Did you ever have anything like that back home?'

'We did, but no one ever had money spare to have a party.'

'Things are looking up now, Mary. We can get on with our lives.'

They both fell silent, Mary thinking about Col and all the other Irish lads who wouldn't be celebrating a New Year, and Chris of all the Army mates he had seen killed and maimed and the terrible carnage in the cities they'd liberated.

'Sometimes I wonder, Chris, if there was any need for so many to die.'

'I sometimes wonder about that too. Some of the things I saw still give me nightmares. But Hilter had to be stopped. He was evil, Mary, downright evil.'

At last all the preparations were done and Maggie, Flossie and Phil declared they were all worn to a frazzle and were almost sorry they'd ever mentioned it. Mary and Breda had helped, as had Carrie and Emily Quinne, and Margaret Dillon who often helped out at the Grapes and was therefore used to coping with a lot of merrymaking customers.

The big surprise was Rosie, who'd also offered her services. And she'd worked quietly and efficiently and had ignored her mother who had declared in a loud whisper to her neighbours that in the old days she wouldn't do a single tap, wouldn't even pick up her discarded knickers. Both Mary and Breda had had smiles from Rosie. She had even made a sort of apology to Breda.

'Would you mind if I came with you next time you and your mates go dancing? I've no friends, you see – though I can't blame anyone for not wanting to be mates with me. I was awful, especially to you.'

'I'll . . . I'll see what the others say, Rosie,' had been Breda's stunned reply.

It was far too cold for the food to be put on tables down the street, so the women who had organised it all laid it out on their kitchen tables and issued strict instructions that there was to be no snatching, greediness or hiding things away. They would have liked to be able to put on a really big spread but they couldn't afford the money or the coupons. The drink was set out in Maggie's kitchen as Gerry O'Hanlon for one wasn't to be trusted with that.

'There's some bottles of port wine that fell off the back of a lorry and some other stuff that passes for wine. Dermot Ryan makes it and it will blow the head off you, so don't be tempted to drink any or you'll be in bed for a week,' Maggie advised them all.

There was to be ginger pop and lemonade for the kids, which had been acquired in the same manner as the port wine, though this time it was a Schofields lorry.

By eleven o'clock the party was well under way, with much loud laughter coming from the block further down and great singing round the Ryans' war-battered piano. Maurice too was enjoying himself. It was very strange, he thought, how you could know someone all your life and yet suddenly not know them at all. Pauline Casey was like that. She'd certainly blossomed.

Some of the younger children had given up the fight to stay awake and had been carried to their beds, but Lily and Kevin, both fighting to keep their eyes open, sat on the front doorstep, Lily clutching her doll and Kevin six of his precious soldiers. His fort and its occupants were the envy of all the lads he knew, but neither of them was going to miss the big event. They'd never been allowed to stay up this late before.

'Will I go and get us some of the stuff the grown-ups are having? I'd just like a bit of a taste,' Kevin said, looking earnestly at Lily.

'You will not, Kevin O'Malley! If I see you with anything,

anything other than lemonade I'll clatter you, so I will. Party or no party,' Mary threatened, having overheard her son. 'Why don't the pair of you get up and dance like the grown-ups? Sure, it would keep you both awake if nothing else. Aren't you like a pair of bookends sitting there. Come here to me, Lily, and give me your doll. I'll mind her and I'll let no one else touch her, I promise.' Mary bent and pulled the child to her feet and took the doll gently away from her. She'd put it upstairs for safety. She doubted either of them would still be awake by midnight anyway, but getting them on their feet might just help.

Chris was sitting on their doorstep, waiting for Mary who'd gone home for what she termed 'a bit of a tidy-up', when Rosie sat down beside him, a bottle in her hand. It was the scrubbed-clean Rosie wearing a brown coat over a brown dress that had a neat little cream-coloured Peter Pan collar.

She smiled. 'Isn't it great, Chris? Fancy them all getting it organised in the first place.'

Chris still felt slightly uneasy about Rosie, for in the past her innuendoes had been far from subtle. The change had been sudden and dramatic, but maybe she'd found a decent lad she was fond of at last. One who hadn't heard her reputation – although it would have to be someone well out of the immediate area for that.

'Yup, great. I hear you helped out too.'

'I did.' She smiled at him again. 'It's my New Year resolution. To help Mam more and stay at home more often. No . . . gallivanting out like I used to.'

'So it's official, then? This is the new Rosie O'Hanlon.'

'Yes, but the resolutions don't start until after midnight, so I can have a few last drinks, can't I?'

She had a bottle of something in her hand.

'What the hell's that? Don't tell me it's lemonade?' he asked, mildly amused.

'No, it's wine. It's not half bad, either. Try some.' She proffered the bottle.

'No, thanks, Rosie.'

'Ah, don't be so miserable, Chris Kennedy. Drink to the future. Things have got to get better from now on.'

He relented. She was right. He took a swig and then nearly choked. After he'd finished coughing and spluttering he looked at her with amusement. 'God, Rosie, where did you get this from? It's like paint stripper.'

'From the Ryans and it's not that bad. I've had a couple of drinks myself and I'm not drunk. Go on, it's better after a few more mouthfuls.'

'Oh, all right. But I've no intention of getting drunk. It's work tomorrow and they dock your pay if you don't turn up for the day.'

'I know. That's why I'm staying sober too,' she replied as he raised the bottle to his lips again.

She wanted him so much. He was so different from all the other lads she'd known, and the fact that he'd ignored all her advances in the past only made her want him more. She'd only been pretending about the wine. She hadn't had a single drop. She was going to make sure that neither he nor herself would be at work in the morning, and then she'd have got him away from that Mary O'Malley for good. When they were found in bed together, her mam's bed, he'd have to marry her. Everyone would insist on it no matter how much he swore and protested. She'd been planning it for weeks. This was why she'd chucked out her make-up and some of her clothes and had acted like a plain Jane and no nonsense. Make-up and clothes could be bought again, when she was

Mrs Rosie Kennedy. Oh, she'd love to see that Mary's face in the morning.

She smiled up at Chris, urging him to keep on drinking. In about ten minutes he wouldn't know what he was doing. She'd have to get him up their stairs soon, before he was too drunk to stand, because she certainly couldn't carry him.

Mary had gone quickly upstairs and put Lily's doll in the bottom drawer of the old chest she'd bought from a pawnbroker who was having a clear-out sale. No one would come up here, and if they did they wouldn't go rooting around. Lily's treasured companion was safe. People were always popping in and out of each other's houses, so doors were never locked, but they would never dream of going upstairs unless invited to do so.

She tidied her hair in the mirror. It had started to come down with all the dancing she'd done. With Chris mainly, but with other lads and older men too. She was wearing her red jacket over her navy blue skirt and jumper, and despite the coldness of the night she was flushed. She'd go down into the scullery and have a glass of water before she went to join Chris again. She'd had two glasses of port and a few sips of 'wine' which had nearly burned the throat off her.

As she turned on the light in the scullery she thought she saw a movement in the yard. 'Now who'd be lurking in the yard with a party going on?' she muttered to herself as she opened the back door.

The yellow light spilled out, throwing the corners into deep shadow, but she thought she had caught sight of someone in the darkness.

'Come out here where I can see you! Right this minute or I'll be after calling Uncle Jim.'

'You won't need to do that, Mary. It's me.' Bryan stepped forward.

'What are you doing out here? I thought you were jigging with Emily Quinne?'

'I was, but I had to come in to use the privy, didn't I? It's all that ale.'

'Then get back if you've finished or your mam will be destroyed thinking you're lying unconscious somewhere after going on a tear.'

She had begun to turn away when her eye caught a slight movement in the corner he'd emerged from, which now she thought about it wasn't anywhere near the privy.

'All right, so who else is out there? I'll not be having any more lies told!'

To her horror it was Breda who emerged from the darkness.

'Holy Mother of God! Breda Nolan, don't you ever learn?'

Breda was going to try to brazen it out this time. 'I . . . we . . . love each other. Can't you understand that, Mary? I know you love Chris Kennedy. Aren't you my sister and haven't I always known things about you without being told? I can see it in your eyes.'

Mary groaned. 'Oh, Breda, that's different. He's a single man.'

'So is Bryan,' Breda shot back with some spirit, wondering why Bryan wasn't backing her up.

'Love, is it? He's your first cousin and you know it's forbidden to marry anyone so closely related. You've no sense at all in that head of yours and didn't you have everyone fooled by your play-acting? Do you want Uncle Jim to have to beat Bryan again? Is that it? Didn't you think of Bryan at all?'

'Yes, but he said . . .' Breda turned to him. 'Tell her, Bryan, tell her that you love me and that we're going to see about a special dispensation?'

Bryan nodded sheepishly. It was something she had thought of doing. He'd tried to persuade her against it but she had insisted that in the New Year she was going to write to the Pope himself if necessary. She would, too. He was in too deep this time and wished he'd left her alone. Now everything depended on Mary and what she intended to do.

Mary's attitude softened a little, but there was great sadness in her eyes.

'You know what this means? We'll have to leave this house, all of us, and what kind of explanation or excuse am I going to have to give for doing so?'

'Oh, Mary, don't be giving out to us, please? Things are bad enough. You . . . we'll think of something if only you won't tell on us. I'll go and see the Archbishop myself,' Breda pleaded.

Mary bit her lip, noticing that again there was no response, no support from Bryan. 'I'm not promising anything. I'll just have to think about all this. Now get back into the street, Bryan, and I think the best place for you, Breda, is bed. Never mind that it must be nearly midnight, get up those stairs and stay there. I'll say you are feeling a bit sick after drinking that poitín that's after being called wine.'

When they'd both gone their separate ways Mary leaned against the wall, depression chasing away her previous happiness. It was here that Albert Fallowfield found her on his way to the privy in the yard.

Earlier on she'd dragged him out into the street to join in, but it wasn't quite his cup of tea and he'd slipped away, not wanting to be included in the kissing and hugging of people who were strangers to him.

'Mrs O'Malley! What's the matter? You look ill.'

'No, I've just had a little bit of a shock, that's all.'

'What kind of shock? Has someone . . .' He was about to say 'molested' but changed his mind. '. . . been upsetting you? Can I help in any way?'

Mary looked up at him, trying to decide if she could confide in him. She decided she could. If he kept his own life so secret then he'd keep her secret too.

'Isn't it my sister Breda. She has me destroyed . . . worried sick,' she amended. 'Isn't she carrying on with her cousin again. I just caught them in the yard. You must have heard the fight that went on before Christmas. Well, now she tells me she loves him and they're going to try to get a dispensation from the Archbishop so they can marry. What am I to do? I'll have to move. I can't tell Aunty Maggie again but I've no excuse for going. None at all.'

He stroked his chin thoughtfully. It was a dilemma but there was no doubt that the best thing she could do was get her sister out of the house as soon as possible.

'It's a bit of a problem, but say nothing for now. I'll try to think of something for you. There must be a plausible excuse.'

'Oh, wouldn't that be wonderfully kind of you. I brought her over here with me so I could keep my eye on her, and haven't I often wished I'd left her behind.'

'Don't you worry, now. I've made a promise and I always keep my promises. Go on back to the party. It's five minutes to midnight and don't worry, it *will* be a happy new year for you. You deserve it.'

'Sure, I'll never forget your kindness. I'll say some special prayers for you, I will.'

'You're a good woman, Mrs O'Malley. Your husband must have been very very fond of you.'

'He was. But as Aunty Maggie says, life goes on for everyone.'

He watched her walk down the lobby and out of the front door, wishing he were younger and had a different job. But at least he could help her to extricate herself from this situation.

Chapter Eight

She didn't need Albert Fallowfield's help or a trumped-up excuse.

She'd gone back outside to join the merrymaking in the street, looking for Chris who seemed to have disappeared off the face of the earth. There wasn't time to go searching every house for him because she was jostled good-naturedly into a huge circle, gripped round the waist on one side by Maggie and on the other by Dermot Ryan.

They all started to chant.

'Ten, nine, eight, seven, six, five, four, three, two, one!' Then the sharp frosty night air was filled with noise. It was as though the whole city and every ship on the Mersey was rejoicing, Mary thought. There were shouts, church bells, steam whistles and laughter, and she was hugged and kissed and wished 'Happy New Year' by what seemed like a hundred people, one after the other.

At last she broke away and went over to Kevin and Lily, who had been mesmerised by the experience. As all the bells rang out Lily had turned to her friend and said with suppressed excitement, 'We stayed up and saw it all, Kev. We *saw* it!'

Mary bent and scooped them both into her arms and hugged them to her.

'Happy New Year, Kevin, and to you, Lily, mavourneen,' she laughed as she kissed them both. 'Now it's time for bed, so off you go.'

'Where's my dolly, Aunty Mary?' Lily asked with concern.

'She's in the bottom drawer of the chest. Didn't I say she'd be safe. Get away with you now. Up the stairs, or dancers as your mammy calls them.'

She sat back on her heels and smiled as she watched them go inside. They were a dear, sweet little pair of innocents and she hoped they'd stay that way for years to come.

The party went on but still there was no sign of Chris. She asked everyone but no one seemed to know where he was. She'd seen Breda, still dressed, creep out of the door and nod to Bryan and then they'd both disappeared down the lobby. She sighed. This was a great start to 1946. The problem of Breda and Bryan and not a sight or sign of Chris.

Gradually people started to drift back to their houses and the street became much quieter until Flossie's yelling and screaming brought them outside again.

'In the name of God, what now?' Maggie said to Jim as they both rushed out of the house, having made sure that all their brood had gone in and to their beds.

Phil and Bob Kennedy and Carrie Quinne had also come back out and they all reached Flossie's doorstep just as she emerged. Her face was puce and tears streamed down her cheeks.

'Flossie, what's the matter, for God's sake?' Maggie demanded.

Flossie couldn't speak. She leaned against the doorpost, her hand at her throat.

'Is it Gerry?' Phil asked, concerned. Flossie looked terrible. Gerry was very drunk, but she'd never seen her friend so upset, even after one of her frequent rows with her husband.

'No! No . . . I wish to God it was.' Flossie again dissolved into tears. 'I . . . I . . .' She couldn't go on, but pointed upstairs.

Maggie and Phil went quickly inside and up the stairs, followed by their husbands.

The sight that greeted them made them both gasp in horror. Phil caught hold of Maggie's arm to steady herself, she felt so dizzy.

In Flossie's brass bed Chris was asleep on his back while Rosie lay with her cheek against his shoulder, one arm across his bare chest. Rosie was pretending to be asleep, Chris was not. He was out cold.

There was a silence so heavy and cold that the ticking of the battered alarm clock sounded deafening. Then Phil darted forward, grabbed Rosie's arm and pulled her away from her son.

'I'll kill him! I'll flaming well kill him! Maggie, help me get him off this little . . . whore!'

Jim appeared in the doorway, followed by Bob Kennedy.

'Christ almighty! So this where he got to,' Bob said grimly.

Phil's face was scarlet with exertion and fury. How could he do this? How could he make such a fool of himself with this little tart, who'd had everyone fooled by her 'new leaf' antics? The worst thing was that he was going to have to marry her now to save everyone's pride, not least her own.

'Go on down to Flossie, the pair of you, and Maggie, make some strong tea. Bob and I will get this young gobdaw back home.' Jim too was seething, but it was Mary he was thinking of. How was she going to take this? There was no hiding it; the whole street would know in half an hour. Flossie was not noted for her discretion and most of the neighbours were out there now wanting to know what was going on. If Chris had been his son he'd have half killed him.

Mary had pushed her way through the little crowd of people gathered round Flossie's front door and was halfway down the lobby when Maggie came downstairs.

'Aunty Maggie, what's the matter? Why is everyone in such a state?'

Maggie's shoulders sagged. She was going to have to tell the girl. Now, before anyone else did.

'Come into the kitchen, luv, I'm going to make some tea. We'll all need it,' she added grimly.

Bewildered, Mary looked around the O'Hanlons' cluttered and none too clean kitchen, the table half covered with empty glasses and stained with spilled beer.

Flossie was sitting in a chair sobbing, her chest heaving. Gerry was standing facing the range, gripping the mantel, considerably sobered by the terrible facts his wife had just yelled at him before breaking down completely.

Phil's cheeks were still burning and anger flashed in her eyes as she stood by the kitchen window with her arms folded over her ample bosom.

'What *is* going on?' Mary demanded as Maggie busied herself with the kettle and teapot. No one had moved a muscle.

'You'd better sit down, luv,' Flossie said through her tears.

Phil's fury exploded. 'It's that bloody stupid son of mine!'

'I'll tell her, Phil.' Maggie's voice was sharp, for Flossie's noisy weeping was grating on her nerves. 'Flossie, pull yourself together and shut up that bloody noise! Things are bad enough without you screeching like a bag of tomcats.'

Flossie sniffed. 'We . . . we should never have had this do. Then . . . then . . .' She shook her head and dissolved into tears again.

'Will someone please tell me what is going on?' Mary begged, beginning to feel anxious. What had Chris done?

'Flossie has just found their Rosie, naked as the day she was born, in . . . in bed . . .' Maggie's voice faltered but she forced herself to go on. '. . . with Chris Kennedy. Jim and Bob are taking him home, as soon as they can get him dressed again.'

Mary's face drained of all colour. Her eyes widened with horror and pain and she clutched the collar of her jacket tightly.

'No! No, he wouldn't do such a thing. Aunty Maggie, say it's not the truth?'

'I'm afraid it is, luv, God blast the pair of them to hell.'

Phil interrupted. 'He's drunk, dead drunk. It's the only way that little tart could have made him do such a . . . thing.' She struggled with her words.

Mary didn't wait. Before anyone could stop her she turned and fled down the lobby, pushing her way through the curious group of people and across the road. As she stumbled inside she collided with Albert Fallowfield. She was blinded by tears and her sobs made her attempted explanation incoherent.

He was shocked.

'Mrs O'Malley! Mary! Who has upset you?'

She was past caring. Slowly, between sobs, she told him of Chris's betrayal.

As he held her in his arms, he realised that she was treating him as a father and he felt very protective and deeply sorry for her plight. A sadness had entered his heart, though. He'd sometimes permitted himself to think there might be some chance in the future of her considering him as a prospective husband, but that had been a pipe dream. As for Chris Kennedy and Rosie O'Hanlon . . . words failed him but the anger bubbled up inside him. He felt that they both deserved to be locked up in Walton Jail, awaiting his ministrations and expertise with the noose. Hanging was too good for the pair of them for shaming and breaking the heart of this young girl who had already known grief in her short life.

'Well, at least now you've no need for any weak excuses, Mary.'

She looked up at him as though he were a stranger.

'You can leave this house now and find somewhere more respectable. You don't belong in a place like this and neither do I. I've no choice but you have. Go, Mary, and find a new and better home.'

She had quietened a little.

'Oh, Mr Fallowfield, how could he do it? How could he do it to me? I'll *have* to go now.'

'You will, child.'

'You're so kind and you after being . . .'

She knew. She knew, he thought. How he didn't know, but it didn't seem to bother her. She was too upset already.

'The public executioner. Someone has to do it, Mary. Go on up now.' Despite his anger he felt hopeful. If she did get somewhere better maybe he, too, could leave and live with her, be a father to her. It was a long time since her own father had died, she'd told him one day when she'd stood talking to him in the lobby. She needed someone older and wiser to take some of the responsibilities of Breda and Kevin off her young shoulders.

She nodded and fled upstairs.

When she reached the room she shared with Breda, Patsy, Lily and Maggie, she flung herself on the bed beside her sister, her shoulders shaking as she buried her face in the pillow and wept. How could he do this to her? He loved her, not that cheap, common little Rosie. He *knew* she loved him too, and yet he'd . . . She couldn't bear to think of him with Rosie.

Breda woke up. 'Mary, what's wrong?' she asked sleepily.

Mary couldn't answer her. Rubbing her eyes Breda sat up and drew her sister into her arms. Mary hadn't cried like this since the day she'd got the news of Col's death. The only words she could distinguish were the names of Chris and Rosie O'Hanlon and she sat rocking Mary in her arms until at last Maggie appeared in the doorway, her face drawn and haggard.

'Aunty Maggie, why is she weeping like this? I can't get any sense out of her at all.'

'She's every right to cry. Twice she's been in love and twice she's lost her man.'

Breda looked confused. 'What do you mean, twice?'

'Flossie has just found their Rosie and Chris Kennedy in her bed. The pair of them naked and drunk. When I left, Jim and Bob were getting his clothes back on to carry him home.'

Breda's mouth formed an O of disbelief.

'No! Sure, it can't have been? He wouldn't do that to Mary.'

'Breda, I saw them with my own two eyes and the shock

nearly made me faint, before I began to feel so mad I could have killed the pair of them with my own two hands! So the poor luv's got a lot to cry about. Move over. I'm that exhausted I could sleep for a week. This is a flaming good way to start a new year, I must say, and there'll be no cheerfulness in Flossie or Phil's houses either. If I were Flossie, I'd swing for that little trollop.'

When everyone had gone and Chris had been removed to his own bed, Flossie pulled herself together.

'Well, what are you going to do about that madam upstairs?' she demanded of Gerry.

'What can I do? The damage is done,' he replied weakly.

Fury began to fill Flossie. 'Oh, it's done all right, and as usual you're whining and trying to shove the responsibility on to me like you've always done. That's why that one upstairs carries on the way she does. Oh, I should have known I'd get no help from you, you bloody useless coward! I know that half the time you were supposed to be out with the other air raid wardens you were hiding under someone's stairs frightened out of your wits. We'll be the disgrace of the whole parish, but you don't care about that, do you, Gerry O'Hanlon? All you care about is your belly and your booze! Well, if you won't do something, I will.' Glowering with increasing rage, she made for the door and he heard her heavy tread on the bare boards of the stairs.

'Bloody women!' he muttered. Always nagging and complaining and trying to shift the blame on to you. All he wanted was a quiet life, but her jibe about his conduct during the war hit home. If she started telling the neighbours *that* he'd never be spoken to by any of the men again. He was a coward, he knew it, but the admission depressed him further.

Rosie had feigned unconsciousness all the way through

the hysterical scenes of the past hour. Now she smiled secretly to herself. She'd soon be Mrs Rosie Kennedy. She'd planned it carefully and it had all gone even better than she'd expected.

She buried her face in the pillow as she heard her mother's footsteps, and then she screamed with pain as Flossie caught her by the bleached hair and yanked her bodily out of bed.

'Mam! Mam! Stop it, for God's sake. You'll have me hair out by the roots,' she screamed.

'I should have known! I should have bloody well known! You've done some things in the past but this is the living end, Rosie! In *my* bed! *My* bed, and with   him!'

Flossie flung Rosie against the wall and Rosie screamed again and tried to cover her head with her arms but her mother caught her hair again and began to rain blows on her, yelling abuse at the same time.

'You've been asking for this for years and your useless da wouldn't do it, but I'm going to. You're going to get the hiding of your life, you little get! And I don't care if you have the whole street up with your screeching! You've shamed me for the last time. You'll marry him and then you'll bloody well behave, like it or not!'

The stinging slaps sounded like rifle shots as Flossie beat her daughter. Shame, anger and frustration with Gerry drove her on until at last she sat down on the bed exhausted. Rosie was on the floor in a corner, whimpering and wondering if it had all been worth it. She'd be black and blue all over for weeks, and her head felt as though it was on fire.

Chapter Nine

Chris awoke with a head that pounded as if it had been pulverised with a sledgehammer and a tongue so furred it felt twice its normal size. God, what had he been drinking? He couldn't remember a single thing after he'd had a couple more swigs out of that bottle that Rosie had given him.

He tried to sit up but his head was so bad he groaned and lay down again as nausea washed over him. He should be at work. He should have been at work hours ago, the weak January sunlight coming in at the window told him that. Gingerly he raised his head and leaned it on his elbow. He'd have to try to make the effort.

As he swung his legs over the side of the bed Phil came into the room.

'God in heaven, Mam, what did I drink? What happened?'

'What happened? What bloody happened?' she yelled at him. 'I'll tell you what happened all right!'

'Oh, God, Mam, don't shout. My head feels as big as Birkenhead!'

'I'll shout and I don't care about the neighbours. The whole bloody street knows anyway.'

'Knows? Knows what? I can't remember most of last night.'

Phil glared down at him. 'You were drunk. Out cold you were, in Flossie's bed with that . . . little whore Rosie! No wonder you don't want to remember, you pig! I hope it was worth it because you've broken Mary O'Malley's heart and mine too and you'll have to marry Rosie O'Hanlon now. You've no choice.'

Despite his hangover Chris was horrified. Oh, God, what had he done? Had he made love to Rosie? He couldn't remember. He just couldn't remember, but if the whole street knew he must have, and what about Mary? He'd have cut his arm off rather than hurt her and yet he'd struck her the cruellest blow of all.

He groaned. 'I'll go and apologise.'

'You will not! You're not setting foot in Maggie's house. She'll throw you out bodily before she'll let you near Mary. Didn't you hear me, Chris? You'll have to *marry* that Rosie and you are not living here. There's no room and I'll not have *her* over my doorstep! The shame! The shame of it!'

'Oh, Mam, I feel like death already, but—'

'And you've every right to,' Phil interrupted him. 'But it's done now and you'll have to face up to the consequences. I'm going to see Flossie.'

'Where's Da?'

'At work, where you should be, but you can lie there and rot for all I care. I'm finished with you!'

Phil slammed the bedroom door hard behind her. The sound made Chris shudder with pain, but it was nothing to the pain he was beginning to feel in his heart. He lay down again. He couldn't take everything in. His brain seemed not to be functioning.

Flossie was up but there was no sign of anyone else when Phil pushed open the front door and walked down the lobby into the kitchen.

'Has she come round yet?' she demanded.

Flossie indicated that Phil sit down, and rubbed her tired eyes. She'd been up all night.

'Oh, she has. She wasn't even drunk, the little bitch! I've given her a hiding she won't forget in a hurry.'

'It's something she should have had years ago. This is all your fault, Flossie – not that I'm trying to shift the blame from our Chris.'

'It's all bloody Gerry's fault,' Flossie answered tartly. 'God knows, Phil, I've tried my best, you know that, but she was born bad, I swear it. What I did to deserve her I don't know. She's a cross I've had to bear.'

Phil glanced around. Gerry must have felt it prudent to go out and get a day's work. There would be a lot of dock workers missing this morning, and the kids had gone to school.

'Ah, I'm dead sorry, Phil. The shame of it. I know I've been ashamed of her before, but this . . . this is the worst and she did it on purpose.'

'Well, I've never been ashamed of any of *my* family,' Phil answered acidly, looking around the untidy, shabby room. Flossie couldn't even keep her house in order, let alone her daughter.

'I've been up all night. What are we to do, Phil?' Flossie asked wearily.

'He'll have to marry her, that's what. The pair of them lying there naked! I've never been so shocked and disgusted in my life. I don't care how much he carries on or swears he doesn't remember, we *saw* them. He'll have to marry her so we can at least hold up our heads again, although God knows what Father Hayes will think.'

'We don't have to tell him?' Flossie suggested tentatively.

'Not tell him! For God's sake, Flossie, the man's not a fool. He'll want to know why. It's so sudden. They've not even been courting, let alone engaged. You can bet your life he'll want to know why.'

'Where am I going to get the money for a wedding from?'

'I don't know. Make Gerry work for a change. I don't know what you ever saw in him, Flossie. You were a good-looking girl when you took up with him.'

'I was, wasn't I? I've asked myself that question a million times over the years.'

'We'll go halves, if Bob agrees. But I'm not having them live with me, Flossie. For one thing I've no room – there's seven of us and only five of you – and for another I won't have her over my doorstep, nor him either once he's married. I could kill him!'

'I very nearly killed her. My arms and shoulders are aching with belting her.'

'So, who's going to take the pair of them round to the church?' Phil asked, anger still evident in her voice.

Flossie groaned. 'Gerry will go to the ends of the earth before he'll do that.'

'I don't know why you put up with him.'

'Because I took my wedding vows, just like you, Phil. Except you got the "better" and I got the "worse". I suppose I'll have to take her – as usual I get the dirty end of the stick.'

'Right, Bob and I will come with you. We'll go early this evening when Bob gets home from work. By then all of the neighbourhood and most of the fellers on the docks will know but that can't be helped. Meladdo will have sobered up by then and if he starts acting up I'll belt him, big as he is!'

Flossie nodded. She couldn't blame Phil for being so angry. Chris was a good, hard-working, decent lad. Phil had brought all her kids up well. What's more, he'd been courting Mary O'Malley, who would have made him a far better wife than their Rosie would. She'd have to face the young widow sometime and try to apologise, but what could she say that would mend that poor girl's broken heart?

Mary and Breda had both gone to work.

'It's better than hanging around here, Mary,' Breda urged, although her sister's eyes were red and swollen from a night spent in heart-rending sobs. None of them had slept much, except for Patsy and Lily.

'You get out there, girl, and hold your head up high. You're not a slut – far from it. You've not brought shame on us or yourself. He doesn't deserve you if that's the way he intended to carry on.' Maggie was still shocked and angry. Chris Kennedy of all people. He *must* have known what he was doing, even if only vaguely. He obviously hadn't thought of Mary at all.

'I . . . I look a fright,' Mary answered. She felt totally exhausted after the torments of the night. She hadn't been able to get the image of his face or the sound of his voice from her mind. She still didn't really want to believe it.

'Put your hair up. I've got a drop of belladonna somewhere. It'll work wonders for your eyes.' Maggie had begun to search through the dresser drawers.

'Aunty Maggie's right, Mary. You've got to show everyone you don't care!'

Mary nodded. 'I know.' She suddenly thought of Albert Fallowfield and how kind and considerate he'd been last night. He'd treated her like a daughter and she was grateful.

'We . . . we'll have to leave, Aunty Maggie. I can't stand the shame of living across the road from him and . . . her!'

'Won't that look as if you're running away?' Breda asked.

'It will not. I'm not going today. I've to find somewhere for us first, and that may take time, so I'll just have to try and ignore everything for now.'

'Mary, aren't you destroyed with it all. Don't think about moving yet. Don't do anything hasty,' Breda pleaded. She didn't want to leave. She'd have to make special journeys to meet Bryan. Last night he hadn't been too keen on backing her up about going to see about a dispensation. But if Mary found some halfway decent rooms she knew she'd have to go.

Kevin and Lily were ready for school, waiting for Patsy to come downstairs. They looked at each other with puzzlement and fear in their eyes and Lily's little hand closed over Kevin's. She didn't understand what had gone on and neither did he.

'Don't go away, Kev. I don't want you to go anywhere without me.'

Kevin looked up apprehensively at his mother. 'Mammy, will we have to leave here? I don't want to go anywhere without Lily. She's my best friend.'

Mary bent and gently stroked his hair. In all the chaos and misery she'd forgotten him. He was her son and he was looking up at her pleadingly with eyes so like Col's. Oh, how cruel it was to have mentioned leaving in front of him. She'd been totally selfish. She'd thought nothing about him but everything about herself.

'Not yet. Mammy will explain when you come home from school, I promise.'

There were tears in his eyes and Lily had begun to kick

her heels against the sofa, a sure sign of an impending tantrum. She looked up at Maggie from under her thick, unruly fringe.

'When . . . when the time comes, can I take Lily too?' Mary asked.

Maggie nodded slowly. It would be less worry for her, although since Kevin came to live here Lily had more or less behaved herself all the time. She didn't want them split up either. It would be downright cruel. She cursed Chris Kennedy again. His bloody selfish lust had hurt them all, even the little ones.

'Yes, luv. When the time comes. Now where's that lazy little madam?' She went to the kitchen door. 'Patsy! Patsy, get down here, or you're all going to be late!' she yelled at the top of her voice.

Mary reached out and touched her arm.

'Thanks. It would have had me heart scalded to separate them.'

'Go on now, off to work the pair of you. I'll see to this lot. Your mammy will come back home to you after her work, I promise,' Maggie added, seeing fear in the child's eyes and open mutiny in Lily's.

It had started to snow heavily as Phil and Bob, both grim-faced, and a dejected, disbelieving Chris knocked on Flossie's front door. Chris, when he'd felt better, had argued and pleaded with his mother but Phil had been adamant.

'It doesn't matter what you say, Chris. It's done! You should have thought of the consequences before you let that one drag you up Flossie's stairs, no matter how drunk you were.'

'God knows what she gave me to drink, Mam. I swear to

God I don't remember doing anything with her. You have to believe me.'

'It's no use swearing to God that you don't remember. The next swearing you'll do to Him will be your marriage vows.'

'But, Da . . .' He was desperate. Rosie had trapped him, he was sure of it. He was absolutely certain now that he'd done nothing with her. He had passed out. He hadn't been capable of anything. She must have put something in that bottle.

'I don't care! We *saw* you! Can't you get that through your thick head? And now you're going to have to marry her and that's my final word.' Bob's voice brooked no argument. He was just as angry and hurt as his wife. The bloody young fool, he thought.

Flossie's expression matched that of her neighbours as she opened her front door, already muffled up against the cold and shoving a shivering, ashen-faced Rosie out before her. The girl looked even worse with the black roots of her hair now showing. Already, even in the dim street light, you could see the bruises beginning to emerge, Phil thought with some satisfaction. It was what Flossie should have done years ago. As she'd expected, there was no sign of Gerry. He'd probably not even come home yet. He'd be propping up the bar in some pub on the dock road.

'Right, the pair of you, walk in front of us so there'll be no running off,' Bob Kennedy commanded.

Chris shoved his hands further into the pockets of his coat, after pulling his cap down as far as it would go over his forehead as a protection against the weather and to try to hide his embarrassment. He'd never felt so ashamed in all his life. His da had judged his mood accurately: he wanted to run. He'd run anywhere and as fast as he could to get out of this mess, but he couldn't run from God, the wrath of the church in the guise of the parish priest, or Mary O'Malley. He felt as though his heart was breaking. He loved Mary and now all that was over. She was lost to him for ever, and all because he'd been stupid enough to believe that Rosie had changed.

'What's this? A deputation? Come in out of the weather but wipe your feet.' The priest's housekeeper held the door wide and they trooped in and stood in the hallway, all of them trying to avoid looking at the huge statue of the Virgin Mary flanked by two small vases of snowdrops set on a large table near the door, a little blue glass lamp burning at its base.

'We've come to see Father Hayes,' Phil informed the woman, who nodded and hurried away through a door.

Within seconds the priest came into the hall.

'It must be important for you all to come out on a night like this. Come into the sitting room. There's a good fire in there; Martha doesn't spare the coal. Will I ask her for some tea? You all look as though you need it.'

'Thank you, Father, but no. We won't be here long,' Flossie said firmly.

When they'd all settled themselves he looked at Bob Kennedy. 'Well?' he asked, even though he knew by their faces what was wrong.

It was Phil who spoke. 'Father, we've come to say that our Chris and . . . and *her* . . . want to get married, as soon as possible.'

Father Hayes looked at Chris and Rosie speculatively. So, he'd been right. He'd never thought of Chris Kennedy as a lad to have anything to do with the likes of Rosie O'Hanlon, whose confession he heard every week, knowing she was there just to keep her mother quiet. In fact, before Christmas he'd been about to tell Flossie not to let her in the door of the church, because she had no intention of making any kind of reparation. Then she'd come and told him she was turning over a new leaf and when he'd seen her next he'd thought she really meant it. Obviously she hadn't.

'I see. You've gone against God's laws and are now faced with the consequences. Is that the way of it?'

'No, Father, that's not it at all. Well, the first bit is, but there's no . . . no baby,' Flossie interrupted hastily.

He was surprised. 'Indeed?'

'Definitely not,' Phil said firmly, glancing at her son. The thought of Rosie O'Hanlon having her grandchild was more than she could stomach.

'Then I'll call the banns on Sunday. We have to stick to procedure no matter what. You'll be married in three weeks, then?'

Bob spoke. 'That will be fine, Father. Now we'll go and leave you in peace.'

At the door Flossie turned. 'Father, will you pray for me? I'm heartbroken.'

'I will, Mrs O'Hanlon,' he said kindly. He'd noted Gerry's absence when they'd arrived. He'd also noted that neither Chris nor Rosie had spoken or even glanced at each other. Well, no doubt he'd hear all about it in due course.

It was the following evening before Chris and Rosie had their first meeting alone in Flossie's front room, which was used as a bedroom-cum-playroom by Jimmy and Carmel.

Chris looked at her with loathing. He felt no pity for her even though her face was a mass of bruises. She'd tricked him. She must have been planning it for weeks.

'Well, aren't you going to say anything?' she demanded, trying to keep the quiver from her voice.

'What is there to say? You've trapped me and I walked straight into it. I'm the biggest bloody fool on this earth. I should have bloody well known that a leopard can't change its spots. I suppose it'll be back to the make-up and the flashy clothes now. God help me, I'll be married to a tart. Everyone's cast-off. Soiled goods.'

'I'm not a tart!' she flung back at him. She hadn't expected him to be all sweetness and light but she did have feelings. She *did* love him and it hurt to see the way he was looking at her. It hurt more than all the aches and pains that racked her body.

'You are. You just don't charge for it, you give it free. At least they admit to being what they are. They don't pretend.'

His words twisted the knife in Rosie's heart. 'I . . . I only ever wanted you, Chris. I swear to God that's the truth.'

He laughed tauntingly. 'When have you ever told the truth, Rosie? What about all the others? I never touched you, but it's me who's going to have to put up with you and your bloody family too. Mam won't have you over her doorstep and I don't blame her. She'd die rather than have the Hornby Street bike in her house. So I'll be lumbered not only with you but with living in this midden too.'

She got up, tears stinging her eyes. Maybe he'd come round in a week or so, when they got married. She would *make* him love her. She was good at *that*, anyway.

'I'll see you at the wedding,' she said flatly before turning and leaving him alone.

He dropped his head into his hands. If it wasn't a sin and a crime, he'd chuck himself off the landing stage. It would be a quick death because of the fierce undertow, and he'd be free of Rosie O'Hanlon, but he'd roast in hell and she wasn't worth that.

Mary had been to Seldon Street off Islington to see some vacant rooms but had rejected them because they were damp and bug-ridden, two things she knew she couldn't contend with. In Dublin there had been houses with those same faults and her mam always said they weren't fit for animals, let alone a Christian soul to live in.

Her head was bent against the icy wind and she picked her way carefully between patches of grey slush, all that was left now of the white blanket that had covered everything three days ago. It had hidden all the dereliction and blackened ruins in the city. She'd turned into the entry because it was less hazardous underfoot than the street, and didn't see Chris coming towards her until he spoke.

'Mary. It's me . . . Chris.'

She looked up. She couldn't avoid him so she stood still and waited for him to come closer to her.

'Mary. Oh, Mary, I'm so sorry.' He reached for her hand but she pulled away.

'Don't touch me. You've the stink of herself's cheap scent on you and I don't want to be contaminated. Your one who I hear you're going to marry soon.'

His eyes and his voice were pleading. 'Mary, for the love of God just listen to me. No one's asked me my side of it.'

'And what side would that be, then?'

'I was as shocked as everyone else. I didn't touch her, Mary, I swear it. She trapped me. She's always been hanging about, making passes at me. She gave me a bottle of that bloody poitin.'

'Ah, so now it's the fault of the drink, is it?' The words

were sarcastic, yet in her heart she wanted to believe him. It was all she could do not to throw herself into his arms and sob against his chest, beg him to tell her it was just a bad dream, a nightmare.

'Not all, but that's how she got me so drunk so quickly. I don't remember a single thing after the third swig.'

'But you took the first one, didn't you? You took a drink from her knowing what she was.'

'I thought she'd changed. Everybody did, even you.'

'Well, none of that matters now, does it? You're stuck with her and it's pity I feel for you now, Chris Kennedy. Pity and anger.'

She made to push past him but he quickly caught her in his arms and drew her to him.

'Mary, I love you! I'll always love you!'

Mary struggled to get free but her heart was ruling her head and her efforts slowly ceased. She still loved him even though he'd betrayed her with Rosie. For a few seconds she clung to him, then she jerked free of his arms and ran up the entry, the tears streaming down her cheeks. He still loved her and she still loved him and there was not a single thing they could do about it.

Chapter Ten

February brought more snow. Temperatures plummeted below freezing and in many homes in the city cold and hunger took their toll on the young, the weak, and the old.

'Nice flaming weather to be having a wedding in,' Phil commented as she sat with Maggie and Flossie in her spotless kitchen, a good fire in the range.

Maggie had been invited because Flossie, left to her own devices, was useless at arranging anything. Not that this wedding needed much organisation.

'You've only to see the way she runs that house to know she's useless,' Phil had commented when asking Maggie for help.

Maggie had shaken her head and told Phil that although she didn't show it, Mary was heartbroken. She would come in from work, have her tea, help Kevin and Lily with what little bit of homework they had, then go to bed almost straight after the children. But she was still awake and sobbing when Maggie and Breda went up.

'It's pitiful, that's what it is, but there's nothing I can do or say to help.'

Phil had shaken her head sadly. 'Oh, I'd have welcomed her with open arms as a daughter-in-law, Maggie, I would.'

'I know, Phil. It's a waste of two good lives.'

'At least this weather's a good excuse for a small, quiet wedding. Everyone's too caught up in their own lives and the extra worries the bitter cold brings. It certainly won't be anything like Katy Ryan's do when she married that Yank. Now that was a good wedding, all right. The dress and veil made by that dressmaker in Bold Street, the food and drink all supplied by him, of course. What was his name, Maggie?'

'Herman or Herbert, something like that.'

Phil sighed. 'I don't know how everyone's going to fit in your house, Flossie.' What she meant was that Flossie should give the place a damned good clean.

'We'll manage. We can set the food up on a table in the front room.' It was slowly beginning to dawn on Flossie what was expected of her, for the couple were to have that room for themselves, that being how most newly-weds started out in life. 'I'll have to shift things round, anyway.'

'I hope so,' Maggie said meaningfully.

'We can put the drink in the kitchen, that way we can keep an eye on that useless husband of mine.'

'What's she wearing?' Maggie asked while Phil raised her eyes to the ceiling.

'A navy-blue two-piece costume and a pink blouse, and I think she's borrowing a hat from Emily Quinne,' Flossie answered.

Both Maggie and Phil were relieved. The sight of Rosie O'Hanlon in a white dress and veil would be an open mockery. White was reserved for virgin brides and Rosie was far from being one of those.

'Will . . . will Mary and Breda come, Maggie?' Phil asked tentatively.

'God knows, I don't. Breda might. You might as well

know, but I don't want it repeated to anyone at all yet, Flossie. Mary's looking for rooms. She can't stand the strain of it all.'

'I can't say I blame her,' Flossie said sadly.

'I'll miss her. I'll miss them all. When she gets fixed up, like, she's going to take our Lily to live with them.'

Phil nodded. That was just like Mary O'Malley. Considerate to a fault. Even though she must be feeling devastated she'd not let her little son or Lily suffer the same fate. A pair of bookends, Mary called them. 'Come here to me, you little pair of bookends,' she often said.

Phil sighed. 'Well, let's get on with the lists, then. I'm just glad St Valentine's Day isn't a Saturday this year. It's more than I could stand for them to get wed then.'

Breda had forced Mary to go into town with her on the pretext that she couldn't choose something for the wedding by herself.

'You don't need me to be making comments. You've never done so before.'

'Well, I want to show your one across the road up. I hear she's got a navy-blue costume.'

'Sure to God you didn't expect her to wear white, did you?'

'I did not. Why don't you buy something too? You are still going? If you've changed your mind again I'll take you apart, so I will.'

'I'm going. Otherwise it'll look as if I'm afraid to face the pair of them.'

'Which you are in your heart,' Breda said shrewdly.

Mary knew it was useless to argue. 'So what if I am, Breda? But you'll tell no one. Not even Bryan.'

Breda flushed. Bryan had become very reticent since the whole upsetting affair with Chris and Rosie. He didn't want his mam upset too, he'd said when she'd mentioned the dispensation again. There had been too much trouble all round.

Breda sighed. 'I promise. Will you look for something? Something very smart and in a bright colour, that will make herself look plain and dowdy. We'll knock the sight out of the eyes of everyone else, too.'

Mary shook her head. She didn't want Chris to start comparing his new wife with his old love. It wasn't fair. Things were bad enough.

'No, I'll get material, and nothing too bright either.'

'What about green? Emerald green, and I'll see if there's something in gold or yellow. Then we'll be nailing our colours to the mast.'

Mary smiled. 'Emerald green. Ireland's own colour.'

'You look grand in any shade of green, Mary, and don't you know it.'

There wasn't much of a choice as the big stores were too expensive for them and the others had all been gutted. Blacklers though had moved into Bold Street, Liverpool's Bond Street, much to the disgust of establishments like Sloan's and Bacon's and Cripps. Mary did manage to get her material there but Breda could find nothing suitable that she liked.

'There's nothing! Nothing at all!'

'Why don't you just buy the material and I'll make you something?'

'No, I'll try the shops in London Road first.'

'Breda, I'm worn out,' Mary complained. She slept very badly these days.

'I'll go by myself and meet you by the station.'

'No, not the station.'

Breda pursed her lips at her own stupidity. At night Lime Street was the haunt of the Maggie Mays, the common prostitutes. Now she'd have her sister thinking of Rosie again.

'On the plateau of St George's Hall, then? I know it's still Lime Street but lots of respectable people arrange to meet there. I'll see you there at four, then.'

Mary agreed and decided to take a walk up Bold Street and scan the windows of the shops that were left standing, although the big church dedicated to St Luke at the top end was a blackened, bombed out shell. She might get an idea for something different from Cripps or Bacon's. Whatever she'd said to Breda, she did in her heart want to look much better than Rosie.

She'd spent half an hour looking in the shop windows and had begun to imagine the lines of a smart costume which she'd trim with black braid. She'd wear her best white blouse under it, and her black shoes and handbag were decent enough. A matching hat would be no problem, either. She'd have pieces left over to make a small hat and she'd begged Mr Scott, the butcher, for the tail feathers of a cockerel. She'd stitch them to one side and the colours would catch the light and make the hat look expensive.

As she walked towards the huge neo-classical building that was St George's Hall, still bearing the scars left by the incendiary bombs that had very nearly destroyed it in the Christmas raids of 1940, she peered through the crowd, trying to pick out her sister's dark head. She had begun to ascend the steps up to the plateau when she was nearly floored by a street urchin clasping an old-fashioned lady's portmanteau to his chest. They seemed to roam the city in tribes, she thought. She heard the cries of 'Thief! Thief!' and a burly-looking man ran past her and grabbed the lad by the frayed collar of his torn and dirty jacket.

The crowd parted, and she saw an old lady lying on the ground. No one seemed to be helping her. Mary pushed through the onlookers and knelt down, helping the woman into a sitting position.

'Are you hurt? Shall I call an ambulance? Don't move now, there may be something broken.'

'My . . . my bag . . .' the woman gasped.

'It's grand. Look, that gentleman is bringing it back. You can't trust anyone these days.' She glared at the small circle of spectators. 'Why don't you go and find yourselves something useful to do instead of standing there like gobdaws!'

The people melted away as the man, an off-duty policeman, came towards them, the bag in one hand and the lad in the other, struggling and kicking.

'Is she hurt?' he asked.

'I don't think so. Just shaken up.'

'Good, because I'm marching meladdo here to the Bridewell in Dale Street.'

'You're a guard . . . a policeman?' she amended.

'I am. Are you sure she doesn't need an ambulance?' He looked at them both with some concern.

'No. I'll look after her. I'll take her home.'

'Thanks, miss.'

She smiled. 'It's Mrs actually, and it's no trouble at all.'

She helped the frail, slightly stooped old lady to her feet, thinking that a good gust of wind would blow her over. She was dressed in the now old-fashioned style of the twenties. Her black felt cloche was lightened by a yellowish cream bow that had obviously become discoloured over the years. The fur collar of her coat looked as mangy as an old mongrel cur, Mary thought.

'Are you certain you've not damaged yourself at all?'

'No, no. I'm a bit unsteady on my feet, and this weather is not much help. It's so treacherous underfoot.' She looked up at Mary, really seeing her for the first time. In all the confusion everyone's faces had been blurred.

'Thank you. Thank you so much. It's very kind of you to be so concerned.'

'Sure, it was nothing at all.'

'You're Irish.'

'I am so, from Dublin. Now let me see you safely home as I promised the policeman.'

'There's no need for you to put yourself to any more trouble.'

'It's no trouble at all. You might slip. Didn't you say yourself that the pavements are a fright? And you'll have to be careful in the future. Next time there may not be anyone like your man just passing and out of uniform. I'll walk you to the bus stop.'

'It's very kind of you, my dear.'

'My name's Mary. Mrs Mary O'Malley.'

'And I'm Miss McPhail . . . Agnes. I came here from Melrose, that's in the Scottish Borders, with my sister a long time ago. When we were just girls really. She died last year. She was two years older than me. Poor Hetty, I do miss her.'

Mary took her arm, noticing that she was still shaking.

'Hasn't it all shaken you up. When I get you safely home you must have some sweet tea, an aspirin and a rest.'

Suddenly she was confronted by Breda, her cheeks flushed from rushing down London Road, knowing she was late.

'Mary! I'm sorry I'm late, but I did manage to get . . .' Her words trailed off as she realised Mary was not alone.

'Breda, this is Miss McPhail. One of that tribe of street arabs pushed her over and snatched her bag. We got the bag back but I'm seeing her home. Here, take this with you and tell Aunty Maggie I'll be in later.' She turned to Miss McPhail. 'Now where is it that we're going to?'

'Exeter Road, just off Balliol Road in Bootle. I have a house there.'

Breda stared after them. Wasn't that just like Mary. Still, she'd managed to get just what she wanted and at a decent price too. A bright buttercup yellow dress which would look well under her good three-quarter-length navy fitted jacket. Fortunately she had a navy and yellow hat Mary had made to go with the jacket, which she'd been saving for some occasion grander than just Mass on Sunday. She'd look ten times better than Rosie, and Mary had that lovely emerald green material. They'd both stand out in the crowd. No one, least of all that creature Chris Kennedy, could fail to notice the pretty, stylish and colourful pair. Everyone would be looking at them and not at the bride with her drab suit and borrowed hat and that awful straw-coloured hair with the black roots. She had lain beside her sister for too many nights, hearing the muffled sobs, to have much sympathy for him. He was an eejit to have let that one trap him. He deserved all he'd got, and his future looked very bleak indeed.

Chapter Eleven

Mary was totally unprepared for the size of the house that Agnes McPhail lived in. Exeter Road was a quiet, very genteel place, she thought, even though it was at the Miller's Bridge end of Balliol Road, a busy main road on which the town hall, the law courts and the public baths were situated. It was also quite near to the railway line and the docks, both of which had suffered badly in the May Blitz. In fact the roadway dipped and ran underneath the railway line to allow lorries and carts and the dockers themselves access to their work.

'You live here alone?' she asked, taken aback.

Agnes McPhail was searching her bag for her keys. 'I do now.'

Mary's eyes travelled upwards. 'But it's so big.'

'It is rather. I have some of the rooms shut off now. When we came here, Hetty and I, Uncle Duncan lived here. You see, we would never have been allowed to come to Liverpool at all otherwise. Mother was very strict like that. Two young girls living unchaperoned in a big city that is also a port and with all kinds of foreign sailors roaming the streets? Och, no!'

She produced a large keyring. 'Uncle Duncan owned the house and was very particular and . . . careful.' There was a slight pause before the last word.

She means he was an old skinflint, Mary thought, but the house, at least on the outside, was very well maintained.

It was a three-storeyed red brick Victorian villa. Seeing the airbricks at its base she realised that it must have a cellar for coal. The brickwork on the gables and above what she took to be a bedroom window was very ornate and quite elaborate for a terraced house.

There was a bay window downstairs and one above it. Another bedroom, she surmised. How many of them were there? There was also an attic window, suggesting that when the house had been built it would have been able to house a family and a servant.

There was a small front garden with a neat pocket handkerchief of a lawn and narrow borders, empty now of plants. It was enclosed by a three-foot-high brick wall and the pathway was flanked, rather grandly, Mary thought, by stone gateposts.

Miss McPhail had opened the front door and Mary followed her inside, glancing furtively round. It felt like stepping back in time to the Victorian era. Everything was dark and heavy. The bottom half of the wall was covered in brown anaglypta, the top half with wallpaper that had a small but very busy pattern of flowers and leaves in cream and brown. The carpet along the hall and up the stairs was also brown and cream.

She followed the woman into a small breakfast room, which was also furnished and decorated in dark colours. Every surface was covered with bric-à-brac, fringed chenille cloths, cream doilies and antimacassars.

'Sure, you don't clean a huge place like this by yourself, do you?' Mary asked.

'Och, no, dear. I have a lady who comes in once a week. I

really need her to come more often but I can't afford it. Will you sit down?'

'Aren't you the one who's had the shock. *You* sit down and I'll make you some tea.'

Thankfully, the older woman sank into an armchair covered in faded chintz patterned all over with deep red Alba roses. She took off her hat but kept her coat on. 'Everything is in the kitchen.'

Mary took off her own coat and hat and went through into a small but very clean and tidy kitchen, which had a door leading into a pantry. There could be no comparison between this and Aunty Maggie's dark, cluttered scullery.

Along one wall were shelves on which all the pots and pans were set out. The gas cooker was old but clean and still serviceable. In a stout wooden press she found the crockery. She put the kettle on after lighting the gas jet, found the teapot and the tea caddy. She placed the dishes on a small tray that had already been set with a starched cloth with a wide cotton lace border, a china sugar basin and a milk jug. It was obvious that Miss McPhail had come from a far better home than herself and was used to a well-ordered lifestyle. An idea was beginning to form in her head and as she poured the hot water into the pot she wondered, should she broach it now or was the poor soul too shaken up? Miss McPhail couldn't afford to pay people to look after her or the house. She couldn't afford to heat it properly. It was deathly cold in that room with only a very poor excuse for a fire burning in the hearth.

She took the tray in.

'Here now, take this. Have you any aspirin or Aspro?'

'In the box in the dresser.'

Mary opened the door of the dark oak dresser. Inside was stored all the table linen in neat piles. It was yellowing with age but all of a good-quality damask. There was an Oxo tin in one corner marked with a label: FIRST AID. She opened it and found that it contained bandages, a bottle of TCP, a small bottle of Dr Collis Brown's Mixture, a tube of Golden Eye ointment, a jar of zinc cream and a tin of Fuller's Earth. Enclosed in a long paper strip were some aspirin tablets and she tore one off.

'Now, take this, and then you must rest. Will I build up the fire? Then you'll be warm and cosy.'

'You're such a kind girl.'

'Sure, it's nothing. Wouldn't I do the same for anyone in trouble. It's quite near to the docks here; you were very lucky not to be bombed.'

'Aye, we were very fortunate, but it was terrifying. The May Blitz was horrifying. It went on for a whole week and for hours on end. We sat in the cellar with the coal and when we came up it looked like a scene from hell. There were flames and smoke and the crashing of buildings falling and the clanging of bells from the fire engines. They were brave men, those firemen, and a lot of them were killed too. I'm certain that it all led to poor Hetty's death.'

Mary glanced at a sepia-coloured photograph in a silver frame that stood on the mantelpiece. Hetty McPhail didn't look a bit like her sister, she thought. She looked strong enough to stand anything, even the might of the Luftwaffe. In fact her expression was so dour and her hairstyle so severe that had a German pilot had to bale out and landed on her doorstep, he'd have wished himself back in his burning plane. She looked to be not the sort of person you would call 'poor' at all. Far from it.

Miss McPhail sipped her tea appreciatively.

'You must tell me about yourself, Mrs O'Malley. You're

very young to be a widow, if you don't mind me saying so.'

Between sips, Mary told her of her life in Dublin with Col, the birth of Kevin. Of how she had pleaded with Col not to go to war, and then his death.

'So when the Emergency was over I decided to come to Liverpool and find work. To try to build a new life. I live with my aunty in Hornby Street, off Scotland Road.'

Agnes McPhail glanced away. It was a terrible neighbourhood, or so she'd heard. There were public houses on the corner of every street and there were always fights. She'd only ever gone along there on the tram or the bus, but she'd seen signs of terrible poverty. Underfed, dirty children with bare feet, even in the depths of winter. Women with shawls clutched around them and some of them had no shoes either. They looked drawn and haggard and old before their time. Now of course many of those streets were just bomb sites, which made the lot of the poor even harder. Despite the poverty she'd grown up in this girl looked clean and tidy and was well spoken.

Mary traced the gold rim of the cup with her finger.

'I . . . I . . . was courting someone that I thought . . . cared for me. In fact I thought he loved me but he doesn't. He's getting married to someone else.'

Agnes winced at Mary's words. Her memory was good and she well remembered Victor Bramwell. She'd been engaged to him although neither her mother nor Uncle Duncan had approved of him. Even after all these years it still pained her to think of him. He'd gone off to France to fight in the Great War and she'd seen him off with kisses and hugs and tears. He'd not come back, although he had escaped injury. He'd written to her telling her he was marrying a French girl, and she'd been left broken-hearted. Only Hetty had been a comfort; everyone else had said 'I told you so'. She had never married. In a way she knew how this poor girl was feeling.

Mary decided to change the subject.

'That was my sister Breda you met briefly.'

'She's a bonny girl. A very bonny girl.'

'She is so, but . . . she's fallen in love with her cousin, her first cousin.' It was now or never, Mary thought, taking a deep breath. 'So, with that situation and . . . and my own, and the fact that we are so crowded, I've been looking for rooms.'

Agnes McPhail gazed at her with interest. 'And have you found any?'

Mary shook her head. 'Nothing decent. There's desperate overcrowding everywhere.'

'Mrs O'Malley, what work do you do?'

'I'm a machinist at Williams's, but I have hopes and plans. You see, what I really want to do is make hats – be a milliner with my own business. I can do it. They're not fancy expensive hats, but I can work wonders with left-over material, so Aunty Maggie says. I make nearly all our clothes and hats. I've even made a small tiara of wax flowers with silver leaves. I'd make smart hats at a price working girls and women can afford.'

Agnes McPhail leaned back in her chair, a slow smile spreading across her face.

'That is what I am . . . or was. A milliner. I worked for Sloan's when Mrs Ada Sloan herself was still in charge. I served my apprenticeship there.'

Mary leaned forward, her eyes full of excitement. 'Oh, Miss McPhail, could you teach me? I'd be so grateful. I could pay you something.'

Agnes was considering the whole situation. It could work.

She only had what she'd managed to save over the years and it wasn't much to live on. There was plenty of room for Mary and her sister and her little boy. They were both working so would be able to pay something for their board. She could see the bairn to school and collect him if needed, she'd always been fond of children. She could help this young girl who had shown her such kindness, whom she'd taken an instant liking to, to make some of her plans and ambitions come to fruition.

Mary was concentrating hard on the pattern of roses around her cup. Oh, if only this frail old lady could help her, wouldn't it be the answer to all her problems.

'Yes. Yes, I'd love to teach you and help you, but there will be no charge. It will be a pleasure. I still have a few contacts in Bold Street. It will be a challenge. I know it's *your* ambition but I'd feel part of it.'

She paused and leaned forward. 'Would you also consider coming here, to live? There's plenty of room and it's a long time since I heard laughter, especially a bairn's laughter. This house has always been quiet. Too quiet of late. It would solve all your problems.'

Mary's spirits soared and tears of gratitude welled up in her eyes.

'Oh, Miss McPhail, aren't you the kindest person I've ever met! To offer us a home and teach me too. Oh, I'd love to live here with Breda and Kevin.' She stopped and some of her euphoria evaporated as she thought about Lily. She'd promised the child. She couldn't leave Lily behind.

'There is just a bit of a problem. Kevin and his little cousin Lily are inseparable. Sure, don't I call them my little pair of bookends. I . . . I couldn't split them up. I promised.'

'How old is she?'

'Seven, the same age as Kevin.'

'And is she well behaved?'

Mary passed over Lily's tantrums, which were few and far between these days anyway. Her manners were better than they had been for she copied everything Kevin did.

'Oh, yes.'

'Then bring the little bairn too.'

Mary was relieved. 'When would you be able to take us?'

'There's no time like the present, poor Hetty used to say.'

Mary thought for a few minutes. 'Will next weekend suit you? By the time I get them organised, see about schools and pack everything?'

'It will. Now drink up your tea and I'll show you the whole house. Maybe we could turn the attic into a nursery.'

A picture of Kevin and Lily in a nursery flashed through Mary's mind and was instantly banished.

'I think they're a wee bit too old. But they could have it as a playroom,' she added hastily. 'That would keep them from getting under our feet.' She smiled. 'How much would you want for our board?'

'Oh, we don't have to talk about that now. We'll discuss it when you move in.'

'What am I to call you? What will the children call you?' she asked, taking the empty cup from her newly found benefactress and placing it on the tray. Both children would have to be kept well away from fine delicate things like this, or they'd go breaking everything around them. Especially Lily, whose curiosity was avid. She turned every new item upside down or inside out, and there were many things here that her little fingers would itch to pick up.

'You must call me Agnes, and I will call you Mary.'

'That doesn't sound . . . respectful, what with you being . . .' Mary became flustered.

'So old?' Agnes laughed. 'Och, don't fret, child. I *am* old, but I've been alone far too long. I've found a friend today. You are a dear kind friend, so you must call me Agnes and the bairns can call me Aunty Agnes. Give me your arm, Mary. I'm full of aches and pains these days. It's the weather.'

Mary was amazed. Apart from the kitchen and morning room, there was a front parlour, so dark it was hard to see exactly what it contained. Heavy dark green velvet drapes hung at the window, looped back and held in place by faded, tasselled cords. They effectively blocked what little light filtered in through the cotton lace curtains.

Her eyes became accustomed to the gloom and she could see that there was an old-fashioned, deeply buttoned brown Chesterfield and matching chairs. The carpet too was dark green, as was the fringed mantel cloth. This was one room the children definitely must not enter. There were far too many delicate ornaments adorning the mantelpiece, the side tables, the high-backed mirrored sideboard. There were bowls and vases of cut glass, china candlesticks and figurines and stuffed birds perched on twigs anchored to a plinth and covered by glass domes.

She took the frail arm firmly in her own as they went upstairs. There were three large bedrooms. Two of them were fully furnished but covered in dust sheets. The third was Agnes's own room and Mary noted how neat and tidy it was. It smelled musty but there was the faint scent of lavender too.

To Mary's astonishment and delight there was a bathroom on the same floor. It was complete with a cast-iron bath on legs, a washbasin with brass taps that were in need of polishing, and – to her the last word in luxury – an inside flush toilet.

They went up another flight of stairs to the attic. It was dim and dusty and filled with old suitcases and tea chests, but it wasn't damp. The house was a little palace. It needed a good clean and all the linen and curtains needed washing – in fact some of them could be removed to let in more light – but it was better than any house she'd ever been into. She didn't know anyone who'd lived in a place like this. There was no back garden, but you couldn't have everything. There was a biggish yard giving access to the very narrow entry and there appeared to be a wash-house of sorts.

She and Breda would share a room and so could Kevin and Lily. She'd make a home of it again, if it had ever been that at all, she thought. Uncle Duncan and sister Hetty didn't sound like homely people. It would be warm, clean, uncrowded and cheerful and she could learn from Agnes, as she must now call her, the skills she needed to become a milliner. But best of all it would be away from Hornby Street, Rosie and Chris and all the neighbours. There would be no need to assume a false, careless attitude day after day, week after week. She'd had enough of that already, and she still felt heart-sore and betrayed.

She could go to the wedding from this house and return here. There would be no one but Agnes to see her tears. God had smiled on her. She must write to Mam and tell her of this minor miracle, after she'd informed Aunty Maggie and Breda. She just hoped her sister wouldn't refuse point blank to move. Uncle Jim would sort Breda out if she asked him to, but neither Uncle Jim or Aunty Maggie knew anything of the continuing liaison with Bryan, or the intention to attempt to gain a dispensation.

Chapter Twelve

She couldn't wait to get back to Hornby Street and she still couldn't really believe it. As she sat on the bus she didn't stare out of the window as she normally did, even though it was dark and the shop lights were being switched off. Her mind was full of plans. Plans for the future, for all their futures. She had not felt so relieved, excited or hopeful since before the disastrous New Year party.

As she came into the kitchen, her cheeks glowing from the cold air and the brisk walk from the bus stop, everyone looked at her.

She certainly had something on her mind, Maggie thought, and it seemed to be good news.

'Mary, in the name of God, where've you been?' Breda asked as her sister came in. She was somewhat annoyed because she'd been waiting impatiently to show off what she now called her 'wedding outfit' to everyone, but she wanted Mary to see it especially.

'I took her home,' Mary replied simply.

Breda was peeved. 'Was there any need for all that? Herself looked grand to me.'

'Well, she would. Anyone would look "grand" to you when your head is full of something else. Aren't I glad I took her home, though. She has a huge house in a nice area, and' – Mary's eyes sparkled – 'she's asked us to go and live with her. You, me, Kevin and Lily. And what's more she's a retired milliner,' she finished triumphantly, glancing quickly at all their faces in turn.

Breda was incredulous. 'Live with her? She's about a hundred and we don't know her at all!' It was beginning to dawn on Breda that she had no choice. If Mary had found them a home she was going to have to go, whether she liked it or not.

'Patsy, put that kettle on. I think we all need a strong cuppa. Now take your coat and hat off and sit yourself down, Mary, and tell us all about it. Breda only said you helped an old lady after her bag was snatched.' Maggie looked grim. 'This city is getting shocking if old ladies can't walk the daylight streets in safety. The police should do something about those street arabs. Nothing but young thieves they are.'

'Aunty Maggie, you know why they run the streets. They're orphans, or their parents are useless. It's the only way they can survive.'

'Then they should be in an orphanage or the workhouse.'

Mary sighed. 'Maybe, but they have to fend for themselves on the streets. She wouldn't have had much in her purse but to that young bowsie it would have been a fortune.'

Maggie was tired of the subject. 'Well, tell us all about this old lady then, Mary?'

'She lives alone in a big three-bedroomed house in Bootle. There's a kitchen with a pantry, some sort of sitting room and a parlour. Everywhere is carpeted except the kitchen. There's a rag rug in there over the red quarry tiles and they only need a mop over them. Upstairs there's three big bedrooms and you'll never guess what else?' She was watching all their faces.

'We won't if you don't tell us,' Breda said pettishly.

'A bathroom!'

'A real bathroom?' Maggie was incredulous. This woman must have money, she thought.

'A real bathroom with a bath and a basin and an inside flush toilet!'

'Jesus, Mary and Joseph! I'd think I'd died and gone to heaven if I had one of those!' Maggie said, shaking her head in awe.

'And there's a big attic room as well that Lily and Kevin can have to play in. There were no children out playing in the street.'

Breda looked decidedly glum. 'That sounds as if it's desperately quiet.'

Patsy came in with the kettle and Maggie busied herself making the tea.

'And how much does she want for all this, Mary?' Maggie asked.

'She wouldn't say. She said we can sort it all out once we're in.'

'You never went and said we'd move in without knowing how much? Sure to God, she'll probably ask a fortune.'

'She won't, Breda. She's just a lonely old lady rattling around in a house so big she can't cope with it all. Two of the bedrooms are shut off and so is the parlour and didn't she have a terrible poor excuse for a fire in that small living room.'

'Where is it?' Maggie enquired as she poured out the tea.

'In Exeter Road, off Balliol Road. It's a quiet road near the docks, and they managed to escape the bombing, although it sounded desperate. She and her sister sat in the coal cellar, she said, and when the All Clear sounded and they came out it was like a scene from hell.'

'It was.' Maggie didn't want to think about the May Blitz. 'So, then, when did you tell her you'd move? And what about those two?' Maggie jerked her head in the direction of Kevin and Lily, both of whom were sitting on the edge of a wooden bench, their little faces a study in concentration and consternation.

'Next weekend. I'll have to enquire about schools and wash and iron and pack. She was quite willing to take Lily and Kevin, after I'd explained about them being inseparable and me promising I wouldn't leave Lily behind.'

'What about me?' Patsy demanded. She didn't feel it was at all fair to be left out. Why couldn't she go with Lily and live in a house with a bathroom that had a toilet so you didn't have to run down the yard with a coat or shawl over your nightdress in the freezing cold or suffer the smell and the flies in summer? Everyone's privy stank in summer.

'Hasn't she enough on her plate without you, melady? Anyway, you're not fit to live in a decent house, what with your snatching and grabbing at the table and the mess you leave everywhere. Just look at the cut of you. Your hair looks like a flaming bird's nest and you've spilled half your dinner down that frock. Lily's table manners have improved a treat since Kevin came,' her mother answered cuttingly.

Patsy stormed upstairs in a huff. Oh, one of these days she'd show them. She'd show them all and she'd make them appreciate her. Make them all take notice of her and what she said and did. Hadn't she fought all Lily and Kevin's battles for them?

Mary finished her tea.

'It all needs a good clean, from top to bottom. Aunty

Maggie, will you help? Breda's not much of a one with the housework.'

'I'd noticed that myself,' Maggie answered tartly.

Breda was incensed. 'Well, aren't you a right beast to say such a thing, Mary O'Malley!'

They both ignored Breda's outburst.

'Of course, luv.' Maggie wanted to see inside this house. 'Will she mind if I bring Phil along too? Many hands make light work, so they say, and it'll take her mind off . . . things.' Maggie could have bitten her tongue seeing the flash of pain in Mary's eyes.

'You're not going to have much time to make yourself the outfit for the wedding,' Breda commented, still in a huff.

'I'll stay late after work. Once it's cut out and tacked it won't take long.'

'Well, now can I show everyone what *I'm* wearing?'

'Oh, go on upstairs and get yourself all done up, then,' Maggie instructed.

'Mam, can I wear my Communion dress for the wedding?' Lily pleaded.

'Only if you promise to behave for Mary when you move?'

'I will, Mam. Honest I will.'

'All right then.'

Lily and Kevin both darted under the table, a favourite, private place for them in what was always a crowded room. Lily pulled at the tablecloth to bring it down so they could have even more privacy. Mary, seeing the cloth moving across the table, was thankful there were no dishes left on it.

'Did you hear that, Kev?' Lily hissed loudly. 'A playroom. A whole room just for us to play in!'

'Will we have to go among strange kids again, Lily?' Kevin was very doubtful about this move.

Her little brow creased in a frown as she considered this.

'I suppose so, but even if they're dead horrible, we don't have to play with them after school. We've got each other, Kev, and we'll have our room. What's an inside flush toilet?' she added.

He was just as mystified. 'I don't know, Lily, honest. I don't even know what flush means.'

'Never mind, we'll find out soon, and I can wear my dress to the wedding. I'll look like a proper bridesmaid then.'

'I don't think they want any bridesmaids, Lily,' Kevin said cautiously.

Lily pushed her hair out of her eyes and shrugged. It didn't matter. They were moving to a big house and would have a special room all to themselves. It would be great to get away from Patsy and her tormenting and their Bryan who always seemed fed up these days. Maurice hardly spoke to anyone anyway, so she wouldn't miss him either.

Maurice took in the news in his usual way, quietly. It didn't matter much to him whether they stayed or went. Mary's cooking was better than his mam's though, he reflected. He ignored the rest of the conversation, wondering if he'd have the courage to ask Pauline Casey from further down the street if she'd go out with him. He could have gone to Goodison Park with the others to see Everton play, but had wanted to save a bit of money, just in case.

Breda's mind was working quickly as she put on the new dress. She'd have to write a note to Bryan, explaining that she didn't want to go to this house in Bootle but had no choice. As from next week they would have to arrange proper meetings, times and places. Then the note must be burned. It was so crowded in this house that you hardly ever got the chance of a private word with anyone, let alone a whole important conversation.

Hastily she scribbled a note with a pencil that Patsy had left out along with some paper which was supposed to be part of her homework. Then she shoved it into the pocket of her three-quarter-length navy jacket. He'd be in soon from the football match with Uncle Jim. She placed the hat Mary had made on her head and tilted it to just the right angle over her right eye before she went downstairs.

Maggie looked at her approvingly. 'Doesn't she look like a picture in one of those women's magazines? Go on then, give us a twirl.'

Breda obliged.

'Oh, you look great, Breda. What's that word she's always using?' Maggie puzzled.

'Sophisticated,' Mary answered.

'Together we'll have them all with their eyes out on stalks,' Breda said, twisting and turning for more effect.

'That's not the point of it at all, Breda, and you know it,' Mary answered, but there was very little conviction in her voice.

'Would you just listen to her, Aunty Maggie? Not the point!'

'Well, it's not,' Maggie said. 'Not really, but I must say that if you want Chris Kennedy and Rosie O'Hanlon and the entire street and congregation to notice you, then you'll do it all right and I don't blame either of you. After all, you'll be living in that posh house by then. You'll have come up in the world. You can have everyone talking and admiring you and saying, "Haven't they done well for themselves, living in the lap of luxury? You couldn't expect them not to look the part."'

Breda turned triumphantly to her sister, the words 'I told you so' on her lips, but the flash of anguish in her sister's eyes forced her to bite them back.

By Saturday morning everything was ready. Battered cases and bundles jammed the lobby and Maggie and Maurice had been commandeered to help, not that Maggie had needed much persuasion. She was eaten up with curiosity. Her son was there under sufferance and made no effort at all to conceal it. All the way on the bus he was still deliberating about Pauline Casey.

All their expressions, except Mary's, changed as they alighted from the bus clutching parcels and cases and followed her round the corner into Exeter Road.

'God almighty! It *is* posh – *and* big,' Maggie said, looking upwards just as Mary had done.

'I wouldn't fancy it myself. It's too quiet around here,' Maurice mumbled.

'No one asked for your opinion. And straighten your cap, you look like a barrow boy,' Maggie stated as the little group went up the path.

Mary knocked and the door was opened almost at once.

'I've been waiting for you, Mary. There's a pot of tea ready and some toasted crumpets.' Agnes McPhail's eyes alighted on the others and she became flustered. 'I . . . I'd no idea . . .'

'I'm sorry. I should have told you that Aunty Maggie and my cousin Maurice were going to help us move.'

'Come in, then. It's bitterly cold out there and I'm sure we can make the crumpets stretch.' Agnes opened the door wide. Mary's relations didn't look too bad and her smile was genuinely warm as Mary introduced the children to her, starting with Kevin.

'Take that thumb out of your mouth and say hello properly, Lily O'Shea!' Maggie hissed at her youngest daughter. They always managed to show you up, she thought. Maurice was standing there like a fool as well. She nudged him hard with her elbow to greet the old lady properly.

Maurice snatched off his cap and muttered a few words to the effect that he was pleased to meet her, which he wasn't, but it kept his mam quiet.

They left all the luggage in the hall and trooped into the breakfast room. Agnes indicated that Maggie and Maurice should sit.

'Mary has told me how kind you were to give them a home when they first came to Liverpool.'

'Oh, they're family, like,' Maggie said, sitting gingerly on the edge of the chintz sofa. The place was a bit shabby but it didn't take much to imagine what it had looked like when it was all brand new. She wouldn't even have minded it the way it looked now. It was far better than anything she was ever likely to have. There were ornaments everywhere and the good but faded chintz curtains matched the suite.

Mary brought in the tray. The tea was passed round and so were the crumpets, cut in half and served on china plates that both Maggie and Maurice were terrified of dropping. God alone knew how the kids would cope with this fancy china, Maggie thought. At least Mary had given them plain white crockery that she'd found somewhere in the kitchen.

'Agnes, I don't want to appear pushy or to be taking over the place,' Mary said, looking at Maggie for support. 'But next weekend will it be all right if Aunty Maggie and Mrs Kennedy come and give me a hand with the attic and the . . . er . . . windows?'

'Of course. I know it all needs a good clean.' She shook her head. 'Nothing much has been done since poor Hetty died, I'm afraid. I get so tired these days. And then there's the arthritis. I'm very stiff in the mornings. Dr Davidson said I should go abroad to live, somewhere where it's always warm, but I couldn't do that.'

'They don't live in the same world as us, Miss McPhail. It's all very well for them to say such things,' Maggie said. She glanced quickly at the photo of 'poor Hetty' and thought that Mary was right. Hetty McPhail looked as tough as old boots. 'It'll be a pleasure to help out, seeing as you've been kind enough to share your home with Mary, Breda and Kevin *and* our Lily. It'll help me no end, too. It'll ease the overcrowding. We're packed in like sardines up there and half the street is just a pile of rubble. I count myself fortunate. I lost my eldest boy on D-Day, but the rest came through and we've still got a roof over our heads.'

'It must have been awful for you. We were very lucky here.'

Maggie gingerly sipped the last drops of her tea but was loath to leave. She wanted to see the rest of the house, especially that luxurious bathroom.

'Shall I give you a hand, Mary, luv?'

Mary knew what was expected of her. 'Would you, Aunty Maggie?'

Maggie stood up, her attitude businesslike. 'Right, you can all take something each. Mary will show us all where things are to go, that's if you don't mind, Miss McPhail?'

'No, of course not.' Agnes was content to sit back. It was pleasant to have company again.

Before Maggie and Maurice departed, every detail of every room was noted, especially the bathroom. All would be relayed to Maggie's neighbours later over a pot of tea.

When they'd gone Mary and Breda set about the unpacking.

'Isn't this grand, Mary? Would you look at the bedspread. It's silk. Real silk!' Breda was incredulous.

'It is. And we'll take it off, because it's also very old and if we use it every day it'll just fall to bits.'

Breda ran her hand over the smooth, dark wood inlaid with a paler wood and mother-of-pearl.

'A dressing table with mirrors! Sure, we'll be able to see ourselves properly. And wardrobes, real wardrobes! No more having to hang things round the room like a hand-me-down place.'

'Breda, you can admire it all later. Now let's get the children's room sorted out. Where are they?'

'Up in the attic. Herself told them they could go up.'

Mary was horrified. 'Go and get them down. Won't they be covered in God knows what and go trailing it everywhere after them and won't that be a fine start?'

Breda pulled a face but went to the door. She'd managed to get the note to Bryan and she'd seen him drop it discreetly into the fire in the range. He'd just nodded and what that was supposed to mean was anyone's guess. It was the only unsettling thought in an otherwise perfect day.

They soon got themselves organised and it was Agnes who took both the children to school on Monday and promised she'd collect them.

Lily had been rebellious. 'We're big enough to come home by ourselves, aren't we, Kev?'

Kevin hadn't answered.

'I know that, Lily, but you don't know this area yet. You'll get lost. Aunty Agnes will collect you until you learn your way around.' There was a lot they would all have to learn in this house, Mary thought. How to tidy all their belongings away after them. Not to go screaming after each other and running up and down the stairs. How in fact to use the bathroom, for she'd seen the look of horror on Lily's face when she'd been confronted with the big bath. The toilet had mystified the child altogether. She'd peered down into it as though it was a huge hole in the Bog of Allen, and when Mary had demonstrated the flush she'd run and hidden behind Kevin, her thumb in her mouth.

Mary's days and evenings were busy. Breda was instructed to make a meal, or at least help to make one, while she stayed on at work to make her costume for the wedding.

'Why me? She can cook and she's nothing to do all day. I'll be in a desperate state with all that china and stuff, and I couldn't keep my eye on those two little eejits at the same time,' Breda had complained bitterly.

'Agnes isn't strong and you *can* cook and look after them. I won't be all night and it's only for a few evenings. I'll do the rest of the sewing by hand,' Mary had replied.

There were only two more weeks to the wedding and she was dreading the ordeal, but she wouldn't back out. She knew that she and Breda would be the centre of attraction, which gave her some satisfaction in one way but not in another.

On the Wednesday night, when John Harvey had locked up and bidden her goodnight, she saw Albert Fallowfield waiting on the other side of the road. She smiled as she crossed over to him.

'Mr Fallowfield, did you come specially? I'm sorry. In the rush of things I never even knocked to say goodbye, did I? I'm a fright and I'm truly sorry.'

'That doesn't matter, Mary. You can hear everything

through those walls and I'm delighted at your good fortune.'
He walked with her towards the bus stop.

'Are you happy there? I mean, is it a decent house?'

'Oh, it's grand altogether. The luxury of the place. There's carpets everywhere and a decent kitchen with a proper stove. In the parlour and bedrooms there's furniture you wouldn't believe the like of. Aunty Maggie and Mrs Kennedy are coming to help Breda and me give the place a good clean at the weekend.'

'I heard that through the wall too. How many bedrooms does it have?'

'Three big ones. Agnes has one.' Mary shook her head. 'I still find it hard to call her by her Christian name. It just doesn't seem polite at all. Breda and I share a bedroom and Kevin and Lily have the other.'

'I see.' He sounded disappointed.

Mary was concerned by his tone. 'Is there something wrong back home? I mean in Hornby Street?'

'No, everything is just the same. It's a bit quieter, except for Patsy and Maurice, who seem to fight and argue all the time these days. I never seemed to hear Maurice's voice when you were there.'

'Sure, Patsy would argue with St Peter himself. She has a temper on her and she wanted to move too.'

'I . . . I was wondering, Mary . . .' He hesitated, then continued, '. . . if Miss McPhail would consider me as a lodger too? I mean, a man's presence in a house is often a deterrent to people who . . . who might wish you harm. I know it's a quiet road, but the main road is only round the corner. The docks are close too and you never know what these foreign sailors get up to, and there's the patrons of the Bedford pub as well.'

Mary stopped and smiled up at him. 'Do you know, that's the very reason Agnes and her sister came to live here when they were just girls. They had to live with their Uncle Duncan, because it wasn't decent for them to be living alone in a big city that had docks too, her mother said.'

'Her mother was right.'

Mary was thinking. He would be an asset and she was sure Agnes wouldn't dislike him for he was quiet, considerate and educated. She couldn't tell her what he did for a living, of course. They could make the attic into a bedroom-cum-playroom for Kevin and Lily, which would leave a bedroom free. She was certain Agnes wouldn't object to his sitting in the parlour to read his books and newspapers; she might even sit in there with him if there was a decent fire. He could eat with them, if he chose to. And she would feel more secure with him there on hand to ask for help and advice should the need arise. She'd never forgotten how kind he'd been to her. As kind and considerate as her father, who had been buried in Glasnevin so long ago.

'I'll ask her. If I put it to her in the right words I don't think she'll mind and I'm sure she'll be glad of the money, even though most of it will go on food and heating. She loves having people around her, I've noticed that, and she'll spoil Lily and Kevin if I'm not careful. Lily is as cute as a bag of monkeys and she'll take advantage of Agnes if I don't watch her.'

'Thank you, Mary. I'd be very grateful.'

'I know Aunty Maggie will be upset with losing all our rent money, but I'll see if Breda and I will be able to give her a little bit. She'll have more room, and there's still Bryan and Maurice at home.'

'And I'll chip in too,' Albert offered.

*   *   *

At first Agnes was perturbed and apprehensive.

'He is very quiet and well educated,' Mary assured her. 'I'm sure you would have plenty of things to talk about. And he would be useful too around the house.'

'It's just that we . . . I've . . . never had a man in the house since Uncle Duncan died.'

'I know you must be a bit worried, but he is very nice and he doesn't really like lodging with Aunty Maggie.'

'Why does he?' Agnes asked, fiddling nervously with the long rope of amber beads she wore around her neck.

Mary was ready for this. 'He's no relations at all and was bombed out of his old place, and you know how hard it is to get decent housing at all. And didn't the poor man have to come through the kitchen to get to the yard and the privy, and to empty his shaving water away in the scullery. I think he must have come from somewhere just like this. He's a true gentleman. I'd trust him with my life, and Kevin and Lily's.'

'Well, then, Mary, he can come.'

'Oh, aren't you goodness itself, Agnes,' Mary enthused, thanking God Albert Fallowfield's occupation hadn't been mentioned. When she wrote to him she'd have to tell him to make up some story. He was paid a retainer which was quite generous, he'd told her once. Maybe he could say he was a gentleman of 'independent means'.

Maggie and Phil arrived early on Saturday morning and when Phil noticed how well Mary looked, and the style of the place she now called home, she cursed Rosie O'Hanlon for the millionth time.

'I believe my lodger is going to be your lodger, Mary? He told me after he'd got your note.'

'He is so. Did he give you the week's notice that I suggested?'

'He did. Anyway, what with the wedding next weekend, he'll have to get organised himself. Our house will be like a lunatic asylum to say the least. Our Patsy's actin' up something shocking. You can't say a word to her without there's tears and tantrums and all because she can't have a new dress. She thinks money grows on trees does that one, and I'm losing his rent money.'

'I'll give you something towards it, Aunty Maggie. Let Patsy have her dress. Somehow, she seems to get left out of things. She's too old for Lily and Kevin and too young for Maurice and Bryan. It will be one fewer thing you've to worry about,' Mary offered, busying herself with the cleaning utensils so as not to think about the wedding.

'Right, luv, where do we start?' Phil asked.

'I think at the top. Now Mr Fallowfield is coming the children will have to have the attic room.'

'She's got some good stuff here, Maggie,' Phil commented as she poked her head around the parlour door.

'I can see that with my own two eyes, Phil. You and me would sell our souls for just a bit of it. Carpets everywhere, even in the bedrooms. Not a piece of old lino or a tatty rug in sight *and* there's one of them vacuum cleaners too to make it even easier. Wouldn't it be as well to pack half of these ornaments and things away, Mary, out of reach of those two? They're bound to break something, especially our Lily.'

'I was going to ask Agnes about that.'

'Well, go and ask her now. It'll certainly make it a lot easier for us,' Maggie instructed.

'I'll go up and make a start. If we take two rooms each we should get it all done in a day,' Phil said. It was a beautiful house, filled with good furniture and every comfort a body could wish for. Oh, Chris was the biggest fool on earth. He could have lived here with Mary in the height of luxury, instead of being cooped up in Flossie's front room having to suffer her cooking and the constant bickering and rows, let alone not having his clothes washed, ironed and aired the way he was used to having them. Oh, he was a real gobdaw . . .

Chapter Thirteen

Half an hour before she was due to make the journey to the church Rosie wasn't even up. She lay in bed staring at the cracks in the ceiling, feeling depressed and panic-stricken by turns. She plucked nervously at the end of the grey army blanket. She'd thought that Chris's attitude towards her would have changed over the weeks. She'd even prayed for it, making bargains with God to be a good wife, but it hadn't worked. When they'd seen her on the street every one of his sisters and brothers had totally ignored her, including Jimmy and Carmel. She guessed that the two youngsters would have been threatened with dire punishments if they even looked at her.

She'd helped her mam to clean out the front room. There was a bed, two kitchen chairs, a very small drop-leaf table and an even smaller wardrobe and chest of drawers out in the yard, covered with a tarpaulin. Her mam had got the bedding from O'Toole's pawnshop. The furniture would be moved after the wedding breakfast. Of course the bed would have to be brought in too, and that would cause a lot of snide and suggestive remarks.

She'd heard, as she was meant to hear, of the carpets, curtains, furniture, linen, dishes and of course the bathroom in the house that Mary and Breda had moved to. They had every comfort now. Oh, yes, they had the luck of the Irish all right, she thought bitterly. And she'd heard the rumours of what they were going to wear today. No colours or detailed descriptions, just that they'd look smart. And they would. They were both natural beauties who didn't need make-up, except lipstick, to enhance their looks, and that Mary was very clever at making things. When Lily O'Shea had made her First Communion she'd been the envy of every kid in the neighbourhood.

Oh, she wasn't looking forward to the day at all. Somehow it had all gone wrong, and she knew everyone in the church would be thinking that poor Rosie O'Hanlon couldn't get a man by fair means. No decent feller would take her of his own accord. No one *loved* the likes of her.

As she came into the bedroom Flossie was annoyed to see her daughter still in bed.

'Get out of that flaming bed now, Rosie O'Hanlon! You've got to be in the church in half an hour. I'll have Emily Quinne here any minute now.'

Emily was the only girl in the street who'd agreed, after a lot of persuasion by her mother who felt sorry for Flossie, to stand for Rosie. Everyone else had refused point blank. Chris's brother Michael was to be best man and he wasn't happy about his role either. He'd wear his dark blue serge suit and the shirt and tie he wore on Sundays, but he'd refused to wear the carnation in his buttonhole and Phil hadn't pressed him.

'The whole bloody day will be more of a wake than a wedding,' Phil had muttered.

'It won't take me long to get dressed and put on that hat,' Rosie replied sullenly. She hated navy blue, it was such a

168

miserable colour. She hated pale pink too. It was too prissy and washed-out looking. And the hat looked awful. She'd dyed her hair so the dark roots were not now visible. Maybe, just maybe he would think her a bit more attractive and she wouldn't have to wear Emily's hat all day.

'Well, this is a nice attitude, I must say. You wanted him and now you've got him, so get up, get dressed and try to look happy about it. It's supposed to be the best day in your life!'

Rosie got up slowly and looked at the navy-blue suit and pink blouse that were on a hanger behind the door.

She'd used to dream of her wedding to Chris. The church would be filled with flowers and music. She'd have a long white dress, a veil and a headdress and carry a big bouquet of flowers, and she'd look beautiful, really beautiful, without much make-up. As she walked down the aisle on her da's arm everyone would turn and admire her and in the front pew would be Chris and he, too, would turn to look at her and smile and take her hand, promising to love and honour her. Now all those dreams lay in shattered fragments. Oh, she'd get to the church on time but nobody would even know she was going to be a bride. You usually walked to church, unless it was too far, and people would come to their doorsteps to wish you well. Shopkeepers and customers and the men in the pubs would come out too and they often gave you money. It was all part of the tradition. But there'd be none of that for her in the hideous suit and hat on her way to marry a man who didn't want her.

Lily and Kevin were both dressed and were sitting on the chintz sofa in the breakfast room. Kevin wore his best clothes, which included an overcoat Mary had made him just after Christmas. She'd trimmed the collar with a bit of old astrakhan fur. He hated it. Lily said it looked too posh and a bit soppy. Lily wore her Communion dress and the socks and shoes that Mary had kept carefully hidden so they wouldn't go to the pawnshop. She was sulking because Aunty Mary and Aunty Agnes, whom she wasn't quite sure she liked yet, had said she must put her coat on or she'd get pneumonia and finish up in hospital.

'No one will see my dress!' she'd complained bitterly.

'Of course they will, once we get back from church. Wouldn't it be a poor thing to bring you to the church looking blue and frozen with the cold,' Breda had intervened.

Lily was still rebellious. 'Our Patsy's got a new frock and *she* won't be wearing a coat over it 'cos she's only got that old one she has for school.'

'Your mammy will make her wear that and then won't she look a fright altogether. Now put on this coat and stop being such a fright yourself, Lily O'Shea.' Breda's voice was sharp. The last thing they needed was one of Lily's tantrums.

She was ready but Mary was still upstairs fiddling with her hair and her hat. Breda looked at herself again in the mirror over the fireplace. She was pleased with her outfit, very pleased. The bright yellow contrasted well with the navy. She'd turned the collar of the dress up and over the lapels of her jacket. Yellow suited her, she being so dark-haired, and her hair and hat were just perfect.

She'd taken ages to do her hair with the curling tongs that were heated over the gas jet of the cooker. The operation was fraught at the best of times. You had to get the heat just right otherwise you singed your hair and it broke off in lumps. She'd secured her hat at precisely the right angle, too. She wanted to look her best. It would be the first time she'd seen Bryan since they'd moved, and today they would be able to make some plans. Everyone else would be absorbed in their own thoughts and feelings.

'You do look very smart, Breda, dear. Very fashionable,' Agnes commented enthusiastically. Breda had promised to relate every detail to her tomorrow. Life was so full now, the old lady thought. A few weeks ago she wouldn't have believed it. She loved having them here, and she'd never be lonely again. Wasn't that nice gentleman, Mr Albert Fallowfield, moving in today, too? He'd called the other evening to present himself for her inspection and she'd been very relieved to see that Mary's description of him was accurate.

Mary had got a couple of nice Dover sole and Agnes was going to cook them for their supper with some potatoes and carrots. Maybe she'd make a sauce too. It was a long time since she'd had anyone to cook for. Then they might talk about themselves. He was a gentleman of independent means but an avid reader like herself. She liked to keep up with what was going on in the world and apparently so did he. To think that only a few weeks ago she had felt isolated and alone.

'I'll just go and see what Mary is doing up there. At this rate we'll be late.'

'And all the guests must arrive before the bride,' Agnes reminded her.

Breda thought about that for a moment. Wouldn't it be great to arrive *after* Rosie and have everyone's attention fixed on *them*. She dismissed the thought. Mary would take her apart.

Before she could go to call upstairs Mary opened the door and both Breda and Agnes sucked in their breath.

'Mary, you'll have them all destroyed with jealousy!' Breda cried.

'Oh, Mary, you look *so* beautiful, dear,' Agnes agreed.

Mary smiled but her heart was heavy. She didn't want to go. She didn't want to go one little bit and she was certain she would have to fight back the tears and nail a smile to her face all day. But she had made a tremendous effort. The emerald green costume was a great success. The jacket was fitted which set off her small waist, the skirt was just on the knee and showed her nice legs to good advantage. She'd trimmed the collar of her white blouse with black braid. She hadn't attempted to battle with the curling tongs, she was too nervous. Even the hairpins to anchor her upswept hair had been hard to cope with. Her green and black hat with the curving, sweeping, iridescent tail feathers looked as though it had been bought in a shop in Bold Street. She carried her handbag and gloves. She took a deep breath.

'Are we all ready then? Come on, my little pair of bookends, and don't be scowling like that, Lily, it spoils your pretty little face. You can take off your coat as soon as we get in the door of the church, will that suit you?'

Lily brightened considerably and caught Kevin's hand. They said goodbye to Agnes and were ushered out to find Albert Fallowfield on the doorstep with two large suitcases.

Mary panicked. 'Is it so late?'

'No, I thought I'd make an early start. It's a bit, well, confused back there.'

'It would be,' Breda said meaningfully.

'I must say you both look very smart. Very smart indeed.' He gave Mary a smile, thinking how brave she was and how beautiful she looked.

'Which is probably more than the bride will.'

'Breda!' Mary reprimanded.

'Well, I wouldn't know about that, but I did hear your mother say that Patsy will look ten times smarter and more cheerful than Miss O'Hanlon.'

Miss O'Hanlon, Breda thought sceptically, but of course he was a gentleman and would address even the likes of Rosie formally.

'Don't the children look well?' Mary placed a hand on Kevin and Lily's shoulder.

'Indeed they do. Lily, you look like a princess, and I see you're wearing your cross and chain. Kevin, you could be called her prince, I suppose, and that's a very nice coat.' He smiled down at them both and a warm feeling rose in him. Suddenly he seemed to have acquired an instant family. He would treat Miss McPhail as he would his own long dead mother, Mary and Breda as daughters and Lily and Kevin as the grandchildren he would never have. Once today was over, for them all, life would settle into a peaceful routine, which was just how he liked it.

There would be no more yelling and shouting. No more arguments. In fact you wouldn't hear a sound through these walls. It was a haven of peace after Hornby Street, and a very clean and comfortable home. Even the children would spend most of their time two floors above in their own room. Yes, things had definitely improved for him since Mary O'Malley came into his life.

They had not improved for Rosie who with her arm through her father's walked with eyes downcast up the street and along Scotland Road to the church. She looked awful, even though she'd put on her make-up and tried to hide her hair under Emily's hat. There were no neighbours to see her, wish her well and comment on her outfit. They'd already gone.

When at last she arrived and the bridal music burst forth from the organ, the first people who turned to see her entrance were Mary and Breda. In that moment she knew that Chris would never love her. Mary O'Malley was so beautiful, so elegant and so composed when she should be absolutely devastated and weeping at home in that posh house. She was even smiling at her. That Breda was too, but Breda's was a smile full of malice. They'd done it on purpose, she thought. Everyone would notice and comment on them, no one would care a fig about her, least of all Chris Kennedy. He'd have eyes for Mary O'Malley, not for his wife.

Somehow Mary managed to get through the ceremony. She fixed her mind on the day she'd married Col, forcing herself to conjure up the images, the scents of that day. Flowers, candle wax and incense. It had been June and the sun had streamed in through the stained-glass windows of St Catherine's, falling in myriad colours on herself and Col as though in a blessing.

She'd had a plain white dress and veil and had made her own headdress, one like Lily's. She'd carried a large bouquet of roses and their scent had been strong and sweet. Col's mother had bought them from the flower sellers in Anne Street and Henry Street. Breda, with Niamh and Maire, Col's young sisters, had been her bridesmaids. They'd had long dresses too. Deep pink because it suited them all. Of course all the wedding finery had been sold but that hadn't mattered. It was only what she'd expected. Both her mam and Col's mam had pawned a great many things to pay for it all.

They'd been so happy then. They'd had no honeymoon, just a day in the seaside town of Bray, down the coast from

Dublin, and were lucky to have even that. She willed herself to go over every single thing they'd said and done, including the way she'd run along the strand at the edge of the sea, her feet bare, her shoes in her hand, laughing as Col tried to catch her, which he did – eventually. She was startled from her dream by the triumphant notes of the Wedding March from *A Midsummer Night's Dream*. It was over. He belonged to Rosie now. She'd lost him for ever. As the newly-weds turned to walk down the aisle she held her head high and placed an arm round Kevin. It was a reminder to Chris that she had been a bride once. That she'd been loved and cherished and that Kevin would always be the proof of that love.

The reception, such as it was, was in Flossie's house, which seemed to be bursting at the seams. Flossie as usual was flustered and disorganised and, as usual, Maggie and Phil helped out, Phil red-eyed, having cried quietly all through the service, especially after she'd caught sight of Mary, who looked like a fashion model, she'd thought.

Rosie and Chris stood beside each other in the kitchen while everyone congratulated them, but Chris looked as though he wished himself a thousand miles away. It was Mary that his restless gaze was seeking out. He had to talk to her, in private somewhere, sometime, before they all went home and he was expected to play the part of a husband. Something he had no intention of doing.

He loathed Rosie. When Father Hayes had joined their hands he'd had to stop himself from shuddering, and when she'd demurely turned and offered her cheek for him to kiss he'd turned his head away. It was like a slap in the face for Rosie and Father Hayes hadn't looked too pleased either, but he hadn't cared. He still didn't.

Breda had managed to get Bryan into a corner of the kitchen. Ostensibly she was looking after Lily and Kevin by removing what would have been their sixth jelly cream, telling them they'd be as sick as pigs and did Lily want to destroy her dress altogether?

'Will we go out next Saturday?' she asked in a low voice as she wiped the sticky red mess around Lily's mouth with her handkerchief.

'Well . . .' he began.

Breda dropped all pretence and rounded on him.

'What do you mean by that?' she hissed, before remembering the children. 'Go off now to your mammy, Kevin, and see that you both behave.' She turned back to Bryan. 'You do still love me?'

'Of course I do, Breda, but it's a bit difficult . . .' he hedged, looking furtively round.

'It is not. I don't live there any more, or had you forgotten?'

Bryan knew he was on a hiding to nothing here. He did love her. At least he wanted to make love to her, but he wasn't keen on marriage and everything that went with it. God, you only had to look at Chris Kennedy's face to put you off the whole thing. He knew this wedding had been forced on Chris, but had it happened to him he would have fled the country and joined the French Foreign Legion rather than have to marry someone like Rosie. Breda was beautiful and loving and she had a great sense of humour, when the mood took her, but he still didn't want to be rushed down the aisle.

'So, will I meet you in the usual place at the usual time?' she demanded.

Bryan nodded. He had missed her around the house and

the smile his agreement brought to her face made his heart turn over. He just didn't want to be tied down yet.

As the day wore on and the merrymaking really got under way, helped by another keg of ale and some more bottles of sherry bought from a kitty all the men had contributed to, Mary's longing to run home to Exeter Road grew greater. The slight ache above her left temple had now become a steady thumping. Her face ached from smiling and she was exhausted from keeping her emotions in check.

Breda seemed to be enjoying herself, though, and she'd seen her whispering in the corner with Bryan, although she hoped Aunty Maggie and Uncle Jim and even Patsy hadn't. She wished she could go home. Flossie had no clock in the room so she asked Father Hayes the time and then went into the lobby, pushing her way through the neighbours, some of whom were sitting on the stairs. She'd just stand at the open front door for a while to get some fresh air and with luck a bit of peace and quiet.

Unfortunately, the party had spilled out into the street and she was obliged to walk to the corner of the entry, where she leaned against the wall and closed her eyes.

She would give it another half an hour, then she would announce that they would have to go. It was almost dark. They had a bus to catch now and the children were tired out, which they were, she thought. In fact there was a good chance that they'd both have to be carried once they got off the bus. At least it wasn't far from the stop to Agnes's house. How she longed for the peace she knew she'd find there. She could drop all this acting and cry and cry. Cry out all the hurt and bitter disappointment. Both Agnes and Albert would understand.

'Mary. I saw you leave. I . . . followed you. I came out the back way.'

She jumped nervously, her hand clutching her throat. 'God almighty! You had the heart across me!'

She couldn't see him clearly but she recognised his voice only too well.

'What are you doing trailing after me, Chris? Shouldn't you be with your wife, enjoying yourself? It *is* your wedding.'

'Oh, Mary, please don't remind me. I'd give anything . . . anything, Mary, not to have to go back in there. The whole day has been a nightmare and things will only get worse.'

'Shouldn't you have thought of that on New Year's Eve?'

'She tricked me, Mary, you know that. God almighty, everyone knows it. I hate her. It's you I love and I always will.' Chris moved towards her.

She stepped aside. 'No, Chris! No! Haven't you hurt me enough?'

'I'm sorry, Mary. God help me, I'm so sorry.'

'It's done, Chris. She . . . she's your wife now.' She couldn't keep the sob from her voice. She wanted to throw her arms around his neck and hold him.

'You'd better go back. I'm going . . . home. It's been a long, desperately hard day for me too and I can't stand any more of it. Goodbye, Chris, and good luck.' And before he could utter another word she had pushed past him and was round the corner, out of sight.

He leaned against the wall and broke down and cried for what might have been.

Chapter Fourteen

Breda wiped the perspiration from her forehead. The sorting room was unbearably hot but Maureen, who stood in the line next to her, assured her that it was always like this in July. It was the worst month; even August wasn't usually this bad because there were often thunderstorms.

She wore her thinnest dress and the minimum of underwear that propriety demanded.

'Leave your stockings off tomorrow,' Maureen advised.

Breda looked horrified. 'I will not.'

'Why?' Maureen demanded. 'During the war we often had no stockings at all. We drew seams up the backs of our legs with eyebrow pencils, after we'd put gravy browning on them. It didn't work, though, because in the rain it just washed off.'

'Well, I'm not going without stockings because it will make me look common, as though I haven't *got* any stockings.' Never mind eyebrow pencils and gravy browning, she thought, she could remember a time when she'd had no socks even and just patched-up shoes or boots. She certainly wasn't going bare-legged now.

'Oh, suit yourself. I just thought it might help.'

Maureen's fingers flicked deftly and rapidly through the letters that came down a long chute.

'I could get you something cool to drink, Breda,' Charlie Higgins said as he came up beside her.

'Why only me?' Breda asked. He wasn't bad-looking. He was tall and fair and had blue eyes like herself. He seemed to be well liked by his boss which would mean that one day he'd be promoted to something better than just Sorting Head Clerk.

'Because no one else is complaining,' he grinned. 'And no one else looks like you.'

'Stop making a mock and a jeer out of me, Charlie. I know I look a fright, it's this heat.'

'I'm not, it was a compliment. Are you doing anything tonight?'

Breda raised her eyes to the ceiling. Sure to God wasn't it the oldest chat line in history. He hadn't much in the way of imagination, and she contemplated using an answer that was just as old and tired. Washing my hair.

'Actually I am. I'm meeting someone.'

'Who?' he demanded.

Breda fluttered her eyelashes and looked at him seductively. She enjoyed flirting.

'No one you'd know, Charlie, and is it any of your business at all?' The words were sharp but her tone of voice wasn't.

'Well, if you change your mind,' he said dispiritedly.

'I'll know where to find you,' she replied. His was a tempting offer. He earned a good wage and could afford to take her out to some of the best places. Bryan always seemed to be skint, as he expressed it, although apart from his clothes she couldn't see where his money went. He didn't smoke, he wasn't fond of going on the jar and she knew Aunty Maggie didn't take most of his wages for his keep.

'You're mad, Breda,' Joyce said. 'He's got plenty of brass in his pocket to spend and half the girls here, including me, are dying to go out with him. And what do you do? You turn him down time after time just for Bryan O'Shea who's always boasting about what he did in the Army. And all this secrecy and stuff about dispensations!' Joyce was a Protestant.

'I love Bryan and he loves me, so why should I go out with Charlie just because he's got money and he's not bad-looking?'

'He's a nice feller too,' Maureen added.

'Well, I'm going to meet Bryan after work tonight, so I'll not hear any more about Charlie Higgins.'

Joyce and Maureen looked at each other and shook their heads. That Bryan seemed to be dragging his feet, and the dispensation nonsense hadn't been mentioned for months. He'd also turned up late a few times and once he hadn't shown up at all and Breda had been livid.

'Honestly, Maureen, I don't know why she bothers with him. He's got no bottle at all, even though he did fight in the war.'

'Only in the last bit when it was nearly over,' Maureen added.

Breda ignored them both and got on with her work.

At lunchtime they got half an hour off and sometimes she walked along Whitechapel and round the corner into Church Street to the city centre shops, but today it was just too hot to walk far. She'd sit in St John's Gardens at the back of St George's Hall.

As she was leaving Charlie met her.

'Are you going down into town, Breda?'

'No, it's too hot. Why, are you?'

'No, and you're right, it's too damned hot.' He ran a finger around his shirt collar. 'Where are you going?'

She felt too drained to start an argument. 'Only to St John's Gardens.'

'I'll come with you if you don't mind.'

'Ah, suit yourself.'

They walked along Victoria Street to St John's Lane in silence and found an unoccupied bench. The gardens were full of people who had had the same idea, but most were sitting or lying on the grass.

Breda turned her face to the sun. 'Oh, isn't it grand to feel the sun and be out in the fresh air.'

'Fresh? I wouldn't call it that. It's full of soot, smoke and God knows what from the factories.'

'Well, it's better than being cooped up in there,' she replied spiritedly.

Charlie remained thoughtful for a few minutes. Then he spoke.

'You know, I . . . I like you. I like you a lot. Is there any chance for me? I know you've got a steady bloke, but . . .' He shrugged.

Breda turned to look at him. Maureen was right, he *was* a nice feller, and she didn't want to hurt or humiliate him.

'I don't know . . . Perhaps one day I'll go out with you, just as a friend.'

'Well, I suppose that's better than nothing,' he said disappointedly. He had been sure that if he got the chance to see her alone she would agree, but it hadn't worked.

He leaned back and turned his own face up towards the sun. If or when she agreed to go out with him he'd treat her like a queen. He'd take her somewhere really posh for a meal first, and have flowers ready and waiting. Then to the theatre or maybe the cinema, in the best seats. When she realised what good company he was and that he could shower her with gifts she might just agree to go out with him as something other than a friend.

The afternoon seemed interminably long. She knew she had damp patches under her arms and her camiknickers were sticking to her. She must look and smell awful.

It was still hot when she left the building and flies hovered over the rubbish in the gutters. Her head was aching and so were her feet, and now she could feel her cheeks burning from sitting out in the sun. She felt grubby and in need of a bath, fresh clothes and something nice for tea. Agnes did the evening meal most nights now. She enjoyed it, she insisted, whenever Mary or Albert warned her about doing too much. She'd taken on a new lease of life, and she didn't need Mary and Albert nagging at her.

They ate together like civilised people with good linen, cutlery and china. Agnes always made everything attractive and she was a good cook. On Sundays, no matter how small it was, they had a joint of meat and Albert always carved. He was still a bit of a mystery and all she got from Mary and Agnes was that he had independent means. Anyway, he was dull and boring and she didn't take much notice of him.

There would be no bath, clean clothes or tempting supper until after she'd met Bryan. They had arranged to meet at six at the pier head which was convenient for them both. They could catch their buses from there, after making proper arrangements.

She walked slowly down to Church Street and then up

Lord Street to James Street which led to Mann Island. Then she crossed the cobbled expanse in front of the Mersey Docks & Harbour Board offices. She was to meet him at the corner of Brunswick Street at the side of the Cunard Building. She was getting impatient with him because he was still dragging his feet, making excuses, although he always swore he loved her. And she *did* love him. Their excursions to the park hadn't been as frequent of late but when he took her in his arms and kissed her, she could forgive him almost anything.

It was a bit cooler standing in the shadow of the two big buildings but her feet still ached. And she felt a fool standing there when the crowds of workers from the offices pushed past her, their only intention to get the bus or the tram home.

Where was he? She walked to the end of Brunswick Street to look up at the twin clock towers of the Liver Building. A quarter past six they showed. She walked back, searching the faces for a sight of him. As she stood and waited she grew more and more annoyed. Just what did he think he was doing? She was worn out already and just standing here made her look a complete eejit. She'd give him a piece of her mind when he turned up. This wasn't the first time he'd been late and there'd been that awful night when he'd stood her up.

She was about to go home, filled with anger and humiliation, when he came rushing towards her.

'Breda, I'm so sorry I'm late, I got a bit . . . tied up, like.'

She smelled the beer on his breath. 'Tied up is it? You've been drinking in the Style House and you *knew* I'd be waiting *and* after having a desperate day and then walking all the way down here. I was just about to go home.'

184

'Well, it was so hot. You wouldn't begrudge me a quick pint.'

'Quick! Quick! I've been standing here for nearly half an hour! I've had a terrible day. I've got a blinding headache, my frock is stuck to me and I'm starving.'

'I've said I'm sorry.'

'Well, you don't look it one little bit,' she snapped. 'Anyway, now you *are* here, what have you got planned for the weekend? The weather is going to be like this, or so I heard someone say.'

Bryan shrugged. 'I promised Mike Kennedy I'd go with him to see the cricket on Saturday afternoon and if the match isn't finished I said we'd go back on Sunday, after Mass. I'll take you along. It's supposed to be very relaxing,' he added.

'Relaxing! Flaming cricket! Isn't it the most boring game I've ever heard of. What am I expected to do? Sit and stare into space?'

'I did promise him, Breda.'

'Sure, you had no right to, Bryan! No right at all until you'd seen *me* and asked *me*. Jaysus, I can't imagine a more boring way to spend a gorgeous weekend. We could have gone over to New Brighton, or taken a day's sail to Llandudno or even gone to Southport on the train. But no, we have to go and watch a flaming cricket match. Well, you can go on your own, Bryan O'Shea, and don't think this is the end of things, it's not. I'm turned eighteen and we've been courting since I came over and that's eleven months ago and we seem to be getting nowhere. Joyce is getting engaged on her birthday next month.'

Oh, God, she was off on that track again, he thought. He didn't care who was getting engaged or married, he wasn't going to give up his freedom for a few years yet.

'That's nice for her and her feller, but . . .'

'But what?' Breda demanded, heedless of the curious glances of passers-by.

'Well, I mean . . .'

Her patience snapped. 'Oh, you're a useless eejit! Go to your flaming cricket match. You obviously think more of that than of me!'

'Breda, I . . .' Bryan reached for her arm but she pulled away and stormed off towards the bus stop.

All the way home she fought back the tears. She loved him but obviously he didn't love her in the same way. She'd never felt like this about anyone before and he was being thoughtless and cruel. Yes, that's what it was, sheer cruelty.

As usual the children had had their tea and were upstairs playing. The table in the morning room was set and Agnes and Mary were in the kitchen. Albert was away for the week. He'd gone to a guest house in Rhos-on-Sea which was smaller, quieter and more genteel than Llandudno.

'Breda, you're so late. But never mind, Agnes has made a lovely ham salad with home-made sponge cake for after, so . . .' Mary's words died as she saw her sister's face.

'Breda, what's wrong now?'

Breda sank down on the sofa and burst into tears. 'Oh, I hate him! I hate him, Mary!'

'Bryan?'

Breda nodded as Mary sat down beside her and took her hand.

'Oh, I'm sorry. I do know how you feel, remember. What happened?'

'He was late. He left me standing there like . . . like a wallflower while he was on the jar in the Style House. Then he . . . he said he was going to a cricket match. He'd already arranged it all with Michael Kennedy. A flaming cricket match! "I'll take you along" he said as though it would be some sort of treat. Oh, Mary, he's a right beast! He knows how much I love him.'

Mary gathered her in her arms and Agnes, who had come to the door, took one look at Mary and disappeared back into the kitchen. This was something poor Breda had to sort out herself, although that young man was treating her very shoddily indeed, she thought. Playing fast and loose with her for nearly a year.

Mary was making soothing sounds, Breda's sobs reminding her that she too had loved and lost.

'Hush now, Breda. It might be for the best. You're still very young.'

'You were the same age as me when you married Col.'

'I know, but things were . . . different. We weren't related and everyone approved. If he doesn't really love you then you are better off without him. He's been dragging the devil by the tail over the dispensation and, to be honest with you, I don't think he even wants to try.'

'But I love him, Mary.'

'I know you do, alannah. All I'm really trying to say is leave him to his own devices for a while. Go out with someone else, that might make him change his mind. You've changed since you came to Liverpool. You were a bold handful back home, you'd flirt with anyone. You had your pick of them all and you can have your pick here, too. You're a very lovely girl, Breda. Don't waste your best years on him. Go out with other boys.'

Breda raised her head, her cheeks wet with tears.

'Charlie Higgins asked me out and Maureen said she

and the others would give an arm and a leg to go out with him.'

Mary smiled at her and gently brushed the damp strands of dark hair from Breda's forehead.

'Then go out with him why don't you? If he asks again. Now go on up to the bathroom and get a wash, then come down for your tea, and after Kevin and Lily have gone to bed we'll talk about it all.'

Breda got up, feeling much better. Both Mary and Agnes knew how she was feeling and that was comforting. Mary was still in love with Chris Kennedy and Agnes had been engaged once and then let down very badly.

The fierce heat of the day seemed to be trapped in Flossie's house, Chris thought as he opened the front door. All the stale smells of cooking and unwashed clothes and bodies assailed him in a single wave. God, how he hated living here. It was a midden. Flossie was a slut, there was no other word for her. Oh, she was a good-hearted, kind soul and she had to put up with a lot, but he'd never seen the house tidy and clean the way his mam's was, and there were more of them. He'd never got into an unmade bed in his life. They didn't have much, not even a wireless as Flossie had, but everything was well cared for and they'd all been brought up to be tidy.

Rosie wasn't much better than her mam. Their room was never neat. She left her clothes on the floor, or thrown across one of the chairs, and on the top of the chest of drawers there wasn't a spare inch between all the make-up and hairpins.

Her hair had at last grown out and when she didn't wear make-up she looked positively plain, not to say ugly. Her skin was pallid and she often had spots too. For most of the time her hair straggled untidily and was dull and lank.

He found that sleeping in the same bed as her was an ordeal in itself. She didn't smell very clean and neither did the faded nightdresses she wore. In all the months they'd been married he could count on his fingers the number of times she'd been to the public baths. Mam had sent them every Friday night, their towels and bits of soap rolled up and tucked under their arms. Once she'd tried to make him take notice of her, to touch her, but he'd pushed her away and turned his back.

He went straight into their room, sat down on one of the wooden chairs and began to undo the laces of his boots. That in itself was something his mam had never allowed. Their work boots had always been taken off in the yard; she wouldn't allow them even in the scullery.

As usual the place was a mess and all he could look forward to was one of Flossie's disgusting meals. He didn't think that Rosie could cook at all. All she seemed to make was tea.

He'd just stripped off to the waist in preparation for his usual wash-down in the scullery when Rosie came in, a mug of tea in one hand and a cigarette in the other. He hated the smell of stale tobacco and this house was full of it.

'Oh, you're in then,' she said flatly, sitting down on the edge of the unmade bed.

'I didn't think you were interested in what time I come in or go out.'

She shrugged. She'd given up on him. He was colder with her now than he'd been before the wedding. He might as well be a stranger. All he did was complain and it had hurt. She'd made an effort in the beginning, she'd even reached out for him one night, but he'd made it clear he wanted nothing from her.

Life now was one long drag. There was nothing to look

forward to, and she couldn't even go out like she used to. She was married and she was expected to lead a virtuous life. She got up, got dressed, went to work, came home, had her meal and went to bed because there was nothing else to do. She might as well be dead, she thought as she watched him. Even now she felt a longing for him. He was a good-looking lad and his work kept him fit. The upper part of his body was burned brown by the sun and the layer of perspiration made his skin glisten. Oh, why couldn't he love her, just a little bit?

'What has your Mam burned for tea today?' he asked tersely.

'I know she's not much of a cook, not like your mam, but there's no need to be so bloody nasty about her.'

'Stop swearing and find something to flick that ash into before it falls on the floor. Not that you'd notice it, the floor's so flaming dirty anyway.'

'Well, if you don't like it here, why don't you go and find somewhere else to live?' Rosie said waspishly, deliberately flicking the ash from her cigarette on the floor. If he thought so much about the state of the bloody floor he could get down on his hands and knees and clean it.

She finished her tea and stubbed the cigarette out in the mug.

Chris watched her with loathing. They lived like pigs. They had no manners, they were ignorant and there was a row nearly every night. Usually between Flossie and Gerry when he rolled in from the pub, or Flossie and Rosie about the washing and ironing. God, he was sick to death of them all. Maybe he would try to find a place of his own. Just a small room would do, but the overcrowding was so bad that there was little chance of a room of any kind.

Rosie left the room, slamming the door behind her, knowing it irritated him.

Chris dropped his head in his hands. He couldn't stand much more of this. Five months they'd been married and his life was one long nightmare and there was no way out. He thought of Mary constantly and it was sheer torture because he always compared her to Rosie. He hardly ever saw her. She did come to visit Maggie now and then but whenever he'd attempted to speak to her she'd turned and hurried away either down the street or into the house. Suddenly he made up his mind. He put his shirt and boots back on and let himself quietly out of the front door which was always ajar.

He walked to the top of the street and then down the entry and stopped at Phil's yard door. He'd not seen much of her or Da or even the kids, although they lived so close. He was certain Mam kept them all in when she knew what time he'd be coming home or leaving for work.

He pushed the door open and went up the yard, noting how tidy it was. Flossie's yard was full of junk. It was like trying to get through an obstacle course to get to the privy. The privy was so bad it defied description. None of them had any sense of personal hygiene and it was a miracle that no one was ever ill. Mam used gallons of bleach and the cinders from the range in theirs and in summer she hung fly papers up.

Gingerly he lifted the latch on the scullery door and walked in. It seemed a lifetime since he'd been in here and as usual everything was clean and tidy. Before he had any more time to think he was confronted by his mother.

'What are you doing here?' Phil demanded sharply. There were times when she felt really sorry for him. It broke her heart when she saw him at Mass with the O'Hanlons. His shirts were never really clean and they were creased as though they'd never been ironed. His good suit looked shabby, the elbows and cuffs shiny. His boots had no gloss on them. She stiffened her resolve. He had made his bed, or Flossie's bed to be accurate, so he had to get on with it.

'Mam, I can't stand it any longer! You've no idea what it's like,' he pleaded.

'Oh, I have,' Phil interrupted. 'I've been in that house often enough to know how they live.'

'No, Mam, you don't, not really. The place stinks all the time. Rosie doesn't lift a finger and Flossie doesn't do much either.'

'That I *do* know,' Phil cut in.

'Rosie flicks cigarette ash on the floor and stubs them out in a mug or a cup or a plate or whatever is nearest. She stinks, too, she never gets a good wash-down. She hardly ever goes to the baths. She just pours cheap scent all over her and thinks that'll cover it up.'

'You knew what she was like before—'

'Well, yes, I did,' Chris interrupted hastily before Phil could start lecturing him. 'But I didn't realise just how much of a slut she is. And the meals! She doesn't cook at all, but her mam ruins everything one way or another.'

'Have you just come here to moan and complain?' Phil demanded.

'No, Mam, I've come to ask . . . to beg . . . you to let me come back home.'

There was a note of desperation in his voice that tugged at Phil's heart.

'You know I can't do that, Chris. How would it look?'

'I wouldn't care how it looked. Everyone knows I hate her, anyway.'

'Well, both me and your da care. You're married, you

192

promised "for better or for worse" and you'll have to get on with it. It would be different if you hadn't known her before or if she lived somewhere else, but it's not and I have my pride. You'd better go now before your da comes in or there'll be blue murder.'

She looked away, not wanting to meet his eyes. If she looked at him she would break down. His plight was tearing her heart apart so she turned and went back into the kitchen. Why oh why couldn't he have married Mary O'Malley before that New Year's Eve party? She knew that they both still loved each other.

Chapter Fifteen

Maurice was in a quandary. Pauline wanted a ring.

'We've been courting for three months now, Maurice. I know it's not long compared to some people, but I'd like something to show that we're serious. We *are* serious?' she asked earnestly.

'Of course we are. You know I said we'd get married when we've got some money saved up. We don't want to start off in someone's front room like Rosie and Chris,' he'd replied. And that was the root of the problem. Money or more precisely the lack of it.

He'd finally plucked up courage to ask her out in July and to his surprise she'd agreed. He didn't earn much, often being unable to get even a half day's work, because, even though the docks were busy, men being demobbed were considered by the blockermen to need the money more than a lad of just seventeen.

When he could he bought her something. Some flowers, a little brooch, but a ring was something he'd never thought to be within his means. In fact this was the first time it had been mentioned. Even the cheapest ring was way beyond his pocket.

His mam did approve of her, though, which was half the battle.

'She comes from a good home. Nelly Casey's a clean, thrifty woman and she's brought all her kids up decently, not like some I could mention,' Maggie had said when he'd first told her. He'd known she meant the O'Hanlons.

Pauline was the same age as himself. They'd been at the same school, lived in the same street. She wasn't stunningly beautiful like his cousins Mary and Breda, but she was pretty in a china doll sort of way. She had a mass of light brown curly hair, a pale complexion and big hazel eyes that were her best feature. The fact that she was tiny, only coming up to his shoulder, always made him feel protective towards her.

He hadn't mentioned marriage to his mam. She'd have a fit and say he was far too young, which he was, although his cousin Mary had been married at eighteen. Maybe they got married young over there, he'd mused.

He sat at the kitchen table well after his mam had cleared it, elbows on the table, his chin cupped in his hands, thinking of ways he could earn more money.

'Do you intend to sit there like that all night? I thought you were going down to see Pauline?' Maggie said.

Maurice got to his feet. 'I am,' he replied, a note of irritation in his voice.

He got changed, put a bit of Brylcreem on his hair and combed it. The fact that the Brylcreem belonged to Bryan he ignored. They could fight about it later on.

Pauline was ready and waiting for him and when she smiled he felt his heart lurch as it always did. She was wearing a blue twinset, knitted by her mam, and a navy-blue skirt.

'I'll just get my coat,' she said. 'Maurice's here, Mam,' she called and Nelly shouted for him to come in and 'put the wood in the hole', meaning he should close the front door.

Their kitchen resembled his mam's, he thought, looking around. Mary had made such an impact from the day she'd arrived that Mam had automatically kept up those standards. It was homely but not scrubbed and polished to death like Phil Kennedy's. You were terrified to even sit down in their house. How their Chris stuck living in a pigsty with Rosie he didn't know. He'd gone from one extreme to the other.

'And where are you out to tonight, then? You do know she's to be in here not one minute after half past nine? She has an early start.'

Maurice nodded his agreement. Pauline worked in a dairy at the other end of Scotland Road.

'We're just going for a sail to Woodside and back.' It was a cheap night out. Just eightpence for their fares and sixpence for two bags of chips, plus the busfare, of course.

Pauline came in with a navy-blue jacket on and a knitted blue tam-o'-shanter over her soft curling hair.

'Right, then, we're off. I won't be late, Mam.'

'You'd better not be.'

Joe Casey lowered his newspaper. 'Is your da going up to the Grapes tonight, lad?'

'I don't really know, Mr Casey. Shall I run back and find out?'

'No, lad, I'll wander up there for the last half hour.'

Nelly raised her eyes to the ceiling.

It wasn't until they had boarded the Woodside ferry and got a seat on the upper deck that the ring was mentioned again.

'I walked up London Road last Saturday afternoon and I saw a really lovely ring in T. Brown's.'

Maurice looked at her with horror. 'I can't afford to go across the door in that place, Pauline. The likes of us don't go in places like that. I was thinking of somewhere like Pobjoys.'

'That's a pawnshop.' She sounded indignant.

'They sell things as well,' he replied, trying to sound hurt.

'Oh, I'm sorry, Maurice, but I would sooner have one from a proper jeweller's.' She put her head on his shoulder and he placed an arm round her. 'I know you don't get much money, Maurice.'

'I do try to take you out and buy you things as often as I can.'

She smiled. 'I know, and it's dead good of you. I'm not moaning, honest. I'd just like something . . . special, like.'

He sighed. Where did she expect him to get 'something special' from? She wasn't always nagging and she certainly wasn't the grasping gold-digging kind who were never satisfied, and he wished he *could* buy her a nice ring. A really lovely one. She had nice hands. They had to be spotlessly clean for work and she looked after her nails. Not like some you saw with dirt embedded under the tips or bitten down to the quick.

'I tell you what, I'll save as hard as I can. I'll see if I can get some kind of other job as well and then maybe by Christmas I'll have enough for . . . something.'

She smiled up at him. 'Will you? Will you honestly?'

'I've said so, but we won't be able to go out much, maybe not at all,' he replied despondently.

'We can go for walks. That costs nothing, and it's only a few coppers to go on the overhead railway. We could do things like that.'

Maurice held her closer to him. She was a really nice, gentle-natured girl and he did love her, but how soon they could get married he didn't know. But if he got her an engagement ring then everyone would know that his intentions were serious, especially her da who was a real stickler for such things. On some occasions they'd literally run from the bus or tram stop so she would be in on time. If she was late she didn't get out for a week.

He was trudging home wearily the following afternoon. He'd managed to get half a day's work and then he'd gone to all the coal merchants down at Wapping to see if he could get work shovelling coal into sacks, but he'd been turned away. There were too many men coming home to their families who needed the work more than he did.

'All right there, Maury, lad?'

The shout made him stop and turn round. It was Hughie Scanlan, the youngest of the notorious Scanlan brothers. They had the neighbourhood terrorised and the older ones were often in jail. One had even been hanged for beating his girlfriend to death after a row. Maurice wanted nothing at all to do with any of them.

Hughie had other ideas. They'd been in the same class at school and as far as Maurice knew had managed to keep out of trouble, so far.

'I hate being called Maury. Me name's Maurice.'

'Oh, gerroff yer high 'orse, lad. Anyway, what are yer doin' walkin 'ome with a right gob on yer? 'Ave yer lost a shilling an' found a sixpence?'

Maurice pushed his cap further to the back of his head. Mam would kill him if she heard of this conversation.

'No. I'm just fed up, that's all. All the fellers getting demobbed are being taken on now.'

'Yeah, I know. Still, look on the bright side. Yer've no worries, no judy ter want all yer money.'

Maurice noticed for the first time how neatly turned out Hughie Scanlan was. The suit was new and so were the shirt and tie and even the shoes, by the look of it.

'What do you do, Hughie? You're all done up like a dog's dinner.'

Hughie straightened his tie with studied nonchalance. 'I've come up in the world. I work with our kid and the rest of me brothers now.'

'And you call that coming up in the world?' Maurice asked sarcastically.

'I've more in me pocket than you 'ave, Maurice O'Shea.'

'Anyway, I do have a girl. Pauline Casey. She lives down our street.'

'Oh, yeah, I remember her. Plain-lookin' bit of skirt.'

'She's not!' Maurice replied hotly. 'And don't call her a bit of skirt or a judy either.'

'All right, all right, don't get yer knickers in a twist! Are 'ers in a twist? Won't she let yer in them? Is that it?'

Maurice realised that Hughie was not going to go away.

'What do you think she is, a tart? We just have . . . different ideas, that's all.'

'What about?' Hughie demanded amiably.

'An engagement ring.'

'Christ! Yer aren't thinking about that already, are yer?'

'Yes, but it'll be ages before we can get married.'

'Yer off yer bleedin' head,' Hughie said with feeling.

'Well, it's my head.'

'Are yer goin' ter get her a ring, then?'

'Not yet. I can't afford it. I'm saving up and hope to get one at Christmas.'

'I might just be able ter 'elp yer there, Maury, lad.'

'How?' Maurice demanded, ignoring the hated nickname.

'I'll 'ave a word with our kid. 'Ow much can yer afford, like?'

'Well, if I saved until Christmas I could pay about two pounds.'

Hughie laughed mockingly.

'Two quid! Is that all? When I gerra steady girl I'll be able buy 'er a ring for about twelve quid.'

'Twelve quid!' Maurice was incredulous.

'Yeah, an what's more I'll go ter somewhere dead posh like T. Brown's or Boodles up Lord Street.'

'God, I could never earn money like that.'

'What if I was ter 'elp yer, like? Get yer one cheap?'

Maurice was suspicious. 'How cheap?'

'Say three pounds for one that would cost yer . . .' he shrugged, 'say ten quid.'

'I still haven't got money like that.'

'Can't ycr borrow offen yer mam or yer brother an' then pay them back, so much a week? Yer judy will be made up an tharral keep 'er from naggin' yer. I mean it, I'll get yer a real good one.'

Maurice was tempted. He knew how the ring was going to be obtained, but then who would know he'd got it from Hughie? He *could* pay three quid back week by week. And he wanted to keep Pauline happy.

'All right, you're on.'

'Good on yer, lad. I'll meet yer at eight o'clock on Friday by them bombed-out warehouses in Dublin Street, just by the alleyway into Saltney Street. Just make sure yer've the money, like.'

'OK.'

'See yer then, Maurice, lad.' Hughie grinned and began

to cross the road and Maurice watched him go, a feeling of foreboding and apprehension rising in him.

'What in the name of God do you want to borrow three pounds for?' Bryan asked. Maurice hadn't had the courage to ask either his mam or his da. There would be too many questions asked, they would start to lecture him on the advisability of getting engaged so young and would want to know how and when he thought he could get married. No, Bryan had been the better choice. Maurice had approached him after he'd come in from work.

'Can you keep your mouth shut?'

'That depends,' Bryan hedged.

'I want it to get Pauline a ring.'

Bryan looked at him with open scepticism. 'You're not thinking of getting married, are you? You're still wet behind the ears for God's sake.'

'No! Well, yes, but not for years and years, but she wants to get engaged.'

'Don't they bloody all,' Bryan replied, thinking of Breda who he'd heard was now going out with a feller she worked with who had been likened to Leslie Howard, and seemed to have more money than sense to spend on her.

'How will you pay me back?' Bryan demanded.

Maurice looked at his brother hopefully. 'Two shillings a week?'

'I'll be collecting me old age pension by then,' he said sarcastically.

'Well, I can't afford any more and she's set her heart on a decent one.'

'You won't get much for three quid. You'll have to get a magnifying glass to see the diamonds.'

'Well, it'll be a ring anyway,' Maurice muttered, hoping Bryan wasn't going to ask where he intended to buy it.

On Friday night he was ready with the three pound notes in his pocket. He hoped that Hughie Scanlan wasn't just having him on, but when he turned down Dublin Street he caught sight of Hughie coming up from the dock road end and breathed a sigh of relief. Thank God he wasn't going to have to hang around here, he thought. It was eerie. There were hardly any street lamps and there were still huge piles of rubble that had been warehouses before May 1941.

Hughie sidled up to him. There was no boastful swagger as there'd been the other day.

'Have yer got the money?' he hissed.

Maurice handed him the notes.

Hughie looked round furtively. ''Ere, put this in yer pocket an' don't bloody open it now. In fact don't bloody open it until yer get 'ome.'

'Christ! Hughie, where did it come from?'

'Don't ask me then yer can't tell any lies. I'm off. Tarrah then, mate.' And he was gone, leaving Maurice standing looking down at the small green leather box.

By the time he got home Maurice was shaking with nerves. He knew it was stolen, but what could he do? Give it back? Take it to the police? He shuddered as he thought of the reaction of Hughie's brothers if he shopped Hughie. He tried to calm himself down and think rationally. There was nothing to connect him with Hughie. Two brief meetings, one on a busy street where no one took any notice of anyone else and the other down a dark, rubble-strewn alley. But Pauline would be so delighted that she'd want to show it off to everyone, including his mam and dad, and they'd want to know how he could afford an expensive ring.

Perhaps he'd keep it until Christmas. He'd tell no one, not even their Bryan. By then he'd say he'd saved for it and got it cheap because the jeweller said it was flawed. They wouldn't question that. He'd have to take it out of the box, though, and burn the box.

When he met Pauline on Saturday he assured her that he was saving hard and at Christmas she'd get a nice surprise. She was delighted with his promise. He was still getting over the shock of the size of the diamonds in the ring. He hadn't taken it out of its box until he'd got home, and then he'd taken it down to the privy, along with the torch they all used to find their way down the yard in the dark. He'd actually gasped aloud. There were five diamonds, two of which seemed huge to him.

'Will I really have a gorgeous one, Maurice?'

'You will. I'm determined. I might get it in a sale. Jewellers sometimes have them. Especially if the stones are flawed.'

'How come you know so much about diamonds?' Pauline looked up at him trustingly.

He shrugged. 'I read it somewhere. In the *Echo*, I think.'

She squeezed his hand and her hazel eyes sparkled. They were going window shopping, something she enjoyed but he did not, but it kept her happy and it cost nothing, so maybe they'd have a cup of tea in the Kardomah later on, he thought.

They were walking across the forecourt of Central Station, a short cut into Bold Street, when Maurice heard the newsvendor's cry. He stopped and his face became ashen. There had been a smash and grab raid on T. Brown's in London Road. He heard two men talking behind them. The thieves had got away with hundreds of pounds' worth of jewellery, particularly rings. The police had caught one member of the gang, Georgie Scanlan. Since then they'd been watching the other members of that family.

'What's the matter, Maurice?' Pauline looked up at him with concern.

'Nothing. I . . . just feel a bit light-headed.'

'Perhaps you're getting a cold or something.'

'I might be. I feel rotten.' That was no lie, he thought. He was riddled with fear.

Pauline patted his hand. 'Right, we're going home now. It's not a very nice day anyway and we don't want you being too sick to go to work on Monday.'

He let her steer him towards the bus stop. He just wanted to go home and hide under the bedclothes. Thank God he'd hidden the ring under the floorboards in the bedroom. He'd taken the lino up to do it and then he'd burned the box. But now he needed an alibi because on Friday night no one had seen him except his mam and dad and they knew he'd only been out for about three-quarters of an hour. They thought he'd just popped over to Pauline's. The only person he could think of who might help him out was Mike Kennedy, though he was much older than him. He'd just have to trust Mike. The alternative didn't bear thinking about.

When he was sure that Pauline had gone indoors he crossed quickly over to Phil's house and pushed open the front door.

'Is your Mike in?' he asked Phil who was baking. Her hands and arms were covered in flour. 'In the yard,' she replied, more interested in the pastry she was rolling out.

'Ta,' he answered.

Mike was breaking up empty fruit boxes and binding the bits of wood together. They'd be used to get the fire going.

You could buy bundles of 'chips', as they were known, but why should they?

'What's up with you? You look terrible,' Mike commented. He was a younger version of his brother Chris and was engaged.

'I feel it. God, you've got to help me out, Mike. I'm in dead lumber.'

'What the hell have you been up to now?' Mike asked, slightly amused. It wasn't like the lad to get into trouble; he was quiet, and terrified of his father. Maybe that was it.

'Are you heading for a hiding from your da?'

'God, it'll be more than that, and not only from Da. Will you say you met me on Friday night?'

Mike grinned. 'You've been two-timing Pauline, have you? You dark horse. Has she found you out and chucked you?'

Maurice was relieved that Mike had come up with something that was believable.

'Yes, sort of.'

'Who?'

'I . . . I can't tell you.'

Mike shrugged. 'OK. How long was I with you and where were we?'

'About an hour. You took me into the Ship at the corner of Woodstock Street for a drink, even though I'm under age. You can say I was worried about Pauline.'

'For God's sake, Maurice, you don't even look twenty.'

'Well, where would you take me?'

'Nowhere.'

Maurice panicked again. 'I've got to have been with you.'

'Oh, calm down, for God's sake. She'll never believe that I took you into a pub.'

'Well, where then?'

Mike was silent for a few minutes.

'Right, how will this do? I went into the Ship and I brought a bottle out for you and one for myself and we stood and drank them, and discussed things. Will she wear that?'

Maurice nodded, so relieved he felt like crying.

'Thanks, Mike. I really mean it.'

'Just don't go playing that girl up, or she'll find someone else. She's a nice girl, too.'

'I won't.'

'Hang on. Who am I supposed to tell all this to?'

'Oh, anyone . . . anyone who asks.'

'Oh, get off home and behave in future.' Mike laughed and broke another orange box across his knee.

It was on the Sunday, after Mass, that two burly CID men dressed in overcoats and bowlers called.

'What do you want our Maurice for?' Maggie demanded.

'I think it's best if we go inside, Mrs O'Shea.'

'You're not putting a foot inside this house until you tell me what you want him for.'

'What's going on, then?' Jim asked, coming up behind his wife.

'These two want to see our Maurice.'

'Mr O'Shea, it really would be better if we came in.' The older of the two looked meaningfully up the street.

'Right, in the kitchen and for five minutes only. This is my home and you've no warrant,' Jim said.

'I hope we don't need one,' one of the men muttered as they followed Jim down the lobby.

Once in the kitchen Maggie faced them squarely and Jim was uneasy.

The older of the two spoke.

'I believe your son, Maurice, knows a Hughie Scanlan.'

'*What!*' Maggie shrieked. Everyone knew the Scanlans and kept well out of their way.

'He was in the same class at school, if that's what you mean. No one in this house has anything to do with any of that lot, and especially not Maurice. He's terrified to even look at *you* lot,' Jim answered.

'Where is he?' the younger man demanded.

'You'll tell me why you want to speak to him first. As I said, you've no warrant.' Jim's voice was cold and determined.

'He's not accused of anything. We just want his help.'

Maggie and Jim exchanged glances. Help, was it? That was usually an excuse for dragging you down to the police station and grilling you for hours on end.

'I'll go and get him. He's over at Nelly Casey's,' Maggie said.

The three men stood in silence, the two policemen glancing round the room. For them, waiting and patience came with the job.

'Mam, what do they want with me?' a terrified Maurice had asked as they'd come up the street.

'How the hell should I know! If you've been in trouble, I'll kill you! Having the bloody coppers turning up on the doorstep on a Sunday. Don't they ever flaming well go home?' Maggie said as she shoved her son down the lobby. The men of the Liverpool City CID were a law unto themselves and everyone knew it, as did their own uniformed colleagues, and it was only two years since Ben Scanlan had been hanged in Walton Jail.

'So, you are Maurice O'Shea?'

'I . . . I . . . yes, sir,' Maurice stammered.

A black leather-covered notebook appeared.

'Do you know Hughie Scanlan?'

'Yes, but . . . but all the kids in our class know him.'

'Did you see him on Friday night between seven and eight o'clock?'

'No! No, I've not seen him for ages.' Maurice prayed he sounded convincing. These two terrified him with their unblinking stares and expressionless voices. You couldn't tell what they were thinking.

'We have the description of a lad seen talking to Hughie Scanlan down Dublin Street, on the corner of Saltney Street.'

'Well, it wasn't him,' Maggie stated firmly.

'If you don't mind, Mrs O'Shea, let him answer for himself.'

Maggie was seething. If Maurice had got caught up with the Scanlans there'd be holy bloody murder.

'On Friday I was with Mike Kennedy from across the road. I was only out for an hour.'

'And what were you and this Mike Kennedy doing?'

'Well, I . . . I was a bit upset because Pauline, that's my girl, wants to get engaged only I can't afford a ring until Christmas.' As soon as he'd said the word ring he knew it was a mistake.

'A ring,' the older man said. 'You need a ring? Hughie, Georgie and Shorty Scanlan took plenty of those from Brown's.' The expressions on the faces of the CID men didn't change. They could and would wait hours for an explanation if need be.

'Here, just a minute. Are you suggesting that our Maurice asked that . . . scum to get a ring for him?' Jim interrupted, annoyed by the implication.

'Not at all. It's a coincidence, though. Go on, lad.'

'Mike got me a bottle of beer from the Ship.'

Jim exploded. 'You're too bloody young to drink!' He didn't mind on special occasions like street parties but actually drinking beer that had been purchased in a pub was going too far, and admitting it to these two was sheer stupidity.

'And Mike Kennedy should have had more sense,' Maggie added. This was the first they'd heard of any of this.

'Right, we'll go and see this Mike Kennedy then.'

The notebook was snapped shut and replaced in the pocket it had come from, and Jim ushered them out of the house and shut the door firmly. They'd be the talk of the street now and so would Phil. He'd have to go over later and apologise to her and Bob.

When Mary arrived with Kevin and Lily for the usual Sunday afternoon visit, Maggie was sitting wiping away the tears. Maurice had denied any connection with Hughie and Mike had sworn he was with him. The description the police had was too vague for certainty but Maurice, who was now upstairs, was warned severely about underage drinking in a public street and mixing with toerags like the Scanlans, even though Maurice denied the latter charge. Jim had belted Maurice and had gone over to Phil's.

'Sure to God, Aunty Maggie, what's wrong?' Mary was concerned. Maggie could cope with almost anything that fate chose to throw in her way.

After Maggie had explained Mary looked as upset as herself.

'He'd not have anything to do with the likes of those savages, surely?' She, too, knew their reputation.

210

'No, but it's worrying. I know that lad, and he *is* keeping something back.'

'What?'

'I don't know, but I do know he wants to buy Pauline a ring. He said he was saving up for one and it was rings that were stolen.'

'Not Maurice. He's so quiet.'

'Still waters run deep, Mary. It's an old saying and sometimes it's true. Our Maurice is deep. He tells us virtually nothing.'

'Lily, get down off that chair this minute before you fall. We've enough on our hands as it is,' Mary said sharply.

Lily had pushed a chair over to the range and was reaching up to the overmantel for something she wanted from amongst the clutter.

'Haven't I enough to cope with without your antics, melady?' Maggie snapped at her youngest daughter.

Mary was thoughtful. If young Maurice was involved with the Scanlans it was very serious. He needed something to shock him, to make him realise just how dangerous it could be.

'If it'll help, I'll get Albert to have a word with him. He'll take notice of him, I know that for sure and for certain. Can I leave these two here and take him back now?'

'Would you, Mary, luv? I'm so mortified. Them standing on the doorstep and on a Sunday too, and poor Phil . . .' Maggie wiped her eyes again.

'Stop worrying. I'll take him down there and then I'll come back for the children.'

Maggie went to the door and yelled for Maurice to come down right this minute.

He looked sheepishly at Mary who shook her head and tutted.

'Get your jacket and cap on, you're coming home with me. We'll have all this carry-on sorted out. If Mr Fallowfield can't talk sense into you, then I don't know who can. Get out that door, you eejit!' She gave him a push as he left the room.

Albert and Agnes were surprised to see her back so soon, with a pale-faced, agitated Maurice in tow. They'd been enjoying their weekly game of chess.

'Albert, could I speak to you for a minute? I'm sorry to interrupt but it is desperate.'

He rose and they went into the hall. Breda was out with Charlie.

'Mary, whatever is the matter? What's he done?'

'Aunty Maggie's in a terrible state. She's had the police round asking Maurice questions about Hughie Scanlan and that smash and grab on Brown's that was in the paper. Apparently Pauline wants an engagement ring and Maurice can't afford one and it was rings they took. Everyone goes there for their rings. They get a free set of special teaspoons and a lucky white heather horseshoe.'

Albert looked serious. 'Do they think he was involved?'

'I don't know what to think. Aunty Maggie is sure he's keeping something back, even though Mike Kennedy said he was with him. Could you talk to him, please?'

'Are you asking me in my official capacity, Mary? Do you know what that means? What if Agnes finds—'

'No! She won't,' Mary interrupted hastily. 'I mean . . . Maurice would be sworn to secrecy and it's a vow he wouldn't break. He'd be terrified.'

Albert thought for a moment, then nodded his head.

Maurice was an unworldly lad compared with that tribe. 'Right, then. I'll see him in the kitchen.'

'Didn't I know I could rely on you. Where would we all be without you?' She reached up and kissed him on the cheek and he smiled. He'd do anything to help her and her family and if giving the lad the fright of his life would help, he'd do it.

Maurice already looked shaken, Albert thought as the lad came into the room, twisting his cap between his hands.

'Right, Maurice, just what have you been up to? I want no lies. I'm an expert at sensing a liar.'

'I . . . I . . . didn't do anything,' Maurice replied shiftily. He was wondering why Mary had dragged him here. Mr Fallowfield was only the lodger, after all. He was more afraid of his da.

Albert took a step nearer and folded his arms across his chest.

'Your mother thinks you did. Do you know what I do? What my official capacity is?'

Maurice could only shake his head.

Albert paused for a few seconds. It would give his next words more of an impact.

'I am the public executioner. The hangman. It was me who hanged Ben Scanlan in Walton Jail. It depends on the skill of the hangman how quickly or slowly you die. He beat that poor girl to death but he had to be dragged kicking and screaming to his own. He didn't help himself, you see. Stay still and the neck breaks like that.' Albert snapped his fingers. 'But Ben Scanlan was a coward and he knew he was destined for hell.'

Maurice had gone even paler. His eyes were wide with horror and he was hanging on to the back of a chair to stop himself from falling. Albert Fallowfield was the hangman at Walton! The hangman who'd sent Ben Scanlan to his death. And he'd lived in their front room for years and now he lived here. Mary *must* know.

'Now, I want the truth. It will go no further if you've done nothing seriously wrong and I have your solemn promise that you'll tell no one what my position is.'

Haltingly, between gulps and sobs, Maurice related every detail of his involvement with Hughie Scanlan and then swore he'd tell no one about Albert, not even Father Hayes.

Albert listened in silence. The lad was a fool. He'd been tempted in a moment of weakness. What good would it do to have him own up and give back the ring? Hughie Scanlan would be caught sooner or later; he didn't have enough of a brain to evade justice for very long.

It would break Maurice's mother's heart and whatever her faults and failings she was a decent God-fearing woman. It would break young Pauline's heart too and those of her family. He'd heard that the police had rounded up Georgie and Shorty Scanlan, the latter being over six foot tall, but they didn't have enough on young Hughie to make a case or get a conviction.

'This time I believe you. I don't think you'll have anything more to do with that family or any of the other villains in the city either. You can give the ring to me. I'll keep it. But you'll have to tell Pauline she can't have it at Christmas. It's going to be a long time before she can have it. If ever.'

Maurice couldn't speak. He couldn't get the terrible image out of his mind of Ben Scanlan kicking and screaming as the man he was now facing put the noose around his neck. He was shivering with sheer terror.

'How much do you owe Bryan? Has he asked you about all this business?'

Maurice shook his head. Bryan would guess, he wasn't a fool, but having loaned him the money in the first place he would keep his mouth shut.

Albert drew some money from his pocket. 'How much?'

'Three . . . three pounds.' Maurice had difficulty in getting the words out.

'Here, take this and pay him back. Give the ring to Mary. Wrap it up in something. Your handkerchief will do. She'll bring it to me.'

Maurice nodded and took the money.

'Now take yourself home and don't ever do anything to upset your mother again.'

When Mary came in he looked pleadingly at her.

'So?' she asked.

Maurice could hardly speak 'He . . . he's . . .'

'The public executioner,' Mary interrupted. 'I know. I've known for a long time. I can see you've learned your lesson. Right, we'll be getting back. Not a word to anyone, Maurice O'Shea.'

'No! Not . . . a . . . word,' Maurice spluttered, still in a state of shock. From now on he'd never put a foot wrong.

Chapter Sixteen

On the Monday morning a very subdued Maurice walked down the street with Bryan and Jim. Mike Kennedy and his father crossed over to join them, a thing they did every morning, but Mike hung back after indicating with his head that Maurice do likewise. When they were far enough behind the others not to be heard, he spoke.

'What the bloody hell do you think you're playing at? You're off your bloody head mixing with the Scanlans and dragging my name into it all. I wouldn't have helped you out if I'd known that. Mam is fuming with me and Da's not too happy either. Neither of them cares about the bottles of beer, it was the mention of Hughie Scanlan they're really mad about. Mam gave me a right grilling after the police had gone.'

'I'm sorry, really I am. It was just that Pauline . . .'

'So you weren't two-timing her at all? It was a bloody ring you wanted and you bought it from that no-mark Hughie.'

Maurice could only nod. He'd slept very badly. His dreams had been invaded by Albert Fallowfield, dressed like a monk in a long black habit with the cowl covering his head, putting a noose around the neck of Ben Scanlan.

217

'So, where is it now?' Mike asked, his eyes firmly on his father's back.

'Mr Fallowfield's got it. Mary's lodger.'

'Why has he got it?'

Maurice was silent, desperately trying to think of a reason. There was no way he'd break his promise to the public executioner.

'Mary thought . . . it would be safer with him.'

'Do your mam and dad know this too?' Mike was not happy about any of this and he'd been shocked and then seething when the police had come knocking on the door.

'No, only Mary and Mr Fallowfield. He gave me the money to pay our Bryan back.'

'Jesus! Is your Bryan in this too?'

'He knew I wanted money for a ring and lent it me. I know he suspects something but he's keeping his mouth shut.'

'Well, thank God someone in your house has some bloody sense. Don't you ever put me in a spot like that again, because if you do, I'll shop you. I don't care how much Pauline Casey wants a bloody ring, but she deserves better than you, you stupid get!'

'Well, I've no money to buy her a ring now and she's expecting a really good one at Christmas.'

'Then she's going to be disappointed, isn't she? And you can explain it away all by yourself. Just leave my name out of things in future.'

For the rest of the way to the bus stop Maurice was silent and dejected. Pauline would be disappointed but he was lucky to have got off so lightly. If he ever set eyes on Hughie Scanlan again he'd run like hell in the opposite direction.

* * *

As the November winds howled around the house and found their way inside through window and door frames, and the rain beat a noisy tattoo against the window panes, Agnes taught Mary all the skills she'd need to become a milliner. Agnes knew where to go to buy all the materials and trimmings, and together after work and at weekends they worked diligently. Agnes commented that she'd never had a more eager apprentice.

'You do have a natural aptitude, Mary,' she said as she watched Mary finishing a small felt hat with a petersham ribbon round the base of the crown.

'There's so much to learn. I'll have to do some fancy hats, just to show I *can* do them.'

'I'll ask Albert to search amongst that pile of junk he put into the wash-house. My blocks are still there and you really do need to block almost all hats at some stage.'

Mary sighed. 'I thought a straw hat was just that, a straw hat. I never knew there was sugar spun straw, panama straw and Bangkok straw and that they all have to be treated differently.'

Agnes smiled. 'And that's not including the felts, velours and furs, which you can't use hot tongs on the brims of like you can with the straws.'

'And then there's all the different trimmings. Braid, ribbon, petersham, grosgrain, velvet ribbon, feathers, artificial flowers. I'll never learn it all.'

'Of course you will, Mary. Having the talent and imagination is half the battle.'

'What I really want to do, Agnes, is to make one of each as a sample and then see if I can get regular orders from a shop.'

'Then we'll do just that. You'll have to show your samples

for inspection. Not only for creativity but workmanship too. You're a very neat sewer, but how will you manage if you do get a big order?'

Mary's brow creased in a frown. 'I'd not thought of that.'

'Of course I'll help you, but my hands are so full of arthritis now that I'll be slow.'

'And unfortunately Breda is hopeless,' Mary added. The dream she'd always cherished was well on the way to becoming a reality but she hadn't thought of big orders or how she would cope with them. She could try to sell to the fashionable shops but she really wanted to sell to working-class girls and women. But to do that successfully, she'd have to rent premises and hire girls, and at the moment everything was too confusing.

'Isn't that a nice thing to hear when you come in dripping wet. Why am I useless?' Breda asked.

Mary sighed. 'I only meant that you don't have the skills.'

'I don't want to make hats anyway,' Breda replied, taking off her coat and hat and going through into the kitchen to put her umbrella in the sink.

She'd gone home with Joyce for tea because Joyce had a gramophone and records of all the popular crooners. She'd been pestering Mary to buy one but Mary said it was a waste of money. She'd argued that they could all listen to it, buy their own choice of records. Mary had replied that records cost money and they already had a wireless and what more did she want?

'Oh, there's a letter on the mantel for you, Breda, dear.' Agnes smiled up at the girl. She was a bit of a handful for Mary, but she had a warm generous nature and loved to chat and gossip.

Breda picked it up. She recognised Bryan's handwriting only too well. She couldn't read it down here or Mary was bound to ask who it was from, because they got so little in the way of mail. Mary wrote to their mother each week and Kathleen replied, and Albert sometimes got a letter from Canada where he had a second cousin who was always urging him to go out and join him, but that was all.

'Look at the state of my shoes! Aren't they soaked through, and I could wring out my stockings.'

Agnes looked concerned. 'Get out of those wet things at once, Breda, or you'll suffer for it when you're as old as I am.'

'I'll go up and change. I'll leave my coat down here to dry – I'll need it for tomorrow.'

'Can't you wear your best one just for a day? That one's absolutely soaking wet, dear. It'll take more than a night to dry,' Agnes said.

Breda nodded and went up the stairs.

She sat on the bed staring at the letter. She'd been going out with Charlie now for quite a while. He was nice and he did buy her things, but it just wasn't the same. It was Bryan she really wanted. She opened the envelope and read the short paragraph. He was terribly sorry for treating her so badly in the past. He missed her desperately as well. He knew she had another fellow but he hoped it wasn't anything serious and would she consider seeing him again? He'd wait outside the Midland Hotel on the corner of Cases Street on Friday night until half past seven and he begged her to meet him.

She flushed, a feeling of triumph rising in her. So, he *did* want her back. He *was* jealous of Charlie, which was the purpose in going out with Charlie in the first place. Should she go or should she make him wait a bit longer? But her heart told her the latter was foolish; she might lose him altogether. No, she'd go and see what he had to say for himself. Maybe now he'd agree with her over the dispensation. Maybe now he'd go with her to see the Archbishop. But she had to think up an excuse and quickly, for Mary would want to know who the letter was from.

When she went back downstairs and into the warmth of the morning room Mary looked up.

'Who was your letter from?' she asked as she pressed a piece of dampened dark blue velour firmly over a wooden block which resembled a head.

'Maureen. She's been off sick and neither of us has a telephone.'

'How long has she been ill?' Agnes asked as she expertly curled the brim of a Bangkok straw with hot tongs.

'About a fortnight. She's had a terrible bad chest and her mam wouldn't let her out the door what with the weather being so desperate. I'm going with Joyce to see her on Friday night,' she lied, her gaze fixed on what Agnes was doing to give the impression that she found it very interesting. She did not, but it served the purpose.

'Her mother's a sensible woman. If she's sick the best place for her is indoors, in bed.'

'And if she's that bad, will she want the pair of you going in on top of her?' Mary asked, balancing the finished straw hat on the tips of the fingers of her right hand.

'Of course she will. Isn't that what the letter was all about in the first place.' Breda quickly threw the envelope into the fire.

'Don't you go and bring any germs home here. Whatever she's got she can keep it to herself.'

'Where exactly does she live, Breda?' Agnes asked.

'In Hunt Street, off Breck Road. I think that's classed as Everton.'

Agnes nodded her approval and Mary got up to make some tea. Albert was sitting in the parlour reading, as he sometimes did. He seemed to like his own company at times. She'd take him in a cup. She was uneasy about Breda and that letter. She hadn't recognised the handwriting but it was such a scrawl that it didn't quite fit in with Maureen's background or job. She herself was fed up working in Williams's. She wished she had the means to start up her own business and she wanted to learn everything quickly.

The wind and rain had abated by Friday night and Breda thanked God for it. There was nothing worse than battling with an umbrella and having your hair look a fright when you finally arrived where you were going. She was relieved when she got off the bus at Central Station and saw Bryan waiting on the opposite side of the road.

He stepped forward, thankful that she'd come. He had thought she might reply to his letter but she hadn't and it had caused him some concern. He had missed her more than he thought he would. He'd been out with other girls but none of them had been as lovely or such good company as Breda. He'd sat and thought it all out one night, staring into the embers of the fire in the range after everyone had gone to bed. He knew she wouldn't stand for any more shilly-shallying so he'd had to make up his mind. It was Breda and marriage – eventually – or a string of girls whose company he didn't enjoy and would begrudge spending money on.

'I wondered if you'd come. I thought you might have replied.'

She looked at him askance. 'Sure to God, how could I do that? Doesn't everyone in that house know my writing?'

'Well, you're here now. Would you like to go for a drink in a pub, a nice one where they have a lounge that's decent?' he suggested eagerly.

'Have you lost your senses altogether, Bryan O'Shea? Do I look as old as twenty-one?'

'You could pass for it.'

'I don't want to *pass* for it and I don't want to be humiliated by being asked to leave.'

'Where would you like to go, then? We can't stand here all night, we'll freeze.'

'Can't we go into the Stork Hotel in Queen's Square? You can have a drink and I can have an orange juice or lemonade.'

She didn't tell him that that was where Charlie sometimes took her and that it was expensive.

Bryan felt a bit dismayed. It cost an arm and a leg for a drink in there. The likes of himself who only worked on the docks didn't go to places like that, but she'd left him with no choice.

'All right, then. I could murder a pint, anyway.'

Breda looked at him from under her dark lashes. It seemed as if he was going to take her seriously now. He'd have never dreamed of taking her into an hotel in the past.

When they were seated in the comfortable and well-furnished lounge bar that was open to the public as well as hotel guests, Bryan gave the order to the waiter and Breda smiled up at the young man, who recognised her.

'We've not seen you in here for a while, miss,' he said pleasantly. Anyone who looked like Breda was never forgotten by any man she came into contact with.

'No, and isn't it a lovely place to be in too, but I'm here now.'

Bryan looked at her with suspicion. 'You never said you'd been in here before.'

'You never asked. Anyway, does it matter where I've been or who I've been with at all? It was you who wrote to me, if you remember.'

Before Bryan could reply the waiter was back with the drinks and Bryan dug into his pocket and counted out the exact money. Breda kicked him under the table and mouthed the word 'tip'.

As she sipped the orange juice Bryan studied her closely. She'd changed. She was far more confident, for one thing, and it must have been that Charlie Higgins who brought her here and tipped the waiter feller. He'd never given anyone money for a tip in his life but that Charlie must be used to it. His mam always tried to save a few coppers for the postman and the fellers who emptied the ashpit at Christmas, but that was only once a year.

'What did you want to see me for, you after being the one who wrote the letter?' Breda questioned. She realised that she was in a much stronger position this time and she certainly intended to use it.

'To ask you if there's any chance of us getting back together again, like?' Bryan was selfconsciously fiddling with the buttons on his jacket.

Breda looked at him steadily. 'I'm not sure. Are you going to be serious this time? Didn't I get fed up with the antics out of you last time. That's why I started going out with Charlie, and a few others as well,' she added, just to let him think she was very popular and could have any man at the drop of a hat, which she could. Even

225

the waiter here would be more than willing to take her out.

'There'll be no more antics, Breda, I promise.'

'What about the family?'

'Well, we'll just have to meet that problem when it arises.'

'And will you consider the dispensation at all?'

He nodded. He would consider it, but he would suggest they got engaged first. He was confused over this issue. He couldn't understand his feelings at times. He *did* want her, yet part of him didn't want to give up his freedom. He supposed he was being a bit of a dog in the manger. If he couldn't have her, then nobody else could.

She smiled and reached for his hand. 'As long as we *are* serious.'

He squeezed her hand and raised his glass. 'To us and being serious.'

She smiled at him again. This time it would work out.

When they left he took her arm and walked her to the bus stop, but as she turned to kiss him goodnight she caught sight of a small figure, hatless and with a shabby-looking coat, and her heart lurched.

'God almighty, isn't that Patsy?'

'Where?'

'Just disappearing round the corner. Look.' She pointed.

'It could have been any kid, Breda,' he replied. The bus was approaching.

'No, I'm sure it was her. Isn't this a good way to start again? She'll go straight to your mam.'

'*If* it was her, Breda.'

'I'm positive. Didn't I get a good look at her? Now what

226

will we do? She'll run straight home and tell everyone, just like Rosie did the first time.'

'Don't worry about her,' Bryan said grimly. 'I'll sort her out. Get on the bus and I'll see you on Sunday afternoon in the park.'

When he arrived home Patsy was sitting at the table, her head bent over a book. Tonight his mam went to her Union of Catholic Mothers' meeting and his da was at the Men's Confraternity, so Patsy would have had time to go out and get back before she was missed. He hesitated, wondering whether it had been her. All he'd seen was the back of someone small.

'Have you been out tonight?'

She looked up at him, her eyes full of spite. She'd sworn she'd make them take notice of her and she'd seen him laboriously writing a letter, something he never did. She'd followed him to Scotland Road where there was a postbox just to make certain. She knew who the letter was for, but she hadn't known the day of the meeting she was certain the letter suggested. So she'd been even more vigilant, and tonight he'd made a special effort with his appearance, so she'd followed him. She'd been frozen stiff waiting for them to come out of that hotel. A posh hotel like the Stork, of all places, and she was sure that Breda had caught sight of her, as she'd meant her to do.

'Can't I go out now?' she snapped.

He ignored her question. 'I said *have* you been out?'

Patsy closed the book. 'Yes. I followed you and you took Breda Nolan into the Stork, and I'm going to tell Mam when she gets in. No one takes any notice of me in this house. It's all you and our flaming Maurice. Well, they will now,' she finished, a note of triumph in her voice.

Bryan's spirits plummeted. Breda had been right.

'All right, how much will it cost for you to keep your mouth shut, you little horror?'

She glared at him. 'It'll cost even more if you call me names.'

'How much?'

'Five shillings.'

'Five bloody shillings! What do you think I am, a bloody king?'

'It's five shillings or else.'

Bryan dug into his pocket and brought out two half-crowns. He could kill her, he really could. She was a spiteful little trouble-maker.

'Here, and I don't want to hear any more about it from you. I'd get to bed before Mam comes in.'

Breda was so convinced she'd seen Patsy that she decided the best plan would be to tell Mary, now, before anything else went wrong.

Mary was sitting on her own in the morning room, patiently folding a piece of broad grosgrain ribbon into a flat bow.

'You're in early. How was Maureen? Is she still badly?'

Breda took off her coat and hat. 'I never went to see her.'

Mary looked up at her sister, knowing instinctively that something was wrong.

'So, where have you been, and who with?' she demanded.

Breda sat down on the sofa. 'The letter was from Bryan.'

Mary closed her eyes. 'Oh, Breda, for God's sake, you're

not after starting all that again, are you? I thought you were serious about Charlie?'

'Charlie's nice, but—'

'Bryan's still your first cousin. Have you forgotten how shabbily he treated you last time? Don't I seem to remember you coming home in tears?'

'No, I've not forgotten that. But this time he *is* serious, Mary. He swore there would be no more antics out of him. And I believe him.'

Mary threw the ribbon down on the table. 'Breda, what in the name of God am I going to do with you?'

'He's even agreed about the dispensation,' Breda said earnestly.

'Breda, I'm sick to death of hearing about the bloody dispensation. Well, it's your life, and if you get hurt again, don't come crying to me,' Mary replied acidly.

'I won't need to come crying to you. Didn't I just say it was serious?'

'Well, then, get up to bed and leave me alone to sort out this damned ribbon.'

When her sister had gone upstairs, Mary leaned her head on her hands. Breda was becoming more and more of a problem. And just when she'd thought the romance with Charlie Higgins was going so well. If it didn't turn out properly this time, she would have to consider taking Breda home to Dublin.

Nothing more was said, but Agnes sensed the strain between Breda and Mary.

'Is there anything wrong, Mary? With Breda, I mean? You both look so preoccupied.'

'Sure, haven't you got the gift of second sight, Agnes. She's started seeing Bryan again. Oh, she said he's promised he was serious about her, but I think it was only to get her away from Charlie Higgins, who *was* getting serious about her. Bryan's always been a bit of a Jack the lad, as Aunty Maggie calls it. He was jealous, but not because he loves Breda but because he didn't want anyone else to be seen to be taking her away from him. He has a great opinion of himself, does Bryan O'Shea.'

Agnes sighed. 'And it's always you, Mary, who has to do the worrying and pick up the pieces when you've so much to contend with already.'

'I know, but she *is* my sister and I promised Mammy I'd look after her. But isn't she more trouble than Kevin and Lily put together.'

'Never mind, I'm sure things will work themselves out. You should be thinking about yourself and your new career. Have you finished the last sample?'

'No, not yet. I was trying to make the ribbon bow until she came in. Oh, I feel so . . . so . . .'

'Frustrated and miserable, though you don't show it? I know you are still in love with that young man who had to marry that dreadful girl.'

The tears welled up in Mary's eyes. 'I am, Agnes. I don't think I'll ever stop loving him, even though he's married. The only comfort for me is the fact that he hates her and always will.'

Agnes patted her hand. 'Better to have loved and lost, than never to have loved at all. That's what poor Hetty told me when . . . Victor's letter arrived. And maybe she was right, Mary.'

Mary wiped away her tears. 'She *is* right, even though twice I've loved and twice I've lost them.'

*　　*　　*

230

Lily hated Sundays. It was the most boring day in the whole week, she complained to Kevin. You had to get dressed up for Mass, then you had to play quietly, then there was that big meal when Uncle Albert took a huge knife and fork and cut the meat. Then Aunty Mary said grace. The afternoons were as bad. Aunty Mary or Aunty Agnes would help them with any homework or do jigsaw puzzles with them. The only good part of the day was the jelly or blancmange and cake that came after the big dinner. And today it was raining.

Lily pressed her little nose to the window pane, which was spattered with raindrops.

'I'm fed up, Kev. Shall we go down into the coal cellar? We've never really been down there. We've only looked from the top step when Uncle Albert has been getting more coal.'

'I wouldn't want to be in the dark, Lily,' Kevin answered cautiously.

'We won't be in the dark. Aunty Agnes keeps a torch in the back place and I *know* they keep other things beside coal in there,' she said triumphantly, her blue eyes full of mischief as she pushed back her thick fringe.

'We'll have to get out of our best things, Lily. We'd be murdered if we got them all full of mucky coal.' He was slowly warming to the idea. He too was bored and it was true they had never been down in the cellar.

'You get the torch and I'll go and get us some old things to wear.'

'How will we change without anyone seeing?'

'I'll throw the things out of the window in our room and you can fetch them from the yard.'

'You can't do that, Lily. They'll get all wet and someone will see.'

'Who?' she demanded impatiently.

Kevin shrugged. 'I'll go and get the torch.'

At least it had stopped raining, he thought. He stood in the yard for five minutes, neck craned, but there was no sign of Lily or any old clothes.

Lily finally crept out of the back door.

'Where are the clothes?' he hissed.

'I couldn't find anything. They must all be in the wash or waiting to be ironed. We'll have to go in these. We won't get too mucky, Kev, honest, not if we're careful.'

He looked at her with apprehension. He could take off his jersey. It would be cold but it was better than getting his good jumper destroyed altogether. But Lily wore a warm Viyella dress in pink and grey check with a pink collar and cuffs and a pink ribbon that kept most of her hair off her face, and she had white socks on and her good black shoes. They were not exactly the kind of clothes you could hope to keep clean in a coal cellar.

'Are you coming or are you going to be a cowardy custard?' Lily asked petulantly.

That settled it. 'I'm coming,' he answered firmly.

It was very dark in the cellar and his hand shook so much that Lily took the torch off him and shone it round the walls. There was coal in a far corner but there were boxes in another.

'Shall we have a look and see what's in the boxes, Kev?' Lily wasn't a bit frightened and had forgotten her dress already.

He followed her and held the torch as she dived into a tea chest and pulled out something wrapped in newspaper.

'What's that?'

'I don't know until I get the paper off, do I?' She started

to pull off the paper, which had yellowed with age. Just as she finally got the article unwrapped, it fell from her hand and shattered on the floor. In the few seconds before it had fallen, they'd both seen that it was a long glass vase and that there was a piece of paper attached to it. The writing was faded but it said; 'For Agnes and Victor, with best wishes on your engagement. Lucy and Tom.'

Kevin was horrified. 'We'll be killed now, Lily! It was Aunty Agnes's vase and it must be very old. Mammy will belt us to bits. And look at the state of us.'

Lily's lip began to quiver and she reached out for his hand. 'What'll we do, Kev?'

He was frightened too. 'I don't know, but if we tell them we'll be clattered.'

'We won't tell them, Kev. We'll run away, that's what we'll do.'

As usual Kevin placed his trust firmly in Lily. 'Where will we go?'

'I don't know. Have you got any money?'

'I've got sixpence. I saved my threepence pocket money from last week.' They both did little jobs around the house to earn their money. Mary had insisted on it. How will they know the value of it otherwise? she'd asked when Agnes and Albert wanted to give them pocket money.

Lily was thinking. It was no use going anywhere near her mam and da, or to any of the houses in Hornby Street. They'd only get clattered and brought back. She tried to think of somewhere far away.

'We'll go to Chester. I heard Aunty Agnes say it was a long way away by train. You can get a bus instead but you've got to go on the ferry first. We'll go to Chester, Kev. No one will ever find us there.'

He nodded and followed her up the steps. Once out in the yard they crept out of the door and into the narrow entry to the top of the road.

'We'll have to get the bus or the tram,' Lily said firmly. She wanted to get away from here very quickly because Kevin was right. They'd be taken apart. She might even get sent back to her mam in Hornby Street and she didn't want that. All she'd get there was her mam shouting and slapping and Patsy tormenting her. Here she had nice things; she'd even got used to the big bath. It was warm and they earned pocket money. There were treats like jelly and cakes even when it wasn't a special occasion, but only Sunday.

They waited at the bus stop, both of them shivering as the wind cut through their clothes. There hadn't been time to sneak in and get some coats. But at last the bus arrived and they got on, scrutinised by the conductor in the process.

'Right, you two, where are you going?' he asked, as he came down the bus collecting fares and giving out tickets from his little machine. When the handle was turned the tickets popped out and it had always fascinated Kevin.

'The pier head,' Lily answered.

'Oh, going for a ride on the ferry, are we?'

They both nodded and Kevin held out his two threepenny bits.

'Does yer mam know?'

Again they nodded.

'Right, that'll be tuppence. Put the rest of your money away, lad.' He grinned as he handed them the tickets and their change. Ten to one their mam didn't know, he thought, but kids were kids and they'd come to no harm on the ferry.

When they got off it was wild and windy and the river looked cold and grey and angry as it hurled itself against the landing stage in clouds of spray. There was a ferry boat waiting.

'I'm freezing, Lily, and I'm hungry and I should have brought my rabbit. I forgot him.'

Tears started in her eyes. She'd left her precious doll behind and she too was cold and hungry.

'We'll be all right, Kev. We can sit near the funnel. It's always warm there, and once we get the other bus we'll be warm too 'cos we'll be on it for ages and ages.' She sounded more cheerful than she felt. It would start to get dark soon.

The man in the ticket office was used to kids going on the ferry alone. They frequently just bought a single ticket and spent hours travelling back and forth until someone, usually one of the deckhands, caught them.

'Are yer just going over?'

'We are, mister, honest,' Lily answered. Her head only just came up to the wooden counter.

'Well, you'd better be, otherwise I'll set the Paddy Kellys on yer.'

'We definitely are,' Kevin added in a grave voice. They didn't want to get caught by the dock police, or the Paddy Kellys as they were known.

It was much warmer down in the saloon near the stairs down to the engine room. It also smelled strongly of oil and once they had pulled away from the stage and were out into the river it was very rough and they huddled together, feeling sick.

'If youse two are going to throw up everywhere, get up on deck an' hang over the side. I'm not cleaning up after bloody kids,' one of the deck hands said, looking down at them.

'We . . . we won't.' Lily's words were far more confident than she felt and she couldn't keep the sob out of her voice.

He peered at them closely. 'Have you got tickets?'

Kevin produced them and they were duly inspected and handed back.

'Do yer live over the water, then?'

They both shook their heads.

'So what are yer doin' on here?' He'd noticed that although their faces and clothes were grubby they were well dressed.

'We're run—' Kevin started before Lily dug him hard in the ribs and he lapsed into silence.

'So, that's it, then? Running away?'

'No,' Lily replied but Kevin had said yes at the same time.

'Which one is it, then?' he demanded.

'We're going to Chester,' Lily said firmly.

'How much money have yer got, then?'

Kevin produced the pennies he had left.

'Well, that won't get yer to Chester.'

Kevin, who was feeling very sick now, started to cry.

Lily put her arm around him. 'Don't cry, Kev, we'll be all right.'

'I feel sick, Lily, and I want . . . . I want to go home.'

The man looked down at them. 'The pair of you stay there until I come back,' he instructed.

Lily was sobbing too now. She was feeling sick and frightened and she didn't want to go to Chester any more. She wanted to go home, even if it meant they would get belted to bits.

When the deck hand returned he looked down at them with pity mingled with amusement. He'd gone to the bridge and explained that they had two runaways on board. Kids who looked as if they came from a decent home. Captain Tony

Murphy had agreed to let them come up on to the bridge where his second officer would keep an eye on them while he got word ashore.

'Right, you're coming with me up to see Captain Murphy, and when we sail again there'll be someone to meet you at the landing stage. Come on, wipe them eyes. How old are yer?'

'Seven,' Lily managed to inform him between sobs.

It was a policeman who was waiting for them on the landing stage and they were so frightened by the size of him that they clung tightly to each other and had to be prodded to move.

'They're all yours now. They live in Exeter Road, Bootle. I know it's not your area, or even your Force, but I'm leaving them with you. Time and tide wait for no man,' Captain Murphy quoted before making his way back to the bridge.

'I'll get them home, even though it's Bootle Constabulary's area,' the constable called before he turned his attention to Lily and Kevin.

'Come on, you'll have your mam out of her mind with worry. Didn't you think about that?' He sounded stern.

'We . . . we . . . didn't mean to break the vase,' Kevin explained.

'No, we was only looking and it slipped,' Lily added.

'Well, you can explain all that to your mam.'

He sat them on the long seat by the door of the bus, while he stood on the platform talking to the conductor. He'd paid all their fares. Kevin and Lily were so thankful to be going home that the time just seemed to fly.

When they reached the bus stop they almost collided with a frantic Mary.

'Oh, thank God! You've had the heart across us all. Where've you been? Uncle Albert is out looking for you and so is Aunty Breda.' Mary knelt and scooped them both up in her arms. Everyone had been destroyed with worry when they couldn't find the pair of them, and Albert had gone down to the cellar and found the broken vase.

'Oh, Agnes, it was one of your engagement presents,' Mary had cried with dismay.

'It doesn't matter, Mary. I should have got rid of all that stuff ages ago. We have to find them. They are much more important than an old vase,' Agnes had replied. She too was very worried and had wanted to go out looking, but Mary had absolutely forbidden it.

She stood up, an arm around each child.

'Oh, where did you find them, officer?'

'I didn't. A deck hand on the ferry spotted them. Apparently they were going to Chester.'

'Jesus, Mary and Joseph! Chester! Do you know how far that is?'

'Mammy, don't be giving out. I'm cold and I want my rabbit.' Tears had formed rivulets in the coal dust on Kevin's cheeks.

'We didn't mean to break the vase, Aunty Mary. Will you make me go back to Mam's?' Lily sobbed, rubbing her eyes with her fists.

'Oh, Lily, no, of course I won't, but you will both say you're sorry to Aunty Agnes for breaking her good vase.'

'You listen to your mam, and in future behave yourselves and don't go wandering off without telling anyone. I'll be watching out for you.'

Mary looked at the constable with gratitude. She was sure they wouldn't run away again.

'Will you come within and have some tea?'

'No, thank you. This isn't really my patch. I'd better get back.'

'Thank you again,' Mary said before turning her attention to the two children. 'Come on inside now. You'll have a hot bath and some tea and then go off to bed. And the policeman's right. Don't go worrying everyone like that again.'

Both Breda and Albert were back as she shepherded them into the kitchen.

'Well, thank God for that,' Agnes cried, getting to her feet.

'Haven't you had the heart across us all with your antics,' Breda said crossly. She'd been getting ready to go and meet Bryan when their absence was noticed. Now it was too late to go at all.

'Where did they get to?' Albert asked.

'Woodside. The captain of the ferry got in touch with the Liverpool police and one of them brought them home and told them off. They were only going to Chester, if you please.'

'Oh, I should never have mentioned the place,' Agnes cried, guilt-stricken.

'Ah, come on out of that, Agnes. Sure it wasn't your fault.'

'Now the pair of you say you're sorry before I take you upstairs.'

Kevin slid his hand into Lily's for support and they both apologised. They were worn out and they were both near to tears again.

'We won't ever do that again, Lily,' Kevin said when they'd been bathed and were sitting at the table eating sandwiches.

'No, we won't, 'cos that scuffer said he'd be watching for us,' she replied.

Mary overheard them and smiled. That was those two sorted out, at least. Now all she had to worry about was Bryan and Breda.

Chapter Seventeen

Christmas was approaching fast. The dark, dismal afternoons were brightened by the street and shop lights. In the shops themselves great efforts had been made but the fact still remained that there was very little to sell. Even bread, the staple diet of the poor, was still rationed. Children with bare feet and tattered clothes pressed their noses against the glass of shop windows and looked longingly at things they would never have.

The weather was mixed. One day it was pouring with rain, the next it was clear but frosty, which made pavements hazardous and caused Maggie to complain to Flossie that the work and expense of Christmas was bad enough without the weather acting up. At least if it snowed you knew where you were. You shovelled it up from outside your own door and threw the ashes from the range over the flagstones to give a good grip. Of course there were the young hooligans who took tin trays or the baking shelf from the oven and used them as sledges, which defeated the object of the shovelling.

Maurice was in a quandary.

'It's not as if you'd sort of agreed, you did *promise*, Maurice.' Pauline had looked up into his eyes and he'd felt his heart drop like a stone. He had promised, but he

241

couldn't afford a ring like the one Albert Fallowfield now had in his possession for safe keeping. He'd managed to save a few pounds, but there were other presents to buy.

'I know I did, but . . . but it's not easy to save up. I only get a couple of mornings or afternoons and I have to give Mam something for my keep. There's Mam and Da and our Patsy and Bryan to buy for too. Money doesn't go far, Pauline.'

He'd had to tell her about Hughie Scanlan. The whole street knew the police had been to their house. He didn't say it was a ring he'd actually paid for, otherwise that would have been the end of everything. He'd said Hughie had approached him with some jewellery. Bracelets, earrings, lockets, things like that, but he'd refused. What use were they to him anyway? He was saving up. Pauline's mam had been very annoyed and had even threatened to part them if that was the scum he mixed with. He'd had a hard time convincing her that he didn't mix, that they'd only been in the same class at school, the way Bryan had been in the same class as Georgie Scanlan.

Things had looked very dangerous for a whole month, because her da had taken him to one side and told him he would give him the hiding of his life if he hurt Pauline. And now she wanted a ring. He couldn't go and see if Mr Fallowfield would give it back. It was too soon. People would catch on, especially her mam and dad when she flashed it around, as she certainly would do.

Her hazel eyes had been moist with incipient tears of disappointment, and that had hurt him.

'I'll see what I can do. I did promise,' he'd said, squeezing her hand as if to emphasise his words.

He'd lain awake for most of that night. It was use-less asking Da or Bryan; their money was already spoken for. He wondered if Mary would lend him three or four pounds. At least she knew all about the affair with Hughie and she was his only hope. He'd rather leave home and go to sea than disappoint Pauline. She was very patient. She didn't ask for much in the way of outings or treats and she was saving hard. She walked to and from work to save the busfare even if she got soaked or was frozen stiff. She took a few sandwiches instead of going to Reiglers for a pie or something. Sometimes he felt guilty and he really wanted to get her a lovely ring to show her that not only did he love her, but he appreciated her sacrifices.

He went to see Mary the following evening.

Breda opened the door to him.

'Maurice O'Shea! What has you down here at this time of night?'

Maurice took off his cap. 'I . . . I came to see Mary. Is she in?'

Breda held the door wide. 'She is. Get inside with you before the wind cuts us both in two.'

Mary came out to him looking concerned. 'Maurice! How are things above in Hornby Street? No one is badly?'

'No, they're all fine, except . . . except it's getting near to Christmas.' He looked pleadingly at Mary, who instantly understood the reason for this surprise visit.

'Come into the parlour. It's warm there. Albert is reading but he won't mind a small interruption.'

'What's wrong with the kitchen or the morning room? Why is he being treated like the gentry? Being "entertained" in the parlour?'

'Breda, for God's sake, do you have to make a song and dance about every little thing?' Mary opened the door and ushered the lad through and glared at her sister. Breda just shrugged and went back into the kitchen.

Albert looked up. 'It's a while since I set eyes on you, young man.'

Maurice went pale but Mary took his arm reassuringly.

'I think he wants to ask us something about an engagement ring. Is that the way of it, Maurice?' She indicated that he should sit.

He nodded and perched gingerly of the edge of the hide sofa. It was very posh in here, he thought, glancing quickly round.

Albert laid down his book. 'If you've come to ask for that one you're going to be disappointed. I told you she might never get it.'

'I know that. I didn't come to ask for that.'

'Well?' Albert waited for a reply.

Mary placed an encouraging hand on his arm.

'I was wondering if . . . if either of you could possibly lend me . . .' He paused and bit his lip. 'You see, she's set her heart on a ring, and she's really great. She walks to work and back and takes sandwiches, just to save the coppers.'

Mary smiled. She liked Pauline and she knew young Maurice really did appreciate the sacrifices the girl made.

'How much?' she asked.

He looked down, twisting his cap nervously between his hands.

'Would three or four pounds be too much? I'll do my very best to have it paid back by summer.'

'That's quite a lot of money.' Albert looked at Mary, who gave a quick nod of her head.

'I . . . I know that, but . . .'

'But if you can't give her the one you got from Hughie,

which is worth at least ten pounds, you'd still like the ring to be a decent one?'

Maurice nodded. Never in his whole life would he forget what Albert did for a job and he was nervous in his company.

'Well, I think between us we can manage four, can't we, Mary?'

'I think so. You're a good lad and you're after getting a grand little fiancée, but you'll try to give Albert something each week until the loan is paid.'

Maurice was so relieved that he could have burst into tears. When Albert left the room he looked at Mary with heartfelt gratitude. 'Maybe . . . maybe later, you could sell the other one, you know . . .'

'Sure, I know full well what you mean, Maurice, and I know it's kindly meant, but the best thing to do with that ring would be to flush it down the toilet. Then no one has possession of it.'

Again he nodded. Albert returned and held out four pound notes.

'Why don't you try some of the smaller, more local jewellers? Get a second-hand ring. You won't pay tax on it so you'll get more for your money,' Albert advised.

'She wants one from a posh jeweller's in town.'

'Then she'll just have to want. Tell her you had to borrow the money, she'll understand. Perhaps you can get a nice little box, fill it with cotton wool and wrap it nicely. I'll do it for you.'

'Would you, Mary?'

'Didn't I just say I would? Now get yourself home before Aunty Maggie thinks you've run off like those two little eejits did.'

When he arrived home, his cheeks glowing from the cold wind, his eyes full of excitement, his mother looked at him suspiciously.

'Where've you been? Pauline's been over and you look like a cat that's got the cream.'

'I've been to Mary's in Bootle.'

'I know where she lives.'

'I'm going to get Pauline an engagement ring. Mary has lent me some money so she can have a really great one.'

'Well, I never had any engagement ring, but I was wondering when you'd get round to making it official, like. You've my full approval. Of course, it'll be years before you'll be able to get married.'

'Not *too* long, Mam.'

'Well, you're not starting out living in my front room. Your da and me have hardly had any privacy for years, and Nelly's front room is out too for the same reason.'

'We don't want to start out like that, Mam. We're saving hard.'

'Good. Did you hear all that, Jim O'Shea? This one here's going to get engaged. I wish our Bryan would pull his socks up. I'll be drawing the old age pension before I get rid of him.'

Jim lowered his newspaper. 'I did. Congratulations, lad.'

'I'm going to give her the ring on Christmas Eve just before Midnight Mass.'

'That's as good a time as any, I suppose,' his father muttered, retreating behind his newspaper which he read from cover to cover every night.

Maggie raised her eyes to the ceiling. 'And you say Mary lent you the money?'

'Well, Mr Fallowfield chipped in too. I promised to have it paid back by summer.'

'You just see that you do.'

'Mam, can we have a bit of a do, like? An engagement party and Christmas party rolled into one?'

'No, we can't. Do you think I'm made of money? And look what happened at the last party that was held in this street. Phil says their Chris won't even go to the same Mass as *her* these days.'

Maurice was disappointed, but then he thought of the delight on Pauline's face when he gave her the ring. She would immediately show it to Father Hayes and most of the departing congregation, and he'd be proud for her to do so.

Patsy had spent the money she'd extorted from Bryan, but not all at once. She'd only bought small things, otherwise Mam would want to know where she'd got the money from. But now she wanted to buy herself a little silver teddy bear brooch that she'd seen in the window of Cooksons pawnshop on Scotland Road. If questions were asked she'd say Bryan had bought it her for Christmas. She'd never had a teddy bear, or any other large toy for that matter, and she'd envied and coveted the doll that Lily had got last Christmas. She'd told herself she was too old for dolls anyway, and it was 'soppy' and babyish, but deep down she had wanted one.

It just wasn't fair the way their Lily got everything, she thought as she trudged home from school on Friday afternoon with the wind cutting through her thin coat. Lily had a great house to live in, nice clothes, ribbons for her hair, and even threepence a week pocket money. Threepence just for doing bits of jobs like tidying up or dusting. No one would give her threepence even if she cleaned the whole house from top to bottom. No, she was determined that Bryan would hand over the money for her brooch.

She waited until early Saturday evening. Maurice was over at Pauline's, Mam had gone down to Cissy Mathews for the margarine she'd forgotten to get and Da had gone to the public baths. Bryan would follow him when he had finished reading the football results in the *Echo*. He wasn't very pleased about them, particularly the match he'd seen. In his opinion (shared by his father) Everton hadn't played well at all. He'd been as vociferous as the other supporters in his protests at the match.

'Hit him with yer handbag!' he'd yelled when a member of the team should have been more aggressive in tackling an opponent, and 'Where's yer white stick, he was wellied!' at the referee who in his opinion (and many thousands of others) had given an unfair decision.

'I've spent the five bob you gave me,' Patsy said bluntly.

'So what?' he answered, still scanning the page.

'I want more.'

Bryan lost interest in the sports page.

'What do you mean you want more, you hardfaced little get!'

'I want more. I spent it,' Patsy repeated defiantly.

'So you spent it.' Bryan was irritated. Patsy was a pain.

'I want a brooch and it's five shillings. It's silver and I saw it in Cooksons on Scotland Road. I'm going to tell Mam you bought it me for Christmas.'

He laughed mockingly. 'What do you take her for, for God's sake? She didn't come over on the last banana boat.'

'Well, I want it or I'm going to tell Mam that you're going out with Breda again, and then you'll be for it.'

Bryan got to his feet, grabbed her tightly by the shoulders and shook her hard.

'Listen, you little blackmailer, you're not getting another penny out of me and you can tell who you like, but if you do I'll belt you from here into the middle of next week! You're a nasty little bitch! God help the feller that gets you, you spiteful, scheming, horrible . . .' He ran out of adjectives but Patsy was upset. She hadn't expected him to go for her like that and when he released her she ran into the lobby, slamming the kitchen door behind her.

She went up the stairs to the bedroom which she now had all to herself. Mam and Dad had the downstairs front room and Bryan and Maurice had the other bedroom. She sat down on the edge of the bed. At first she'd been delighted that at last she had a room to herself and she'd boasted to her classmates who all had to share with some member of their family. But the novelty of that had soon worn off and sometimes, although she wouldn't admit it, she was lonely.

He was the nasty one, she thought, his words still ringing in her head. She was only nasty and spiteful because no one ever took any notice of her in this house. Bryan had Breda and Maurice had that Pauline Casey, whom she didn't like and considered stupid to even look at someone as dull and boring as Maurice. Their Lily had Kevin and that big house which she hadn't minded at first, it had been such a relief to get rid of Lily. It was only when they came visiting on Sundays that she began to see that Lily's dresses were far better than her own and she had more of them.

She got up, dragging a blanket off the bed and pulling it around herself. It was freezing cold. She stood looking down into the street through the rain-streaked window pane.

If people were nice to her then she wouldn't be spiteful.

It was the same in school, she was always left out of things. All the others had best friends or were in a group, but no one wanted her. She'd only got a new dress for Rosie O'Hanlon's wedding because Mary had given her mam half of what it cost. And she'd had to wear her awful brown rag of a coat over it when their Lily, who had a smart coat, had been allowed to take it off, thereby revealing the Communion dress. That too had been coveted. She'd had to make do with a plain one and a bit of limp net for a veil and there hadn't been a flowered tiara for her. Everyone she could think of seemed to hate her. Tears of self-pity rolled down her thin cheeks. She was skinny and had black straggly hair that no amount of rag curlers would make curl, and they were agony to sleep in anyway. Lily had thick golden hair that curled all by itself and she was going to grow up pretty, you could see it now. All she wanted was a little brooch, and their Lily had that cross and chain.

An idea was beginning to take shape in her mind. If Bryan wouldn't cough up the money, then she'd try Breda. Why not? Breda always seemed to have money to dress smartly and she was sure that Mary and Mam didn't know that those two were at it again. For the life of her she couldn't understand why Breda wanted her brother. He was awful. He was a slimy creep who thought he was God's gift to women. Breda was as beautiful as a film star. And that wasn't fair either. Why couldn't she have been born looking like Breda Nolan?

She dashed away the tears with the back of her hand and threw the blanket on the bed, determination showing in her thin, pinched, plain little face.

She'd cadged the bus fare from her da when he'd come in.

She'd complained that she never got anything, not even the odd penny for sweets when she knew Mam had plenty of sweet coupons.

As she got off the bus on Balliol Road she thought how different it was around here. There were bomb sites, and the docks were just down Miller's Bridge, but the side streets were quiet. It was raining heavily and she had no hat or umbrella, so she ran the short distance and hoped that someone would answer the door quickly.

It was Breda herself who opened it.

'Jaysus! Come on in before you're soaked altogether!'

Patsy was only too glad to obey.

'Now what is it that has you out on a night like this? Will you look at the cut of you. You've water dripping from your hair. Where's the hat and scarf and mitts Mary made you?'

Patsy looked sullen. 'I dunno. I came all the way to see you.'

'What for?'

'There's a brooch in Cooksons that I want and our Bryan won't give me any more money, so I've come to get it off you, or I'm going to tell Mam about you and him.'

Breda's eyes flashed with anger. 'Aren't you a terrible poor excuse for an innocent child! Get back home now before I lose the run of myself and kill you. You're not going to get a penny out of me either.'

Patsy was cold, wet and determined. 'Then I want to live here, like our Lily does.'

'Then you can bloody want. You're not coming in on top of us. Two rowdy children are enough.'

'Breda, who was it hammering down the door—' Mary caught sight of Patsy.

'God in heaven! Patsy, what's the matter? You're soaked!

Get into that kitchen and take off those things, otherwise it'll be the hospital for you.'

'There's nothing wrong and she's going home now,' Breda said emphatically.

Mary looked hard at them both. Patsy was up to something, and despite Breda's furious expression she was guilty of something. Mary knew her sister too well.

Agnes and Albert were sitting in the parlour before a roaring fire having a nostalgic conversation about the city and the way it was when they were young. Lily and Kevin were upstairs and judging from the noise were having an argument. She'd have to go up to them soon and sort them out.

'Get into that kitchen the pair of you!' she commanded in a tone that brooked no further argument.

She stripped off Patsy's coat, hung it over the back of a chair which she placed in front of the fire and gave the child a towel to dry her hair.

Breda stood twisting her hands together. Patsy was by far the most malicious and troublesome child she'd ever come across.

'Now, it's the truth I want. Patsy, what has you out on a terrible night like this, and does Aunty Maggie know where you are?'

'You can be sure she does not,' Breda interrupted.

'I'll speak to you, Breda, when your one here tells me why she's come all this way in the rain.'

Patsy didn't feel quite so cocksure of herself. Mary had changed, seemed older, more commanding than when she lived with them. 'I . . . I . . .'

Breda couldn't control her temper. 'I'll tell you why. She's nothing but a cheap little blackmailer. She took money from

252

Bryan and now she's come here wanting money from me, otherwise she'll tell you about Bryan and me, which you know already. So go on back out there, you little fright, and get home. It's a wasted journey you've had.' Breda turned back to her sister. 'And isn't she after wanting to come and live here too.'

Patsy's face had fallen. She'd had no idea that Mary already knew.

They were interrupted by a red-faced Kevin. His hair was sticking out and his jersey had been pulled so hard that the neckband was twisted and lopsided.

'Mammy, Lily took my chalk, my best blue one, and broke it up.' He was near to tears.

'So that's what's been going on above. Get back up those stairs this very minute, Kevin O'Malley, and tell Lily that if there's any more fighting you'll both be clattered and there'll be no pocket money this week. Upstairs with you – now!'

It was the words 'pocket money' that affected Patsy most. She was cold, wet and miserable, and she'd failed. She'd never have the brooch now and it had been so pretty. Tears started in her eyes.

'There's no use you starting to weep and wail like a banshee, Patsy O'Shea,' Breda snapped.

Mary looked at the child, then thought of Lily and some of her anger subsided. Patsy was so plain compared to her younger sister, and no one took much notice of her. Yet she couldn't be allowed to get away with conduct like this. Mary sighed heavily. All she saw was a skinny, soaking wet, plain child dressed in a skirt that was too short and a jumper that didn't fit her. Her coat was steaming before the fire and it was the one she had to wear for school and Mass alike. It was the only one she owned and the sleeves were too short.

'Sit down there by the fire and dry your hair properly. Will I get you some tea and a slice of bread and jam? Are you hungry?'

Patsy nodded miserably.

Breda was incredulous and outraged. 'Glory be to God, you're never going to let her stay here?'

'No, I am not. When she's dry I'm going to bring her out in the rain again and take her home myself. And I want a word with you, Breda. Now, in the morning room!'

When Patsy was settled in front of the fire, a blanket round her and a cup of tea and a jam butty set on a stool beside her, Mary grimly followed her sister to the morning room.

'This is all your fault, Breda.'

'Why so? Isn't she a desperate child altogether? The little sneak, coming here demanding money.'

'Because if you weren't hell bent on carrying on this romance with Bryan, she'd have nothing to say about anyone.'

'Mary, I've told you we're serious.'

'*You* might be, but I doubt *he* is. Has he approached Father Hayes, even? No, he has not. After I've sorted out those two in the attic above, I'm going to take Patsy home, and what do I tell Aunty Maggie? Will you tell me that, please?'

Breda was sick of all the pretence, the secrecy but most of all Patsy.

'Oh, I don't care what you tell her. I love Bryan.'

Mary stared at her closely. Breda might think she loved him, but she'd shown none of the signs, the little gestures and smiles that Mary and Col had shared. She was sure it was a case of 'forbidden fruit', the excitement of the secret meetings or simply infatuation. Maybe if they got the whole thing into the open it would be sorted out once and for all.

'Right then, it's time for the truth. Wait now while I sort out those two, then find Albert's huge black umbrella. That'll cover us both.'

She was still angry as she went upstairs, leaving Breda staring after her.

She flung the attic door open.

'Would you look at the mess of this room! You'll clear it all up, right this minute, or it will all go into the bin and then you'll have nothing to fight over. And when you've done that, Aunty Breda will get you to bed. Be thankful that I'm too worried with other things or I'd take the pair of you apart, so I would. Is it bent on annoying Aunty Agnes and Uncle Albert you're after? Pick up those things now, and Lily, you tormenting little rossie, give Kevin back his chalk. You've chalks of your own.'

As she went back downstairs, Agnes came out of the parlour.

'Mary, dear, what is going on? You don't usually shout at the children.'

'No, I don't, but tonight they are desperate and, well, I've other things on my mind.'

'Who was at the door?' Agnes queried. For the most part she had left Mary and Breda to their own devices of late. They deserved some sort of privacy, some time to just enjoy being sisters. She and Albert had a lot in common but sometimes they just sat in restful, companionable silence. He had fitted in so well and he was concerned for them all, even down to Lily, who would play everyone up except him. These last few weeks she'd not felt well but she'd had a terrible fright when Lily and Kevin had gone missing. You read such terrible things in the newspapers these days and the whole experience had given her a few sleepless nights.

'It's Patsy, Lily's sister. Soaked to the skin she is.'

'Isn't she the somewhat malicious one her mother worries about?'

'Yes, but I think I can understand how she feels. She always seems to get left out. I think she does these desperate things because she's lonely and is looking for attention, even if it's the wrong kind of attention. I'm taking her home.'

'Oh, the children today would have you worried sick. What will you say to her mother?'

'I don't know yet.' Mary prayed for forgiveness for the lie. She knew exactly what she was going to say to Maggie.

Suddenly Agnes swayed and clutched at the door frame.

Mary forgot her worries. 'Agnes, what on earth is wrong? You're sick, you've gone a terrible colour. Here, let me help you.'

She supported the older woman and called for Albert, who immediately came out into the hallway.

'Oh, I'm sorry. Please don't fuss,' Agnes begged, her breathing shallow and obviously laboured.

'What's wrong?' Albert asked with concern. He was genuinely fond of the old lady.

'She's gone a bit faint,' Mary replied, looking to him for guidance.

'Right, straight to bed and I'm going for the doctor.'

'No, no, I don't want to drag the poor man out on a night like this. I'm just a little tired. It's the weather, I expect. I hate the winter months.'

Mary smiled at her. 'You can always do what Dr Davidson suggested.'

Agnes managed a weak smile. 'And miss the first real family Christmas in this house? Miss seeing the children's faces on Christmas morning? Not for all the tea in China.'

'Breda will help you. I've to get Patsy home or they'll be worried, and we know what that's like from the last escapade of those two above.'

She called Breda into the hall.

'Help Agnes to bed. She's had a little turn.'

Breda nodded, tight-lipped, her eyes full of anger. She could kill Patsy with her own two hands, but she hoped Aunty Maggie would save her the trouble.

Patsy's coat was still very wet, so Mary bundled her up in an old but warm jacket that belonged to Agnes. She'd tucked Patsy's hair under a pixie hood belonging to Lily. The jacket swamped the child and only served to make her look more forlorn, Mary thought as she took Albert's big, black umbrella out of the elephant's foot stand in the hall. They then braved the weather, Mary holding the child against her to keep her dry as they walked to the bus stop.

When they finally arrived in Hornby Street Patsy was shivering, not with cold, she told Mary, but with fear.

'I didn't mean to do it, honest, Aunty Mary. She'll kill me.'

'She will not, but you do deserve a punishment of some kind after the antics out of you. It was a terrible thing to do, Patsy. Blackmail is a crime as well as a mortal sin.'

When the door opened Maggie's face in the dim light coming from the kitchen looked even more drawn than usual, Mary thought.

'Jesus, Mary and Joseph! Has she dragged you out on a night like this? I was wondering where the little madam had got to. Get in, melady. And where's your coat?'

'It's here. She was soaked. I've dried it off as much as I can, but you'll still have to have it in front of the fire all night.'

Bryan looked startled as they all came into the kitchen. Then he cast a venomous glance at his sister.

Maggie stood, her hands on her hips, and asked for an explanation.

'Right, Patricia Mary O'Shea, what have you been up to now?' she demanded, using her daughter's seldom heard full Christian names.

'Apparently she asked Bryan for money to buy a brooch, and when he wouldn't give it to her she came to Breda.'

Maggie's brow furrowed in a frown. 'And just why would she be doing that?'

Bryan froze. Mary was going to let the cat out of the bag now.

'Because my eejit of a sister is seeing her cousin again, and this bold one found out and started to ask for money. Blackmail is what it is.'

Maggie sat down on a wooden chair. 'Am I to get no peace at all out of the pair of you? You, meladdo, are the living end! Up to the old tricks and the old lies. And as for you, melady, I'm taking you to see Mother Superior tomorrow morning! Blackmailing your own brother! I've never heard the flaming like of it. It's a good job your da's gone to the Grapes or it would be his belt you'd get. Mary, luv, what am I to do with them?'

Mary sighed. 'To start with, I'd send Patsy to bed and then we can get the other thing sorted out.'

Patsy needed no telling. She ran from the room and straight up the stairs. She didn't relish the visit to Mother Superior, but it was ten times better than getting a hiding from her da *and* Mam had said nothing about dragging her to see Father Hayes. She'd got off lightly in her opinion and Mary did seem to care about her.

Maggie closed the door. 'Right, that's her sorted out for now. What's going to become of her I don't know.'

'Aunty Maggie, the child's lonely and feels left out of things. She's terribly jealous of Lily, but I can't take her as well.'

'I know you can't, luv. But why is she lonely?'

'She thinks Bryan and Maurice get all the attention.'

'She's got a room all to herself now. What more does she want?'

Mary chose her words carefully. It was difficult to give advice and still appear to be respectful. 'Just a bit of time with you and Uncle Jim. Someone to talk to, to make her feel she's wanted, and maybe a nice present for Christmas. She's set her heart on that little silver brooch. Lily's got the silver cross and chain that Albert gave her. Fuss over Patsy a bit. Ask her about school, things like that.'

Maggie sighed. 'Kids today want everything. There were twelve of us and there was no fussing over any of us.'

'I know, but it might help. You don't want her turning out like . . .' She couldn't speak Rosie's name aloud, it was too painful.

'If that's all it takes, we'll do it. I *don't* want her to end up like *that* one. Now what about you, meladdo?'

'Breda told me they were serious about going to the Archbishop to try to get a dispensation.' Mary passed her hand over her now aching forehead. 'Aunty Maggie, you've no idea how destroyed I am with the pair of them and this flaming dispensation.'

Maggie's nerves had already been stretched by Patsy and her antics and she turned on Bryan.

'Is this true? *Are* you going to see the Archbishop?' she demanded forcefully.

'Er, well . . . I suppose so,' he muttered, refusing to meet his mother's eyes.

'Oh, that sounds dead keen, doesn't it? Very serious I'm sure, and you a feller of twenty-four,' Maggie said scathingly. 'You mean you can't make up your mind.'

'Aunty Maggie, I don't think either of them really loves the other. I don't think they know the meaning of the word. Breda thinks it's a sort of game.'

'And do you think it's a game, meladdo? Playing fast and loose and promising God knows what else when it's a pack of lies you've been telling the girl? I know you, Bryan O'Shea. There's only one person you love and that's yourself!'

Bryan didn't answer. He wished he'd gone out as he studied the toecaps of his shoes.

'I'm going to have to make a decision about all this and soon. Breda is getting beyond my control, so I'm thinking of taking her home.'

'Back to Dublin?'

'Yes, we'll all go. Breda, me and Kevin.'

'Mary, luv, what about your hats? All your plans? You've worked so hard.'

'I'll try to sell to the posh shops in Grafton Street. Switzers, maybe.'

'But what about Agnes and Albert?'

'Albert is well able to look after Agnes, and she's fond of him too.'

Maggie shook her head. 'It's not fair on you, luv, but maybe it's for the best.'

They were both thinking of Chris Kennedy.

Mary nodded slowly. 'I know. It might be for the best on that subject too. I won't go before Christmas. I couldn't disappoint the children or Agnes. She's really looking forward to it all. She's had a bit of a desperate life. No love in it at all after her fiancé up and married someone else.'

'Well, if you decide to go you can bring our Lily back. You'll have enough to cope with, with Breda, Kevin and your mam.'

'Oh, Aunty Maggie, that's another problem I'll have to face. Kevin's going to be heart-scalded.'

'Well, you can leave that problem sitting over there, gazing at his feet like a fool, to me and Jim,' Maggie said firmly. 'It'll be one less for you to worry about.'

Chapter Eighteen

She'd tell no one that she was thinking of going home. She would let them all have this first Christmas together, for she owed it to both Agnes and Albert. She'd thought it all out on the bus back, oblivious of the driving rain that beat on the windows. She was furious with Breda.

'How is Agnes?' she asked when she came into the morning room.

'Asleep, as far as I know. Sure, isn't it only to be expected at her age, having "little turns" now and then.'

'And aren't you the considerate one, you bold strap! Mam's right, that's just what you are. And don't start carrying on about that flaming dispensation because I'd try to get used to the idea that Bryan O'Shea doesn't love you one little bit and certainly has no intention of marrying you, dispensation or no dispensation.'

'Who said that?' Breda demanded, jumping to her feet.

'Aunty Maggie. When she asked him about it all he could do was stammer and stutter and give no real answer at all. Aunty Maggie says he loves no one but himself and I think she's right. So, don't go pestering him again and making yourself cheap. He doesn't love you, Breda.'

Breda's eyes filled with tears.

Mary was ready for this. Breda could dissolve into tears at the drop of a hat.

'And don't be turning on the crocodile tears either. Aren't the pair of you selfish. There has to be a lot of give and take in a marriage and both of you will do all the taking and no giving and you'll end up fighting all the time and life will become hell.'

Breda snatched up the hat that Mary had been helping her to trim and stormed out of the room. She'd wanted to get the hat finished to meet Bryan tomorrow but now it looked as though it was all over, thanks to that little cat Patsy.

There was little time in the weeks that followed for Breda to fret. She'd not seen nor heard from Bryan and yet strangely it didn't really bother her now. Not really. Oh, she'd cried a lot and begged Mary to go and see Aunty Maggie, but Mary had flatly refused.

Both Mary and Agnes had spent a great deal of time cooking and baking and sewing. Albert had gone into town and come home with a big Christmas tree and a huge bundle of holly with which they'd decorated all the downstairs rooms. Mary had taught the children how to make simple decorations. The more complicated ones, such as cardboard angels covered with silver paper, she did herself.

Both Kevin and Lily were bursting with excitement and Mary had a hard time keeping them under control. Making the ornaments helped a little.

She knew that both Agnes and Albert had bought presents for them which were duly wrapped up and placed under the tree. She had bought Kevin a second-hand scooter, the paintwork of which needed tidying up. 'A bit of a quick going-over' was how she'd described it. Albert had other ideas. He was going to repaint it completely. For Lily she'd got a second-hand doll's pram, and this too had been polished and painted. She and Agnes had made a pram set for it and some new clothes for Lily's doll. Both toys were at the back of the wash-house covered with an old blanket and newspaper.

As she'd sat sewing late at night, her thoughts always turned to the prospect of going home. She really didn't want to. The children were so settled and this *was* a happy home. Somehow a lonely man; an equally lonely old lady; a little boy who, although he barely remembered his father, still felt deprived and bewildered; a little tomboy of a girl; her handful of a sister; and herself had, against all the odds, become a family. Everything would have been perfect if she could have had Chris beside her, but these days she had learnt to keep all thoughts of him at the back of her mind. It was an effort, but she had to do it to keep her sanity. No, news of her decision would ruin the holiday.

After lunch on Christmas Day she'd take Lily and Kevin to Hornby Street while Agnes rested and Albert read the Father Brown stories that had been her present. Breda could stay and clear up. Then on St Stephen's Day, or Boxing Day as the others called it, she had a little outing planned for them all. A trip to New Brighton, weather permitting.

Agnes, herself and Albert would go into the Tower Ball-room and listen to the organist who was giving a special performance of Christmas songs, while the children could have some rides on the fair, supervised by Breda who would put up with anything to avoid having to sit still and listen to what she called 'boring music'. Had it been Bing Crosby then she'd have been queuing up outside.

On Christmas Eve everything was ready. The vegetables

had been cleaned, peeled and put into bowls of cold water, as had the potatoes. They were all now on the draining board. The turkey was on the cold slab in the larder stuffed with a parsley, thyme and breadcrumb mixture that Agnes had made, awaiting the roasting in the oven in the morning after Mass.

Albert was taking Agnes to their church, but before that they were eager to see the faces of Lily and Kevin when they unwrapped the gifts under the tree. Both children had been warned severely that if there was any poking or tearing of paper to see what was inside, Santi would see them and leave no toys for children who cheated.

They'd both looked at Mary with solemn expressions when she had lectured them.

There were other gifts under the tree too. Gifts from Agnes to Mary, Breda and Albert. From him too and from Mary and Breda. Mary wondered if there would be anything for her sister from Bryan, but so far nothing had arrived, nor had Breda mentioned the subject.

She was awakened in the dark, early hours by shrieks of delight and thudding running footsteps, and then both Kevin and Lily hurtled into the room like small tornadoes.

'Mammy! Mammy! You'll never guess what Santi's brought us!' Kevin cried, clambering on her bed. 'A scooter! A scooter all painted red and yellow with shiny wheels and handlebars!'

'And I've got new clothes for my dolly and a pram! A pram! It's just like a big one with pillows and sheets and everything! How did he get that down the chimney, Aunty Mary?' The little face was full of wonderment.

Mary smiled. 'Doesn't he have magic in his fingers, Lily? He can do anything. Anything he wants to, but only for children who are good and well behaved, especially at Mass.'

'Can we open the others now?' Kevin's face was glowing.

Mary shook her head. 'No, you can not! Do you know what time it is? It's still the middle of the night. You can open the others later.'

'Will I get more from Mam?' Lily asked. It was the best Christmas ever, she thought. Last year she'd got her precious doll and now she had a pram and everything to go in it. Her, little Lily O'Shea who had run barefoot at times, with a *pram*!

'Lily O'Shea, aren't you a greedy little rossie? Haven't you enough already? Now go back upstairs both of you and get into bed, or you'll catch cold and you'll wake Aunty Agnes and Uncle Albert.'

They disappeared with great reluctance and she hoped they'd not ignore her warning and start making a noise that would have the house up.

She lay back, thanking God that she had been able to bring pleasure and happiness into their lives, but soon her thoughts turned to Chris and this time she couldn't push them away. What kind of Christmas would he have in that overcrowded and none too clean house, with Gerry drunk and Flossie's terrible cooking and . . . Rosie? She lay awake, tears sliding down her cheeks, staring at the ceiling, consumed by such a longing for him that she knew there'd be no more sleep this morning.

Chris too lay looking at the cracked and damp-stained ceiling. The grey fingers of the December dawn that he could see through a chink in the curtains depressed him still further.

He'd tried the previous night to drown his sorrows, to blank out for a few hours his miserable existence, but no matter how much he drank it seemed to have no effect on him. He wished now he'd had a bottle of Dermot Ryan's 'wine'. Half a bottle of that and you wouldn't wake up until Boxing Day.

Rosie lay beside him asleep. She stank of body odour, stale cigarette smoke, cheap scent and the beer she'd drunk last night. She at least had achieved her goal, he thought bitterly. She'd been paralytic, barely able to stand, and he'd picked her up and thrown her on the bed, still fully dressed. She'd have a terrible hangover when she woke, he thought maliciously. Gerry had arrived home in the same state. There were times when he felt genuinely sorry for Flossie.

He hated his life. God, how he hated it. There was no comfort or companionship in it now. The only friends he had were his workmates. He tried hard to look as clean and as decently dressed as he'd been at home. It had become almost an obsession, the determination to show everyone that he hadn't sunk to *their* level. Rosie for her part seemed determined to be as shrewish and as slatternly as possible. She'd taken to going out with her mates from work a few times a week and did make a token effort with her appearance on these occasions. He couldn't care less where she went.

He turned away from her but the sight of the untidy room with its stale odours caused frustration to burn up in him. This was going to be the worst Christmas of his life. He couldn't believe that twelve months ago things were so very different. Then he'd slept in a clean bed in a clean and tidy house with his mam's Christmas dinner to look forward to. He could remember a time when they were all young when the meal had been a scratch affair and there'd been very little in the way of presents, the memory of which only increased his affection for his mam. Not a minute passed when she was idle. She worked harder than any man on the docks and always had done. She had cleaned offices in the evenings when all the staff had gone home, and that after a full day's work at home. She'd joined the army of cleaners who descended on the Cunard ships when they docked. His mother-in-law could have done the same, but she never had. She was too lazy.

And then there was Mary. He closed his eyes, remembering every detail of her appearance. Oh, God, he loved her so much it was a physical ache. Desperation claimed him again. There must be something he could do. There must be something she or his parents could do to extricate him from this living hell. He had never laid a finger on Rosie; even the thought had made him shudder with revulsion.

He sat up as an idea hurtled into his mind. Would it be possible to get the marriage annulled? It had never been consummated. The fact that their alleged affair had taken place before the wedding would be taken into consideration, and that would take time, but he could wait.

Hope surged through him. Why hadn't he thought of this before? It was a way out even if it took months, maybe even years. He could stand that if at the end of it it meant he could marry Mary.

Eagerly, he leapt out of bed, pulled on his clothes and raced down to the church, determined to speak to Father Hayes as soon as possible. He found the priest in the vestry, in the act of putting on the gold and white chasuble, the appropriate colours for Christmas morning. A small group of altar boys in starched white surplices were getting restless and noisy.

'Father, I'm so sorry to barge in like this, but I just had to come now. Is there . . . can I have a private word?'

'It'll have to be quick,' Father Hayes said before he turned to the boys. 'You will all go and stand near the door so you'll be ready, and there'll be less noise out of you too.'

Under a gaze they knew from experience meant trouble, they silently obeyed.

'Now, what has you down here all in a state?'

'Father, you know I never loved Rosie O'Hanlon. She tricked me.'

The parish priest nodded slowly. The true story had got back to him eventually.

'She did, but you're married, Chris, you took sacred vows.'

'I know that, Father but . . . I've never laid a finger on her in my life. Even at that party I never touched her. I was out cold. Could . . . could the marriage be annulled?'

Father Hayes stroked his chin. If all Chris Kennedy said was true, there would be grounds for annulment.

'You mean have it annulled because it has never been consummated?'

'Yes. Please, Father, would there be any chance?'

'That would depend if Rosie agrees with you.'

'I'm sure she would. She hates me. We hardly ever have what could be called a conversation.' His heart was racing. Oh, to be free of Rosie and that house.

'Go home and have a talk to her, unless you're staying for Mass?'

'No, Father, I'll be at the eleven o'clock with Mam and Dad, as usual.'

The priest nodded. 'It will take a long time, Chris. Don't expect it to be finalised next month, or even next year.'

'I won't mind how long it takes. Thanks, Father.'

'Happy Christmas, Chris.' The priest had already started to walk towards the group by the door.

'It is now, Father!' Chris called after him.

When he returned home Rosie was still asleep. He shook her hard.

She opened her eyes slowly. 'Oh, God, me head! Me bloody head!'

'Never mind your head. You brought it on yourself, which is more than I did last New Year. I want to talk to you.'

Rosie grimaced and raised herself up on her elbows.

'You've never wanted to before. Do you want to say "Happy Christmas"? Because if you do you can go to hell!'

It was just the right moment, he thought. She must be feeling terrible.

'I've been to see Father Hayes. I asked him about getting this sham of a bloody marriage annulled. I've never touched you. People think we slept together at that damned party, but we didn't, and anyway that was before I married you.' His eyes were bright, his voice full of conviction.

Rosie looked up at him. She felt awful and he hated her, he always had, and now she hated him for spurning her love. For spurning her. Well, he wasn't going to get away with this. He wasn't going to shame her by saying he'd never even kissed her, never mind anything else. Half the parish would be whispering and pointing and saying she was such a slut it was no wonder he wanted rid of her. It would be back to the old gossip that Rosie O'Hanlon couldn't get a husband without resorting to trickery.

Her eyes narrowed. 'You can do what you like but you'll not get me to agree to that! I'll say you and I often made love.' She laughed, then grimaced with pain. 'Love! That's a laugh, but she'll believe it. That one living in Bootle that you *do* love. Go to hell with your bloody annulment.' She lay back and closed her eyes. She could almost feel his anger and disappointment but she knew he would never raise a hand to her. It wasn't in his nature. She smiled to herself. Serve him right. He wasn't shaming her.

Chris stared at her. He could kill her! He could put his hands around her scrawny, dirty neck and squeeze the life out of her, then he'd be free. He'd be rid of her for ever. He should have known she'd not agree to anything that would let him go to Mary. She'd always hated Mary, but he'd never realised just how much until now. Hope had died, snuffed out by her malicious refusal. He slammed the door hard as he left the room, hoping it would increase her headache, but the sound only reminded him that she'd slammed the door on his only means of escape. He closed the front door behind him. The street was deserted as he walked up towards Scotland Road. If he had to walk the city streets all day and all night, he'd do it. He wasn't going to Mass with the O'Hanlons. It would hurt his Mam, his absence from church on Christmas morning, but he was too hurt and disappointed to care.

'It's a good thing it's only once a year,' Albert said jovially as Lily and Kevin tore off the paper to reveal more presents, their eyes shining, their cheeks flushed.

'Aren't you the lucky ones to have so many toys,' Mary laughed as she cleared up the paper after all the presents had been opened and hugs and thanks had been dispensed.

She'd put the turkey into the oven, and it should be nearly cooked when they all returned from church.

'That turkey smells delicious,' Albert said.

'As does the pudding,' Agnes added. She had made it

herself and it was now being steamed over a pan of hot water, wrapped in its muslin cloth. There were silver threepences in it as well as candied peel, raisins, sultanas and glacé cherries. Her face had lost the tired, pallid look that had worried Mary so much of late.

'Won't we all be as fat as pigs,' Breda added. There had been a card from Bryan but nothing else, which had peeved her. But then she hadn't bought him anything either and the feeling hadn't lasted long. She'd see him later on when they went up to Aunty Maggie's. She'd told Mary that she wasn't going to be left clearing up all by herself.

'Aren't we entitled to be for the day that's in it?' Mary laughed, but it was a laugh that contained a note of sadness.

It wasn't until after they'd all come back from New Brighton that Mary noticed that Agnes looked far from well. They'd all had a good time, and the weather had been kind for the ferry crossing. The river had been calm, and what wind there was was generated by the movement of the ferry itself. The buildings of the Liverpool waterfront stood out against a pale, duck-egg blue sky and rebuilding work on the church of St Nicholas had started.

'Agnes, you look badly.'

'Oh, I'm just tired, Mary. It's all the excitement of yesterday and today. I've never had such a good Christmas, and the look on the children's faces was a joy and a gift in itself.'

'Well, you go and have an early night. I'll bring you up some cocoa.'

'That would be nice. You know, yesterday morning at church, I gave thanks for all the happiness you've given me. Your company and Breda's, the children and Albert. I'm such a lucky old woman, for there's poor souls who have

273

no one and nothing. I would have been like them but for you, Mary. Come here and kiss me. I prayed too that you'd find someone.'

Tears started in Mary's eyes as she hugged the frail old lady. 'There's only one I want, you know that, and he . . . he's so far out of my reach that he might as well be thousands of miles away, like Albert's cousin in Canada. Go on up now, you need your rest. I feel worn out with it all myself,' she said, smiling though her tears.

She stood watching the pan of milk on the stove. If you didn't catch it just at the right moment it boiled over, and then the kitchen and the morning room would reek of it, the top of the stove and the pan would have to be scoured clean . . . but all such thoughts fled when she heard Breda's screams.

She dragged the pan off the stove and rushed up the stairs to find Breda on the landing, white with shock and trembling like an aspen in the wind.

She caught hold of her sister by the arms. 'Breda, in the name of God, what's the matter?'

Breda could barely speak. 'Agnes . . . Agnes . . .' she stammered.

Agnes's bedroom door was wide open and releasing Breda Mary pushed past her and nearly tripped over the limp form on the floor.

'No! Oh, Agnes, please, please don't leave us!'

She fell to her knees and took the hand of her benefactress in her own, but she knew she was too late. Everyone was too late. Agnes McPhail, who had been goodness itself to her, was dead. Time seemed suspended, then Albert was beside her and she looked up at him through a mist of tears.

She shook her head. 'She's . . . gone. I was making her

some cocoa just a few minutes ago and now . . . oh, Agnes! Agnes!'

Albert bent and took the old lady's other hand and felt for the pulse. There was none and he shook his head sadly.

'You're right, Mary. She's with God and her other family now. It was quick, and I'm sure she . . . wouldn't have suffered.'

He was shocked, although he told himself he shouldn't be. He'd seen so much of death. All during the war he'd been an air raid warden. It had often been his lot to bring the broken bodies of men, women and children from the rubble, and there had been some with horrific injuries. Then there were the lives he himself had snuffed out, but that was different. They'd been tried fairly and been sentenced by the law of the land.

He sighed heavily. 'I'll go to the phone box and ring the undertakers.'

Mary was still shaking her head in disbelief. 'She was good to me . . . to us . . .'

'She was, Mary. She was a good, kind, gentle woman and we must thank God that she lived to see what was the best Christmas in all our lives. You gave her that, Mary, and she blessed you for it, she told me so.'

Mary sat back on her heels and tried to pull herself together. She still held the tiny, claw-like hand.

'Tell Breda that when she's calmed down she's to go up to Aunty Maggie's. Do you not bring her to the church to lie?'

'No, we don't. It's not a custom here. She will be laid in her bedroom or the parlour, or the funeral people will take her to lie in a chapel of repose, I think it's called. It's a modern notion, I believe.'

'No . . . no, I couldn't let her lie alone in a place like that.

She'll lie here with us all until it's time to bring her to the church . . . and then . . .' She couldn't say 'the cemetery'. The words choked her and she began to sob quietly.

Albert picked her up and held her in his arms, as he'd done once before when fate, in the form of Chris Kennedy and Rosie O'Hanlon, had been so cruel to her. This time it was different, at least for him. He'd just lost a very dear friend and she'd gone to her rest not knowing about his profession. She'd given him a decent home and the pleasure of her company, and shown him every kindness in one form or another.

Mary had quietened a little when he took her out on to the landing where Breda still stood, white with shock. The two children were clinging to her, confusion and fear in their eyes. Lily had her thumb in her mouth, a habit they had thought had been broken.

He bent down. 'Kevin, Lily, your good, kind Aunty Agnes has gone to heaven.' He struggled with the emotion in his own voice. 'She was very old and God wanted her even more than we did. She's happy now, with her sister Hetty and her mother and father, so there's nothing to be frightened of.'

He stood up. 'Breda, child, get yourself ready and go on up to your aunt in Hornby Street. Tell her . . . tell her that everything here is rather chaotic and confused and could she possibly help us?'

Breda nodded wordlessly. She wondered dazedly if they were all going to be expected to stay the night in Hornby Street. Bryan would be there and she hoped he would be a comfort to her, but they'd have to share the room with Patsy. She was confused. She didn't even know if she wanted to go to Maggie's at all.

After they'd all gone, Breda and the children to catch the

bus and Albert to the phone box, Mary knelt by Agnes's side. Albert had lifted her from the floor and placed her gently on the bed. She smoothed the grey wisps of hair from the old lady's forehead. Oh, how she'd miss her. She'd given her much more than a home, she'd given her help and comfort and the benefit of all those years of millinery experience. This house had become home, a haven of peace, a place of warmth where the joyful laughter of children's voices had echoed through the rooms. She leaned over and kissed the parchment-like cheek.

'Thank you, Agnes, for everything. Your friendship, your kindness and generosity to take in the likes of us. You were a lady. May God be good to you.' She crossed herself and began the 'De Profundis'. Agnes hadn't been a Catholic but she knew that the Latin prayer for the dead would be well received.

Maggie had immediately agreed to come back with Breda. She had suggested that the children stay in Hornby Street but Breda knew they would have trouble with Lily and she couldn't stand any of Lily's screams or the stamping of feet. She'd smack the child and that wouldn't solve anything.

Albert opened the door to them. 'Mrs O'Shea, it was good of you to come yourself.'

'God luv her, she was the salt of the earth. Where's Mary?' Maggie dabbed at her eyes. She'd had great respect for the old lady.

'In the morning room. I made her come down while . . . they are up there.'

'That's the best thing,' Maggie agreed. She had come to offer the services of herself and Phil but could see they were not needed. 'Will I make a pot of tea – or will you do that, Breda, while I get these two to bed?'

'No, I'll take them in to Mary. It's best she puts them to bed. Sure, I haven't the heart to cope with them.'

Hadn't the heart, Maggie thought, and this was the one who was going to try to move the might of the Catholic Church, in the form of the Archbishop, to get married.

Maggie busied herself in the kitchen. Her mind was not on Agnes McPhail but on the good fortune of Mary. She had a home now, providing she was allowed to stay, of course, and Agnes had taught her everything there was to know about making hats. Yes, the woman had been kindness itself. She'd ask Father Hayes to say a Mass, even though Agnes McPhail had been Church of England, or Church of Scotland in her younger days. But her generosity would count for more than the difference of faith.

'She was a good woman. The sad thing was that for all these years she had no one, except the one with a face like the back of a bus up there on the mantel. She'd have made a good wife and mother,' Maggie said, passing a cup to Albert.

'She would,' Albert said shaking his head. 'You should have seen her face on Christmas morning, though. It was radiant with happiness. Her cheeks were like two rosy apples. She enjoyed every single minute of the day, as I did too. I've spent too many lonely Christmases.'

Maggie looked at him closely. He still baffled her, although he'd changed. He was more open, more chatty, more amiable.

'You know you were always welcome to join in with us. We never had much but we'd have shared it.'

'I know, but I wouldn't intrude. You wouldn't have

wanted me there if . . .' Grief and shock had made him vulnerable.

'If what?' Maggie sat down with her teacup.

Albert gazed down at his tea. Was it time to tell her?

'Have you no family at all?' Maggie was curious.

'A cousin who lives in Canada.' He was in control of himself again. This was not the time. There had been enough shocks of late.

'I see. When will it be, then? The funeral?'

'On Monday the thirtieth, at Christ Church in Hawthorne Road. Will you be attending, Mrs O'Shea?'

Maggie looked a bit worried. She'd never in her life set foot in any church except her own. She wasn't even sure how Father Hayes would react, but she nodded. Agnes McPhail had been a really good person, so she reckoned that God wouldn't mind an hour spent in a Protestant church.

Albert seemed to have read her mind. 'There is only one God, Mrs O'Shea, it's just that there are so many different paths to travel to reach Him.'

She nodded again. It was a very comforting thought.

'I'll go round the neighbours and see if anyone else wants to come. We usually go round the doors and collect a few coppers from everyone for a wreath, like. No matter how poor we are we all pay into the burial fund. Phil runs it. It's mortifying to be laid in a pauper's grave, really mortifying for everyone.'

'That's very kind of you, considering no one knew her in Hornby Street.'

'Well, those that did admired her, and even the ones who didn't heard only good about her from me and Phil.'

The following day Mary sent Breda to work and began the task of draping all the mirrors and picture frames in black.

She placed a wreath of laurel leaves intertwined with black crêpe on the front door. The curtains on all the windows that faced the road she closed over. It was a task convention demanded but she found heart-breaking.

Agnes was lying in her coffin upstairs in her room. On the third finger of her left hand Mary had placed the engagement ring she'd found in a small leather box in one of the drawers of the dressing table. The sight of it had brought on a fresh burst of sobbing. It looked so pathetic on the waxy, gnarled finger and she wished Victor Bramwell to hell and back. There were other things in the drawer but she'd ignored them. They'd keep until later, after the funeral when everything would have to be sorted out. Thank God she had Albert to help her.

They'd all been in to pay their respects, even the children. She'd taken them in and they'd stood in silence, hand in hand.

'She was good to us all and we loved her. Doesn't she look as if she's just asleep? And that's what it is and she'll wake up on the last day and we'll all be there with her in heaven.'

They'd both nodded and Lily dropped her silver cross and chain, which she'd been clutching tightly in her hand, into the coffin.

'I want her to have it now,' the child said simply.

Knowing how much Lily treasured it, Mary vowed to replace it. She picked it up and carefully arranged it on Agnes's breast.

They had just settled in for the night when there was a knock on the front door.

'Who on earth is this? Are we to get no peace at all?' Mary said wearily as she went to open it. Maggie and Jim and Phil and Bob Kennedy had already called to pay their respects and to tell her that they would be at the funeral on Monday, as would Flossie and Gerry.

'Our Bryan wanted to come too but I gave him the length of my tongue. He never knew her, he only wanted to come and see the other one,' Maggie had said sharply and Mary had nodded her agreement.

It was a wild night. There was no rain but it was blowing a force eight, Mary surmised, adding a quick prayer for anyone at sea tonight.

Chris was standing on the doorstep, his cap in his hand, his dark hair blown by the wind.

'Mary, I've come to see—'

She was astounded. 'No! You never even knew her.'

'Will you let me finish, please? It's you I've come to see.'

She stared at him, confusion in her eyes, a tide of sorrow washing over her.

'Mary, can I come in?' He was desperate. He knew how she must be feeling and wanted to take her in his arms and hold and comfort her.

'What for?'

'Because I know how much you cared for her and how upset you must be. Please . . .'

She took a step backwards. 'No, Chris. Haven't you caused me enough heartache already?'

'I hate Rosie, you know that. I hate her and I hate that house, it's like a pigsty! No one knows me around here, Mary, so I thought . . .'

'Albert knows you, and so do Breda and the children.' Her eyes widened as she began to grasp what he was trying to say. 'Sure to God, you haven't come here to ask can you stay?'

Life with her in this house would be paradise, even if he was only a lodger like Albert Fallowfield. And with Albert there to act as chaperon, he'd thought it would be possible.

'I . . . I thought . . . with Albert being here too . . .'

'For God's sake, Chris, go home! I'm a respectable widow. What future is there for us? Go home to your wife and for the love of God leave me in peace.'

She shut the door, but not before she had glimpsed an anguish and love to match her own in his eyes. She leaned with her back against the closed door. Oh, why had he come? There would never be a time for them. They had no future together, yet they loved each other passionately. She closed her eyes while the tears slid down her cheeks and she could taste their bitter saltiness on her lips.

Chapter Nineteen

Everything was confusing. Mary felt empty and drained, yet the others looked to her for support. She was glad of Albert's help and guidance. She knew she couldn't have coped alone. He had gone to Brougham Terrace to register the death after Dr Davidson had issued a death certificate. He had dealt with the undertakers and the vicar at Christ Church.

Maggie had been down to enquire further about the arrangements and to offer to do the refreshments.

'We'll all chip in with coupons, luv. How many will you be expecting back at the house?'

Mary tried to concentrate. 'I don't know, Aunty Maggie. I think it will be just family.'

'It's hardly worth bothering with, then. You three and the kids.'

'Yes, I know, but I have to do it, Aunty Maggie. It's what she would have wanted. For most of her life she had no one but your one over there who looks as if she's sucking a lemon and that skinflint uncle. I have to give her a decent funeral. I owe her that much, although it's a poor payment for what she's given me.'

Maggie had agreed and gone home to drum up support and coupons, wondering if they would ever be able to purchase things without the blasted ration books or whether they'd all go to their graves with the flaming things.

After she'd gone, Albert told Mary that she should visit Mr Grey, the solicitor.

'What for?' She didn't understand the need. Lawyers were people the likes of herself never visited. They were too high and mighty and charged a fortune.

'Agnes made me promise that if anything happened to her you would go and see him.'

'Why?'

'Because I think she's left you something in her Will. She told me she'd made a new one.'

'No, I don't want to go. I don't want anything. Haven't I enough already? All the things she gave me and taught me, and her understanding over Chris.' A thought crossed her mind for the first time. Would she have to leave this house that had been such a happy home for all of them?

'Would you ignore her request, Mary? Go against her wishes?' Albert said gently.

Mary sighed and shook her head. Put like that, how could she refuse?

'We'll go after the funeral. I'll come with you. These lawyers use about twenty fancy words to tell you what could be said in two or three in plain English. I've some experience with them.' His experience was strictly in the line of business. Usually there was one with the governor when a person was hanged.

Mary looked up at him with tears in her eyes. 'Where would I be without you? Where would we all be without you?'

'I miss her too, you know, Mary.'

'I know. We seemed to have turned ourselves into a real

family. I'd feel the same way if it were Aunty Maggie who'd died. But isn't it a wonderful thing to have you to lean on, to share my worries with. I hardly knew my da at all. Did I ever tell you that?'

Albert reached for her hand. 'Mary, I'm so . . . pleased and flattered that you consider me as a surrogate father . . . a sort of stepfather,' he added, seeing by her eyes that she didn't understand the word 'surrogate'. 'If only . . .'

She knew what he was thinking. If only there were some way she and Chris could be together.

'I know, but it's just not possible. At least I've got you and Breda to console me, although she's more of a hindrance than a help.'

'Is she still determined on Bryan?'

'Yes, but I don't think he's as keen as she is.'

'Don't worry, Mary, these things have a way of sorting themselves out. Just wait. Time resolves most things.'

Monday morning dawned grey and dismal with needle-fine rain pouring down steadily from a sky the colour of gun-metal. It made the pavements and the cobbles glisten and soaked into everything.

'God, isn't it a desperate day,' Breda said wearily, looking out into the street before she closed the curtains again. She had no heart for anything. Even Joyce and Maureen and Charlie couldn't jolt her out of this depression. And Bryan had been no comfort at all. In fact, apart from the few words they'd exchanged at Maggie's on the night Agnes had died, she'd not seen or heard anything from him. She supposed he was working and she'd heard what Maggie had said to him.

'Isn't it a huge church of theirs? At least, it looks huge from the outside, and I bet it's freezing cold inside.'

'Breda, for God's sake stop moaning. It's going to be a bad enough day as it is. Go and see that the children are ready.'

She'd been unsure about the wisdom of taking Kevin and Lily to a funeral, but Maggie had said it was the custom. Wasn't she herself present when her da had been buried in Glasnevin? Mary had tried hard to remember that day but she couldn't recall it.

Kevin and Lily would wear their best clothes but she had made a black armband for each of their coats. She and Breda had both taken a dress and a coat to be dyed by Johnson's, and Mary had stripped two black felt hats of their coloured ribbons and replaced them with black ones.

They were going in one car. Maggie, Phil and Flossie had brought up the sandwiches and pies and they were now in the larder with damp tea towels over them to keep them fresh. The neighbours from Hornby Street would make their way straight to the church. A lovely wreath had arrived early that morning with a simple message on the card: 'From everyone in Hornby Street. RIP.'

It had brought tears to Mary's eyes. Agnes would have been so pleased to think that people she hardly knew, complete strangers half of them, had been so kind and generous.

'Mary, the carriage is here,' Albert shouted up to her and after glancing in the mirror she went downstairs. Stairs that Agnes McPhail would never descend again.

All along the road to the church men in the street took off their caps and women stood, as they always did for any passing funeral, shaking their heads. Mary took some comfort from that mark of respect from perfect strangers.

Albert, with a black Cromby overcoat over his dark suit, a black tie that made his white shirt seem brighter and a black bowler hat on his head, sat between the children, holding their hands as they looked round, confused, upset and mystified by the behaviour of the people in the street. They didn't really know what it was all about.

'Do you think she can see us from heaven, Lily?' Kevin had asked as they'd sat on the sofa in the parlour, waiting for the hearse and car to arrive.

'I dunno, Kev, but we'd better be dead good in case she can. For today anyway. We go back to school soon so we'll have to behave then,' she replied sagely.

When they arrived Albert left them. He'd asked to help with carrying the coffin into church. It was his last mark of respect and gratitude to a woman who'd given him a home, the pleasure of her company and the small confidences and advice.

As Mary followed him into church with Breda and the children she saw Maggie and Jim, Phil and Bob Kennedy, Flossie and Gerry, all wearing black armbands and standing in the front pews. Then Mary's heart lurched. Chris Kennedy stood alone in the back pew, his cap in his hands. Their eyes met and then the tears that she had managed to control for the sake of the children overcame her and everything was a blur. Oh, why had he come? Didn't he know how upset she'd be? Or was it an attempt to comfort her by his presence? It was hard to tell, but she knew she wanted to run to him, throw her arms around his neck and sob out the grief and longing. She turned away from him and guided the children towards the empty front pew. The neighbours all crossed themselves as the coffin passed.

In the pew Kevin pulled at her coat and she bent down. 'What is it?'

'Mammy, there's no statues, and no pictures or candles

and lamps. It's cold, and why isn't the priest wearing the purple cloak thing? Won't Aunty Agnes be upset?'

'No, she won't be upset. Sure, they've taken them all away just for today. It's the sort of day when statues and pictures and candles and purple vestments don't fit in.' She sighed to herself. Lily too was looking at her for answers. How could she explain to them the differences in religion, when they'd been taught from their first day at school that there was only one true, Catholic and apostolic church?

Mercifully the service was short. The vicar extolled Agnes's virtues and gave thanks that the last months of her life had been enriched and made happy by Mary and Breda, Albert and the children.

As she followed the coffin back down the aisle, her neighbours followed her out, Phil and Bob Kennedy glaring at Chris.

'Fancy him having the sheer nerve to show up when poor Mary was so heartbroken,' Phil fumed to herself. Well, he'd feel the lash of her tongue later on. At least he'd had the sense to stand at the back and had not joined them in the front pews.

Mary held the two children closely. Kevin buried his face in her coat and Lily had her thumb in her mouth. Her hair had managed to escape from her hat and looked untidy. Albert had his arm round Breda's shoulder as the gravediggers lowered the coffin into the cold, damp earth. Mary wished she'd left Kevin and Lily at home. They were both in tears. They were too young for all this, far too young to take it all in, but maybe that was a blessing in disguise.

Again the prayers were few compared to a Catholic burial, but Mary was thankful. They were all cold and wet. Albert asked the vicar to return to the house with them but he refused politely.

'Can you see any of them down at the presbytery turning down an offer like that? And wasn't it all quick? He spoke very well of her, though, but didn't it feel odd?' Maggie hissed to Phil.

'It doesn't feel right, I'll say that,' Phil agreed. 'And I'm going to give meladdo there the length of my tongue for turning up here.'

Maggie nodded her agreement. Just what did Chris Kennedy think he was doing? He'd not known the woman; it was as plain as the nose on your face that he'd come just to see Mary.

As they left the graveside Phil turned away, looking for her son. She saw him making a beeline for Mary and the children and deliberately rushed to place herself between them.

'Don't you even think about it! You're not going to upset that poor girl still further. Why aren't you at work? Why did you come?'

Chris looked at the figure of Mary disappearing down the pathway towards the road.

'Mam, I had to come. I had to see her. I wanted to speak to her, that's all, I promise,' he pleaded.

'Well you can't. She's gone. She's gone back in the car to Exeter Road and don't you even think about showing up on the doorstep because if you do your da will throw you out unless I get there before him and do it myself!'

He looked down at her, pain and despair in his eyes, and for a second he saw it reflected in his mother's eyes.

'Oh, Mam, I'm so miserable. I wish . . . I wish I could emigrate, but I'd never see Mary again. On Christmas Day I tried to get *her* to agree to an annulment, but she wouldn't. She hates me but she still won't go along with it.'

'I think we've all heard enough about dispensations without starting on annulments too,' Maggie intervened. She'd had a row with Bryan that morning and it was over Breda. Like Chris Kennedy he'd only used the funeral as an excuse.

'Chris, leave Mary alone. Hasn't she enough on her plate?'

'Mam!' he pleaded.

'If you land on her doorstep I'll tell Mr Fallowfield to deal with you,' Maggie added.

Chris glanced from one to the other and knew he'd failed yet again. Now he had no inclination to go back to work. He'd head for the nearest pub and stay there until he was either thrown out or clean out of money.

He spent the hours after the burial in the Bedford pub but by two o'clock his money had run out and he was far from being as drunk as he'd hoped to be. He'd just have to make his way home, he told himself morosely. But he'd go slowly, at a snail's pace. Home, he thought, some 'home' in one dirty, smelly room where it was impossible to keep his things decent and tidy, thanks to his equally dirty, smelly and unattractive wife.

Try as he would he couldn't get the sight of Mary out of his mind. Even dressed entirely in black she'd looked elegant and beautiful. Her eyes had been full of tears when she'd looked at him in the church. She was everything Rosie was not.

He knew that Flossie and Gerry would stay on at Mary's house. His mam would too, but his da would go back to work, as would Jim O'Shea. They needed the money. It was a measure of the depth of their respect for the old lady that they'd given up a morning's work. When they returned this evening there would be a good fire in the range and a decent meal ready to be served to them. And what would be waiting for him? Nothing and no one. He'd had enough. No one wanted him, except Mary, and even though she loved him the fact that he was married kept them apart. Everything was such a bloody mess and he was desperate enough to leave. He'd pack what few things he had and get the hell out of that midden.

By the time he alighted from the bus he'd sobered up a little and he'd made up his mind. He was going. There was nothing left to keep him here now. As a skilled man he'd have no trouble getting a job in another town. Nearly all the cities in the north had suffered from the bombing. Hull, he'd heard, was in a worse state than Liverpool, as was Coventry. He'd have no trouble getting work.

He never carried all his money on him, it wasn't safe. It was his mam's advice to him when he'd first started work and he'd always adhered to it. He had some savings because he only turned up enough to Flossie for his own keep. Rosie worked and he wasn't bloody well keeping her, he'd yelled at her when the subject had first arisen. Having to share the same room with her was bad enough. He kept his money in an empty Brasso tin under the floorboards, which were covered by the filthy lino, and Rosie didn't know about it. He had enough to get him to Hull and pay for lodgings for a week. He'd have work by then. He'd make a fresh, clean break. Try to rebuild a life for himself, away from Rosie and her family but also away from Mary.

As he pushed open the front door the familiar odours assailed his nostrils. God, it would be great to come home to a house that didn't smell like a sewer. As he put his hand on the doorknob he thought he heard noises coming from inside the room. He paused. The kids were both out, *she'd* gone to work and his parents-in-law were up at Mary's. There was nothing in Flossie's house that was worth stealing, except maybe the wireless set and that was so heavy that no one in their right mind would bother taking it. He turned the knob cautiously and the door opened silently.

On the unmade bed Rosie lay half naked while Joe Fletcher from Portland Street was straddled across her.

A fury began to rise in him, so violent that it made him start to shake uncontrollably and a red mist seemed to cloud his vision.

'You bloody little whore! You lying, cheating bitch! Gone back to your old habits, have you?' he roared, making a grab at Joe Fletcher's hair.

Rosie screamed as Joe twisted away out of Chris's grasp. He grabbed his clothes and lunged past Chris, running at full belt down the lobby and out of the front door.

Chris made no attempt to stop him. His anger wasn't for Joe Fletcher. It was centred directly on his wife who was now clutching the grey army blanket to her to hide her nakedness.

'You're . . . you're supposed to be at work! Why are you home?' Rosie was quaking with fear. She'd never seen him like this. In fact she hadn't thought he had a temper.

Chris crossed to the bed and stood looking down at her.

'Because I went to a funeral. So, how long has this been going on? How many times have you been rolling around in that bed with anyone who'd have you? I suppose you charge these days.' It wasn't the fact that she'd been unfaithful he cared about, but the position she'd put him in.

He grabbed her by her shoulders and yanked her out of bed.

'You were a whore when I married you and you'll always be a whore! How many fellers will be in the pubs boasting how they've had it off with *my* wife?'

'None! It was only Joe and it was only a couple of times. I was lonely, you never wanted me, and I love you!' she sobbed.

'Love! A bitch like you doesn't even know what love is. To you it's lying on your back getting screwed by anyone who can stand the smell of you. And I lost Mary because of you!'

For a second the pain of losing Mary gripped him, then was added to his fury. Rosie screamed again as his hand caught her across the side of her head. Lights danced sickeningly before her eyes but she hadn't time to even scream before the second blow caught her, knocking her off balance. She fell heavily, her head catching the corner of the cast-iron fire grate.

It was fully thirty seconds before Chris realised she wasn't going to get up. The sight of her sprawled at his feet didn't bother him; she'd done this before. She'd been acting and acting well on the night she'd trapped him. Then she'd feigned a drunken stupor, now she was pretending to have fainted. Well, he was up to her tricks now.

'Get up, you bitch! You don't fool me, I know you too well.' He prodded her inert form with the toe of his boot. She didn't move so he bent down and caught her by the shoulders, trying to drag her to her feet. Only when her head lolled to one side and he saw her wide and staring eyes did he begin to panic.

She couldn't be dead. It was a trick. She'd fainted.

He hadn't hit her that hard. Just two sharp slaps, that was all.

'Stop this bloody nonsense, Rosie! Stop it!' he yelled, shaking her. But to his dawning horror he realised that she wasn't acting. She was dead. He let her fall back to the floor and it was only then that he saw the dark stain on the edge of the fire grate. He started to tremble again but this time it was with fear.

I've killed her! Holy Mother of God, I've killed her! I never meant to. Sweet Jesus, I never meant to kill her! She was a cheating little whore. I was only doing what any husband would do! I didn't even beat her up. It was only two slaps. Oh, God help me! Panic took hold of him. He'd be arrested, tried for murder and hanged. Even now he could feel the rope cutting into his neck. He had to get away from here as quickly as he could.

Distractedly he stuffed a few clothes into a brown paper carrier bag, the only thing he could find. Then he pulled and dragged at the lino and prised up the floorboard. Snatching up the tin that contained his savings he stuffed it into his pocket. He'd go out the back way, down the jigger. No one would see him. The kids hadn't come in for their tea yet, most of the neighbours would be working or out shopping. He'd get down to the pier head and sign on for any ship that was leaving Liverpool. By the time someone found her and they'd thought of him, he'd be away, sailing down the Mersey towards the open sea, and he would never come back.

His heart was pounding in his chest, making breathing difficult, and as he at last reached the junction of Vostock Street and Hornby Street he collided with a small girl whom he instantly recognised as Patsy O'Shea. He caught her by the shoulders and shook her hard.

'You've not seen me, Patsy, do you hear? You never set eyes on me. Promise!' He shook her so hard that her teeth chattered and she nodded with terror in her eyes. Chris Kennedy was one of the quietest people she knew, and here he was acting like a lunatic. She'd skived off school for the afternoon. Everyone was out so she'd get away with it. She'd just sidled out when a lad she'd never seen before had come running out of the O'Hanlons' house. He had trousers on but no shirt or jacket or boots. She'd watched him stop, put on his boots and shirt, then run again and now it looked as if Chris Kennedy was going mad too.

Patsy ran as soon as he'd released her and didn't stop until she got to the top of the jigger. When she looked back over her shoulder he had gone.

Chapter Twenty

It was Carmel O'Hanlon, the youngest of Flossie's kids, who came running to Maggie with tears streaming down her ashen face and terror in her eyes.

Maggie caught the child to her. Carmel was shaking and close to hysteria.

'In the name of God, Carmel, luv, what's the matter?'

'It . . . it's . . . our Rosie. Where's me mam and da? I want me mam! Our Rosie's lyin' on the floor and she's got blood in her hair and she's not moving,' the child informed Maggie between racking sobs.

Maggie crossed herself and disentangled herself from Carmel's clutches.

'You stay here, child. Don't cry. It's probably just a fainting fit. Hush, now. Our Patsy will be in soon.'

Maggie knew that there'd be no sign of Flossie yet. She had been determined to stay in Bootle as long as Gerry and so divert him from wandering into the nearest pub on the way home. After the scene in the churchyard Chris had presumably gone back to work and by rights Rosie should have been at her job too. What in God's name had happened?

There was no answering cry as she called all the O'Hanlons'

names in turn. The door to the front room was standing wide open and she could see a pair of bare legs protruding from behind it.

She went inside and gave a cry of horror as she realised that Carmel had been right. She bent down over Rosie and touched the powdered and rouged cheek. It was barely warm, and she'd seen too much of death not to know that Rosie's soul had left her body. Then she saw the dark stain that had spread on to the lino and was now congealing.

'Oh, God almighty!' she cried, crossing herself. Who would do this kind of thing to the girl? She could now see that Rosie was half naked. Just what had been going on? She sat back on her heels, her face white and drawn with shock. Oh, Liverpool was often a violent city, but nothing like this had ever happened around this neighbourhood.

She got up, dragged the quilt off the bed and covered Rosie with it, closing with difficulty the girl's sightless eyes. She'd send Patsy for Father Hayes and she herself would have to call the police. The girl had been murdered, but it seemed to her that Rosie hadn't put up much of a fight. Maybe she'd known whoever it was. A sudden thought hurtled into her mind. Chris! She racked her brains: what was it he had been saying? Something about Rosie and an annulment? But no! No, it couldn't have been Chris. He wasn't capable of doing something like this. Not even when he was drunk, which wasn't very often at all, would he use such violence. Flossie often said he must be a saint to put up with their Rosie and not raise a hand to her.

She looked down at the girl, wondering whether she had been here with someone else. She wouldn't put it past her, but she'd have to go back now and see to the kids before going to the police.

Patsy was in and she was as white-faced as Carmel, who was still sobbing.

'Get yourself down to see Father Hayes. Tell him that Rosie O'Hanlon is . . . dead. Go on now and be quick about it.' Maggie's voice was sharp.

Patsy looked up at her with terror.

'What's the matter with you, for God's sake? Go on! I'll have to go to the police station so they can at least get Flossie and Gerry back home.'

'Mam . . . Mam . . . I saw a feller come dashing out of their house an' he only had his trousers on. He stopped to put his boots on. I've never seen him around here. An' . . . an' then . . . Chris Kennedy . . .'

'Chris Kennedy what?' Maggie demanded, leaving aside Patsy's truancy and the mystery man for now.

'He was running down the jigger and . . . he . . . shook me and made me . . . promise I'd say . . . I'd . . . not seen him! Oh, Mam! Carmel said . . . is she really dead?'

Patsy was clearly shaken and it would be best to give her something to do to take her mind off Rosie.

'Yes, she is. Now get off with you, and I'll sort you out later, melady. On your way, ask Carrie Quinne to come up here to look after Carmel and Jimmy, when he decides to come home, that is.'

Dragging on her coat Patsy ran from the room. It was terrible, terrible. Rosie had been murdered. She knew it. Carmel and her mam wouldn't say Rosie was dead if she wasn't, and Mam was going for the police. She was glad that when she returned she wouldn't be on her own. She would have the parish priest with her.

Maggie was almost gasping for breath by the time she reached Athol Street police station and pushed open the door.

'What's up, luv? You're in a right state about something.' The desk sergeant looked at her with concern. She had neither coat, hat nor shawl and it was freezing. Obviously it was serious trouble.

'I . . . I'll be . . . fine . . . in . . .'

'Here, sit down on this bench and get your breath before you tell me what's wrong.'

Maggie nodded her thanks and sank down on the long wooden bench against the wall which usually seated members of the criminal fraternity, drunks, ladies of the night and pimps until such time as they were removed to the cells.

He came and sat beside her.

'Is that better now?'

She nodded again. 'There's been a death . . . a murder. Number fifteen Hornby Street, opposite our house. It's a girl named Rosie O'Hanlon . . . Rosie Kennedy,' she amended.

The sergeant looked grave. A certain Gerry O'Hanlon of the same address had spent a few nights here in the past.

'Flossie and Gerry are at a funeral in Exeter Road, Bootle. They . . . they . . . don't know. Her younger sister found her when she got in from school. Then I went over.'

'Did you touch anything?'

'No. Only her, to see if she was . . . breathing. I . . . I closed her eyes and covered her up.'

'How do you know it was murder?'

'There was blood on the floor, on the lino and the fireplace. Look, can't all these questions wait? Can't you get her mam and dad home? Me nerves are in pieces. God help her poor mam, because you can bet your life Gerry will be no use at all.'

The sergeant nodded, his expression grim. 'I'll phone Bootle Constabulary. They'll go out to them. Now you get back home. I'll send one of my lads down to stay until the CID arrive. There will be a Scene of Crimes Officer too, so don't move anything.'

'My girl, Patsy, saw a feller running away from the house. She'd never seen him before.'

'I'll make a note of that.'

Maggie got up. 'When those fellers in Bootle tell them, can you tell them that I'll be waiting at the top of the street for them, by the bus stop. Oh, poor, poor Flossie. She's had a rotten life, and now this.'

'I'll do that. Now you go home, Mrs . . . ?'

'O'Shea. Maggie O'Shea. I live at number eighteen.'

'You should have put a coat or a shawl or something on. You've had a nasty shock, so get some sweet tea down you when you get home.'

She left and walked home as quickly as she could. When she arrived Father Hayes was sitting in the kitchen.

'Maggie, just what has been going on? The girl is dead, but I've anointed her just the same.'

Maggie sat down opposite him. Of Patsy and Carmel there was no sign.

'Where are the kids, Father?'

'They're upstairs. I sent them up. I told Patsy to wrap Carmel and Jimmy up in a blanket or quilt.'

'So, he's home.'

The priest nodded. 'I stood at the door to catch him before he went into the house. He knows his sister is dead, but that's all.'

She sighed. 'I don't know what to believe, Father. I know Rosie was a little tramp and our Patsy said she saw a strange feller running, half dressed, from the house. Then she says she met Chris Kennedy running down the back jigger and he made her swear she'd not seen him. The police will be here soon. What am I to tell them, Father?'

Father Hayes remained silent as he digested Maggie's words and their implications. Rosie had been a little tramp and obviously she was being unfaithful, but he couldn't see Chris Kennedy, a lad he'd always liked and felt sorry for, doing anything as dreadful as this. Perhaps he'd come home early and caught Rosie. Or maybe the murderer was the man Patsy saw running away and Chris had come in and found Rosie already dead, panicked and run.

'The truth, Maggie. That Carmel came to you, you went over and then Patsy told you she'd seen this man running from the house.'

'But what will I say about Chris Kennedy? I don't want him blamed. You know he'd never do anything like that, Father.'

'I know, but Chris could have come home and found her already dead. Can Patsy say how long it was between her seeing this man and meeting Chris Kennedy?'

'I just don't know, Father. Will you stay with us when they come? You know what those CID fellers are like.'

He nodded, knowing also that before long Jim O'Shea and Bob Kennedy would be home. He got to his feet.

'I'll just go over and see Mrs Kennedy.'

'I told the police I'll wait for Flossie and Gerry at the bus stop, but tell Phil to come over here.'

'I will. Now get your coat on, it's freezing out there.'

Mary was with them when they at last alighted from the bus. She'd left Albert and Breda in charge of the children.

She hugged her cousin. 'Aunty Maggie, poor Mrs O'Hanlon is in a terrible state. Is it true? Is she really dead? The police came and took them into the parlour.'

'It's true, Mary. It's . . . terrible. Come here, Floss, luv, hold on to me and Mary,' Maggie instructed her distraught neighbour. 'Gerry can hang on to anything that comes to hand or he can crawl. Bloody drunk again. Mary, why didn't you chuck him out?'

'Albert wanted to but I couldn't. Mrs O'Hanlon was having a pleasant afternoon and I just hadn't the heart to spoil it for her!'

'Never mind him now. Let's get poor Flossie home.'

Together they supported Flossie, followed by a swaying, staggering Gerry, until they reached Maggie's house. There was a black police car outside the O'Hanlons' house and in Maggie's kitchen a worried-looking Phil was talking to a uniformed policeman.

'Mary, luv, put the kettle on. We all need something to steady our nerves. Will you have one as well?'

'I will, thanks, missus,' the policeman replied.

'What are they . . . doing . . . over there?' Flossie managed to get the words out with difficulty.

'Oh, looking for fingerprints, looking for a weapon, things like that.'

'When can I . . . see her?'

'They'll come for you before they take her to the city mortuary.' Seeing the added distress his words had caused he carried on: 'Don't let that upset you, luv. The doctor has to see her, an inquest will be opened and then the coroner will give a verdict and she'll come home to you for the funeral.' He hated this part of his job. He didn't mention that the doctor would be a pathologist and that Rosie's body would be, in all probability, cut open. It was a matter of course at a post-mortem, but she'd be sewn up again and made to look decent. The undertakers would be called in and they'd make her look as if she were asleep.

Flossie wiped her streaming eyes and turned to the priest. 'Oh, Father, who'd do such a thing? I . . . I know she wasn't perfect, but . . .'

'Calm yourself now, Flossie. That's what the police are doing over there. Trying to find out who would do such a thing by looking for fingerprints, any clue at all . . .'

Phil's eyes met Maggie's and Maggie saw fear in them and she knew Phil was thinking of Chris. She wished she could say to her friend that he was at work and would be home shortly, but would he?

Mary handed round the cups of tea, just as shocked as the rest of them. It couldn't have been Chris, she thought. She knew it. It just wasn't in his nature.

For a while silence reigned until a CID inspector came into the room.

The constable hastily placed the cup on the floor and stood up.

'Which of you is the girl's mother?'

'I . . . I am, sir,' Flossie said with a sob in her voice.

'Then you can go over now. They've finished, for the time being anyway. The ambulance will be here soon.' He turned to his uniformed colleague. 'Have you informed her of the procedure?'

'I have, sir,' he replied, thinking how bloody cold and officious the man was. In fact they all were.

Flossie got to her feet, aided by Maggie. She turned to the priest.

'Father, will you come across with me? Gerry's . . .'

'Drunk again,' Maggie interrupted acidly. Poor Flossie would get no support from him, as usual.

'You come back over here when you're ready, Floss. We'll see to the kids as well, you're in no fit state. Gerry can flaming well see to himself.'

When they'd gone the inspector turned to Maggie. 'I believe your daughter saw someone leaving the house?'

'She did. Shall I get her down?' Maggie was praying that any minute Jim would walk through the door, for she needed his support. Bryan and Maurice would have to fend for themselves for a meal tonight.

'If you don't mind, Mrs O'Shea.'

As if in answer to her prayer Jim and the two lads walked into the kitchen.

Jim glanced around the room. 'What the hell's going on here? Why is the street crawling with you lot?' he demanded of the inspector.

Maggie spoke first. 'Maurice, get down to Pauline's, and Bryan, go and get Bob. Phil needs him here.'

The lads did as they were told and then the inspector informed Jim of the circumstances of Rosie's death.

'What was our Patsy doing running the streets instead of being in school?' Jim demanded of his wife.

'I haven't got round to that yet. Don't be too hard on her, Jim, she's frightened and shocked as it is. I'm going up for her now.'

Jim stood with his back to the range, stunned, and as Bryan appeared with Bob Kennedy he just shook his head, not knowing what to say, trying to think of something informative, but nothing that would throw any suspicion over Chris whom no one seemed to have set eyes on, unless he was just late home from work.

Patsy was terrified and shaking, despite her mother's protective arm around her.

'Now, young lady, will you tell me just who you saw, what they were doing and, if you can remember, something about the time.' His voice was much softer and kinder.

'Go on, luv, you tell him. There's nothing to be frightened of,' Maggie urged.

Haltingly Patsy told them all she knew, and as she did so Phil caught her husband's arm and clung to it.

'But you don't know how long it was after you saw this man running away that you met Chris Kennedy in the entry?'

'No. No, sir, I wasn't noticing.' Patsy continued: 'I . . . I had skived off . . .' She looked up at her father. 'I did it because they wouldn't let me go to the funeral, like our Lily.'

'That's all right, Patsy. And funerals aren't picnics, anything but. Can you tell this officer what the man looked like?'

Patsy did her best and it was all written down. Then Mary intervened. She was worried sick about Chris.

'It was the funeral of a lady I lived with who had shown me great kindness, Miss Agnes McPhail. We live in Exeter Street – myself, my sister Breda, my son Kevin and Aunty Maggie's little girl, Lily. And Mr Albert Fallowfield.'

The effect Albert's name had on the faces of the policemen was very noticeable and she prayed they wouldn't tell everyone here just how they knew about him.

'Thank you, miss.'

'It's Mrs. Mrs Mary O'Malley.'

Both notebooks were put away and the CID man turned to the uniformed constable.

'Get back to the station and run this description through the mugshots. If it fits then go and find the bloody culprit.'

'I'll need a warrant.'

'You won't need a bloody warrant. Just haul the bastard in and I'll see to him.'

They both left as quickly as they'd arrived, the constable tight-lipped and resentful.

Maggie sent Patsy back upstairs with the jam butties Mary had made for the children. Mary seemed to be the only one who was doing anything. Everyone else was sitting in silence, just staring at each other.

Flossie had calmed down a bit and between them Jim and Bob had got Gerry home and to bed. Rosie had been taken by ambulance to the mortuary at the Royal Infirmary.

'I can't take it in. I . . . I just can't believe . . . that she's . . .' Flossie again broke down in tears.

Maggie went to comfort her while Phil and Mary took the dirty cups into the tiny scullery.

'Oh, Mrs Kennedy, sure to God he couldn't do such a thing?' Mary was distraught.

'No. No, I know he couldn't do it. It's just not in his nature. He's like Bob. He'd be furious inside but he would say nothing, let alone do anything. He must have walked in and found her dead and then panicked. Oh, I just wish he could walk in the door this minute, then we'd know for certain. I . . . I was so hard with him for turning up at the funeral. He wanted to speak to you, but Maggie and I stopped him. God knows where he is now. All we can do is pray he went to work, or maybe stopped off at a pub where someone would tell us how long it was before he left.'

'What will we do if he doesn't come back tonight?' There was fear in Mary's voice.

'I don't know, Mary. Oh, I wish he'd married you before that bloody party!'

'I wish he had too. There have been so many nights when I've cried myself to sleep over him. I love him, Mrs Kennedy, and I always will.'

Phil hugged her and Mary clung to the woman she had once thought would be her mother-in-law.

'Will we make more tea?' Phil asked. 'I'm awash with the stuff but what else is there to do?'

'I'll do it. You go and sit in with them. Poor, poor Mrs O'Hanlon. I feel so sorry for her. Oh, it's been a desperate day altogether.'

A few minutes later, when Mary appeared in the doorway with the teapot, she walked into a row, for everyone's nerves were in tatters.

'For God's sake, Flossie, she was a little tart and she was at it again! Didn't Patsy tell the police that she saw that feller running away, half dressed? What was he doing down here, and why was she home from work in the afternoon when she knew everyone would be out? She tricked our Chris. You know that. We should never have forced them to get married. We were only thinking of our pride. He begged me to let him come home. He hated her! She was a dirty little slut.'

'She didn't deserve to die, Phil! She wasn't much good, I'll say that myself, but she didn't deserve to have her head bashed in. I saw her. She . . . she . . .'

'All right, the pair of you, that's enough,' Jim said firmly.

Flossie ignored him. 'Then where is he? Where is that precious bloody son of yours who can do no wrong?'

'Hiding somewhere, frightened to death to come home in case he'll be blamed instead of that feller.'

'I said that's enough, the pair of you! Tearing each other apart won't help anyone!' Jim thundered.

Mary handed round the cups of tea with shaking hands. Oh, Chris, where are you? Please, please come back. I'm sure you've nothing to fear. Just come home, she prayed silently.

Chapter Twenty-One

The appointment with Mr Grey was for eleven o'clock the following Monday and it wasn't something Mary was looking forward to even before Rosie's death. She was still upset over Agnes and now Chris seemed to have gone missing.

'Mary, it's best if you occupy your time,' Albert had advised, and so the next day they started the harrowing task of going through all Agnes's things.

Sorting out her wardrobe was particularly painful for Mary as she'd seen Agnes wearing most of the dresses. She held each one tightly, pressing it against her cheek and breathing in the smell of lavender before adding it to the pile on the bed.

'What will I do with all these things? They're too good to go to the rag man. Some of them are beautiful. Look at the beadwork on this. I can't let it go, it would break her heart, I know it would.'

Albert was sympathetic. 'Then anything you think you can utilise keep, the rest we'll send to the Salvation Army. They'll find a good use for them.'

'Oh, this is desperate, really desperate. I feel like some kind of a vulture picking over her things.' Mary shuddered.

'I don't like it either, Mary, but it has to be done. We'll start on the dressing table next.'

They worked in silence, Mary's heart heavy with grief for Agnes and worry for Chris. Every minute she expected to hear a knock on the front door and find Aunty Maggie or Phil standing there to tell her that he'd come home. She brushed away a tear at times as she thought of him or she discovered one of the laced-edged handkerchiefs Agnes had favoured or a rope of beads that harked back to the '20s but which Agnes had often worn.

'Albert, will you help me? Isn't this drawer stuck fast. I think there's something jamming it.'

Albert peered at the drawer, weighed up the problem and then decided the best way to get it open was just to use brute force. It gave at the second pull and gloves and lace modesty vests were scattered all over the floor. Carefully Mary gathered them together. All the gloves were so tiny that they would have fitted Lily, but she had no intention of giving them to the child. They were all well worn, and anyway Lily would lose them. She might be able to use the lace to trim something for the child, though. Agnes would like that, she thought sadly.

'What's the matter with the drawer?' she asked Albert who had failed, despite much manoeuvring, to replace it.

'There's something stuck at the back of it. Probably something from the next drawer down that's obstructing it.' He put his hand inside the space and felt around.

'It's a book, or some papers or something. I've got it now.' He pulled out a thin and battered leather-bound booklet with a faded piece of lined writing paper sticking out of the top.

'What on earth is that?' she asked.

Albert opened it and the letter fell to the floor. Mary picked it up and read it.

'It's from Henrietta – Hetty – McPhail to Agnes. She says if she should die first Agnes will have the money Uncle Duncan left. She says she won't give it to her now – that must have been years ago – because Agnes tends to be extravagant!' Mary was incredulous. 'Extravagant! Sure, Agnes was far from that. Didn't she offer us a home to help pay the bills? Didn't she tell me when I first brought her home here that she could only afford to pay someone to clean for a couple of hours a week?'

'Well, if she'd known about this she'd not have worried, or had any need to take us all in.'

Mary looked at him quizzically. 'Why so?'

Albert passed her the book. It was a bank book. A Martin's Bank book and Mary gasped at the neat row of figures.

'She . . . she left three hundred pounds and ten shillings. More than three hundred pounds hidden away and Agnes couldn't afford a decent fire!'

'She was a very parsimonious woman, I'd say.'

Mary's brow furrowed in a frown. 'A what?'

'Mean. Hetty McPhail was as mean as their Uncle Duncan by the look of it. But why did she hide it like that? She must have known Agnes might never find it. She never needed to pull the drawers right out. She was tidy. The furniture might have been sold and then the money might have been lost for good.'

'What will we do with it?' Mary asked.

'Take it to the solicitor and see what he says. I suppose technically it should be included in Agnes's estate.'

'Oh, to think she stinted herself when she could have

lived in luxury. Wasn't that a desperate thing to do, to hide it?'

Albert nodded. 'But then we would never have become a family of sorts. And you, Breda and the children made her so happy. She loved the children especially. I think I'll always remember her face on Christmas morning.'

'Don't forget the hours you gave her. You enjoyed the same things. *You* made her happy too.'

'She . . . all of you have brought joy and purpose into my life. Something I never expected.' Albert fought to control his emotions. He loved them all.

Mary wiped her eyes. That sight on Christmas morning was something she, too, would remember for the rest of her life. It was worth far more than all the wealth. Something even her love and anxiety for Chris couldn't dim.

Mr Grey's name was very apt for his office. It was a dim, dusty, poky affair on the second floor of a building in Castle Street. He himself looked grey and dour too, Mary thought as he bade them sit down. Grey hair, charcoal grey suit and an old-fashioned winged collar and grey cravat. He smoothed a piece of paper out on his desk.

'Before you start, sir, I'd like to say that we found these amongst Miss McPhail's belongings. We think you should see them.' Albert passed over the bank book and the letter.

Mr Grey read the letter carefully and then examined the bank book just as carefully.

Mary felt completely out of her depth. She was happy to let Albert do all the talking.

'We believe . . . in fact we know for certain that Miss Agnes did not even suspect let alone know of their existence.'

Mr Grey nodded. 'Then it will be included with the contents of Miss Agnes McPhail's Will. Are you Mrs Mary O'Malley?'

'Yes, sir, I am,' Mary said quietly.

'Then I am going to read out Miss McPhail's last Will and Testament which she had drawn up in August of last year.'

Mary sat in silence while in a flat, detached tone he told her that the house and all its contents now belonged to her, as did the money in the bank book. There were small bequests for Breda and Albert and even Kevin and Lily.

Mary couldn't take it all in, but one thing did stand out in her fogged mind. She wouldn't need to replace the silver cross and chain that Lily had placed in the coffin. Agnes had left the child a gold one. For Kevin there were five gold sovereigns, which were getting scarce these days. For Albert there was a gold half-hunter watch and chain that had belonged to Uncle Duncan, and for Breda a silver brooch set with amethysts and earrings to match – the first pieces of expensive jewellery either of the girls had owned. All the rest was cheap and cheerful, except for Mary's wedding ring that was now just a memory.

'Do you understand it all, Mrs O'Malley?' Mr Grey asked gravely.

Mary was dazed. 'I . . . I think so.'

'Then I'll draw up the necessary documents to transfer the deeds of the property to you. I will also see that a new bank account and book is opened. I think that covers everything for now.'

They rose and Albert took Mary's arm to steady her. When they got outside she looked up at him.

'Was that right? Did I dream it?'

'It was and it was no dream. The house, the furniture and the money are yours now, Mary.'

Mary pressed her hands to her cheeks. 'Oh, Holy Mother of God! I didn't want her to die. I didn't want her house or the money. How can I ever thank her now?'

Albert patted her shoulder. 'She knew when she changed her Will that you'd be grateful, Mary. That you'd see to the upkeep of her house. Her home,' he amended.

'Grateful is it? Don't I owe her everything! She took us in, she taught me all her skills. She told me all about Victor Bramwell and how he deserted her, so she helped me to cope with being rejected and shamed by the man you love in front of everyone in your life. Oh, Albert, I'll miss her so much. She even thought of Kevin and Lily. I'll keep the sovereigns and the cross and chain until they are old enough to appreciate them. Oh, God bless her.'

'I'll say amen to that, Mary.'

Tears of gratitude sparkled on Mary's dark lashes. 'She couldn't give me the thing I wanted most so she's given me everything else. I'll never have to worry over money now or a roof over our heads.'

'Ours?' Albert questioned.

'Yes, ours. Sure to God you didn't think I'd put you out? It's your home . . . it's *our* home.'

He smiled down at her. 'Thank you, Mary.'

'There's no need for thanks. Don't we all look to you for advice and much, much more. Don't you know you're head of this assorted family of children who run away, a bold rossie who has her heart set on someone who doesn't really love her, and a staid, desperately staid, widow?' There was a wry smile on her lips.

'Mary, I'm proud to be head of such a family. And you,

Mrs O'Malley, are definitely not staid. You're twenty-five and a beautiful young woman.'

The smile spread across her face and she took his arm as they crossed the street and for a few minutes she forgot about Chris Kennedy.

Chris had very little time to think about anyone. The only ship available was a floating rust bucket of a tramp steamer called, inappropriately, the *Gardenia*.

'What can you do?' the bored, middle-aged man behind the desk at the shipping pool had asked.

'I'm a bricklayer by trade,' he'd answered, trying not to sound too furtive or desperate for a job.

'Oh, aye, that'll be dead useful, that will,' had come the sarcastic reply.

'I'll take anything. Anything at all.'

The clerk had looked at him more closely over the top of his horn-rimmed glasses.

'What's the big rush for, then? Are the scuffers after you?'

'No. No, it's nothing like that. It's the wife—'

'Oh, that's it, is it?' the man interrupted before Chris could finish. 'You'll have to leave her an allotment.' He drew a form across the desk and produced a well-worn fountain pen.

'That one's getting nothing from me.' Chris was trying to keep his voice steady and his expression calm.

'Well, you've got to leave one to someone or if you go down with the ship they'll get nothing. No one signs on without having left an allotment. What about your mother?'

Chris nodded. 'All right, my mam, but is there any way

you can not tell her where I am or what I'm doing? She doesn't know, you see, about . . . Rosie.' He found it hard to speak her name without emotion.

'What do you think I am? Part of the bloody secret service?'

'Will you try, please? It's Mrs Philomena Kennedy, nineteen Hornby Street, that's off Scotland Road.'

'I bloody know that. Half of that entire neighbourhood are employed on anything that floats as crew of some kind or another.' He wrote down the name and address with a great show of reluctance.

'You could have it paid here, I suppose,' he conceded, 'but it's highly unusual. Are you sure you're not wanted by the police?'

'I'm bloody certain. Now what have you got?'

There was the same suspicious look and then the man opened a large book from the pile stacked on a shelf behind him and leafed through it.

'The *Gardenia*, sailing for Lisbon, that's Portugal, and then Uruguay – eventually. That's South America.'

'I don't need a geography lesson. What will I do?'

'Deckhand, general dogsbody, gofer.'

'That'll do. When does she sail and where from?'

A pocket watch was taken out of the shabby waistcoat pocket.

'In about an hour, so they're desperate. You should sign articles but I don't think her master will be too fussy about that. I'd be surprised if they even meet the Board of Trade regulations. You should also have a discharge book. Have you got your identification card?'

'I fought in a bloody war and there weren't this many regulations.'

'Don't take that attitude with me. Thousands of men sailed out over the Mersey Bar and never came back, my own lad amongst them. He was on the *Ceramic*, the first one to be sunk and the bloody war only just announced. There was only one feller who lived. Anyway, the *Gardenia* is down at the Sandon Dock. You'll have to sign on here and sign the allotment form.'

Chris hadn't read either form closely. The wage was a pittance compared to what he'd been earning but the money didn't matter. He'd signed half of it to go to Phil.

When he'd first set eyes on the *Gardenia* his heart had sunk like a stone. She didn't look in a fit state to get across the Bay of Biscay, let alone the Atlantic Ocean. If things were too bad maybe he'd jump ship in Lisbon.

Once out of the comparative shelter of the Mersey estuary things got very bad. The little tramp steamer was tossed about like a cork and Chris did no work for two days. He lay in his narrow, grubby bunk wishing to die. It would have been worth staying at home to face the music rather than endure the sheer misery and wretchedness of seasickness.

'What the bleeding hell they sent you for God knows. Fat lot of use you're going to be. Every day you're lying on your back will be deducted from your wages,' the bosun informed him when he came down to see what Chris was doing.

Chris couldn't care less. They could take the bloody lot, he just wanted to die.

By the morning on the third day he felt well enough to get up. The ship was still pitching and rolling but it didn't seem to have the same effect on him. He was hungry but the box-like cabin was filthy so he went in search of the bosun and asked for a bucket, scrubbing brush, bleach and disinfectant.

'We're not a bleeding ship's chandlers. There's a bucket, a brush and a mop but you'll have to make do with a bit of Aunt Sally.'

Chris nodded. It was the brand name of a sort of concentrated liquid soap but it was better than nothing.

First he washed all the clothes he'd been wearing for the past two days and nights and then went up on deck to see if there was anywhere to hang them to dry. He was in the process of rigging up a clothes line with a piece of rope attached to a ventilator and a small winch when there was a bellow of rage from above.

'Take that bloody thing down! It's not a bloody Chinese laundry!'

Chris glanced up and caught sight of a red-faced and angry captain. He made do with spreading the garments out on the hatch covers.

He worked all day, not only on his own cabin but on the companionways and the deck too. His efforts were rewarded by a fry-up that the cook dished out on to an enamel plate, which had to be eaten standing up. There was no crew mess at all. He presumed the captain would be the only one who sat at some sort of table to eat.

It was later that evening as he stood on deck with the cold Atlantic wind whipping his hair, the collar of the well-worn but still serviceable duffel coat turned up, that he thought about Mary and his mam.

They'd have found Rosie days ago. There would be a police search going on now. He gripped the ship's rail tightly. Dear God, he hadn't meant to kill her. He'd just lashed out in temper and hadn't he a right to do that, the way she was behaving? Why had she fallen so badly? Why had a sharp corner killed her instead of just grazing her? There were so many whys. But he couldn't go back, not yet, maybe not for a long time. Maybe never. The wind seemed to whisper Mary's name in his ear and he thought of the way she'd looked at his fiasco of a wedding and then at the old lady's funeral and that increased and compounded his misery.

The inquest had been opened on the day Rosie died and Maggie and Phil had been left to arrange the funeral as Flossie was in no fit state to do anything yet. Gerry had suddenly had an urge to work.

'Bloody typical!' Maggie had snapped at him when he imparted this news. 'You're a useless waste of space on this earth, Gerry O'Hanlon, and always have been. She could have had her pick of lads, she was a lovely girl, but no she has to waste her life stuck with you. Anyone would have been better than you.'

'She'll be better when it's all over. It must be terrible for her while everything's just hanging in the air,' Phil had remarked, glaring at Gerry.

After the inquest the CID inspector came to the house.

'What now?' Maggie demanded when she opened the door. Both she and Phil were spending more time at Flossie's than they were in their own homes. Flossie had gone to pieces and there were Jimmy and Carmel to see to. Between them they'd given the place a good going-over and said in private that, good-hearted though she was, Flossie had never been much of a one to do a thorough clean.

'Is Mrs Florence O'Hanlon in?'

'She is, but she's in no state to be harassed by you lot.'

'I've come to tell her the coroner's verdict.'

'Come on in, then,' Maggie instructed, wondering what it was and how it would affect Flossie and Phil. 'He's come to tell you what they said about your Rosie,' she informed her neighbour.

Flossie's eyes filled up again and Maggie patted her on the shoulder.

'So?' Phil asked apprehensively.

'Accidental death,' he said flatly. 'There were no other injuries, we couldn't trace the feller seen running off and we believe her husband is away at sea. It's the first thing we check when they do a runner. The pool and the big shipping lines.'

Maggie heard Phil's sigh of relief. 'So what you're telling us is that she tripped or something and she cracked her head on the fire grate?'

'That's it. We've no evidence to the contrary, despite a missing husband who may or may not have been intending to find a job at sea. Case closed.'

'You . . . you're telling me it was an . . . accident?' Flossie managed to get out.

'That's right.'

Flossie was incredulous. 'But someone must have hit her or pushed her.'

He turned to Maggie. 'That's as may be, but who? We've only got your daughter's word to go on, and we wouldn't want a child of her age to be questioned in an open court.'

'Thanks be to God for that,' Maggie said fervently. The Lord alone knew what kind of effect something like that would have on Patsy.

'So, you can go ahead and organise the funeral.'

'We've already done that. It's on Friday.'

He nodded and turned to leave but Phil caught his sleeve.

'Did you say Chris is at sea?'

'Yes.'

'On what ship? Where to? When will he be home?'

'It's a ship called the *Gardenia* bound for Uruguay.'

'Where the hell's that?' Maggie asked.

'South America. Before you ask, I've no idea how long it takes to get there or get back.'

Phil showed him out while Maggie made a pot of tea.

'I . . . I . . . suppose all we can do is accept what he said,' Florrie said in a voice full of child-like resignation.

'From what he told us we've got no choice. That coroner feller must be right. He's a sort of judge,' Maggie said firmly.

Phil nodded, feeling a little easier in her mind just knowing where Chris was. It was useless to try to speculate on how long it would be before he came home.

Mary wasn't at all pleased when Breda announced that she too was going to Rosie's funeral.

'You hated her! Aren't you a hypocrite, wanting to go along too for the spectacle of it.'

'Hypocrite, is it? What about you? You hated her just as much as I did. In fact most of the people going hated her, and she died before she could repent, so why all this fuss anyway? Why all the flowers and Mass cards and a church full of gawpers? We all know that she'll have gone to hell, the carry-on out of her. And how many more fellers were there, I'd like to know?'

Mary rounded on her. 'Breda Nolan, that's a desperate thing to say! It's wicked. Aunty Maggie, Mrs O'Hanlon, Mrs Kennedy and I like to think she had time for a few words of contrition. Even just a "sorry" would have done. Don't you dare go saying anything like that to anyone!'

Breda raised her eyes to the ceiling and went to look for the black coat and dress she'd worn for Agnes's funeral. She'd pin the lovely brooch Agnes had left her to the lapel of her coat. It would look just right. Not flashy, just expensive and tasteful.

Every word she'd said to Mary had been true. No one was going because they had really liked Rosie. What was there to like about her? Oh, her mam would be upset and the rest of the kids, but no one else. And she certainly didn't think Rosie had had time to say sorry to God. She herself was going because Bryan was going too. Most of the residents in the street were going, not for Rosie, but for Flossie's sake. A young person's death was tragic enough but Rosie's still had everyone guessing and speculating. Breda herself had questioned Patsy.

'Tell me again, Patsy, what did your man running off look like?'

The child had looked at her quite calmly. She'd become something of a celebrity at school since Rosie's death, being the only one who had actually seen anything.

'I told the scuffers, Breda, you know I did. He was sort of fair and medium build.'

'In the name of God, Patsy O'Shea, you must have noticed more than that!'

'He wasn't very tall, not like our Bryan, but he looked . . . heavy.'

'Oh, isn't that a great help? Can you not remember how long it was before you saw Chris?'

'If I knew I'd have told them by now, wouldn't I? I'm fed up with all the questions. That's all I get at school, questions. I haven't got a bloody watch so how would I know?'

'Don't you use language like that or I'll clatter you myself and then tell Aunty Maggie. It's too cocky you are.'

'Well, I was the only one who saw anything,' Patsy had replied smugly so Breda had let her alone.

Mary and Breda were ready to leave well before the appointed time. The children were at school and Albert would keep his eye on them until the girls returned, for as Mary had said they couldn't just go rushing off home. She knew that the neighbours were putting on a bit of a spread because, as usual, Flossie was broke. Gerry had decided he was unfit to work as suddenly and conveniently as he'd decided just before that he wanted to, and spent his time drowning his sorrows with drinks bought for him by men who wanted to show some sympathy. Mary herself had contributed to the food and drink and she'd ordered a large wreath to carry the message: 'From Mary and Breda. RIP.'

'Does this hat look better tilted over one eye or not?' Breda asked, studying her reflection in the mirror on the wall of the hall.

'It's not a fashion parade! Leave it alone and get out of that door,' Mary replied sharply.

It was a big affair by local standards. There were many floral tributes and as the hearse passed the houses in the street, the black plumes of the black horses bending before the cold wind, people fell into step behind the family and immediate neighbours to walk to the church.

Flossie was supported by Maggie on one side and Phil on the other. Bob Kennedy and Jim O'Shea supported Gerry, who needed help just to stand up, and Cissy Mathews, who'd closed her shop for the day, and Carrie Quinne had their arms round Jimmy and Carmel.

'Aren't some people desperate,' Mary said to Breda as they took their place behind the immediate family. 'Sure, they never knew the girl at all. They've only come because of the circumstances surrounding her death, the gossip and the speculation.'

'We're not supposed to go passing out sandwiches and beer to them as well, are we?'

They had both volunteered to help with these tasks.

'We are not. Won't Aunty Maggie make sure of that!'

'Would you look at the cut of himself. He can hardly stand and it's only ten o'clock in the morning. Out on the jar at this time. Where did he get it from? The drink?'

'Very probably the crowd who frequent the Grapes had a collection and bought him a bottle of something to get him through the day.'

'Well, it looks as though he's gone and drunk the lot. Isn't he a disgrace? Let's hope he doesn't think it's a wedding and start singing, wouldn't that cap it all?'

Mary nodded her agreement.

The Requiem Mass seemed to go on for hours, even though Father Hayes did his best to keep his sermon short. There was very little good to say about Rosie and he spoke mainly about her childhood and called her 'a lost soul' which Maggie thought was very generous of him. At least it seemed to comfort Flossie.

For Mary and Breda it seemed interminable, but for different reasons.

Mary was trying to think kindly of Rosie, helped by the parish priest's sermon. She even prayed that Rosie had indeed gone to heaven, but thoughts of Chris wouldn't be banished, no matter how hard she tried.

Breda's mind was not on Rosie at all. She had managed to catch Bryan's eye as they got to the church door. It was the first time she'd seen him for ages.

'Later. I'll see you later,' he'd hissed and she'd nodded. She was still unsure of her feelings for him – or his for her, for that matter. They'd have to be careful. Aunty Maggie and Mary would be watching them, but with any luck at some stage in the day they could speak.

The opportunity arose in the early afternoon. The crowd of people who had been packed into Flossie's front room and kitchen had mainly left. Aunty Maggie and Uncle Jim were talking to Father Hayes, and Mary and Phil were collecting up the dirty dishes and cups and stacking them in the scullery. She'd caught Bryan's eye and jerked her head in the direction of the scullery while both her sister and Phil were in the front room, clearing up and talking to people. She went straight through the scullery and into the yard, which was full of rubbish.

Bryan followed her and they managed to squeeze into a corner behind a stack of orange boxes and the flock mattress off the bed Rosie had shared with Chris.

'Isn't it terrible? I still can't take it in that she's dead – that I'll never see her face with all that make-up plastered on it again. I'd known her all my life, from when we were kids playing in the street.'

Breda exploded. 'For God's sake, have you come out

327

here to talk about her? Haven't you a short memory, Bryan O'Shea? Look what she did to us – and what was even worse, what she did to Chris and Mary.'

'I heard he was away at sea.'

'I don't care what you heard about anyone! It's *us* I want to talk about.'

'Oh, yeah. Sorry,' Bryan said, forgetting all about Rosie.

'Mary says you'll never marry me. She says you don't love me and Aunty Maggie said you only love yourself.'

He was caught unawares. 'Of course I love you! They just don't want us going out together, that's all,' he blustered.

'Going out! Is that what you call it?'

Bryan was becoming impatient. 'Oh, come on, Breda, you know what I mean. I'm not a feller who goes in for flowery words or speeches, like. You know that.'

'So you do still love me, despite what they say?' she demanded.

'Of course I do.' He reached out and took her in his arms and kissed her, wishing that his mam and Mary would stay out of things that really didn't concern them. But still, it gave him more time to stall. He wasn't ready for domesticity yet, and then there was Sally Riley in Hopwood Street. He'd taken her out a couple of times. She was great company, and there was none of all this intensity.

Mary and Phil worked efficiently side by side. Every plate, cup, mug and glass had been borrowed from the neighbours. And this was the first chance Mary had had all day of having a private conversation with Phil.

She placed a pile of plates on the draining board. 'And they said it was definitely this Uruguay place he's headed for?' she asked.

Phil was up to her elbows in soapy water. 'It is. Bob went to the library and got a map and found it. It's nearly the other side of the world. It's thousands of miles away.'

'Oh, I wish there was some way we could reach him. Just to tell him to come home, that . . . her . . . death was an accident.'

'I know, luv. I asked Father Hayes to help and he said he'd find out what order of priests are in – oh, that place with the heathen-sounding name. He said he'd write to them asking them to look out for Chris and to tell him to come home. But they might not find him or he mightn't believe them and anyway it could all take months. We don't even know if he's got there yet.'

'But it's a hope and it's all we have to cling to. We have to believe they will find him and convince him. If only I could write to him.' Mary pushed a strand of dark hair from her forehead. It had been a depressing day and she wished it were over so that she could nurse her fear and sorrow at home, alone.

'I know, Mary. I thought of that myself. I *knew* he didn't do it. He wouldn't harm a fly, our Chris. I'm sure he came in and found her and panicked, and when I think about what he must be feeling I . . . just keep praying for him, that's all we can do.'

Mary nodded. It was a small comfort to know roughly where he was and that he was innocent, but it might be months, as Phil had said, before anyone found him, or he might get another ship and sail to God knows where. It might take years to trace him. It might never happen. Chris may never come home. The thought upset her so much it brought tears to her eyes, and she didn't want Phil to see how upset she was.

'I'll hang these tea towels on the line in the yard. They really should be washed out but there's no soap and I don't think they'll stand up to it without falling apart. There's more holes in them than a sieve.'

'I wouldn't use them as floor cloths. But stick them on the line anyway, we've finished now. I'll sort out what belongs to who later tonight.'

The washing line looked grimy and sagged in the middle and Mary could only find a couple of loose pegs scattered on the floor. She was so intent on her task of finding more pegs that it wasn't until she was a foot away that she noticed her sister locked in a passionate embrace with her cousin.

'Breda! Breda Nolan, get in that house now!'

Bryan hastily pushed Breda away from him and went on the defensive.

'It wasn't what it looked like, Mary, honestly it wasn't.'

Breda rounded on him.

'What do you mean by that, Bryan? Not what it looked? You've just told me how much you love me and that next week we'll go to see the Archbishop, and now—'

Mary felt the anger begin to rise. She was tired and upset and she was at the end of her tether with her sister. It had been a long, harrowing day, trying to keep up the appearance of concern for Flossie and trying not to look worried about Chris.

'You are not going to see anyone, Breda! I've had enough of all this. I've made up my mind. There's only one place you are going and that's home. Back to Dublin and out of harm's way. Or more precisely out of *your* way, Bryan O'Shea, and I think your mam will have a few well-chosen words to say to you over all this as well as Uncle Jim. I'm destroyed with the pair of you! Get in that house now,

330

Breda, and get your coat and hat on and don't you start weeping and begging to stay because I'll have none of it. You're under twenty-one and you'll do as I say. You've disgraced yourself and me for the last time. The carry-on out of the pair of you and Father Hayes still in the house! Get inside, Breda, now, this minute, or I'll lose the run of myself and drag you home without your coat and hat! Get inside!'

Chapter Twenty-Two

All the way home on the bus Mary had fumed and Breda, her cheeks burning with embarrassment at being publicly castigated and hauled off like a naughty child, had also remained tight-lipped and silent.

Albert opened the door to them.

'Mary, you look worn out. It's a good job the children are in bed.'

'Worn out is it! Wouldn't anyone be worn out with the antics of this one here!'

'Aren't you the one to talk about antics!' Breda exploded. 'She dragged me out of the house, shouting that I was going back to Dublin on the next boat, in front of everyone!'

Albert took both their coats and hung them on the row of hooks behind the door.

Mary sank down on a chair. 'Breda, I'm at my wits' end with you! He doesn't love you and never will and I won't stand for any more. It's humiliating, that's what it is, and not only for you but for me too. Aren't they all whispering that he's just stringing you along with this dispensation nonsense.'

Tears pricked Breda's eyes. Even though she tried to fight it down, in her heart she knew that all Mary said was true. It was the public humiliation of being dragged off home that had upset her most.

Albert sat down beside Breda. 'Breda, Mary's right. You're a lovely girl, so don't go making yourself the subject of all the gossip in Hornby Street. Have some self-esteem and shut him out of your mind completely.'

Mary sighed. 'I'd better send a telegram to Mam. There's not much to see to here.'

'What about the children, Mary?' Albert asked anxiously, wondering about his own future. Would he have to find new lodgings? Lodgings like the room in Hornby Street? He'd become so fond of this house. It was restful and comfortable, and he'd grown used to facilities like a decent bathroom.

'I'll take Lily back to Aunty Maggie's, for the time being at least. Kevin will be broken-hearted, I know, but if I can promise Lily I'll send for her it might not be too bad.'

'You're serious, Mary, aren't you?'

'I am, but don't look so miserable. I won't be selling the house, and anyway it's your home now. I might come back soon so you'll just be minding it for me.'

He breathed a sigh of relief as he nodded, knowing it was the thought of Chris Kennedy coming back that was uppermost in her mind.

Breda spent the night tossing and turning restlessly and there were the occasional bursts of tears, but they were tears of anger. Oh, Albert was right. What a fool she'd been, running after Bryan, making a spectacle of herself when at the mere flutter of her eyelashes she could have had anyone!

She didn't want to go home, although she was certain that now Mary had money they'd be leaving the Liberties for a much better area and a decent house. She just didn't want it to look as if she was being dragged off like a child. Well, when they all came to see her off, as no doubt they would, she'd hold her head high and imply that she was glad to be going back where she would have her pick of well-set-up Irish lads who were not related.

Mary too spent a restless night. She didn't want to go back either, just in case Chris came home. She didn't care that people might think they were both running away with their tails between their legs, Breda over Bryan and herself over Chris. No, people could think what they liked.

She stared at the ceiling for hours, worrying, wondering, praying that he was all right and that he would come back one day. Oh, Chris! Chris! I love you so much! Where are you? Please come back to me, my love. The words and entreaties went round and round in her head until she finally fell asleep just before dawn.

Before they went to school Mary took Kevin and Lily to one side.

'Sit down on that sofa now, I want to talk to you both.' Her stomach was churning as she saw the serious expressions on their little faces and anxiety in their eyes.

'We have decided, Uncle Albert, Aunty Breda and me, that it will be best for us to go back to Granny Nolan in Dublin. We won't be staying in her house for very long, though. Mammy will find us a grand little place in a nice area.'

'Why do we have to go?' Kevin demanded, his bottom lip trembling. 'I . . . we . . . like it here.'

Mary sighed. 'Because both Mammy and Aunty Breda want to go and it's just . . . just not possible to stay here,' she lied, watching their faces closely. Her heart was breaking as she saw the bright tears fill her little son's eyes.

'As soon as we're settled in a nice house, I'll write to Aunty Maggie and tell her to send you over, Lily.' She plunged on before either of them could speak. 'Aunty Maggie or your da will bring you. They'd love the outing. Did you know your da was born in Dublin, Lily?'

Lily didn't reply. She didn't care where her da had come from. Her lip too was trembling and she reached for Kevin's hand.

'I . . . I don't want Mam to bring me! I want to go with you! You promised! You promised that Kev and me will always be together!' The child's voice turned into a heart-rending sob and the tears started in Mary's eyes.

'Oh, come here to me, my little bookends!' she said in an unsteady voice, kneeling down and catching them both up in her arms. 'It won't be long, Lily, I promise you!'

'You . . . you promised last time!' Lily sobbed.

'I know I did, but we have to go. I can't explain it, and if I tried to you wouldn't understand it anyway. But I will send for you, Lily. Come on now, dry your eyes. Uncle Albert will walk with you to school.' She didn't want a repeat performance of the day when they'd decided to go to Chester.

Reluctantly they were pushed gently into the hall and she heard Kevin say emphatically, 'Don't cry, Lily. I'll *make* her send for you, I *will*. *I* promise you. You'll come and live with us for ever.'

As the front door closed behind them Mary sank down on the sofa and dropped her head in her hands. They'd come here with such high hopes and fate had smiled on them until Rosie O'Hanlon had appeared on the scene. After that everything seemed to have gone wrong. Now she had to warn her mam, get tickets and book a cabin.

This time she had the money and, if she'd achieved nothing else, they were going home in style. She'd get their things packed and then she would go up and see Aunty Maggie. Breda had left for work looking far better than Mary had thought she'd look after a restless night.

Maggie was over with Phil and they were still sorting out the dishes.

'I'm sure that Carrie Quinne has taken four cups that belong to Maudy Halliday.' Maggie was looking worried, for simple things like this could turn into a huge row. Then as she looked up and saw Mary she smiled.

'Mary, come in, luv,' Phil said, leaving aside the task of trying to reunite the respective dishes with their rightful owners.

Mary sat down and Maggie pushed the teapot across to her.

'Pick a cup, luv. I'm past caring what belongs to who. They can all fight it out themselves. How are things down in Bootle this morning? Meladdo's gone to work with a flea in his ear, I can tell you. His da's not pleased with him, not one little bit!'

Mary poured herself a cup of weak tea. 'Aunty Maggie, I've decided for certain that I'm going back to Mammy and I'm taking that strap of a sister with me, and Kevin of course.'

Phil leaned across the table and patted her arm.

'You know, luv, that if I get any news, anything at all, I'll let you know. I promise faithfully.'

Mary nodded, close to tears.

'Does our Lily know yet?' Maggie asked.

'I told them both this morning before they went to school. Albert took them there.'

'And I suppose that little madam had one of her screaming tantrums.'

'No. She was upset and Kevin was upset, but I promised them both that when I got sorted out I'll send for her.'

'Mary, luv, you don't have to. This is her home and I'm her mam. You've been goodness itself with her. She's spoiled rotten.'

Mary sighed. 'I know, and sometimes I think it's unfair on Patsy.'

'Well, that one will soon bring our Lily down off her high horse,' Maggie said firmly.

'I don't want that. I want both of them to be happy.'

'Stop wishing for the moon, Mary. This is Hornby Street, remember. We've come through a war and some lost everything, even their lives. "Happy ever after" is in short supply round here, luv.'

'What are you going to do now, Mary?' Phil asked.

'Send a telegram to Mam, I suppose.'

'God above! Don't do that. It'll terrify the wits out of her!'

'No it won't. The Emergency's over and the lads that went to fight in the Great War are middle-aged now, those who came back,' Mary reminded her.

'I'd write if I were you, just the same. Will you be moving, then?'

'We will. We'll go out to Blackrock or Rathmines or even Bray.'

'But what about your hats, luv? After all that work and the great gift you've got for colour and the like, it's a shame to waste it all.'

'Oh, I'll take some samples to Switzers or Brown Thomas in Grafton Street, but it really doesn't matter now. I don' need the money as badly as we used to. Albert is staying on in the house. It's his home now. I couldn't put him out in the street, he's been so good to us all. And . . . well, one day I might come back, if . . .'

Again Phil patted her arm and Mary managed a smile.

'I'll go down and book our passage and this time we'll be travelling in style, with a cabin.' A sad little smile played around her lips.

'Won't that be just great, Phil? Those ferries are like flaming cattle boats and God help you if it's a bad crossing. When we came over for your da's wake it was shocking. I'd never been so terrified in my life.' She laughed. 'God help us, we didn't know the meaning of the word then.'

'I'll book first and then write to Mam.'

Maggie shook her head. 'When will you go, luv?'

'I don't know.'

'I think the sixteenth would be a good day. You'll be home in time for St Patrick's Day. The emigrant returning with a small fortune in her pocket and as smart as new paint. There won't be many going home like that, Mary.' Phil smiled, but there was sorrow in her smile too.

Mary finished her tea and got to her feet. 'Well, I'd better go then.'

Maurice and Pauline announced that they were going to set a wedding date. Saturday June the fourteenth.

'Congratulations! But you've not left your mam and me much time to get organised, have you?' Maggie smiled, while Jim shook his son's hand and gave Pauline a bear hug.

'So, whose front room will it be?' he asked.

'Neither, Mr O'Shea. We've just enough saved to pay

for a room for two months. We'll start off on our own. Well, nearly on our own,' Pauline added.

'Well, if that doesn't beat all! You've a good girl here, lad. See you treat her right.' Jim glanced over to Bryan who looked away to avoid the scorn in his father's eyes. 'And you can stop calling me "Mr O'Shea". From now on it's "Da" or "Dad".'

'That's as well as maybe, but let's get things properly organised before we start worrying about what to call each other.' Life was all go at the moment with Mary leaving and now these two setting a date, Maggie thought.

'Can I be a bridesmaid, Pauline?' Patsy asked timidly, her opinion of her future sister-in-law having improved over the months.

'Of course, Patsy. Our Kate and Molly and you. And you'll have really lovely dresses. Pale blue, I think. That will suit all of you. And I'll pay for you to go and have your hair done in a real hairdressing place.' Pauline had a generous nature and had often felt sorry for the child.

'Oh, I'll never be able to do anything with her now!' Maggie said laughingly.

'What about our Lily?' Patsy asked. Their Lily had had everything but she'd be coming home to live very soon and she didn't want her younger sister taking the shine off her big day. Fancy Pauline saying she could go to a real hairdresser!

Maggie looked grim. 'No, that one has had enough of the attention. She's spoiled rotten as it is and she'll get her legs slapped if she starts her antics here! She gets away with murder up there . . . Oh, God! Phil, I'm so sorry. I didn't mean it to sound . . . well . . .'

'That's all right. I *know* he's not a criminal. But don't go mentioning the word murder to Flossie.'

It was a blustery night, with cold drops of rain in the fiercely gusting wind, when Albert and the neighbours came down to the pier head to see them off. Kathleen had written back immediately saying they'd all be welcome and didn't they know that too. In the end two cabins had been booked, one for Mary and Kevin and a single one for Breda. Mary had taken pity on her sister, who had finally faced up to the fact that she was not in love with Bryan O'Shea at all. It had been a case of forbidden fruit all along, the excitement of secret meetings and stolen kisses.

The blue-grey smoke issuing from the *Leinster*'s black and green funnel was caught by the wind and whipped away into the night sky. Mary was clutching the tickets and all three of them had tears in their eyes.

'Oh, take care of yourself and write to me soon,' Mary said as she hugged Albert. The same sentiments were addressed to Uncle Jim and Aunty Maggie, and were even more emotional on Maggie's part.

'I'll send a telegram if there's ever any news at all,' Phil promised as she held Mary to her. It was still her fervent wish that one day Mary would become her daughter-in-law.

Kevin and Lily stood facing each other. Kevin's cap was in danger of being blown away and Lily's unruly locks were confined under a knitted pixie hood, tied firmly under the chin. Tears were streaming down both their cheeks. The sight almost broke Mary's heart in two and she said a silent prayer that all would go well in Dublin and she could send for Lily sooner rather than later.

'I don't want you to go, Kev,' Lily wept, holding tightly to his hand.

'I told you I'd *make* Mammy send for you,' he gulped between sobs. He pushed his knitted rabbit towards her. It was still his favourite toy. 'You take him, Lily. You look after him and bring him with you when you come to Granny Nolan's.'

Lily took the battered and grubby toy and hugged it. 'No one's going to take him away, Kev. I'll look after him and I'll bring him with my dolly to your nan's house.'

There were tears in everyone's eyes at the sad little farewell scene being played out before them. Even Jim and Bob had to swallow hard, and Albert blinked rapidly.

'You'd best get aboard, Mary, luv. It looks like they're getting ready to haul up the gangway,' Jim advised and, with hugs all round again, Mary, Breda and a very tearful Kevin reluctantly climbed the wooden gangway. Mary was wondering if she would ever make the return journey.

Unfortunately the weather was very rough and the crowds going home had already been toasting the imminent national holiday in fine form.

'Aren't I glad now I got us cabins. Isn't the state of this lot a disgrace even before we get under way, let alone into Dublin Bay,' Mary said as a steward ushered them down the stairs from the saloon.

Breda too was very grateful for the privacy and comfort. A cabin all to herself. It just showed what money could do to help life along. Granted, it wasn't very big. In fact you could hardly swing a cat in it, but the sheets and top cover looked crisp and neat. There was a tiny washbasin with a small mirror attached to the wall above it.

She undressed and laid her folded clothes across the foot

of the bunk. She brushed her hair, washed her face and after a tussle with the sheets, which she began to think were nailed down, got into the narrow bunk.

The noise and vibrations from the screws made a restful night look impossible and before long she was fretful and bored. Sleep eluded her as one after another the small items around the washbasin slid and crashed to the floor.

She sat up. Oh, this was desperate, she thought. At this rate, by morning the place would be destroyed altogether. She got dressed again, carefully avoiding the broken glass on the floor, and locking the door behind her made her way along the companionway towards the stairs and the upper deck. She'd go outside for a bit of fresh air. The ferry was packed and she felt claustrophobic. Judging by the pitching and rolling it was blowing a gale, but she needed time to think more clearly about her future.

She had a struggle with the door, and when she got outside the wind was screaming around the funnel and the rigging. The deck was wet and slippery and the cold spray crashed over the bows as if determined to show how puny were man's efforts to tame it. She clung tightly to the rail. She'd been a complete eejit to come out here. She was terrified by the violence of the storm and there wasn't another soul out on deck. If she let go of the rail she would be washed overboard, and no one would even miss her until morning when Mary came to get her up. Fear paralysed her, and her tears mingled with the salty, wet spray until she could hardly see.

Suddenly she was gripped tightly round the waist and she looked up into the face of a young man with green eyes and dark auburn hair. He was bareheaded and the gale was blowing his hair into his eyes.

'Oh, Holy Mother of God! I'm terrified. I must have been mad to come out here,' she cried with a sob in her voice.

'Didn't I have the same thought myself. But when I saw you hanging on for dear life, well . . . what could I do but help?'

She fought down the terror. 'Will we go back?' she shouted, her eyes full of trust. They both had to shout over the noise of the wind and the sea.

'We will so. Keep tight hold of me, even if you only hang on to my coat, and somehow we'll manage it.'

Breda clung to him like a limpet, staggering and slipping, until at last they were inside and safe. She then disentangled herself from his arms.

'Ah, now isn't that the pity. There I was all alone with a beautiful girl in my arms and now . . .'

Breda blushed. She must look a terrible fright but he had still called her beautiful. She felt suddenly shy and tongue-tied. He was tall, with classic Celtic good looks, and by his dress and speech he was obviously not hard up.

'What's your name?'

'Breda. Breda Bernadette Nolan.' She managed a smile.

'I'm Niall Peter Patrick Joseph Fitzgerald. Isn't that a mouthful? When I was baptised I'm sure half the congregation had dozed off before the Father had finished with that lot. I live in a village near to Clonmel. Were you ever there?'

She shook her head. She'd never been out of Dublin, let alone that far down in the country in Tipperary.

'What about you?'

Instinctively she raised a hand to try to tidy her hair. 'Oh, I was a clerk in the main sorting office in Liverpool,

344

but Mary – my elder sister – decided we couldn't leave Mammy on her own much longer.' There was no way she was going to let him know the truth. He was very handsome, she thought, even though he was windswept and the salt was crystallising on his eyebrows and lashes.

'What was it that had you in Liverpool?' she asked.

'I wasn't in Liverpool at all. I was in a mill town called Bolton. I'm an accountant, for my sins, and I could earn more and see more of life over there. Except that there wasn't much of life to see in Bolton, unless you are fascinated by cotton mills. I went to Trinity College.'

She was surprised. 'They let you go in there?'

'They did, even though the Archbishop said we were to boycott the place.'

Breda nodded. For centuries Catholics had been excluded from Dublin's oldest university. Most went to University College, if their families could afford it. She glanced up at him under her thick lashes. She'd never met anyone like him before. An accountant, for God's sake. He didn't look like one, but then she'd never had reason to set eyes on one before. She felt drawn to him. It was a totally different feeling from any she'd had for Bryan. But she felt different altogether now that they'd left. She felt older, steadier now. Despite what Mary said about her, she knew she'd lost the inclination to flirt with every lad who came her way. And Niall Fitzgerald wasn't a lad. He was a man and one she liked. One she wasn't going to put on simpering smiles or go through silly and obvious performances to impress.

'Is your mother still in Dublin?'

Breda panicked. 'She is.' She wasn't going to tell him where. Practically everyone in the Free State knew what kind of a neighbourhood the Liberties was.

'This is my cabin. Thank you . . . thank you for saving me and bringing me here.' She looked up at him and her wide deep blue eyes were his undoing.

'I know this will sound crazy, and maybe it *is* crazy, but, Breda Bernadette Nolan, will you meet me again? Go out with me?'

She was taken aback. 'I . . . I . . . don't know you!' she stammered.

'Not yet, but I feel as though I've known you all my life. And you are very, very beautiful, you know.'

She blushed. He was right. It was crazy, and yet there was a feeling that she had known him always too.

'Have I a chance at all?' he asked quietly.

She couldn't speak. She was trembling but she managed to nod.

'I'll have to go on to get the train when we disembark, but will you wait for me, Breda?'

She was confused. 'Wait? Where? When?'

'A week. I'll meet you under the clock at Clery's in O'Connell Street on the last Monday in the month at three o'clock.'

'What . . . what will I tell Mary?'

'Would you like me to speak to her, to explain?'

'Oh, please. She wouldn't believe the daylights out of me just now. I've been a bit of a problem to her lately.'

'Will I go now?'

Breda nodded. 'She . . . she's next door with Kevin, her little boy. She's a widow, you see.'

'Mrs . . . ?'

'O'Malley.'

'Will I come back and tell you what her feelings are?'

'Oh, that would be grand.' Breda's heart was pounding.

She'd never met anyone like him before. Bryan was a mere shadow, and one who couldn't make up his mind either, while Niall . . . well, he'd literally swept her off her feet, or a dangerous deck at least.

She heard the voices in the next cabin as she sat on her bunk, clasping her hands tightly. Oh, she hoped Mary wouldn't go into the long catalogue of things she'd done and the real reason for their coming home. She found her hairbrush and with some difficulty brushed her tangled curls into some kind of order and washed her face.

She didn't have long to wait before there was a knock on the door and when she opened it both Mary and Niall were standing there.

'Come in. It's a bit of a mess; everything's smashed to pieces . . .'

'Isn't that only to be expected with us being hurled from pillar to post since we left Liverpool Bay,' Mary said.

'So . . . ?' Breda looked pleadingly up into Niall's eyes.

'So, your sister has agreed that it will be permissible for me to meet you on the thirty-first.'

'I'm not terribly happy about all this, Breda. Just think carefully before you finally agree.'

'I have. I want to meet Niall again.'

Mary just nodded curtly and with a warm smile he made them both a mock bow and walked away.

'What were you doing out there, for God's sake? And aren't you the lucky one to get hauled to safety,' Mary hissed as she pushed her sister into her cabin and closed the door behind them.

'I was not "hauled".'

'This is terribly sudden, Breda.' Mary was full of doubt and misgivings.

'I know, but I suppose I like him. I must have looked a fright, too, with my hair like a bird's nest and the spray half blinding me.

'He told me about himself, briefly. He's been called home, his father has just died. He has the largest share in a co-operative creamery down there so he's not short of money. He asked if I would object to you going to meet his family – in time. He seems sincere.'

'Meet his family!' Breda repeated. He must really be serious about her, and that knowledge caused a pleasant yet somehow subdued excitement to wash over her. Strangely his education and the fact that he had money were unimportant. Things like that had once been paramount, but no longer. Niall Fitzgerald was a man she was attracted to and one who was obviously attracted to her. So much so that he wanted her to meet his family.

'I want you to get to know each other. There's to be no nonsense this time.'

'Isn't all that behind me now? It was stupid. I didn't love Bryan, it was all the sneaking out to meet him. It was childish, that's what it was.'

Mary smiled. 'Now get to bed and try to sleep. I've to go back to Kevin, the poor lamb is badly. Thank God I'm not, but I'll have a few bruises by morning from being hurled all over the place. It's easier to sleep on the floor.'

As she closed the door behind her, leaving her sister with her daydreams, Mary felt her heart lighten. Niall Fitzgerald seemed a very genuine young man. He was twenty-five, well educated, with property and a thriving business, and Breda appeared to be acting sensibly for a change. She only hoped it would last. She knew there would be remarks about him being a 'culchie', living down there, but he was far from being backward. Maybe it had been the best thing all round to bring Breda home. Well, only time would tell.

Chapter Twenty-Three

Their arrival next morning couldn't have been more different from their departure, Mary thought as they all stood on deck. It was hard to believe that for over nine hours the *Leinster* had battled her way against the gale and the mountainous seas. Now there was no wind to speak of and only a fine drizzle, which her mam would call 'a soft morning', as the ferry came alongside at the North Wall.

All around them were the activities of a busy port with gangs of dockers and stevedores loading and unloading. Carts and lorries were parked in lines as the docks stretched along the banks of the Liffey. In the grey, miserable light the dome of the Custom House dominated the skyline.

She'd slept badly, her mind on the future, her own and Breda's. Her comfort and care of her poor little seasick son had been constant. She was very tired now, she thought as she watched the gulls wheeling and swooping overhead, their raucous cries mingled with the other noises from along the quays. She longed for the comfort of her mother's arms, her shoulder to cry on. It seemed so long, the time she'd spent in Liverpool, and yet it was only a couple of years and she'd coped with all the worry and the bereavement, the heartache and then the trauma of Rosie's death and Chris's disappearance, by herself.

As she heard the familiar accents, the shouted instructions and commands and the witty replies, her spirits lifted and she smiled to herself. She was home.

'Can I offer you ladies a ride anywhere? I'll be getting a cab myself to Heuston Station.' Niall Fitzgerald's voice cut through Mary's thoughts.

Breda looked at her sister with apprehension.

'That's very kind of you, but we're going in the opposite direction.' Mary smiled up at him. They too would get a cab but she wasn't going to ruin Breda's day by accepting a ride to the Liberties. She glanced sideways at her sister and smiled again. 'And has the cold light of day changed your mind?'

He shook his head. 'Not at all. Even in the cold light of day I still want to see her. Again and again and again.'

Mary laughed. 'Ah, Mr Fitzgerald, do you just know what you're letting yourself in for? She's led many a one a fine dance.'

'And don't they deserve such a fate being so foolish,' he replied.

Breda's gaze went from her sister's face to his. Wasn't that just like Mary, but he'd taken it all as a joke. He still wanted to see her again.

She too had lain awake all night, unable to believe what had happened. He was everything Bryan, and every other boy she'd met, was not. He was well educated, handsome and full of confidence. The fact that he was a professional man with shares in a creamery didn't seem to matter. If he'd been a coal heaver like Col O'Malley she knew she would feel the same way about him. The most astounding thing was that she loved him. All the terror as she'd clung to the rail on the open deck had gone as soon as his strong arms had encircled her. She'd known it then and now she was certain. It was love at first sight, for them both.

Nothing had changed much in the time she'd been away, Mary thought as the jarvey deposited them at Mam's. The area was still a festering slum no matter how hard the women tried to keep the place clean and tidy. The decrepit state of the houses made all their efforts futile and many had given up. Still, by late this afternoon she hoped to have found somewhere decent for them all. Three hundred pounds wasn't a vast fortune. Not enough to buy a house outright, but she'd find decent rooms or a house for rent. Then she'd try and pick up the threads of her life.

Kathleen met them at the open front door that was sagging on its hinges below a broken, flyblown fanlight.

'Thank God you've arrived safe. Wasn't I only saying to Theresa Donaghue God help you in that storm last night. Were you badly?'

Mary hugged her mother. 'Kevin was. He was frightened and sick.'

Kathleen bent down and picked up her grandson. 'Ah, it's good to have you home again, child. Haven't I missed you all. Come on in, that mist will have you soaked in seconds.'

Breda wrinkled her nose at the mingled odours that assailed her nostrils. When she'd lived here, or indeed at Aunty Maggie's, she'd not noticed them, but after living in Exeter Road they came back with powerful effect. Thank God Mary would, with luck, have them out of here by tomorrow.

Everything in Kathleen's rooms was spotless, but the place was desperately furnished, Mary thought as she put down her case and took off her coat. The room was cold and smelled musty and the fire in the elegant Georgian fireplace was too small to heat it.

'Wait now while I wet the tea and then we'll have some rashers and dipped bread.' Kathleen bustled around with the teapot, kettle and heavy frying pan.

'Mam, just wet the tea for now. We'll have the rashers later on. On second thoughts, will we all go to O'Neills for a breakfast?'

'We will not. I won't have you wasting your money on the prices your man charges. Oh, I've heard all about himself and what he pays for his meat and what he charges people for the pleasure of eating it. There'll be none of that, Mary O'Malley.'

Mary sighed. She really should have known better than to even suggest it.

She accepted the tea, as did Breda.

'Mammy, as soon as I've seen to Kevin and unpacked, Breda and I are going to find us somewhere decent to live. I got a copy of the *Times* on the way here. Nothing too grand, though.'

'The *Times*, is it? Nothing too grand, is it? Where did you have in mind?'

'I'd thought Rathmines, Ballsbridge or even Blackrock.'

'In the name of God what would I want to live way down there for?'

'It's nice and the sea air would do us all good.'

'It'd do my arthritics no good at all. And when, may I ask, would I be having the time to get to see my friends at all?'

'You can get a tram or bus or even a cab. I know they can't afford the fares, but you can.'

'You mean *you* can.'

'Oh, Mammy, don't be giving out already. I've the money and I can work, and Breda—'

'I've met a really special person. His name is Niall Fitzgerald,' Breda announced. She'd been bursting to tell her Mam the news.

Kathleen stared at her hard, then turned to Mary.

'You said nothing about any special person.'

'I didn't know! She only met him on the boat. In fact he saved her from being swept overboard. Eejit that she is, she wanted a bit of fresh air – in a force eight gale with waves crashing over the deck!'

'Surely to God that doesn't make him special? Wouldn't any half-decent man have done the same thing?'

Breda was impatient. 'Oh, Mammy, let me have my say?'

Kathleen crossed her arms over her bosom and leaned back in the chair.

'He did save me. Then he asked would I see him again. Then he even went to Mary to ask would she have any objection to me meeting his family. I . . . I think I love him and I think he loves me. I know now that I never loved Bryan. It was just the excitement of—'

'Forbidden fruit,' Mary interrupted hastily. Breda had forgotten that that relationship had been kept from her mother.

'Bryan?' Kathleen looked puzzled.

'A lad she met at work who was a Protestant.' Mary directed a warning glance at her sister.

'And just who did you fall in love with, then?'

'His name is Niall Fitzgerald. He's twenty-five. He went to Trinity and is an accountant, but he's been called home to take over the family business because his father died.'

'Glory be to God! Is she telling the truth, Mary?'

'She is, and I have to say he seems well set up and declares that his intentions are serious. I think he means it. I knew as soon as I set eyes on Col I wanted to spend my life with him. He asked to see Breda again about ten minutes after meeting her.'

Kathleen was astounded. 'Trinity! An accountant! A family business!' She shook her head after each pronouncement.

'It's a creamery down in Tipperary, near Clonmel.'

'So, he's a rich culchie?'

'Mammy, I'd thank you not to go calling him that,' Breda snapped.

'So when are *we* going to meet him?'

'I'm going to meet him on the thirty-first. We'll have moved by then so I'll bring him for your inspection. Surely to God there can't be anything for you to complain about.'

'Did I say there was?' Kathleen turned her attention to her grandson, who was still pale and looked very close to tears.

'Come here to me, Kevin, and give your granny a big hug. Haven't I missed you all the long time you were over there.' She sat him on her knee and as she held him to her he began to cry.

'Mary, where's his rabbit? The one Santi brought him a few years back and he took everywhere?'

'He's left it behind with Lily. You remember I told you about the pair of them? He gave it to her to mind. She'll bring it with her when Aunty Maggie comes here.'

'Is that so? Well, it's years and years since I saw Maggie – or Jim, for that matter. You stay with me, child, and you can tell me all about that big place over there where you lived. Your mammy and Aunty Breda have to go out and find us a new place. Come on now, dry your eyes. Will we go and see Mrs Kavanagh in the shop?'

Mary sighed with relief as she saw the first sign of animation in her son's eyes.

At the end of a long, cold day they returned to the house in the Liberties.

'Thank God we've got something to show for all the tramping the streets of this city,' Breda said wearily.

Mary had paid a month's rent in advance for all the ground-floor rooms in a well-maintained house in Rathmines. Tomorrow they would go shopping for furniture and linen and other household necessities. This would be their last night in the Liberties and as she looked around her in the dismal light she thanked God for the generosity of Agnes McPhail.

The next few days were spent in furnishing and equipping the house, and when they finally left with the few odds and ends they were taking there was a crowd of neighbours to see them off.

'You mind yourself now, Kathleen,' Theresa Donaghue called.

'God and all the saints smile on you, Mrs Nolan. Sure don't you deserve it.' Mrs O'Hara patted her arm.

'Mary, take good care of her now.' This from Mrs Cusack.

'Sure we're not taking her to the moon. It's only a few

miles away and you can all visit. You'll all be welcome,' Mary said.

Kathleen wiped her eyes. Times had been and still were hard, but they'd all helped each other along and she'd miss them. She held Kevin tightly on her knee.

Breda raised her eyes to heaven. 'It's a wonder they don't hold an American wake for us and be done with it,' she muttered.

'Don't you go making a mock and a jeer out of them. American wakes are all too frequent,' Mary chided.

For an American wake parents, grandparents, family and friends got together for a big party when a son or daughter was emigrating. It was a bit like a real wake because everyone knew they would never see the emigrant again. They'd get letters and parcels, but they would never be able to hold the son or daughter in their arms again, or hear the familiar voice. Unless of course the emigrant became a millionaire and came back, which didn't happen often.

The house and location were not dissimilar to Exeter Road, and Mary had been to see the parish priest about Kevin's going to school. Even though it was only a few days since they'd left Liverpool, he was already asking when Lily would come.

Mary had decided to approach the buyer in Switzers with her sample hats. She was very apprehensive as she went through the doors of one of the most prestigious shops in Dublin. In the past she'd only been able to look through the window. Unless you were smartly dressed and looked as if you had money to spend, you wouldn't get past the doorman.

Although she had no appointment, she was eventually

ushered into the small office where Miss MacRory worked. She was a small woman who reminded Mary of Agnes, except that this one had a face like Hetty McPhail.

'Thank you for seeing me at such short notice. I do appreciate it.'

Miss MacRory indicated that Mary should sit.

'You are a trained milliner, Mrs O'Malley?'

'In a way I suppose I am. I learned everything I know from a retired milliner, Miss Agnes McPhail, who worked all her life in Sloan's, one of Liverpool's most exclusive shops.'

'I see. Well, let me have a look at your samples.'

Mary carefully removed them from the hat boxes and one by one placed them on the desk. There was one of every material and they sported every type of trimming. They looked well, she thought, but judging by the look on the buyer's face she didn't find them attractive.

'They are very well made, and I particularly like the straws, but they are a bit' – she searched for the right word – 'ordinary, if you can understand that?'

'You mean that they are not for the ladies who come here to purchase their hats and clothes?'

'Exactly. I would suggest you try the smaller, less expensive shops.'

Mary returned them to their respective boxes. She really wasn't disappointed. She had said to Agnes that she would prefer to make hats for working-class women and girls.

'Thank you for seeing me, and for your advice.' She held out her hand and Miss MacRory looked taken aback, although she did extend her hand. She'd never met anyone quite like this young woman before. She was well dressed and obviously confident of her talents. She certainly didn't look as though she needed the money, she was far too well dressed. Yet there was a strong Dublin accent.

Mary walked purposefully down Grafton Street. She'd try Clery's in O'Connell Street. She should have gone there in the first place. It was a shop frequented by those who didn't have the money for Switzers or Brown Thomas or the shops in Nassau Street.

When she enquired she was told that unfortunately the buyer was not in, but the middle-aged woman took down her name and address and asked her to call again.

At least it was hopeful, Mary thought on the way home.

When she got in it was to find Breda in a state of high excitement and her mam in despair.

'Hasn't she got me destroyed altogether, Mary, with all the clothes she's got. Wanting my opinion of what to wear when she goes to see this young bucko that went to Trinity.'

Breda appealed to her sister. 'Mary, what'll I wear? I don't want to look too . . . flashy, yet I don't want to look dowdy either.'

'Dowdy, is it? You spent most of your life looking dowdy. It was all I could do to keep you in shoes after your poor da passed away. God rest him and God bless the mark afterwards.' Kathleen crossed herself, remembering her husband.

'Wear the dark green costume with your good cream blouse. I'll lend you my black bag and shoes and you can wear that green and cream hat. The one herself in Switzers thought wasn't good enough for the high and mighty who shop there. The cream blouse and hat will contrast with the dark green and flatter your complexion.'

'Mother of God! Haven't you learned some fancy ways of going on from over there,' Kathleen exclaimed.

'Won't you need a coat? Where will he take you, do you think?' Mary asked, ignoring her mam.

'I've no idea, but I hope it's somewhere nice.'

'Take a coat. It might only be a walk through the Green, or Herbert Park, or along the quays, and it might rain.'

'Oh, Mammy, for heaven's sake look on the bright side, please?' Breda said.

'Haven't I been doing that for most of my life and look how far it's got me. Only for Mary, we'd all still be in that two pair front.'

Monday the thirty-first was a bright but cold day for spring and Breda shivered, partly with cold and partly with nerves. She had firmly refused to wear a coat. It would spoil the entire effect, she said, which had had Kathleen giving out about beggars not being choosers. She had asked just what was meant by that. They were no longer beggars.

'Only because of the goodness of that poor lonely old woman, God rest her. So don't go getting airs and graces,' had come the stinging reply.

She did look smart, she knew that from the expressions of the passers-by as she alighted from the bus at the top end of O'Connell Street and began to walk down towards Clery's department store, almost opposite the neo-classical General Post Office whose walls still bore the bullet marks from the Easter Rising.

He was waiting under the clock of what used to be the Imperial Hotel, and as she caught sight of him her heart turned over. Yes, she wanted to spend the rest of her life with him – providing he asked her, of course. It might take a few more meetings like this, but she would wait. She smiled. It was a dazzling smile, full of love and hope that lit up her face as she caught his eye.

'Breda, you look . . . stunning. Aren't you going to take the place down there by storm.' He tucked her arm through his and they began to walk down the wide thoroughfare.

'Tell me again where exactly is "down there"?' she asked.

'Kilsheelan. A village about five miles out of town. The River Suir runs past it, dividing us poor culchies from his lordship who lives and owns the other side. He has an enormous house they call a castle. They're Anglo-Irish, of course. More Anglo than Irish, photos of themselves with King George and Queen Elizabeth and old Queen Mary, so I hear tell. The creamery and the house are just a mile from the village, up the lane past St Mary's church, but there's the trap if you want to learn how to drive it. If you want to learn to drive the car I'll teach you myself. And won't *that* be a great laugh!'

'It'll terrify me! Me, driving a motor car! God in heaven, I've not even had a ride in one.'

'Women and girls drove lorries and ambulances during the Emergency.'

'Were you over here or over there when all that was going on?'

'Over there. They couldn't conscript me but I joined the Civil Defence and took a lot of abuse too, but I could understand that and it was no use telling women who'd lost husbands and sons that Ireland was no longer part of the Empire.'

They had reached the O'Connell bridge, which was as long as it was wide. Threading their way through the pedestrians and traffic, they walked on towards Grafton Street, passing the magnificent buildings of Trinity College.

'I have fond memories of that place.' Niall smiled. 'Sure, there were those who looked down their noses at me but I couldn't have cared less. Their class and culture is dying out and the remnants will go back across the sea from where they came. But it's not a history lesson you'll be wanting from me. What would you like to do?'

'I don't know. Isn't that an odd thing and me living here all my life.'

'Will we take a walk in the Green and then tea in the Shelbourne?'

At the mention of Dublin's most exclusive and expensive hotel she almost gasped aloud. God, the Shelbourne! When she'd been younger she used to stand and stare at the wealthy people arriving and departing.

She nodded and they headed for the park with its lake and bridges, arbours and little pavilions. The trees were just beginning to sprout and some of the shrubs were evergreens, so it wasn't completely devoid of greenery.

'Would you like to sit down, Breda?'

'Would you?'

'Yes. I've got something to ask you.'

'What?'

'Not until you are sitting down.' He propelled her gently in the direction of the nearest bench.

'Breda, I know we only met on the boat, but . . . but I fell in love with you. I couldn't help myself. I spent the rest of that night thinking about you.'

She looked down at her tightly clasped hands resting in

her lap. He did love her. Her instincts were right. All her dreams, her fantasies, were coming true.

'Is there a chance?'

She looked him full in the face and there was no guile or flirtatious expression on her face. Her eyes told him everything he wanted to know.

'Yes, Niall. I . . . there's . . . Oh, I love you! I really do! Mary wants me to wait, have a proper courtship as she calls it, but I don't want to!'

He took her hand. 'Neither do I. I don't want to travel the length of the country to see you. I want you by my side. I want to marry you, Breda Bernadette Nolan. Will you marry me? I'll get down on one knee if that's what you want.'

'It is not!' She smiled at him. 'Yes, I'll marry you, Niall.'

He leaned towards her and took her in his arms and kissed her. She loved him. She'd agreed. Oh, to hell with convention and the bloody clergy, he thought.

When at last he released her she felt dizzy.

'Close your eyes,' he instructed.

'Niall, what in God's name for?'

'Do as you're told. Close your eyes and hold out your hand. Your left one.'

Breda did as she was bid and he took a ring from its box and slipped it on her finger. It was too big but that could easily be remedied. He'd been praying ever since he'd bought it that she would agree to his proposal. He'd been far from certain, but he loved her.

'Now you can open your eyes.'

'Oh, Jesus, Mary and Joseph! Niall, it's gorgeous!' she gasped as she studied the gold ring set with a single flawless diamond.

'You like it then?'

'Like it! Didn't I just say it's gorgeous? Oh, Niall!' She turned and kissed him on the mouth, and for a few seconds all that could be heard was the noise of the ducks on the lake and the sighing of the wind through the trees.

'So, Breda, will I take you to meet my mother and sisters?'

'I never heard you mention sisters before.'

'I haven't, but there are a lot of things I haven't mentioned yet. Will you come? Won't they be impressed with their sister-in-law to be?'

Breda felt apprehensive. 'How many sisters are there?'

'Only two, sure it's not a rake of them.'

'All right, I'll come. When?'

'What about Saturday? The trains don't seem to be as bad on Saturdays, but Sundays you might just as well walk half the journey before they decide to fire up the engine and get a move on. One of these days this country is going to be run efficiently.'

When she arrived home Breda was full of it. As she stretched out her left hand both Mary and Kathleen were stunned by the size of the diamond in the engagement ring.

'You've only met him once before, Breda,' Kathleen cried.

'I know, but I *love* him, Mam.'

'Breda, are you sure? Really sure? Mam's right, you have only met him briefly.'

'I'm sure. I've never felt like this before. Didn't you love Col from the minute you set eyes on him? I love him and he loves me. And we went to the Shelbourne! The Shelbourne, Mam! You should have seen the style of the place! I was terrified that the cream and jam would spurt out of the scone all over me and him too.'

'So?' Mary urged.

'So I said I'd go down and meet his mam and sisters.'

'Won't that be a bit of an ordeal?' Mary enquired.

'It will so. I'll be paraded up and down like a tinker's hack at a horse fair. I'll have to be on my best behaviour and watch what I say and how I say it.'

'Well, you'll have to remember not to go saying "your one" or "your man", but don't you go giving yourself a posh accent. There's nothing wrong with the one you've got,' Mary advised.

'Oh, I don't know whether to go now. I'll be destroyed in case they don't like me.'

'What is there not to like, might I ask?' Kathleen said indignantly.

'Mam's right, Breda. You'll be marrying him, not that tribe of women. You'll be a fool to even think of not going.'

Breda nodded. 'What will I wear?'

Mary smiled. Breda was over the worst of her doubts. When she began to talk about clothes she was her normal easy-going self.

Chapter Twenty-Four

The preparations for Breda's visit to her future in-laws drove Kathleen to distraction. Her head was spinning with all her daughter's questions.

'What if they think me a poor excuse of a fiancée for Niall?'

'Will I wear my best things all the time or will that look too grand?'

'What if the sisters are little cats and make a mock and a jeer of me?'

When she couldn't bear it a minute longer, Kathleen took a tram back to see her old neighbours, to whom she could complain and gossip for hours. They were all agog, wanting to know what life was like in Rathmines and all the details of the big society wedding down in the country. None of them had been outside Dublin in their lives.

'Sure, it sounds like heaven, Kathleen,' Theresa Donaghue commented.

'Well, I wouldn't fancy it myself, Theresa. All those open fields and boreens, and they have strange ways of going on too,' Eileen Cusack had stated.

'And what kind of ways would they be?' Theresa had demanded.

'I heard there are a lot of Protestants down there.'

'In the name of God, haven't they a right to live where they choose? Aren't they just as Irish as we are?' Kathleen had replied.

'Aren't you very . . .' Theresa had searched for the right word '. . . tolerable.'

'Tolerant,' Kathleen had corrected her.

Sometimes she took Kevin along with her but he didn't seem to want to go and play with his former friends. He kept asking when Lily was coming.

'Mary, you'll have to do something soon. He's fretting after your little one over there.'

Mary sighed. Her mam was right. 'I know, but I just want to get Breda organised first.'

'Well, you'll never get *that* one organised. Not until the wedding is over and done with.'

'Oh, God, Mam. I don't think I could stick it out that long. It's not exactly going to be next week and Kevin is looking washed-out and miserable.'

'He doesn't like the school here, he told me so. All those boys look down their noses at him because he wasn't born and reared here or in Donnybrook.'

Mary sighed again. Things didn't seem to be improving at all.

Late on the Sunday night, Breda arrived back in a cab. She was bursting with excitement.

'I can see by the look on your face that the outing was a success,' Mary laughed.

'A success! Oh, you should see the style of the place! It's a huge old stone farmhouse, but inside it's got everything, absolutely everything. And to wake up in the mornings and not have all the shouting and the rattling of carts going by is wonderful. There's green fields all around and we went for a walk to the village and stood on the little stone bridge over the river and it was so quiet, and you could smell the air and it was sweet.'

'That's all very well, but what did you think of herself and the sisters that you were so worried about?'

'She's nice, Mam. Well, fairly nice,' she conceded.

'Only fairly?' Mary probed.

'Well, you don't expect the woman to welcome a future daughter-in-law with open arms when she's only been told a few weeks ago that she's to have one at all.'

'Do you think you could live together without belting one another to bits after a couple of weeks? Two women into one kitchen don't go, Breda, or do you intend herself to do all the cooking?'

'Oh, Mam! What a thing to say. Of course we'll get on. Like I said, it's a surprise, and I think she was expecting someone a bit . . . different.'

'Someone without the temper you have on you at times.'

Breda ignored her mother's remark and turned instead to her sister.

'The sisters, Maire and Niamh, are sixteen and fourteen. Maire works in a drapery on their O'Connell Street. Isn't that strange that there's two?'

'Not at all. Isn't it named after the great man himself and wasn't he a Protestant,' Kathleen added, thinking of Eileen Cusack's remarks.

Breda ignored her and carried on. 'Niamh is still with the nuns at the Presentation Convent. Niall wants her to get her Leaving Certificate in six subjects and go to university in Dublin to be a doctor or a librarian. She's quiet, always got her head in a book. Maire's much more spirited. We got on like a house on fire.'

Kathleen was looking a bit overawed, Mary thought, but there was no stopping Breda now.

'I know it's very unusual, but I want to get married down there in St Mary's, Irishtown. That's just a district. You go through the little archway of the old West Gate and it's a grand church. There's St Peter and St Paul's in the town itself, but St Mary's is far nicer. I'll have to have permission from Father Grogan. In fact we'll both need permission, because Kilsheelan has its own church, but it's a bit small.'

'And what, may I ask, is wrong with St Catherine's?' Kathleen demanded.

'Nothing, Mam, really. It's . . . it's . . .' Breda shrugged.

'She doesn't want the whole of the Liberties turning up to gape at the Quality up from the country, that's what's wrong with St Catherine's,' Mary said scathingly.

Breda tossed her head. 'Well, what if it is? Wouldn't I die of shame at the cut of them?'

'Breda Nolan, I'll not have you turning into a snob. "The cut of them" indeed! Just you remember that the Liberties is where you come from, and don't we always do our best to be decent and the men out of work half the time.'

'So, we all have to traipse down there? And where will we stay?' Mary asked.

'There's a nice hotel called Hearns. I thought—'

'Glory be to God, now she wants to waste money by putting us into a hotel.'

Mary sighed. If this was what Breda wanted then she for one wasn't going to argue. In a way she could understand her sister. They'd both come a long way from the Liberties and it was not a bad thing for her sister to aspire to a better lifestyle.

'Will you be inviting Aunty Maggie and Uncle Jim?'

'If you don't mind, Mary.'

'No, we'll have to sport some family or it'll be a poor show. What about the rest of them?'

'You mean Patsy and Bryan and Lily?'

'Yes.'

Despite her efforts a smug expression crossed Breda's face. Wouldn't Bryan O'Shea sit up and take notice. She was having a big wedding, marrying a professional man and a man of property. Not that she cared for Bryan now, but she'd enjoy seeing his face. 'Will you have Patsy as a bridesmaid?' Mary asked

'I will not. Isn't she a fright.'

'No, she's not. No one ever takes much notice of her. Please, Breda, just for me?'

'Oh, all right, but I'm not having Lily as well. I don't want it to look like a May procession.'

'What about Phil and Bob Kennedy and Flossie and Gerry O'Hanlon?'

'I am *not* having those two. Not after what Rosie did to you and Chris. Besides, they'd show you up, and what would herself think then? No, just Mr and Mrs Kennedy. At least they know how to behave.'

'And Albert?'

'Well of course I'll have Albert. Isn't he almost family and an educated man?'

'And just who is going to pay for all this?' Kathleen asked.

'I'll pay for the hotel and the outfits and half of the

reception,' Mary said. 'Once she's settled I'll try to start up with the hats again. Agnes's money won't last for ever.'

'At the rate you're spending it it won't, Mary. You're usually so thrifty.'

'I know, Mam, but it will be worth it to see her settled.'

'Mam.' Breda hesitated.

Kathleen's eyes narrowed. 'What now?'

'Will you . . . well, Niall says . . .'

'What is the matter with you, Breda?'

'Will you come and live down there with us? There's a nice little stone house by the ruins of St Sillan's church on the river bank. It's empty but they own it.'

'What would I want to do that for? I don't know anyone down there. And what about Mary and Kevin? No, Breda, I'm staying put here in Dublin.'

Breda shrugged. It was the reply she'd expected.

'I suppose you'll get your dress in Grafton Street?' Kathleen said with resignation.

'No, she will not. Isn't there a wonderful woman just off Dawson Street who makes dresses just as good, in fact better, at half the price. She'll do the bridesmaids' dresses too.'

'That's a relief. I thought she was going to bankrupt you, Mary,' Kathleen said. 'Will you have Kevin as a pageboy, do you think?' she asked Breda.

'God almighty, you don't want him dressed up in a sailor suit, do you? He'll be destroyed altogether if you do,' Mary replied, thinking of her son's embarrassment.

As the *Gardenia* sailed slowly into the wide estuary of the Tagus past the Belem Tower, Chris knew he had had enough. He doubted the ship would get to South America. The dreaded Bay of Biscay had lived up to its reputation and he was full of bruises after the battering the little ship had taken. He had no intention of drowning, so he'd jump ship and think about getting home. He'd never been so homesick, not even when he'd been in the Army. Now he longed for the sights and sounds of home. His mam and dad, Mike and all the other people he knew, but most of all Mary.

He knew he'd forfeit his pay, so he'd have to rely entirely on his savings.

Once away from the docks he began to realise what a beautiful city Lisbon was. Mosaic tiles covered the outside of many buildings. There were palm trees and exotic flowers blooming in the wide streets and the Rossio, the main square, whose pavement was also of tiles.

It was hot and the clothes he had were dirty, creased and far too heavy for this climate. He'd have to buy some new ones, then find a barber's shop and somewhere to stay, and he didn't speak a word of the language. When he'd sorted all that out he'd go down to the docks again and see what he could get in the way of a ship.

He felt much better in his new clothes. His hair had been cut and he'd had his first decent shave since he'd left Liverpool. All this had been achieved by a sort of sign language. He'd paid for a room in a house close to the Jeronimos Monastery in Belem, the old quarter of the town, which was very pretty. The room was sparsely furnished but it was clean and there were wooden shutters which closed to keep out the sun for the windows opened inwards.

He sat on the bed and went over his position. He had

no identification except his wartime ID card. He'd no discharge book which would mean he'd have a hard time finding a ship. And when he got home what would he do? It wouldn't be long before the police found him and he'd be facing the death sentence, but now he didn't care. Waves of misery and longing washed over him and he lay dejectedly watching a small lizard on the wall until the light faded.

When it was completely dark in the room he'd made up his mind. He'd go back, even if he only had a couple of days or even hours to wander the beloved streets again. Then he'd have to sign on for another ship and it would be just like the one he'd left.

On the following evening he made his way down to the docks again. It was a pleasant night with a soft breeze coming in down the estuary and rustling the fronds of the palms and palmettos, and the smell of flowers was heavy in the air. He caught sight of a policeman and, taking a deep breath and summoning up all his courage, crossed over to him.

'Sir, are there any British ships in?' he asked. Surely a dock policeman would understand him.

He did. 'Two. The *Athenia* and the *Hildebrand*, down there.' He pointed with a white-gloved hand and Chris thanked him. He'd try the *Hildebrand* first. She was one of the Booth Line ships and would be on her way back to Liverpool after sailing up the Amazon to Manaeus. Billy Jones from Athol Street sailed on her sister ship, the *Hilary*. If he was turned down he'd try the *Athenia*.

At the top of the gangway a deckhand stood smoking a cigarette.

'Can I come up, mate?' Chris shouted.

The man looked over the rail at him. 'What for?'

'I'm looking for work. Trying to get back to Liverpool.'

'Yeah, all right then.'

When he reached the top of the gangway the man looked him up and down. 'Where in Liverpool do yer come from, then?'

'Everton,' he lied. 'Who do I see about a job? Any kind of a job? Waiter, steward, deckhand?'

'The chief steward, a bloke called Hayes. Ben Hayes. He's a sound feller, and so is the barber, but the rest of them . . .' He shrugged and threw the cigarette butt over the side.

Chris followed the instructions he was given and marvelled at the decor of the ship. There were beautiful wood-panelled bulkheads, fine pictures and some small statues, potted plants and soft carpets, for she carried passengers as well as cargo. He stopped at a door with 'Chief Steward' engraved on a small brass plate and knocked.

A voice from within instructed him to go inside. Although it was only a small berth it was pristine and tidy, as was the man with light ginger hair wearing immaculate tropical whites who sat at the desk; in reality just a flap of wood that when folded fitted smoothly against the bulkhead.

'Well?'

'I . . . I've come to see if I can work my passage home, sir.'

'That's an accent I know well. You're a Scouser.'

'I am. I'll do anything. Any kind of job at all.'

'Have you sailed before?'

'Yes, sir, on the *Gardenia*.'

'God almighty, that old rust bucket's not still afloat? She

375

should have been impounded and scrapped by the Board of Trade years ago.'

'It was all I could get. They were desperate.'

'They'd be bloody desperate to get anyone at all. Have you any experience?'

'Only as a deckhand. I'm a brickie by trade.'

'So, what is a bricklayer doing in Lisbon?'

'It's the wife, sir. We . . . we had problems.' Chris was hedging. He hadn't been dismissed out of hand yet.

The chief steward stared at him hard, thinking of his own wife who had a temper you wouldn't believe. He was glad to be away for nine months of the year. Any longer than a couple of months' leave when there was money enough for parties, outings to the theatre, clothes and jewellery, and they'd fight like cat and dog.

'You don't have to explain *that*. Half the men in the merchant navy are away at sea to escape their better halves. Right, you can sail as a deckhand. Where's your discharge book?'

Chris's spirits drooped. He'd been doing so well so far. 'I don't have one. I left in a hurry and as I said, sir, the captain of the *Gardenia* was desperate and no one asked me any questions or asked to see any documents. I've only got my identity card.'

'I see. Have you got it on you?'

Chris dug into the inside pocket of his jacket and produced the card for inspection.

'What regiment?'

'The King's Liverpool, sir.'

The man nodded. He'd seen action in the Royal Navy in the first war and had sailed in the Arctic convoys in the second.

The card was returned. 'It's against company regulations, to say nothing of the Board of Trade and Immigration, but you seem genuine enough. Any nonsense out of you and I'll throw you in the brig and turn you over to the police when we dock.'

Chris breathed a sigh of relief. 'You'll have no trouble from me. When do we sail, sir?'

'Tomorrow morning at seven. Be aboard by five at the latest.'

'Thank you, sir, I really do appreciate it. I've not many belongings to collect from the room I've been staying in. I'll be aboard by half past four.'

The chief steward nodded and turned his attention once more to the sheaf of papers on the desk.

The journey home was pleasant even though Chris saw very little of the luxurious cabins and public rooms. They carried ten passengers with two stewards and one stewardess to attend to their needs. Chris was confined to the crew's quarters, the open deck or the engine room. With each day his spirits rose, despite the threat that hung over him. Just to see that familiar waterfront again would be enough. He'd have a wander around the city centre and then go back to the pool for another ship. At least he did have experience now and Mr Hayes had written him a reference which would enable him to get a discharge book, the sailor's passport in which the master always commented on such things as behaviour and standard of work.

Oh, it was so good to see the familiar landmarks, even the bomb sites, a lot of which had been cleared. Building work had already started and he wished he could stay. He'd have no trouble getting a job at his own trade in this city.

After a wander across the pier head and around the main

streets he had a quick and much relished pint in the Style House and went back to the pool. His feet felt like lumps of lead, so reluctant was he to turn his back on his native city after such a short stay, but he didn't dare linger any longer. The sight of a policeman, even one on point duty, brought him out in a cold sweat.

He pushed open the door to what was in effect the seamen's employment exchange with a feeling of dread in his stomach.

'Christ! Where the hell have you been?'

Chris was struck dumb as he faced his younger brother, Mike.

'Shut up, for God's sake! Do you want them to call in the scuffers?'

Mike looked at him in astonishment. 'What the hell do you mean by that?'

'I'll be seen and caught, that's what I mean.'

Mike grabbed him by the shoulders and pushed him back outside.

'There's no scuffers looking for you, you fool! They held an inquest on Rosie and the coroner gave a verdict of accidental death. You're in the clear, so for God's sake come home and see Mam. She's worried to death about you.'

Chris was so stunned and then so relieved that he couldn't speak.

'I see you made your way back in some style, anyway.' Mike nodded in the direction of the *Hildebrand* which was now being edged back into the river by the tugs.

'They told us you'd sailed in the *Gardenia* bound for South America. I think Mam has almost given up hope that she'll ever see you again.'

'What about Mary?' Chris had a hard job keeping his

voice steady. He wasn't a wanted man. He was home and he could stay home. He could walk the streets of Liverpool without fear. It was a minor miracle.

'She went back to Dublin. Oh, for God's sake don't look so bloody miserable, Mam and Maggie O'Shea have got the address. Breda was acting up and Mary was still so upset about you that she left.'

'But she's all right? She hasn't met anyone else?'

'She's fine and no, she was too cut up about you to be bothered with anyone else. So get back in the pub and we'll have a pint before we go home.'

Chris shook his head in wonderment. 'Home. God, but it's good to be back, Mike. And free! Bloody free! What were you doing in there, anyway?'

'Same as you, looking for a ship. I'm fed up with the docks. They've given me a job as a deckhand on the *Empress of Scotland*. A Canadian Pacific ship that takes passengers, mainly immigrants, to Canada. I sail in two days.' Mike slapped his brother hard on the shoulder. 'You bloody fool, but it's great to have you back!'

Chapter Twenty-Five

Phil stood stock still for a second before crying out, bursting into tears and throwing her arms around her eldest son. He'd been away for five months.

Chris hugged her. 'Oh, Mam, I'm so glad to be home. I've missed you all so much.'

When Phil calmed down she patted his arm.

'There was no need for you to go, son. No one blamed you. Patsy O'Shea said she saw a man running away from Flossie's house.'

Chris ran his hands through his hair. 'But I did hit her, Mam. I . . . I came home from the funeral and caught her with that Joe feller and I lost my temper. I slapped her twice across the face, not very hard but she fell. They were just slaps, Mam.'

'I know, son. She had no other injuries, or so they said.'

'I knew she was dead. I was terrified and I panicked and ran. I'll never be able to forgive myself for it. Never. I didn't mean for her to die.'

'She was no damned good, the little trollop, and given the circumstances even if you'd stayed you'd only have been tried for manslaughter,' Mike added.

Phil reached up and touched his cheek.

'Oh, Chris, you're not a murderer. You were provoked beyond the point no decent man could stand. It's all behind us now, son. You're home safe and that's all that matters.'

'Mike tells me that Mary's gone to Dublin. Have they all gone?'

Phil nodded. 'Aye. She was shocked and heart-broken over you, and that little madam of a sister was driving her mad, so she up and left. Albert Fallowfield is still in Exeter Road, though. He's looking after the house. She vowed she wouldn't sell it. I know for a fact she hoped that someday you'd come back. And she wouldn't put Albert out. She looks on him as a father. Now sit down while I get you a meal and you can tell us all about wherever it is you've been.'

Chris laughed. 'I didn't get very far. I'd had enough by the time we arrived in Lisbon.'

Phil's heart was bursting with happiness as she started to get a scratch meal together for him. She wasn't having him wait until Bob and the others came in. He looked so thin and gaunt. Never mind; at the end of the week on payday they'd have a slap-up do to welcome him back properly. Flossie wouldn't be happy but that was just too bad. Chris's name had been cleared at the inquest. It was Flossie's misfortune to have reared that little tramp Rosie, who had ruined so many lives and brought nothing but heartache to her poor mam.

Maggie and Nelly Casey were sitting at Maggie's kitchen table with Pauline on Pauline's afternoon off, making plans for the forthcoming wedding, when Mary's letter arrived in the second post.

'Put the kettle on again, Pauline, luv, while I read this.' Maggie tore open the envelope.

'The price of stuff these days! I don't know how they've got the nerve to charge such prices,' Nelly said indignantly, looking at the list they'd drawn up of guests and food and drink. They'd already pooled their coupons.

'We'll all have to starve,' Maggie had said earlier.

'It looks as if we won't have to pay for anything just yet, Nelly.' Maggie laid the letter on the table in front of her.

'Why?' Nelly asked, while inexplicably Pauline's excitement had begun to wane.

'It's from Mary. She says that Breda is going to marry the feller she met on the boat. You know, the one with all the money and the posh education she wrote about.'

'So?' Nelly queried.

'So she's getting married on the tenth of June and she's invited us and we *are* the only family she's got. Apart from our Kathleen and Mary.'

'Doesn't she know about our Pauline and your Maurice?' Nelly demanded. Breda Nolan was a madam and a half in her opinion. She'd never envied Mary's guardianship of the girl.

'I can't remember, Nelly, what with all the fuss that was going on at the time.'

'Oh, Mam, our day will be ruined! No one will turn up!' Pauline was very near to tears. Oh, trust that Breda. Not only was she marrying money but she was demanding that everyone went over.

'Now don't get upset, luv.' Maggie patted the girl's hand. 'You'll have your big day and it'll be a great day. We'll be able to have more food and drink, and you might even get a cab to the church. Just put it off until, say, September? It's only a couple of months.'

Pauline began to cry. 'It's three whole months!'

Nelly, although annoyed, could see the sense in this.

'Come on now, Pauline, Maggie's right. It's better to have it later when everyone can come. Even Breda and her rich husband if you want them. At least she'll have had her day. You'll get all the attention.'

Reluctantly Pauline nodded. 'I will still be having Kate and Molly and Patsy and a nice wedding breakfast?'

'Of course you will, luv. Nothing has changed just because Breda's getting married. And it *is* over there, so there'll be no fuss here.'

'She's inviting our Bryan and won't that alter his gob. You can bet your life she'll rub it in that he missed his chance, though I doubt they'd have been happy. They are both too selfish. And Mary wants our Lily. Well she can keep that little madam over there, I've had enough of her. Spoiled rotten she is and I'm worn out with her tantrums. She's learned some fancy notions living in Bootle and if she can't have her own way there's murder. She says she's not going to no public baths. *They* have a bathroom! I ask you! Oh, and Breda wants our Patsy as a bridesmaid. That's a turn-up for the book. And she's inviting Phil and Bob, but not Flossie and Gerry.'

'I can't say I blame her for that. Could you just see the cut of Gerry? He'd be blind drunk for days on end, and Flossie's no manners at all. God bless her, it's not her fault.'

'I don't think that's the real reason. I think both Breda and Mary are still upset over Rosie.'

'And who could blame them? I tell you, it's going to be a dear do, Maggie.'

'I know. Mary says that she'll pay all our boat and train fares.'

'Train? Where is she getting married then, for God's sake?'

'Down in Tipperary, a place called Clonmel.'

Nelly was incredulous. 'Where will you all stay? Surely your Kathleen can't put you all up.'

'In an hotel, would you believe. God in heaven, we're not used to hotels! The likes of us don't stay in places like that. We haven't even got a decent nightdress between us. Oh, I'm starting to dread it already and I've those two madams of mine to cope with. Our Patsy will torment the daylights out of our Lily because she's going to be a bridesmaid and Lily isn't. Then there'll be murder and that's before we even set off! We'll all have to have new outfits and where am I going to find the money for those?'

'If she wants you to go, then she should pay for the outfits,' Nelly said firmly, thinking that maybe Pauline was right to complain.

'She says she'll pay for all the expenses. I presume that covers clothes.'

'And what does he do, this Niall feller?' Nelly enquired.

'He went to some big university in Dublin, then he worked over here, and then . . .' Maggie's words trailed off. Her eyes widened and she clutched a hand to her throat as she caught sight of Chris standing in the doorway.

'Mary, Mother of God! Is it you, lad?'

Chris grinned. 'It's me, Mrs O'Shea! Safe and well and back from Lisbon.'

Maggie hugged him to her while Nelly sniffed and Pauline wiped her eyes. It was turning into a really miserable day for her. First Breda Nolan and now him.

'Did your mam send you over? How long have you been back? Where've you been?'

Chris disentangled himself. 'She did, about two hours and I've been to Portugal. Does that cover everything?'

'I can't believe it! I just can't believe it! You know they said it was accidental death? Our Patsy couldn't remember how long it was between seeing the feller and seeing you and they couldn't identify the feller either.'

'I know, Mam told me.' He wasn't going to reveal all the facts of Rosie's death outside his immediate family. Let them all believe what they liked.

'Is it Mary's address you want?' Maggie beamed at him.

'How did you know?' He smiled back.

'That's a letter from her, just arrived. I've been reading it out to Nelly. Breda's getting married in June to some rich bloke she met on the ferry going home.'

'But Mary hasn't . . . isn't . . .'

Maggie's voice and expression softened. 'No. Mary still loves you, Chris. Will you go to her now?'

'I'll be on the next boat.'

'Then for God's sake take our Lily with you, she's driving me mad. Mary promised she'd send for her and all I get is "When, Mam? When? When?" She's like a cracked gramophone record!'

The night couldn't have been more of a contrast to the night before St Patrick's Day when they'd all gone to see Mary, Breda and Kevin off, Maggie thought. It was quite a warm evening for the first of May so no one was muffled to the eyes or huddled together against the wind and rain.

They'd all come down, even Flossie who had been

convinced by Maggie and Phil that it must have been that Joe who'd killed Rosie and Chris had panicked. All of Phil's family, Mike, Lizzie, Theresa and Joey, and Bryan, Patsy and Jim plus Carmel and Jimmy O'Hanlon. Even Pauline and Maurice and Nelly and Arthur Casey had gone down to the pier head to see them off.

Lily's eyes were dancing and her little face was full of excitement. She'd hated living with Mam again. She hated Patsy who was going to be a bridesmaid twice and who never stopped talking about blue dresses and hairdressers and usually ended by saying 'and you're not!' At which point Lily often flew at her sister like a small fury, scratching and kicking until Maggie intervened and they were both slapped.

She held Kevin's grubby rabbit tightly. She'd never let Patsy even touch it. Despite her joy, however, she had one small fear. She hoped the crossing wasn't going to be like their experience on the Mersey ferry. She didn't want to feel sick and frightened.

'Lily, now give our Patsy a kiss and let's have an end to all this nonsense,' Maggie instructed.

Lily glared at her sister. 'I won't. I hate her! I hate her!'

'And I hate her too!' Patsy yelled back.

Maggie slapped the pair of them. 'Oh, isn't that a nice way to go on and in public too? Love thy neighbour, it says in the Commandments, and that means each other, especially sisters like the pair of you!'

Under the gimlet eyes of their father they made a show of kissing each other, Patsy hissing. 'I still hate you' and Lily hissing back, 'I'll have a better frock than you, Aunty Mary will see to that!'

Patsy made a grab at the knitted toy and Lily screamed at the top of her voice.

Maggie was furious. 'Oh, now what? Patsy, pick up that flaming rabbit and give it back or she'll not get on board the damned ferry!'

Patsy did as she was told and judging by the look on her father's face knew she was in for a hiding when she got home. She didn't care. She wouldn't have to share her bedroom with Lily ever again. And she was to be bridesmaid twice and Pauline had promised blue and a visit to the hairdressers. Breda had said nothing about any of that, but hers was to be a big affair, so Patsy assumed that the bridesmaids' dresses would be very fancy.

Phil hugged her son to her. 'Oh, Chris, I'm so glad for you. You bring her back here as your wife and my daughter-in-law, for that's the way I've always looked on her.'

'I will, Mam, I promise. Come on, Lily, hold my hand tight now. By morning we'll be there and you can give Kev back his rabbit. Have you got your doll?'

Maggie had given strict instructions regarding the treasured doll. 'If that damned thing is lost or broken she'll make your life a flaming misery,' she'd warned.

'She's in the bag,' Lily replied. Her mam, after packing all her things into a big canvas holdall, had said the doll would be safer in there. She would have enough to do looking after the rabbit, because if she managed to lose it she wouldn't be very welcome at all.

They all stood in a group and waved as the gangway was hauled up. The customary three blasts of the ferry's steam whistle rent the dark spring air and the ferry pulled away.

On deck Chris lifted Lily up so she could wave to her

mam and dad while a lump in his own throat stopped him from shouting the way Lily was doing. He wanted to cry and laugh and he was shaking with emotion as he held her hand and found a seat in the saloon. There wasn't the luxury of a cabin for them.

The sun was beginning to rise in a cloudless blue sky as they stood on deck next morning. Mary didn't know they were coming and all night Chris had held Lily on his knee as she slept, the ludicrous, battered little rabbit clutched tightly to her. Asleep she looked like a little angel, awake she was a holy terror, or so her mam had warned him.

His heart was pounding now as the ferry cleared Ireland's Eye, the small island just off the coast. He'd asked directions from a priest who was on board and knew which tram or bus to get out to Rathmines.

At last the gangway was lowered and he picked Lily up so she wouldn't get lost in the crush. The crowds streamed down, into and out of the huge shed-like building, and they followed them.

'Are we really here?' Lily asked, looking up with apprehension. This didn't look anything like what Kev had described.

'We are, Lily. Now we have to get either a tram or a bus to a place called Rathmines and then—'

'You're sure I'll see Kev?' she persisted with a stubborn set to her chin.

'Lily O'Shea, your mam said you sounded like a cracked gramophone record and you do. Now shut up while I look for the right queue.'

The journey seemed interminably long. The streets were unfamiliar to him but there were a lot of houses like the ones in Rodney Street at home, although those in Rodney

Street, Liverpool's Harley Street, were well maintained while the houses here in Dublin looked to be in danger of falling down.

At last they alighted and walked up the road. It was a beautiful May morning and his heart was singing. It was going to be a perfect day.

Kathleen opened the door, wondering who would be calling at this hour of the morning.

'Mrs Nolan?' Chris asked, his cap already in his hand while Lily clung to his jacket, her thumb in her mouth.

'I am. And who are you?'

'This is Lily O'Shea and I'm—'

Before he could finish there was a shriek and Mary, with tears streaming down her cheeks, threw herself into his arms.

'Oh, Chris! Chris! I never lost hope! I always thought you'd come back one day!'

He held her tightly, the way he'd dreamed so often he would. 'Oh, Mary, I've missed you so much!'

For the first time Mary saw Lily.

'Lily! Did you bring her, Chris?'

'I did, and she's harped on and on all the way!'

'Oh, Mam, take her to Kevin, please?' Mary was loath to leave the circle of Chris's arms, and as Kathleen took hold of the child's hand and led her away she raised her lips to his. 'Chris! I love you so much. Did you hear the verdict?'

He nodded before bending to kiss her again.

When they heard the shouts and screams from the back of the house they drew apart.

He looked down at her. 'Mary, will you marry me, now, this minute?'

She smiled up at him, a smile so radiant it made his heart beat faster. 'I will so, but the "very minute" is out. Won't they have to call the banns first?'

'Then take me to see your priest.'

'After I've really made sure you are flesh and blood and not just a dream. One of my many dreams of you, Chris.'

His arm round her waist, they walked into the kitchen where Lily and Kevin, flushed with excitement, were holding hands and doing a little jig, to the accompaniment of Kathleen and Breda's encouragement and clapping.

Breda smiled at Chris.

'Come here to me, if you're going to be my brother-in-law, and give me a kiss. And promise to be "the wild rover no more",' she laughed, using a line of a folk song. 'All I ask, Mary, is that you don't upstage *my* wedding.'

'We won't do that, I promise,' Mary answered. 'Ours will be a quiet wedding.'

'And long before yours. In three weeks to be exact.' Chris laughed although he meant it. As soon as the banns were read, this time he wouldn't let her slip through his fingers. He loved her too much.

Chapter Twenty-Six

They were married three weeks later in a quiet ceremony in Mary's new parish. Mr Brannigan from the old neighbourhood gave Mary away. Breda and young Bernard Donaghue were the two witnesses. Kathleen's eyes misted as she heard her eldest daughter plight her troth for the second time in her young life, and she prayed that this marriage would be as happy as the first had been and last far longer.

Mary, at Breda's insistence, had bought a cream dress trimmed with navy from Brown Thomas in Grafton Street.

'I could have made it myself for half the price,' Mary had complained.

'Mary, for once in your life stop thinking of the cost. Things aren't on ration here now,' Breda had said impatiently.

'Oh, she's off already! I knew it wouldn't be long before she started with the high and mighty way of going on,' Kathleen had remarked, and Mary had insisted on making her own hat.

Pure happiness made Mary look radiant and when Father Kelly said to Chris that he might now kiss his bride only his arm round her kept Mary from swaying dizzily. She looked up at him with shining eyes.

'Oh, Chris, I love you so much,' she said quietly.

'I'll never leave your side again, Mary, I promise.' His voice too was full of emotion.

'Could I have a kiss too, do you think?' young Bernard asked.

'Indeed you cannot! Oh, take no notice of him, Father. Isn't he a desperate trial to me,' his mother interrupted, having left her seat in the second pew where she was sitting with Mrs Dunne and Mrs Cusack.

There was a small reception at Mary's house before the newly-weds were to catch the overnight ferry to Liverpool, leaving Kevin and Lily with Kathleen.

Kathleen, with a newly found air of confidence and pride, showed her old neighbours round her ground-floor rooms.

'Will they come back here, do you think?' Mrs Dunne asked.

'Only to visit. She's that house over there, don't forget, and she's really going to try to get a business going. All this and Breda's wedding is costing a fortune. That Albert Fallowfield is going to help her and Chris will be working too. Did I tell you he's a bricklayer by trade? He won't go short of work over there.'

'Sure, won't you be rattling around in all these rooms, especially with Breda going too?' Theresa asked.

'Well, there's one thing you can count on for sure and for certain: I'm not moving down there to live in a stone house on a riverbank. I'm taking no grace and favour house from that lot down there.'

'Mam, will you not speak like that about Niall's family. It's . . . derogatory,' Breda chided.

Kathleen raised her eyes to the ceiling. 'What am I to do with her at all, using all these fancy words, hoping to sound educated. I can tell you I'm not looking forward to this do one little bit.'

Kevin and Lily, both still in their best clothes, although Lily had already lost her hair ribbon and had red jelly down the front of her dress, were sitting under the table, a habit they'd reverted to despite the fact that they now had their own room.

'Do you think they'll forget us, Lily?'

Lily looked scornful. 'They promised, Kev, and Aunty Mary always keeps her promises. Didn't I come over like she said?'

Kevin nodded and bit into his fourth fairy cake. 'What will we call him?' he asked, his mouth full of sponge.

Lily pondered this. 'I can call him Uncle Chris, I suppose.'

'Will I have to call him Da?'

'Only if you want to. Now come on out from there this minute. Look at the cut of you, Lily O'Shea. Sure, I'll never get all those stains out,' Kathleen scolded as she whipped up the tablecloth to reveal the two small fugitives.

Mary was instantly by her mother's side and she sank down on her heels to be on their level.

'What do you want to call him, Kevin?' She searched his face for signs of doubt and unhappiness.

Kevin looked up at Chris. He'd not really known him when they'd lived in Hornby Street but his mammy said she loved him.

Chris smiled at him. He'd made no ostentatious show of interest or affection. The child must make up his own mind, he'd told Mary when this had been discussed. 'I'll call him Da,' Kevin said firmly.

Chris grinned and bent down to hoist Kevin on to his shoulder. They were both laughing.

'Me too! Me too, Uncle Chris!' Lily shouted, tugging at Chris's jacket.

'This is turning into a circus, so it is. Put those children down or they'll be sick. Haven't the pair of them been at the jelly and cakes like a couple of little pigs!' Kathleen demanded, but there was laughter in her eyes.

They were blessed with a calm crossing. As usual the ferry was filled mainly with men and boys. The Free State had given them freedom but it couldn't yet provide them all with jobs.

As they watched the incandescent wake of the ferry catching the moonlight, making it resemble a pathway of silver, Mary laughed quietly.

'What is so funny, Mrs Kennedy?'

'Breda and Niall. I was thinking of the weather last time. He must love her if he thought she was a great beauty and she drenched to the skin with salt water. But I think she's settled down. She seems more . . . grown up. Mind you, I can't see him putting up with the antics she used to use to get her own way.'

'She's young, Mary, and she loves him.'

'So I am old and settled?' she asked, but her eyes were shining and her cheeks were flushed.

'No, you're young and beautiful, but yes, I hope you're settled. I've waited a long time for you, Mary.'

She reached up and softly stroked his cheek. 'Then we'll waste no more of that time. Will we go down now?'

He took her face gently between his hands and kissed her as he'd so often dreamed of doing.

*   *   *

They went first to Exeter Road to tell Albert because they both knew that once in Hornby Street they'd not get away for hours.

Kathleen had said that Mary must write and tell him but both she and Breda thought it would be best to surprise him.

'Haven't I known people of his years to drop down dead being "surprised",' had been the terse reply.

He was indeed surprised.

'Mary! Mary, why didn't you write? Come on in.' Then he noticed Chris and a broad smile spread across his face. 'So you came back? And do I have the pleasure of calling you "Mrs Kennedy", or is that being premature?'

Mary hugged him. 'No, it's not. I am Mrs Kennedy.'

Albert took her left hand in his and scrutinised the gold band.

'Well, congratulations to you both. You've both been to hell and back. Does Mrs O'Shea know?' he asked as he ushered them into the shabby morning room.

'No, we came here first,' Mary said.

'To sort of gather our wits and strength before the onslaught, if you know what I mean,' Chris added.

Mary took off her jacket and went to make a pot of tea, her hands trembling at the sheer joy that filled her.

'Take care of her, Chris, or you'll answer to me. I love her like a daughter and she's had enough sorrow in her life.'

'I swear I will.' Chris leaned forward. 'I never loved anyone but Mary. That . . . mess with Rosie . . .' He shook his head. 'I didn't love her. She tricked me. I hated her.'

'At the time I was so angry that I thought hanging was too good for you.'

'I don't blame you. In your shoes I'd have felt the same way.'

Albert shook his head. 'Chris, you wouldn't ever have wanted to be in my shoes.'

'Why?' Chris was confused.

Mary came in with the tea in time to hear Albert's last words. She put down the tray and went over to Albert and took his hand.

'Chris, I've looked on Albert as a father, as did Breda. To Kevin and Lily he was like a grandfather and they love him as much as Breda and I do. He's a kind, generous, wise and thoughtful man.'

Albert looked up at her and gave a slight nod.

'He is also the public executioner,' Mary said quietly.

For a few seconds there was silence and then Chris ran his hands through his hair and stood up.

'That must be the best-kept secret in Liverpool.' He shook his head. Never in a million years would he have suspected Albert Fallowfield of holding such a position. 'How did you get to be . . . that?'

Mary watched Albert's expression. It was a question she'd often wanted to ask herself.

'From my father. I felt it was my duty to take over from him. Mother died young and then Father just seemed to . . . fade. It was a duty and I endured it. It's something that's usually kept in the family. It's . . . embarrassing, you see, having to tell people outside your family what your father does.'

'And you never married?' Chris asked.

Albert shook his head. 'I just didn't meet the right person. And it really does have to be the right one.'

'I think we all need the tea. Will I pour?'

'No, you will not, Chris. Aren't your hands shaking so much you'd drop Agnes's best china.'

'Your china, Mary,' Albert corrected.

'No, *our* china.'

Albert smiled. 'Mary, I'm fifty-six so I've got quite a few years left, please God, and I'm sick of death. I've come through two wars – in the first, I served in the Liverpool "Pals" Regiment and I was lucky to escape with a leg wound. In the last one, I was an ARP warden – and then . . . well, we won't go into what followed. I'm retiring. I've posted my letter of resignation. I'd thought of going out to my cousin in Ontario. He lives in Beamsville. It's in the fruit-growing belt, and while I'd like to spend the rest of my days surrounded by trees and vines and not smoke-blackened buildings, bomb sites, dirt and grinding poverty, I just couldn't leave you and the children. Not to see them grow up would break my heart. But I think you and Chris need some time together, it's only right, and it's not much use going all that way for a couple of weeks. I thought I'd go in September and come back just before Christmas. Can you put up with me until September?'

Mary hugged him but there were tears in her eyes.

'Hasn't this been your home from the day you left Aunty Maggie's house? It'll always be your home.'

'Thank you for that, Mary. I shall always regard it as such. But you'll need the place to yourselves for a while,' Albert said. 'And the children. Have they come with you?'

Mary smiled. 'Now wouldn't that be a nice thing? Trailing two children with us on our honeymoon? No, aren't they driving Mam mad, but it won't be for long. Everyone will be coming over for Breda's wedding. Have you had your invitation yet?'

Albert consulted the watch Agnes had left him. 'No, but it's a bit early for the post.'

'Well you will, and I won't hear a word about you refusing it. Haven't you been like a father to her too. In fact if I'd had a say you'd have been the one to give her away instead of Uncle Jim, who is dreading it, so I hear.'

'And so would I. No, Jim O'Shea is family, real family, Mary. But I'll definitely be there.'

'Before I go on to Hornby Street, would there be a chance of taking up a certain item there was such a fuss about? I believe, according to Aunty Maggie, that young Pauline was very upset about having to postpone her wedding because of Breda's.'

Albert nodded slowly. 'I think so, but tell her not to be too keen on flashing it around. In fact you could advise them to sell it and with the money they could have a better start to married life.'

Chris looked at Mary with curiosity.

'I'll explain it all later,' she said as Albert left the room.

Although it was still early there was uproar in Hornby Street once it was known that Mary and Chris were back as man and wife.

All the neighbours came out to congratulate them and were reluctant to leave Maggie's house, where Mary and Chris had gone first.

Phil was so happy that she was in floods of tears and had to be calmed down by Lizzie and Bob.

'It's the answer to all my prayers,' she said between sobs.

'Well, it doesn't sound like it by the way you're crying, Mam,' Chris laughed.

'Have you seen Albert?' Maggie asked.

'Yes. We'll be going back there later.'

'How long will you be staying?'

'Until the weekend. We're hoping to have a few days together in Llandudno. I've been told it's very nice there. Then I'll have to go back or Mam will have killed them all.'

'I'll put the kettle on again. There's some things about the wedding we want to discuss.'

Jim, Bob, Maurice and Bryan made for the door.

'Come on down the docks with us, lad. You'll get no peace with this lot now that the Wedding of the Year has been mentioned,' Bob urged.

Chris laughed. 'Da, we've only just arrived.'

Mary smiled at him. 'Go on back to Exeter Road and you can have a peaceful morning with Albert. Maurice, will you call at Pauline's and tell her to pop in on her way to work?'

In all the commotion Patsy had been ignored until she tugged at Mary's sleeve.

'Patsy O'Shea, shift yourself or you'll be late for school,' her mother instructed.

'No, wait. What is it, Patsy?' Mary asked.

'It's . . . when . . . well, Breda's wedding. What will I wear?'

Maggie tutted but Mary saw a rather plain child who hadn't had much in the way of happiness in her life.

'Come here to me and sit down, Patsy, while I tell you all about it.'

The child's expression changed.

'Well, there will be three of you. Maire and Niamh are grown up, and they will be wearing long peach taffeta dresses with frills round the hem and neck, and they'll have bouquets of roses and carnations and a band of flowers in their hair. But you'll be special because you're the youngest.' Seeing Patsy's expression she carried on. 'You're to have white organza over peach satin and all around the neck, the sleeves and the hem there'll be little bunches of blue forget-me-nots. You'll have a basket of flowers to carry and you'll have a headdress like the one Lily had for her Communion only a bit more fancy. Oh, and white socks and buckskin shoes. And I hear that Mrs Power who's supposed to be great with the hairdressing down there will come to the hotel to do everyone's hair, if they want her to.'

'Glory be to God, Mary, this must be costing you a fortune! Hotels, posh frocks, hairdressers! I never heard the like!'

'Not as much as you think. Haven't I got a good deal from Hearns? Because we're practically taking over the hotel they're giving me everything at half price. And Mrs Power doesn't charge the earth. The Fitzgeralds are paying for the church, the flowers and half the wedding breakfast, which will be in the hotel. They don't need transport; they already have a car, a trap and some sort of old-fashioned carriage that's been dug out of a barn and is being cleaned up.' Mary laughed. 'Mr Kennedy is right, it will be the Wedding of the Year. They're not short of money.'

As she went upstairs Patsy was thrilled. All *that*! She'd have them all green with envy at school. Two bridesmaid's dresses and two real hairdressers to do her hair.

She'd barely disappeared when Pauline, looking a little apprehensive, came in the back way.

'Maurice said you wanted to see me?'

'I do. Aunty Maggie, do you think we could use the front room for a few minutes?'

Maggie nodded sagely, thinking Mary was going to try to cheer the girl up. She'd need it, by the sounds of it. After seeing what kind of a wedding Breda was having the poor girl would be devastated.

'Pauline, I'm so sorry about Breda's wedding clashing with yours, and haven't you been goodness itself to change your date.' Mary delved into her handbag and brought out a small leather pouch and passed it to Pauline.

'Go on, open it. It's for you. It's a present from Chris and me.'

Pauline gasped at the sight of the ring, knowing instantly how valuable it was.

'It's . . . it's . . . for me?'

'It is so. You've already got a very nice ring, so if you'd like to sell it and use the money for something else we won't mind one little bit. It came from a very expensive jewellers in Grafton Street, Dublin,' she lied.

'Oh, I couldn't sell it!'

'It's up to you, Pauline. It's yours.'

'I don't know what to say. Thanks! Oh, thanks!' Pauline was near to tears.

Mary hugged her. 'I hope you'll be as happy with Maurice as I am with Chris. Get off now or you'll be late for your work.'

Well, that was two of them happy, she thought. Now there was only Aunty Maggie and her new mother-in-law to sort out with outfits and accommodation at Hearns, Clonmel's foremost hotel. It had been a car or coaching depot run by Charles Bianconi who eventually established a nationwide transport system over a hundred years ago, so Breda had read. Breda was determined her new family were not going to think her ignorant of the history of the place she was coming into.

Chapter Twenty-Seven

They had taken over the whole hotel and at eight o'clock on the tenth of June chaos reigned. All the men had had a 'drop of the good stuff' the night before and most were looking under the weather, especially young Maurice who had had a dressing down from his mam, plus a clip around the ear which made his already throbbing head worse.

'I blame you, Jim O'Shea! Fancy letting him get bevvied like that. Pauline's going to be mortified.'

'For God's sake, Maggie, give it a rest. Does this bloody collar have to be so tight? It's choking me.'

'Yes, it bloody does. Now where's that flaming hat pin? I've got a head like Birkenhead already.'

'You put it on that table thing,' Patsy informed her while preening before the mirror on the outside of the wardrobe door. She looked wonderful. Her dress was gorgeous and so was her headdress. It was far nicer than Lily's Communion one. It was like a crown. Mrs Power had washed her hair, trimmed it, dried it and then coaxed and teased it until it was a shiny bob with a fringe which suited her. Then her headdress had been placed securely over it. She'd tormented Lily with her new image and only the timely intervention of Mary stopped it all ending in tears.

Mary seemed to be the only one to have some measure of calmness and Chris thanked God for it. His own mam was wearing a very smart and slimming royal blue dress with a matching hat and Maggie was transformed by a sage-green two-piece costume trimmed with cream braid and a large cream and green picture hat.

Maire and Niamh were ready and were bored and then excited in turns. Maire declared she could eat a horse, to which Niamh had replied that if she ate even a crumb she couldn't go to Communion and then Mam would take her apart.

Kathleen, who was uneasy wearing the dusky pink grosgrain dress that had cost an arm and a leg, had to endure an unforgettable twenty minutes of Mrs Power's ministrations.

'Why in God's holy name I have to have you to do my hair at all I don't know. Won't it be destroyed under the hat? And that's another thing. I won't be able to get through doors without difficulty. Sure, it could be used as a wheel on that fancy carriage she's to go to the church in.'

Mrs Power had, up to now, been very pleased with her handiwork on the bridesmaids and Phil and Maggie and was looking forward to arranging the bride's dark curly hair. These disparaging remarks caused her to look pained.

'Won't you be taking that grand hat off later on?' she stated.

'The sooner the better or I'll have a headache from the weight of it,' Kathleen replied, ignoring the hairdresser's petulant tone of voice.

'Then you won't want your hair looking . . . untidy.'

'Won't it all be flattened?' Kathleen was still not happy. What if this woman made a complete fright of it, for all her professional airs? Mary was doing her own and Breda was only going to have her hair tidied and her headdress and veil put on.

'Nothing that a quick flick of a comb won't cure. Of course it wouldn't even need that if I'd have had time to give it a marcel wave.'

'And what might I ask is that?' Kathleen was getting irritated by the woman's patronising tone.

'It's a perm. I would have thought you'd have known that, living above in Dublin.'

Kathleen sniffed. 'Not everyone in Dublin spends their time "dressing up",' was her acerbic reply.

The hairdresser decided to ignore the rebuff.

'Well, it's a process where you wrap the hair around special curlers and then use chemical pads and heat and it produces "Permanent" waves. It's very popular and fashionable and it takes skill.'

'That's as may be, but if the good Lord had wanted me to have waves and curls, wouldn't I have been born with them like Breda and Mary.'

Mrs Power pursed her lips. There was no conversation between them until the hat was placed over the new coiffure.

Mary, already dressed but without her hat, gloves and handbag, fully approved of the hairdresser's work.

'Mrs Power, doesn't she look grand?'

Mrs Power nodded, glad that at least someone approved.

'Mam, go and get your accessories while I pay Mrs Power for all her hard work. She has only Breda to see to now.'

Feeling more confident now that she'd had a truthful opinion from her elder daughter who was used to such a way of going on, she nodded curtly in the hairdresser's direction.

'After you've seen to Herself here, will you do something to liven up those two rossies who are lounging around out there? I'll try and keep Patsy and Lily from killing each other. Our Maggie's at her wits' end with the pair of them. You've spoiled that child, Mary. Weren't they at it again when I saw them last and after all you said to them not ten minutes ago? Am I to see Breda at all before she goes to the church?'

'Of course, Mam. After Mrs Power here has finished I'll send someone for you but there's to be no weeping and throwing your arms around each other or both of you will end up with red eyes and ruined outfits.'

Kathleen raised her eyes to the ceiling. She'd be glad when all this palaver was over. Sometimes Mary could be a bossy strap but she'd inherited that from herself.

Despite Mary's instructions, after she'd told her two young nieces in detail what she would do to them if there wasn't an end to the fighting she went in search of Breda and almost collided with her brother in the corridor, to the detriment of the angle of the hat.

'Glory be to God! Is that you, our Kathleen?'

'It is so and you've just ruined half an hour's work, Jim O'Shea. Now I'll look desperate in this fool of a hat.'

'Gerroff, you look dead posh. You all look like the "gentry" as you insist on calling the future in-laws. Posh ladies from Liverpool and Dublin.'

Kathleen, who had been trying to return the hat to its former angle, looked at her brother with open scepticism.

'Ladies! Are you making a mock and a jeer out of me?'

'I'm not, honestly.'

Kathleen smiled. 'Well, we won't be disgracing her by letting *them* think we've no manners on us at all. Anyway, where are you off to, creeping around the place?'

'To escape the tribe of women. They seem to be everywhere.'

'I hope you're not thinking of heading for the bar. If you can't go to Communion and you after being the one to give her away, Maggie will kill you and so will I. There'll be no "drop of Powers" this morning.'

Jim pulled a face. 'Don't I know it. I've already had the Riot Act read to me twice.'

Kathleen grinned and left him.

She reached the door of Breda's room just as Mrs Power was leaving and, totally ignoring the look the hairdresser gave the hat, she went straight in.

'Mary, will you do something with this fool of a hat. It's all wrong, didn't Jim nearly knock me off my feet just now and . . .' Her words trailed off and tears misted her eyes as her gaze alighted on Breda.

'Oh, Mam, don't start or I'll be in floods of tears myself.' Breda sniffed. 'Oh, I'm destroyed altogether. I'll trip over this train or fall up the church steps or forget what I'm supposed to say and . . .'

Mary took them both in hand although her own tears were not far away.

'It doesn't matter that our backgrounds are different from theirs. It's the style and the turnout that's the thing. And your vows, Breda. They are the most important thing of all.'

'Oh, they are, Mary. I love Niall but I'm terrified, I really am. What if something awful *does* happen and I make a show of . . . everyone?'

'Breda, it *won't*. You'll be the most beautiful bride Clonmel has ever seen and he'll be delighted with you. You look gorgeous.' Mary smiled at her sister. 'Take a deep breath and let it out slowly while I get the bridesmaids organised or we'll all be late. Aunty Maggie's watching Kevin and Lily and Pauline is giving Maurice a good talking to.'

'And won't it be the first of many. He hasn't got much go about him, has he? I said so to our Maggie, but didn't she bite the head off me.'

'Mam, for God's sake let's not have any fights today! Just keep Breda calm.'

Mary turned at the door and then went back to her sister and kissed her cheek.

'God bless you, Breda, and I mean that with all my heart. Mam, you're to stay here until everyone except Breda and the bridesmaids have gone to the church. The car will come back for you.'

'Oh, Mother of God! Me in a car! Isn't my head spinning with the palaver of it all already.'

'Ah, come on out of that, Mam. You're enjoying every minute of it.' Mary laughed and then kissed her mother's cheek.

'Are you ready, Breda, luv?' Jim asked, taken aback by the girl's appearance. Kathleen had set off to the church already. All brides looked beautiful, so Maggie had told him and Breda had always been beautiful, but now . . . 'You look like a princess.'

'Do you really mean that, Uncle Jim? Oh, I'm shaking.'

'Of course I mean it and you love him, don't you?'

'Yes, of course I do.'

'Then what in the name of God is there to be nervous about?'

Breda smiled and began to feel calmer. She did love Niall and it was him she was marrying in fifteen minutes' time.

'I'll get our Patsy and the others in here to help with all this.' He airily waved a hand indicating the dress and veil. 'Then we'd better go down and wait.'

Breda looked stricken. 'How will we manage to get all this material into the carriage, just you and me?'

'Stop getting in a state again, Breda, we'll manage and you'll have his sisters and our Patsy to sort it all out when we arrive.'

With the help of Mrs Power and Biddy Kelly, the barmaid, who had lingered in the passageway hoping to be asked for assistance, they got Breda installed in the open landau. On her journey to the church everyone stopped to stare in amazement and call out to her as they drove down O'Connell Street and through the narrow stone archway to St Mary's. Shopkeepers, publicans, women on the street, men going about their business, all wished her well.

The church spire soared upwards towards the blue sky and the bells began to ring as Maire and Niamh helped her out, while Patsy held the bridal bouquet of white lilies, roses, carnations and trailing smilax. Now that the big moment had arrived Patsy was trembling with nerves and half wished she'd never agreed to be a bridesmaid at all.

The church looked lovely, Kathleen thought as she took her place in the front pew on the left-hand side. The flowers of summer were riotously plentiful and contrasted with the pale tones of the interior. It was a big church with a long aisle which meant that everyone would have a good view of Breda as she passed. Joy, pride, love and satisfaction: all were mixed in her breast. Everyone on her side of the church looked very smart and elegant. Her gaze softened as she looked at Mary, Chris, Kevin and Lily. Mary had always been a grand girl who deserved the happiness now shining in her eyes. Today particularly she had dressed down, so as not to take any of her sister's glory away.

Mary caught her glance and smiled back as Chris's hand closed over her own. Kevin and Lily, now quite happy with a bribe of a penny bar of Cadbury's chocolate later, stood close together as they always did. Mam looked great, she thought. She was totally transformed and looked the equal of Niall's mother and aunts, of which there seemed to be a large number. A couple of them were nuns and dressed in the habits of their different orders. One cousin was a priest who had come over from Waterford to assist. This gathering of clergy was Mrs Fitzgerald's trump card. Every Irish family was extremely proud of their relations who had taken Holy Orders of any kind and paraded them at every important occasion.

Before she had time to dwell on this the organ thundered out the first bars of the Bridal March and every head turned.

Breda was almost calm now; her triumphal journey had replaced her fears with composure. This was *her* day and Mary was right, all that was important were her vows and Niall's happiness and pride in her. She gripped Jim's arm tightly and glanced up at him and he winked and she felt the last vestiges of nervousness fall away. Then she saw Niall's face and everyone else's faded into the background. She saw only the flowers, the candles and *him*.

Phil nudged Maggie. 'Oh, God, Maggie doesn't she look – well, she's like . . . a dream.'

Maggie nodded. 'I'm lost for words myself, Phil. I've never *ever* seen anyone more beautiful.'

The gleaming white satin sheath of Breda's dress, with its simple neckline and long sleeves, around which was a design worked in pearls and bugle beads, gave her an air of grace and class while the eight-foot-long train that was attached by a huge bow to the back of the dress drew loud gasps of admiration. Over her shining dark curls was a tiara. The stones that glittered so brightly were only paste but that didn't matter. It anchored the yards and yards of tulle that formed her veil and she now held the simple but effective bouquet.

Patsy looked timidly at her mother when they reached the end of the aisle and then managed a smile as she saw Maggie nod her approval. Patsy felt beautiful herself. It was the new hairstyle and the gorgeous dress, she told herself, arranging her features into a more serious expression as the parish priest came down the altar steps and Niall stepped forward to greet his bride.

Everyone was excited and starving hungry by the time they got back to Hearns for the wedding breakfast. The parish priest had accompanied them, officially to say the Grace and a few words.

Pauline, somewhat stunned by the whole thing, held onto Maurice's arm but made sure the large diamonds in her ring were plainly visible.

'Mary, Mother of God, these shoes are crippling me. Me bunions are throbbing unmercifully,' Maggie confided to Phil as they both sat at the long formal table with their families and sipped the sweet sherry they'd been given on arrival at the hotel.

'I've got a throbbing headache with this hat. It's too tight but that Mrs Power told me that's as it should be.'

'Our Kathleen told me not a few minutes ago that she wouldn't believe the daylights out of that woman. I can't say I like *this* sherry, it's dead sickly. It's supposed to be the best but I've had better. Oh, thank God for that,' Maggie sighed, having finally eased her feet from the pincer-like grip of the new shoes.

'You'll never get them back on, Maggie.'

'I don't flaming well care. When the meal's over I'm straight upstairs for my old ones. Neither Mary or Breda will care by then.'

'Is there any sign of the food yet, Mam?' Mike Kennedy asked his mother in a loud whisper.

'Wouldn't you know one of them would show us up. Just wait and stop moaning,' Phil hissed back.

'This looks like it now, Phil. It's soup anyway,' Maggie replied, craning her neck to see what the smartly turned out young waitresses had on their trays.

'I could murder pie and chips,' Bryan added. He had had a moment's regret when he'd seen Breda in all her finery but it had passed. Niall's sister Maire looked a more interesting prospect.

'Tharral do from you too. Just don't eat like a pig and make sure you clap loudly when your da finishes his speech.'

The matter of his speech had lain heavily on Jim's mind all day. He was an ignorant working class man. He'd had had no education at a university like Niall Fitzgerald, but he'd do his best not to let the family down. Maggie had said to ignore all those priests and nuns, it was only Niall's mother's way of showing off. Now he couldn't help thinking about them and he wished his wife had kept her comments to herself. He glanced across the table. Well, they didn't look too bad a lot. Hopefully the 'drop of the good stuff' on arrival and the beer and wine to be served with the meal itself would mellow them a bit more.

On his left sat Mrs Fitzgerald – senior now, he thought. Dressed to the nines, of course, but Kathleen's outfit did put it in the shade a bit. They'd exchanged a few pleasantries during the morning but now he thought it prudent to try a proper conversation.

'Is everything to your liking, Mrs Fitzgerald?'

Margaret Fitzgerald, who had never let anyone shorten her name to Maggie or Peggy, nodded. She was very relieved that Breda's family and friends appeared quite civilised. She'd feared the worst. In fact she'd had words with Niall over it and he had called her a snob, which in her opinion she was not. She liked Breda and this wedding would be talked about for years to come. Her sister Mary had indeed done her proud.

'Tell me, Mr O'Shea, are you nervous about your speech?'

'I am. I'm flaming – sorry . . . I'm terrified. This is the first time I've had to do anything like it.'

'But it won't be the last. Your son Maurice is engaged to that rather pretty girl wearing a magnificent ring, so your wife told me while we waited for the photographs to be taken.'

So, she'd noticed or rather Maggie had drawn her attention to Pauline's ring.

'Yes, but it won't be anything like this.' He took a sip of beer. He could do with a tumbler full of whiskey but a couple of sips of beer would have to do until after the dreaded moment was over.

'Shall I give you a tip? My husband, God rest him, gave speeches from time to time.'

They both crossed themselves in memory of the departed Mr Fitzgerald senior.

'I'd be glad of anything.'

'Don't look around the room. People's faces and reactions can distract you. Look at the wall at the other end or directly at someone you can trust, like your wife.'

'Thanks, I'll look at the wall. Our Maggie's not to be trusted at times like this.'

'Oh, and don't make it too long. People start to fidget.'

'I'll bear that in mind.' The advice was getting to be as bad as his speech, he thought.

He would have enjoyed the substantial meal of soup and warm bread rolls, roast beef and potatoes and vegetables and the choice of sherry trifle or fruit salad to follow if the thought of his speech hadn't been hanging over him.

As the meal progressed the noise level increased. Everyone looked as if they were enjoying themselves, particularly the bride and groom. Everyone except himself. Well, if he could cope with this he could cope with anything, he thought as the hotel manager rapped sharply on the end of the table with a gavel and silence descended.

Big Jim O'Shea got to his feet, as nervous as on his own wedding day, many, many years ago now. Fixing his eyes on the far wall, he took a deep breath.

'Ladies and Gentlemen, Reverend Fathers and Sisters, I'm not going to go on and on for ages, it's a short speech. It should have been my brother-in-law standing here today, but my sister Kathleen has been a widow for many years.'

He paused while custom prevailed and the long deceased Mr Nolan was remembered in short prayers.

'So, it was my pleasure to give Breda away in marriage and I'm sure you'll all agree that she's a beautiful bride and that Niall has got himself a lovely wife.'

There were nods and quiet words of agreement, mainly from Breda's family.

'I give thanks daily to God for the happiness of my own marriage and the blessing of a family of three sons and two daughters, although the Lord in His wisdom saw fit to take our eldest son to Himself for Davie's efforts to stamp out the evil that has swept the world for six years. I hope that Niall and Breda will have a marriage just as happy as mine, despite our loss. But this isn't a time for remembering sadness. No, today we should all be happy for the newlyweds, and I know Breda won't mind me including her sister Mary, recently married in Dublin, in the toast, so will you all raise your glasses to two beautiful sisters and two happy and, we hope, fruitful marriages.' Jim took a deep swig from his glass and sat down amidst loud clapping.

Mary's eyes sought those of her sister, afraid Jim's words had upset Breda, but Breda was smiling and between them there was a bond of pure happiness.

EPILOGUE

The evenings were drawing in and there was the smell of autumn in the air, Mary thought as she drew back the bedroom curtains. She'd been married a little over four months and her love for Chris had grown stronger every day.

They'd settled down now as a family. Kevin and Lily were back at school and her business was growing fast. She had started with just one young girl to help her and they'd worked in the breakfast room. Orders hadn't been slow in coming in, not after she had persuaded the buyer from Blacklers to just 'try a few'. They'd gone like hot cakes and now she employed two trained milliners and another young apprentice and she was already planning the styles for next spring. Very soon now she knew she'd have to rent somewhere as a proper workroom. They'd 'overflowed' into the kitchen and parlour.

'Is it that time already?' Chris asked sleepily, trying to focus on the face of the alarm clock on the table by the bed.

'It is, so I'll thank you to get out of that bed and get washed, shaved and dressed,' Mary laughed.

'Only if I get my good morning kiss.'

'Well, just a small one. Isn't there so much to see to today. And . . .' She paused.

'And what?'

'I've a surprise for you. You're going to be a father.'

Chris gasped and then caught her in his arms and pulled her down on the bed beside him. 'You're sure? It's not a joke?'

'A joke is it! Why would I joke?'

'Oh, Mary, I didn't mean it to sound like that.' He enfolded her in his arms. 'Now I'll be the happiest man in this city today.'

She kissed him. 'That's your good morning kiss.'

'When will we tell everyone?'

'I thought we'd leave it until just before Albert goes up the gangway, but that might upset him.'

'No, I don't think it will. He'll see us as a complete family now.'

'What about the children?'

'Tell them at the same time. Right, I'm getting up to make you a cup of tea, you lie here and rest.'

Mary pealed with laughter. 'I'm pregnant, not sick and aren't you after forgetting I've been through it once before. I know what to expect.'

'Well, stay there anyway and I'll bring us both the tea. I don't believe it! I still can't believe it! A son . . . my son . . .'

'Or daughter,' Mary reminded him.

The autumn day was dying in a burst of orange sunlight that was reflected on the waters of the Mersey and tinged with gold the white-hulled *Empress of Scotland* as she waited to embark her passengers, Albert amongst them.

'You'll have a calm crossing judging by that sky. Red sky at night, sailors' delight. Red sky in the morning, sailors' warning,' Chris quoted. 'And our Mike's aboard if you need anything.'

Albert shook Chris's hand warmly. He'd liked Chris a great deal as he'd got to know him better. Mary was safe and happy with him, which was a great relief.

Mary hugged him with tears glistening on her dark lashes.

'We've a surprise for you, haven't we, Chris?'

Chris nodded. 'Go on, luv, tell him.'

'I . . . we are having a baby.'

A surge of emotion filled Albert and he reached out for her.

'Mary, I'm so happy for you . . . for you both. You will take things easy until I get back? Will you write to me and tell me how things are going?'

'Of course I will. Now you'd better go or they'll be sailing without you,' Mary urged.

'Not until *that* lot get aboard.' Chris laughed and pointed to a group of men, crew and a couple of junior officers, all rushing from the Style House pub, summoned by the long blast of the ship's steam whistle.

Albert bent down and hugged both the children. There was a certain misty look in his eyes, Mary thought. He was so fond of them.

'Why is he leaving us, Aunty Mary?' Lily had demanded when she had tried to explain his departure.

'He isn't leaving us, Lily. He's going on a long holiday. He wants to see his cousin again.'

'Will he ever come back, Mammy?' Kevin had been very concerned.

'Of course he will, Kevin. It takes days and days crossing the big ocean even to get there, so he'll be away for a long time.'

'Doesn't he love us any more?' Lily's lip had trembled.

'Of course he does, Lily. He *is* coming back and he'll write us long letters and they'll have foreign stamps on them too,' Chris had added. 'You could start a collection.'

'Can we, Da?'

Chris had nodded. Every time Kevin called him 'Da' he felt a tenderness for his little stepson.

They all followed Albert down to the landing stage. There were the final hugs and kisses for a man they all loved. The gangway was towed away, the hawsers were slipped from their moorings and the three blasts from the beautiful white-hulled ship sounded over the Mersey: the traditional 'goodbye' of all merchant ships.

Chris hoisted the two children on to his shoulders so they could get a better view of the crowds lining the ship's rail and the profusion of coloured paper streamers which linked the passengers to their loved ones but which broke as the tugs manoeuvred the white *Empress* out into the river.

Both children were in tears as Chris set them down and Mary held them both to her.

'Hush now, Uncle Albert wouldn't want all this misery. He'll be back before Christmas. He wants you to be happy and you will.'

Chris took her hand. 'Remember what we told Uncle Albert? The surprise? You're going to have a baby brother or baby sister after Christmas, won't that be great?'

'Why do we have to wait so long? I want a brother. Our

Patsy says you go to the hospital to get one,' Lily asked, her thoughts diverted from Albert's departure.

'No, you don't just go and get one, Lily, you sort of . . . order it.'

'I want a brother too,' Kevin said firmly. Lily was his sister, almost.

Chris put his arm around Mary's shoulder and she held both children's hands as with one last dazzling burst of golden light the ship was silhouetted against the dark clouds.

'It's the start of a new life for us all, Mary. The baby, these two, us. The war is over, the rebuilding of the city has started. Yes, when tomorrow dawns it will be the opening of a new and happy era.'

They stood in silence until the ship was lost in the gathering dusk and they turned away, their arms around each other. Chris was right, Mary thought. When tomorrow dawned it *would* bring new life, new hope, new dreams.

Headline hopes you have enjoyed reading WHEN TOMORROW DAWNS and invites you to sample the beginning of Lyn Andrews' compelling new saga, ANGELS OF MERCY, available soon in Headline hardback.

Chapter One

1912

'You can't wear a hat in the house!' Kate Greenway's voice penetrated her mother's reverie. 'Mam, tell her she can't wear a hat, she'll look daft.'

'No, she won't,' Peg Greenway answered. 'No one decent goes out without a hat if they've got one. You'd better pin it on well, Evvie, the Pier Head can be a windy hole on a raw December Saturday.'

Peg was still a handsome woman, despite the years of hardship. Physically she'd always been big-boned but now there was more flesh on those bones. Her features were even, her eyes large and brown, her thick hair, untinged by grey, worn in a tight knot at the back of her head. She inhaled deeply and nodded with satisfaction at the appetising smell that permeated the kitchen, smiling as she stirred the big pan of scouse that stood bubbling gently on the open range. It was a smile that encompassed her seventeen year-old twin daughters as they took off their heavy shawls, hung them on the hook behind the door and plumped themselves down on the old sofa.

Peg glanced at them briefly, thinking what a fortunate woman she was. Things were far better these days with all the family, except young Joe, working. For most of her married life she'd had to manage on Bill's small wage from the Tannery in Gardners Row. It wasn't a very pleasant job and his work clothes stank but at least it had been a steady wage. She could count on it each week, unlike many women she knew who had to try to keep a family on whatever their men had managed to earn down at the docks.

She'd not lost any of her children either and, in a city where so many died before the age of ten, it was a miracle she thanked God for every day of her life. What's more, the girls had been very fortunate where looks were concerned. It was Ma McNally, the local midwife, who had first called them 'Angels'. When she'd placed the two tightly wrapped identical infants in Peg's arms, she'd beamed with joy.

'They're like a pair of angels, God love them,' she said, then as she busied herself collecting up the stained newspaper, old bits of towels and all the other items scattered around the room of confinement, she'd added sagely, 'mind, you'll have yer work cut out now, Peggy girl.'

The name 'Angels' had stuck, for, as they'd grown, Katherine and Evangeline as they'd been christened, were the image of two cherubs and as alike as two peas in a pod.

Peg took the big ladle from its place on the wall, stirred the stew again and smiled once more at the twins. They'd inherited none of the characteristics of either herself or Bill. Their hair was not a coppery red like her own or Tom's, her oldest son, or dark brown like Bill's or young Joe's. It was blonde. Almost silver white in some lights and it curled naturally. Nor were their eyes brown as were those of the rest of the family. They were blue. A startling cornflower blue.

'I'll never know where I got you two from,' was a comment often heard in number fourteen Silvester Street.

'I'm the one who should be saying that, Peg,' Bill often joked, but in reality they both knew where the twins' head-turning looks came from. His mam. In her youth blonde-haired Nelly Greenway had been considered a great beauty around the Scotland Road area of Liverpool. It was a pity she'd not lived to see them Bill often said. She'd have been as proud of them as he was, for all his sisters had died young, as had two of his brothers, back in the days when cholera had raged regularly through the slum-ridden city, decimating the poor.

Bill was a quiet man who worked hard and left the day-to-day management of the family in the capable hands of Peg O'Riorden, as she'd been before he'd married her. Now, after twenty-three years of marriage, they were proud of their family: Tom was a fine lad, young Joe was a bit of a tearaway but there was no badness in him. Peg glanced again at her daughters and felt a quiet sense of achievement. She'd often caught her husband looking at them in the same way. The 'Angels of Silvester Street' as they'd come to be known, though angels with dirty faces when they'd been growing up.

After she'd tasted the stew, Peg nodded. It was almost ready.

Kate pursed her lips in annoyance and raised her eyes to the ceiling while Evvie grinned at her mother.

'Mam, you've not been listening to a word I've said. I don't mean she shouldn't wear her hat when we go and meet Tom tomorrow. I mean she can't wear a hat for Maggie McGee's party.'

'Oh, that,' Peg replied tersely, sawing a large loaf with the carving knife and heaping the slices on a plate. 'Well, all I can say is that Hetty McGee must have more money than sense. Fancy wasting it on a "do" for their Maggie an' her only seventeen. I mean, it's not as though she were twenty-one, like, now is it? Now *that's* a birthday to really have a "do" for. If you can afford it. That's the time to go to Skillicorn's for the cakes and Pegram's for the boiled ham. Not now, when that little madam is only seventeen.'

Kate and Evvie exchanged glances. Peg's views matched those held by most of the neighbours. It was something the whole of Silvester Street was talking about, for there was hardly ever any spare cash for such frivolities. For big occasions, like a coronation, they all clubbed together for a communal affair but most of the time everyone just managed to scrape a living.

'Mrs Holden from the shop was saying that it's a disgrace. A terrible waste, spending all that money on Maggie, and it will only give her more airs and graces.'

'Aye, well, Ivy Holden's got a mouth like a parish oven, but this time I have to agree with her. Get the dishes on the table, Kate, yer da will be in any minute an' he likes his meal ready. Evvie, shift yerself, girl. Take the big jug and the bucket out to the tap, I've no water left for the kettle, and don't stand jangling with Josie Ryan,' Peg instructed, bustling about the small kitchen that served as a living room for the entire family.

'Ah, Mam! Can't our Joe go for it, I'm worn out?' Evvie complained. Even though she was thankful to have a job, standing all day in Silcock's Feed factory was not a soft occupation.

Peg shook her head angrily. 'That little sod has scarpered again an' I told him I needed him to go down to the tap. Yer da will have to take him in hand – he's running wild. We'll 'ave the scuffers hammering on the door for him one of these days. Go on, Evvie, be quick if you want a cup of tea.'

As Evvie reluctantly fetched the jug and bucket from the dank, airless scullery, Peg sighed, pausing for a moment to glance around, the Fry's Cocoa tin that served as a tea caddy clutched to her chest. Materially, she didn't really have much to show for more than two decades of marriage. Apart from the bits and pieces in the bedrooms, all the rest of the furniture was in here. The scrubbed table stood against the window wall, with two long benches pushed beneath it until they were needed. A ladder-backed chair and the old sagging sofa were against the opposite wall. A food press with a mesh front, a plain dresser, two three-legged stools, were all crammed in. Rag rugs covered the floor and her pans hung above the range. Above them was suspended the slatted clothes rack that worked on a pulley and rope system, which often collapsed and festooned anyone who happened to be in the room with damp clothes. On the overmantel was a cheap clock, a couple of brass candlesticks, complete with candles, a pair of china dogs and a statue of the Virgin Mary.

Peg wore herself out day after day, scrubbing and polishing, but day after day the house defeated her efforts. It was the way they were built, she knew that. They were old, some were very damp and some even looked as though they would fall down any minute, burying their occupants in debris. The kitchen floor was flagged and the chimney often smoked. There was no running water but at least they had their own privy at the bottom of the yard, an earth closet that was emptied once a week. All the houses had their share of bugs. It didn't matter how many times the Sanitary men came and stoved them, the bugs came back. Bill frequently used a blow lamp to burn them off the iron frames of the beds. The houses all needed knocking down and new ones built, but there was fat chance of that happening.

Like all her neighbours, Peg daily scrubbed the steps, the window ledges, even the section of pavement outside her door, then she went over the steps with a donkey stone. They were all poor but they took pride in keeping the decrepit, dilapidated houses as clean as was humanly possible.

Often she would get up off her knees in the street, her back aching, her hands raw with harsh soap and soda, and she'd glare with heart-felt venom at the clouds of smoke that poured from the factory chimneys and those of the Clarence Dock Power Station, known locally as the Three Ugly Sisters. In an hour, less if the wind changed direction, the smuts would undo all her hard work and there was nothing she could do about it. It was the same on wash day. She'd cursed Tate & Lyle's sugar refinery at the bottom of Burlington Street up hill and down dale, but it didn't make the washing any cleaner.

Suddenly Kate let out a sharp cry and darted into the scullery. Peg, jerked back to reality, looked up in time to see Joe and Mickey Ryan tottering precariously on the wall at the bottom of the yard that led into the entry, or jigger as it was known. She crossed to the window and banged hard on the glass pane with the tin.

'Geroff that wall, the pair of you!' she yelled.

Kate had been quick. She'd caught her brother's jacket and had hauled him down bodily, then she marched him into the house by his ear.

Peg glared at her youngest son, taking in the rip in his jacket, the scuffed boots and the woollen socks hanging untidily around his ankles, revealing dirty scraped knees.

'Just look at the state of you! I wear meself out washing,

432

ironing, mending and scrimping so you'll have boots on your feet, and what do you do? You go playing silly beggars with that Mickey Ryan. A pair of flaming little hooligans, that's what you are! You could have fallen and broken your neck, or worse, landed in the midden! You wait until yer da gets in, Joe Greenway!'

'It wasn't all my fault, Mam! He dared me!' Joe cried indignantly, rubbing his ear but knowing that it would sting even more if his da heard of his escapades. He didn't see what was so bad about Jumping the Jigger Walls as it was called, all the kids did it. It was a popular pastime and had been for years. Even his da had admitted to doing it when he'd been a lad, an admission Joe looked on with great resentment, seeing that that game was now forbidden to him. Of course you could end up in Stanley Hospital with a broken arm or leg, and some of his mates considered such injuries were worth it, if it meant no school for a goodish time, but it wasn't often that that happened. It rated as one of the better games, along with Ollies and Flattie Throwing, although the latter was likely to result in a hiding. Still, it was good fun to hurl your cap between the legs of the horses or the wheels of the carts. If you judged it right, it went clean through to the other side of the road. If you didn't, it meant you lost your cap and got belted when you got home.

'If he dared you to jump off the landing stage, I suppose you'd be daft enough to do it. Sometimes you're as thick as the wall, our Joe!' Kate remarked acidly.

'Oh, go and get yourself cleaned up and don't mither me any more tonight with your antics,' Peg said wearily. Kate was right, sometimes she wondered if Joe had any brains at all. If he had then he certainly didn't use them very often.

'There's no water. I saw our Evvie going down the street,'

Joe said brightly, seeing a reprieve but totally forgetting that it was him who should have fetched the water in the first place.

Peg's temper flared again. 'Don't be so hard-faced, meladdo! Go and help her bring it in. I asked you to get it for me!' She made a swipe at Joe with the piece of sacking she used as an oven cloth but he darted past her and into the lobby and they heard his boots clattering on the scuffed lino.

Peg shook her head and returned to her preparations. 'I'll swing for that lad one of these days, so help me I will!'

'Oh, he's not bad, Mam, he's just easily led,' Kate consoled her.

'I know, Kate, but if I don't watch him he'll be the death of me.'

Kate looked up from setting the table as the backyard door opened.

'Here's da now, he's early tonight.'

'Wouldn't you just know it, when there's no water for him to get washed in and it'll take a while to boil. If tha young hooligan had gone for it when I asked him to, thi wouldn't have happened.'

Bill had removed his boots and left them in the scullery He left his jacket in there too as it stank to high heaven, a Peg often commented.

Bill gave his wife a peck on the cheek. He looked tired Peg thought.

'I'm sorry, luv, but there's no water yet. Our Evvie an Joe have gone for it and you'll have to chastise that littl horror too.'

'Now what's he done?' Bill asked wearily.

'Jumping the jigger walls, not doing what he's told, sneaking off before he fetched in the water, to start with.'

'I'm starving.'

'We all are, Bill, but there'll be no tea until you get a wash and change your clothes,' Peg stated firmly. They might not have much in material things but she did have standards.

After the meal was over, all the chores completed and Joe suitably chastened by his father, Kate and Evvie went up to their tiny bedroom. The house only had two rooms upstairs and Tom and Joe shared the other. Peg and Bill slept in the parlour, an arrangement that grieved Peg sorely. It had been her lifelong wish to have a 'best' room. Somewhere to entertain Father Foreshaw, the parish priest, when he called. It gave you standing amongst the neighbours, but until she 'got rid of them all', as she put it, the downstairs front room had to serve as a bedroom.

The twins' room was cold and smelled musty and until Kate lit the gas jet and replaced the clear glass mantle the only illumination came from the street lamp on the corner of Limekiln Lane. The flickering flame threw long shadows over the room.

'It's freezing in here, we should have stayed in the kitchen,' Evvie complained, pulling the blanket from the bed around her shoulders.

'And have our Joe listening to every word and telling Mickey Ryan and then having the pair of them skitting and sniggering at me? No, thanks very much!'

Evvie sighed. Kate had always been more outgoing, more confident than herself. Ideas and plans were always instigated by Kate, she just followed, usually meekly. There were occasions though when she did dig her heels in, if the current idea really didn't appeal to her.

Kate, who had wrapped the faded patchwork quilt around her shoulders, was standing by the window, looking out into the street. The rows and rows of soot-blackened terraced houses, their roofs the colour of gunmetal and shiny with the sleet that had been falling since tea time, ran all the way down to the River Mersey. It was too dark to see the river and the forest of masts, spars and funnels of the ships that crowded the six miles of waterfront.

She wanted to get away from here some day, maybe on one of those ships. She certainly didn't want a carbon copy of her mam's life. Oh, Da had a steady job in the Tannery. In fact he and Alf McGee, who worked for Bent's Brewery, were the only two men in the street who did have one, but it was still grinding hard work for Mam.

When they'd been young, Mam had gone out office cleaning in the evening to earn a few extra shillings. And that after an exhausting day at home. It wasn't unusual, all the women in the street either went cleaning or took in washing to make ends meet, apart from Ivy Holden at the corner shop.

Kate wanted more from life – just what exactly she did want in the long term wasn't clear, but, she told herself, there was plenty of time.

Apart from Ivy Holden, the only other woman with any status was Hetty McGee. She was a dressmaker and over the years she'd gathered a few loyal clients who paid for clothes made on Hetty's Singer treadle sewing machine that stood in pride of place in her front room, her 'Fitting Room' as she so grandly called it. With only three of them in the family there was no overcrowding in their house. The kitchen wasn't cluttered and their Maggie had the enviable luxury of a bedroom to herself.

Kate sighed deeply. 'You wouldn't think it was Christmas in a couple of days, would you? There's not a lot of "Glad Tidings of Great Joy" out there.'

'Oh, what's up with you, Kate?' Evvie snapped. 'You've had a cob on all day. It's not like you to be so sharp with people and you nearly bit Josie's head off this morning.'

Josie Ryan didn't work with them but they all walked to the tram stop together.

'All she said was that she really liked that Frank Lynch from Athol Street.' Even as she spoke, Evvie became acutely aware of the reason for Kate's bad humour. 'So that's what's the matter with you. That's why you were so sharp with Josie. You like him, too, don't you?'

Kate felt the blood rush to her cheeks. She should have realised that Evvie would know. They were so close that it was a wonder Evvie hadn't guessed before now. She turned back to the window and idly traced a pattern in the condensation that misted the pane of glass. 'So what if I do? It's not a crime, is it, or a mortal sin? And he's not engaged to Josie, is he? He hasn't even asked her out yet and I hope he doesn't. I *do* like him, Evvie. Whenever I see him, I feel sort of on edge, and when he looks at me, my heart just turns over. Do you think . . .'

'What?'

'Well, is there such a thing as love at first sight?'

'I don't really know and you don't really know him. I don't think I could love someone I didn't know.'

'Oh, Evvie, you're so . . . wary.'

'I'm not. I just feel as though I have to *know* someone before I said I loved them. Do you love him, Kate?'

Kate sighed. 'Oh, I don't know. I think I do but what about Josie?'

'He hasn't asked her out yet but he hasn't asked you either.' Then, seeing the look that came into Kate's eyes, she added, 'Oh, all right, don't get aereated with me, too!'

'Well, don't you say anything to anyone. Promise me, Evvie, please? I'd feel such a fool. He hasn't asked me out, and if . . . if he doesn't like me . . .'

'Of course he likes you. I've seen the way he looks at you when we leave church on Sunday mornings,' Evvie said firmly. Josie had been her friend for years but her first loyalty was to her sister.

'Promise me just the same?' Kate pleaded.

'Oh, all right, I promise. God's truth.' Evvie crossed herself to show she was sincere.

Kate sighed again and sat down on the bed they shared, twisting a strand of hair around her finger, a habit they both had when anxious or upset. She wore her hair in a loose chignon while Evvie's was swept up into a soft roll that framed her face. It was the only way people could distinguish between them. When they'd been younger they'd often mischievously changed places, Kate saying she was Evvie and vice versa. Only immediate family didn't fall for this trickery. Mam could tell them apart just by the sound of their voices.

Kate was thinking of how Frank Lynch's eyes had swept over her with what she hoped was interest and admiration. Of course it had been after Mass and she'd been looking her best.

'I wish I had something new to wear for this party,' she said wistfully.

'Can't you afford anything? Not even a blouse?'

'How can I? We turn up our wages to Mam and I'm still paying off my Sturla's cheque with my pocket money.'

Evvie brooded in silence. She was in the same position herself. A lot of people used the 'cheque' system. It was a form of credit. You went along to Sturla's Department Store in Great Homer Street, picked what you wanted and then paid a set sum each week until it was all paid off. Often though, the things that had been purchased were worn out before the debt was paid. She'd used her 'cheque' to buy Christmas presents. 'You know I'd lend you something if I could.'

'Oh, I know and I suppose I'm just being daft. I mean, you can't have everything, not on what Silcock's pay us, and Mam can't sew like Mrs McGee.'

'Maybe our Tom will have got us something, something to wear, from New York.'

'And pigs might fly. He doesn't earn a fortune, Evvie, and he is good to us. We'll get the usual bottle of cheap scent. He doesn't get tips like a steward or a waiter.'

Evvie nodded her agreement. Working as a trimmer in the stokehold of the *Carmania* was her idea of hell. As the ship ploughed its way regularly from Liverpool to New York and back, Tom worked like a thing possessed, shovelling coal in temperatures that would make a hot summer day appear cool by comparison. It was hard and dirty work, done in shifts of four hours on, four hours off and when he got to New York, like nearly every other member of the stokehold, he went on a drinking spree. You couldn't blame them, they had to have some relaxation. But somehow he always managed to find the time to get them all the requisite little gift. It was almost a tradition on Merseyside, that the seafarers brought home presents, no matter how small or insignificant. He always managed to keep a few shillings of his wages too, which was more than most of them did: he left Mam an allotment that she collected from the Cunard Building by the week. All in all, though, he could never be called well off.

'Ask him to lend you some money then, he won't mind,' Evvie suggested, for Kate's mood had affected her own spirits.

'How can I when I won't be able to pay it back for months? No, I'll just have to make do with my blue skirt and white blouse. I'll give the blouse a dip in Robin starch and press it. That's if I can get it dry without it getting covered in smuts.' Her thoughts returned to the matter of Evvie's hat. 'And you can't wear a hat. You'll have to try and find a bit of ribbon or something for your hair instead. Apart from looking daft, you'll get it ruined. It'll get knocked and if you take it off someone's bound to sit on it.'

Evvie nodded. It had just been an idea and not a very good one, for it was her only hat. However, she was determined to think of something to smarten up her appearance. 'I'll see if I can get a bit of ribbon and maybe an artificial flower in Great Homer Street market tomorrow and I'll pin my hair up. I bet Maggie will have something that looks as though it's come from Cripps in Bold Street,' she added wistfully. Not only was Mrs McGee clever at sewing, she often found ingenious ways of brightening up old clothes, adding a velvet trim on a jacket or a piece of pleated muslin at the neck of a dress. Maggie, too, was clever with materials. It was one of the reasons she'd been accepted as an apprentice seamstress at Sloan's in Bold Street, the Bond Street of Liverpool.

'Her dress is pale green foulé with a narrow black stripe trimmed with black buttons and braid. That's all I could get out of her. "It's gorgeous and it's going to be a surprise," she kept on saying. Sometimes, I really envy her!' Kate finished trying to imagine herself in a pale green dress, trimmed with black braid. She'd certainly catch Frank Lynch's eye in something like that.

'I know, so do I. It must be great to be able to make your own clothes,' Evvie consoled her sister, but she thought it best not to say that Josie Ryan had a new blouse, the front of which was frilled and pin-tucked and embroidered with tiny rosebuds. She'd got it cheap because there was a scorch mark on the back but Mrs Ryan had treated that with bleach until it was barely noticeable.

Evvie, Kate and Josie were firm friends and had been since they were toddlers. Maggie had never been classed as a real friend. She was that little bit younger and had been spoiled in comparison to the rest of them. She just hung about on the fringe of their group and was often a pain in the neck. However, the appearance of Frank Lynch on the scene seemed about to change things between Kate and Josie, Evvie thought, for they were both obviously smitten with him. She didn't see what either of them saw in him; he was a bit of a loudmouth and fancied himself as a ladies' man. Still, it looked as though this birthday party of Maggie's was going to be interesting to say the least. She just hoped there wasn't going to be any serious argument or irrevocable rift between Kate and Josie. It would be such a shame if they came to blows over Frank Lynch. Perhaps Josie didn't want him as much as Kate obviously did. She'd never known Kate to say she loved any of the other lads who'd drifted in and out of her sister's life over the last year. Maybe it would be left for Frank Lynch himself to choose.

The front door banged shut and Evvie got up. 'That's Da off down the Royal George. I'm going down before I freeze to death.'

Now that she had unburdened herself to Evvie, Kate felt better. 'I could do with a cup of tea myself and I'm going to shove a couple of bricks in the fire and then put them in this bed. It's like the flaming North Pole up here.'

Now you can buy any of these other bestselling books by **Lyn Andrews** from your bookshop or *direct from her publisher*.

FREE P&P AND UK DELIVERY
(Overseas and Ireland £3.50 per book)

My Sister's Child	£5.99
Take These Broken Wings	£5.99
The Ties that Bind	£5.99
Angels of Mercy	£5.99
When Tomorrow Dawns	£5.99
From This Day Forth	£5.99
Where the Mersey Flows	£5.99
Liverpool Lamplight	£6.99
Liverpool Songbird	£6.99

TO ORDER SIMPLY CALL THIS NUMBER

01235 400 414

or e-mail orders@bookpoint.co.uk

Prices and availability subject to change without notice.